IN SAFE HANDS

KATIE RUGGLE

sourcebooks
casablanca

Published by Sourcebooks Casablanca, an imprint of Sourcebooks, Inc.
P.O. Box 4410, Naperville, Illinois 60567-4410
(630) 961-3900
Fax: (630) 961-2168
www.sourcebooks.com

Printed and bound in the United States of America.
LSC 10 9 8 7 6 5 4 3

*For everyone at the Rochester
Minnesota Police Department*

*Thank you for all that you taught me, and for
your daily acts of courage and selflessness.
Fire might get all the glory (and calendars), but
cops are still my favorite real-life heroes.*

Prologue

ANDERSON KING PUNCHED THE NUMBERS INTO THE burner phone. As it rang, he resisted the urge to pace. The shadows of the lawn shed hid him, but movement could catch someone's attention. It rang twice more, and King was starting to think he'd be sent to voice mail, when someone finally answered.

"It's me," King said quietly.

There was a pause. "A lot of people are looking for you."

"That's why I need to get out of here."

"Why are you calling me?"

"Because"—he eyed the light seeping out around the edges of the closed blinds in the upstairs window—"to leave, I need money."

"Again, why are you calling me?"

"I found Price. We had an interesting talk."

The silence on the other end continued too long, forcing King to speak again.

"He told me some things about you."

"What do you want?"

"Just to have a chat." King grinned. The conversation was going exactly as he'd imagined. "Meet me tomorrow at that empty white house on Alpine Lane with the for-sale sign out front. Two a.m. I'll make sure the back door is open for you."

He ended the call, still smiling. With a final glance at the window, he turned and disappeared into the shadows.

—◊◊◊—

The killer was late.

Anderson King prided himself on his patience, but his stomach had begun to curdle at the thought of his plan going to hell. It was one thing to leave the country with money, and a whole other thing to go on the run broke. No brother, no cash, cops on a county-wide manhunt, sleeping on the hard floor of a vacant house, his body bruised and aching from George Holloway's fists…how had everything gone so wrong?

Nervous energy forced him to pace the living room until Anderson realized his boots were clomping against the hardwood floor. Appalled, he stopped abruptly. A final echo of the sound reverberated through the empty space. How had he gotten so sloppy? Was he losing his stealth and nerve along with everything else?

"Anderson."

He whirled toward the voice. Anderson had been so preoccupied that he hadn't heard anyone else enter the vacant house. The moonlight filtering through the windows wasn't very bright, but Anderson had no problem making out the handgun and its attached silencer. He reached for his pistol holstered at the small of his back.

"Don't." The single word wasn't loud, but there was an authoritative crack to it. That and the pistol pointed at him made Anderson reconsider drawing his weapon.

"About time you got here," he blustered. "I was beginning to think you didn't care if I handed all this evidence over to the state investigators."

"What evidence?"

As the other voice calmed, growing quieter and more

conversational, Anderson found himself getting agitated. *Relax*, he told himself. *You're holding all the cards here*. "Photographs Willard Gray took."

"Of what?"

Anderson leaned a shoulder against the fireplace mantel. "Pretty, pretty fires."

"That proves nothing."

"There are letters, too."

The silence stretched an uncomfortably long time, and Anderson forced himself not to fidget. During poker games, he'd always been good at bluffing. Now was not the time to develop a tell.

"Letters?"

And there's the tug on the baited line. Biting back a triumphant grin, Anderson confirmed, "Yep. Gray sent them to that crazy buddy of his, Baxter Price. There's all sorts of interesting information in those letters. It's funny. He may be dead, but Gray still can give his eye-witness testimony."

"Where are they?"

That was the flaw in his plan. With Baxter Price missing, there were no letters or pictures—at least not in Anderson's possession. No one had to know that, though. "In a safe place."

That disconcerting silence fell again.

"You don't have any letters." He sounded certain.

"Sure I d—"

Time slowed as he saw the gun flash and felt the punch of the bullet entering his chest, cutting off the lie midword. This was it, then. The gun fired once more, and he began to topple face-first toward the floor.

At least he'd get to see his brother again soon.

With a sigh, Sheriff Rob Coughlin lowered his gun. He was tired, and it was late. The last thing he wanted to do was deal with yet another body. There wasn't any alternative, though. He'd made the mess, so he'd clean it up. That's what responsible people did.

Quietly, methodically, he got to work.

Chapter 1

IT WAS ALMOST MAY, AND IT WAS STILL SNOWING. DAISY made a face at the fat flakes clinging to the window. It wasn't like she had to go out into the snow, but she hated that it drove everyone else *inside*. With her neighbors sheltering against the cold, her special version of reality television had been reduced to what she could see through the windows of the few houses in her line of sight.

There was no use whining about it, though. It would have to do until spring finally came to the Rockies.

She peered through the curtain of snow at the house directly across the street. It looked like most of the Storvicks were in their family room, watching a movie. Only the oldest son, Corbin, was missing. Daisy spotted him through one of the upstairs windows, talking on a cell phone while pacing his bedroom. From the way he yanked on his hair with his free hand, there was more drama happening between him and the tall, redheaded girl who visited his house on an off-again/on-again basis.

As she watched the teenager end the call by throwing his phone against the wall, Daisy leaned closer to the window, making a mental note to tell Chris that Corbin and his girlfriend were fighting again. Last time they'd split, Corbin had spray-painted misspelled epithets on the girl's garage door. Daisy wasn't sure why his girlfriend had taken him back after that. Maybe Corbin was a good apologizer.

Since the teen had crammed in his earbuds and thrown himself on his bed, Daisy figured he'd be moping for at least a few hours. With the excitement at the Storvick house over for the night, she checked out Ian Walsh's place. To her disappointment, the new shutters were closed, blocking her view.

The window coverings and the girlfriend had been installed around the same time. Although she was happy that Ian had found someone, those shutters had put a definite damper on any vicarious thrills. Firefighter Ian Walsh had been in the habit of walking around in nothing but boxer briefs, and Daisy missed her personal Chippendales show.

The house to the right of the Storvicks', 304 Alpine Lane, was empty and had been for almost eight months. The for-sale sign was looking a little faded, especially with the frosting of new, bright-white snow lining the top. Daisy wished someone would move in soon and give her one more channel of neighbor TV. It looked like tonight's entertainment would be a book or the Internet, neither of which excited her.

With a resigned sigh, she started to turn away from the window, but a movement in her peripheral vision brought Daisy's focus back to the empty house. She squinted through the falling snow. There might have been a flicker of motion by the back corner of the house, but the darkness and the veil of snow made it hard to see. As her gaze traveled over the shadowed edges of the yard, she shivered and wrapped her arms around her middle. Without any moonlight, the forest on the far side of number 304 disappeared into absolute blackness. Anything or anyone could be lurking just past the tree line, and Daisy would never know.

Dragging her gaze away from the encompassing darkness, she forced herself to leave her window seat.

"No more horror movies for you," she muttered under her breath. Ever since her friend, Chris, had told her about the headless body found in a nearby reservoir a few months ago, Daisy had been even more on edge than usual. As she scanned her bookcase for something light and funny to read, Daisy couldn't help shooting a wary glance at the window. There were dangerous, terrifying things in the world beyond the safe walls and locked doors of her home. She knew this all too well. If she let herself dwell on those horrors, though, the nightmares would get even worse.

Picking one of her comfort reads, Daisy sat on her bed with her back toward the window. As she started on the first chapter, she was quickly lost in the book, and Daisy was almost able to shove away any worries about the unknown dangers creeping around outside her safe haven.

Almost.

⁓

Daisy recognized the knock, but she still pushed the intercom button. Messing with Chris was one of her few pleasures in life.

"May I help you?"

"Dais. Let me in." He sounded crabby. That was unusual.

"Is that how you announce yourself? Shouldn't you be shouting 'Sheriff's department' or something?"

"I'm not serving a warrant." Chris was *definitely* cranky. "If you don't let me in right now, you're not getting your very heavy present."

"Present?" She hit the button to unlock the exterior door. "Why didn't you say so? You know 'present' is the magic word." Tipping her head close to the wood panel, she listened for the dull thud of the outer door closing and the click of the lock reengaging. Once it was secure, she opened the four dead-bolt locks and two chains as quickly as possible. Finally yanking open the interior door, she grinned when she saw the big box Chris was carrying.

"Out of the way," he grunted, walking forward so she was forced to retreat a few steps. As soon as he was through the doorway, she closed the interior door, careful not to look at the outer one. Just the sight of that flimsy barrier between her and the outside world made her dizzy.

After refastening the locks, she turned toward her gift and its bearer. Chris had set the box on the kitchen floor and returned to the door to remove his boots. As Daisy hurried toward the mystery box, she stepped on a chunk of melting snow. With a yelp, she hopped over the remainder of what Chris had tracked in.

"I think the cows already escaped," she said, watching through the arched doorway between the kitchen and the entry as he pulled off his boots.

He blinked up at her. "What?"

"Closing the barn door? Boots? Snow on the floor?"

With a snort, he unzipped his coat. "You're a strange one, Daisy May."

"You do know that's not my middle name, right?"

"Sure." He offered her a crooked grin. His bad mood

seemed to have disappeared as soon as he was inside. "*Daisy May* is just more fun to say than *Daisy Josephine*."

"If you say so." She curled her fingers under the box's cardboard flaps and looked at Chris, waiting anxiously for his okay to open it. When he waved a hand, a smile tugging at his mouth, she flipped the flaps over, revealing a sheet of bubble wrap. Pushing it aside, she spotted the flesh-colored torso and shrieked with excitement. "Grapple Man!"

Wrapping her arms around the dummy, she pulled him out of the box, scattering packing material as she did so. He was heavier than she'd expected, probably about fifty pounds, and Daisy grunted as she hoisted him upright. Looking at Chris, she saw he was wearing a proud grin.

"This is awesome, Chris! If I didn't have my arms full of this marvelous specimen of fake manhood, I would hug you so hard! Where'd you get him?"

"The department upgraded, so I snagged this one for you." He leaned against the counter and crossed his arms over his chest. "He needed a new sparring partner, and I figured you could use a training buddy for times when I'm not here."

She was distracted for a second by the way Chris's biceps bulged, stretching the tan fabric of his uniform shirt, and it took a moment for his answer to penetrate. "He's the best present ever. Thank you, Chris." She hugged the dummy, since the man she really wanted to hug was several feet away and didn't always accept physical affection gracefully. "I shall call him…Maximillian. Unless…" Daisy looked over the dummy's shoulder so she could see Chris. "Did you guys already name him?"

Smirking, he shook his head.

"Huh." Bending her knees, she heaved Max over her shoulder into a fireman's carry. "How could you have worked with him for *years* without naming him? It's unnatural."

"Unnatural? Naming some dummy you're about to kick in the face is what's unnatural. I'll get him, Dais." Chris reached to take Max, but Daisy spun out of reach, tottering slightly before catching her balance.

"We're good." She patted Max's behind as she headed for the training room. "I can't wait to practice my kicks on him. With the bag, I never know if I'm landing them in the right spot. Did I mention that this is the best gift *ever*?"

"I think you did a couple of times." He followed her through the doorway.

"Well, thank you again." She eyed the hook dangling from a chain next to the heavy bag. "That should be a good height for Mr. Max, don't you think?"

"Looks about right." Chris maneuvered the dummy so the ring at the back of his neck slid onto the hook. Max's feet almost touched the ground.

"Perfect." Eyeing her new piece of training equipment, Daisy excitedly bounced on her toes before turning back to Chris. "He's so great. *You*'re so great. Thank you, thank you, thank you!"

She couldn't stop herself from reaching to hug him, but he dodged and grabbed her outstretched hands instead. Although she felt the usual dart of hurt, Daisy's delight in Max was too great to be squashed so easily. She squeezed his hands, instead.

"You're, uh, welcome," he said, glancing away. Ever

since she'd given in to a moment of impulsive stupidity and tried to kiss him a few months earlier, awkward moments had occurred between them on a regular basis. Daisy hated that.

"Are you hungry?" she asked, releasing his hands and turning toward the doorway. "I can make us some lunch."

"That's okay." He followed her out of the training room. "I'll just swing by my house and grab something quick."

Disappointment settled over her, and she fought to keep her smile. "Since you used your break to bring me my new favorite man, the least I can do is feed you. Plus, then you can fill me in on all the latest Simpson gossip."

"Gossip?" he grumbled. "I don't gossip. I'm with the sheriff's department, not Fire."

Daisy laughed. "If we call it 'important local news,' instead, will you tell me the latest on the hermit guy's new girlfriend?"

Although his affable smile stayed in place, a shadow darkened his expression for just a second before he reached for his coat. "Sorry, Dais. No time. Got to keep Field County safe from jaywalking tourists and vagrant bighorn sheep. I'll stop by on one of my days off so we can train."

"Sure? There are leftover crab cakes from last night. Not to toot my own crustacean-cooking horn, but they're pretty tasty."

His smile widened, but he didn't pause as he pulled on his boots. "I'll have to try them another time."

"Okay." Daisy watched as he unfastened the multiple locks. Although she wanted to push him again to stay, it would just make her seem lonely and desperate. "Thanks again for Max."

"You're welcome again." With a final crooked smile, he was gone.

And she was alone once more.

Sweat ran into her eyes, making them sting. Her knee connected with Max's outer thigh. If he'd been a real boy, the nerve strike would've rendered that leg useless for a while. Moving back, she practiced front and side kicks until her legs were like noodles, and then moved to punches and palm-heel strikes.

When her wrapped hands felt too heavy to lift, she leaned against Max and gasped for breath. He swung away from her weight, so she wrapped her arms around his middle to stabilize them both. When she realized how they must look, Daisy gave a breathless laugh and forced her body to straighten.

"You really are the perfect man, Max," she said, patting his belly. "I wake you up at two in the morning, beat you to a pulp, and you're still willing to cuddle. How many men would put up with that?" A certain deputy sheriff came to mind, but she pushed the thought away before she got mopey. Looking down, she made a face as she pulled her sweat-soaked tank away from her skin. "Now I'm disgusting and need a shower. Good night, Max. Thanks for letting me assault you."

The stairs loomed in front of her, mocking her with their steepness. Daisy wished she'd left a little juice in her leg muscles for the climb. With a whimper that almost made her glad no one else was within earshot, she forced her wobbly quads to lift high enough for her feet to clear each step.

She stopped in her room to get clean pajamas. As she passed the front window, the one she referred to as her "TV screen," she stopped and moved closer. There was a sheriff's department SUV parked at the curb in front of the Storvicks' house.

"Corbin, you budding little psycho," she muttered. "What did you do this time?"

Forgetting her aching legs, she scurried over to turn off the overhead light and then returned to her window seat. The Storvicks' place was dark, and Daisy frowned. Had the deputy not gone up to the house yet? She'd been expecting shouting parents and a crying Corbin, not the current sleepy silence.

No one was in the driver's seat of the SUV, though, so the deputy had to be somewhere. Maybe Corbin hadn't done anything to his ex-girlfriend after all. Daisy looked around the area. Despite her immediate assumption that Corbin was the reason for the deputy's visit, the squad SUV was actually parked closer to the for-sale house than the Storvicks'. Daisy thought of the movement she'd seen the previous night, and she wondered if there was a homeless person living there. The deputy could be responding to a trespassing call.

Daisy drummed her fingertips on the wall next to the window, trying to remember when Chris's days off started. If he was working, then his shift started at seven a.m., so she could call him in a few hours, and he wouldn't threaten to kill her. If he *wasn't* working, however, he tended to sleep late to start getting his body ready for the approaching night shift. She knew from experience that, when woken, Chris was as grumpy as a bear that had been punched in the face.

Besides, his recent standoffishness had pushed her off-center. Daisy wasn't sure where they stood at the moment. He'd been her friend—her only real-life, in-person friend—since she'd been sixteen. After eight years, they'd developed an easy, comfortable camarade-rie, but she'd managed to mess that up in one impulsive second that she'd regretted ever since. It'd been movie night a few months ago, and they'd laughed in unison at some funny line. When she'd turned to look at Chris, she'd caught him staring at her with a strange, almost hungry expression. Her amusement had died, replaced by a longing so intense that she couldn't stop herself from leaning closer and closer until their lips barely touched. She could have sworn he'd wanted to kiss her as much as she'd wanted to kiss him.

But then he'd jerked back as if she'd given him a static shock. Muttering some excuse, he'd escaped from her house as quickly as possible, leaving her to wallow in regret and humiliation. Ever since that night, Chris had been acting…weird. Except for the day of her mother's murder, Daisy had never wished so hard for a do-over.

The thought of losing Chris was scary, so she shoved it out of her head and concentrated instead on the scene in front of her. An almost-full moon and a couple of streetlights illuminated the SUV and the yard immedi-ately next to it. If she squinted, Daisy could make out the shadowed impressions of footprints in the day-old snow, leading around the far side of the house. Those must've been made by the deputy, she decided.

Daisy tried to figure out why uneasiness was

simmering in her belly. Everything was so quiet and still, with everyone sleeping—everyone except for her, at least. The squad vehicle just didn't fit with that peace. In her experience, cop cars brought action and noise and movement—or at least a visit from Chris. That must've been why the empty SUV seemed so eerie.

She shivered and blamed it on her sweaty, quickly drying tank top. Darting across the room, she grabbed the hoodie draped over her desk chair and pulled it on as fast as possible so she wouldn't miss anything that might happen outside. As she was about to rush back to the window, her cell caught her eye, and she reached for it, sliding the phone into her hoodie pocket.

Daisy curled up on the window seat again. She knew from experience that she wouldn't sleep if she tried to go back to bed after exercising, plus that odd, uneasy feeling hadn't gone away. Resting her chin on her up-drawn knee, she watched, waiting for the deputy's return.

The wind picked up, rushing past her window and making the pine tree branches scratch against the side of Daisy's house. She pulled the hoodie more tightly around her and tucked her fingers under her arms to keep them warm. Clouds crept over the moon, darkening the shadows surrounding the house.

"No," Daisy groaned. The streetlights mostly just lit the narrow circle of space around their poles, so it was much more difficult to see anything with the moonlight gone. The encroaching darkness sent her imagination into overdrive, making it too easy to picture all sorts of things hiding in the shadows. She leaned toward the glass, trying to make up for the dim lighting by getting as close as she could to the action—or lack of action.

She'd resisted getting binoculars in the past, since that always seemed like it would've pushed her neighborhood-watch activities out of "quirky" and right into "creepy." Now, she regretted having qualms. In fact, a pair of night-vision binoculars would've been even better. So what if that shoved her squarely into creeperhood? At least she'd be able to see what was happening.

A break in the clouds revealed someone walking along the side of the empty house. Sucking in a startled breath, Daisy rose to her knees and pressed her forehead against the cold glass. She stared hard at the furtive figure.

The person's shape was wrong. It wasn't just the distortion of the shadows. Either an ogre was walking next to the empty house, or... Wishing once again for binoculars, she shifted, trying to find a better angle.

Then the wind cleared the clouds away from the moon, and she could see more clearly. The misshapen form was actually someone with a large bundle over his or her shoulder. Peering at the person, she decided from his size and the way he moved that he was definitely male.

After a half step of hesitation, he walked into the puddle of light circling one of the streetlamps. The lights on the SUV flashed, and the back hatch door lifted. Balancing the burden over his shoulder with one hand, he reached with the other to move something around, maybe making room.

"What?" Daisy muttered, confused. The man next to the sheriff's department vehicle wasn't wearing a uniform. He was dressed head to toe in black, rather than the tan deputy uniform. Even their department-issued winter coats were tan. The wrapped bundle over his shoulder caught the glow of the streetlight, gleaming a familiar, semiglossy blue. Whatever the guy was carrying was wrapped in a tarp.

Closing her fingers around her phone, she pulled it out and tapped on the video app. The scene was strange enough that she felt like she needed to record it, even if it was just so she could watch it in the morning. In the light of day, the ominous feeling would be gone, and she could laugh at the way her overactive imagination had turned something innocuous into a nebulous threat.

No matter how she shifted, raising up or dropping low, Daisy couldn't find the right angle to get a glimpse of the man in black's face. Even if she had gotten a clear view, though, she probably wouldn't have been able to identify him. She only knew Chris's coworkers through his work anecdotes. She zoomed in her phone camera, but the image just got darker and grainier, rather than clearer.

Leaning forward, the man half-dropped, half-shoved the large bundle into the back of the SUV. The rear of the vehicle sagged a little, which meant the object must be heavy. There was an unsettling familiarity in the way the tarp-wrapped item fell, bulky and weighted, that sent a shiver across the back of her neck.

The black-clad man shoved at the bottom of the bundle. He'd managed to tuck the majority of it into the SUV when something dark escaped from the bottom of the rolled tarp, tumbled over the rear bumper, and fell to the ground.

Daisy sucked in a breath hard enough to scrape her throat. From her vantage point, that dropped item looked very much like a boot.

Chapter 2

STUNNED BY THE POSSIBILITY THAT THERE WAS A *BODY* IN the back of the SUV, Daisy froze. She didn't move as the man grabbed what was definitely a boot and chucked it into the back with what *couldn't* be a dead human being...could it? He closed the back hatch door quietly. Any click or thump it might have made was buried under the whistling groan of the wind.

It wasn't until the man opened the driver's door and looked directly at her window that Daisy returned to life, leaping away from the glass so violently that she stumbled over her backtracking feet and fell, dropping her phone. It took her a few moments before she could scrape up the nerve to stand and approach the window again. By the time she got close enough to see the street, the SUV was gone.

"Stupid," Daisy scolded herself, frantically looking in one direction and then the other, vainly trying to make out the red glow of taillights. There was nothing but darkness. "You could've gotten a good look at his face if you weren't such a chicken. He couldn't have seen you up here in the dark." Giving up on getting another glimpse of the SUV, she slumped against the window. "At least you could've looked at the plate number."

She rushed over to where her phone had fallen. Grabbing it, she pulled up her pathetically short list of contacts. Her finger hovered over Chris's name first, and then her father's. Her dad was in Connor Springs, installing solar panels on a new, high-end condo project. He was scheduled to be back that evening.

Her finger, poised above the screen, retreated before it tapped on either contact, and her arm dropped to her side. It was sinking in that she didn't have anything concrete. There was no plate number, no way she could identify which deputy had tossed a human-shaped bundle into the back of a squad SUV, and no certainty that there was, in fact, a dead body currently being transported who knew where. All she had was some indistinct video footage of a dark form putting *something* into an SUV.

If she called either her dad or Chris tonight, they'd think she was imagining things. Worse, they might believe she'd expanded the boundaries of crazy-town, adding delusions to her current phobia. Her father would look at her with angry, helpless eyes and scratch his beard. In the short time he'd be staying at the house before leaving for another installation job, conversation would be infrequent and awkward. Daisy cringed at the thought.

Chris, on the other hand... Daisy wasn't sure what he'd do. He'd been acting so squirrelly lately, and he might use this as a sign that he should stop telling her about his cases, especially the one revolving around the headless guy found in Mission Reservoir a couple of months ago. Worse, maybe he'd stop visiting her altogether.

Her breathing quickened, becoming harsh and shallow, and she closed her eyes. Daisy imagined hiking on a rocky trail, winding higher and higher until she reached the summit. In her mind, she turned around and could see the entire county spread out beneath her. The jagged edges of the lower peaks, furred with evergreens and aspen, smoothed into the flat plains. A distant herd of pronghorn grazed, and a pair of hawks circled in the impossibly blue sky. Daisy's heart beat faster, not in fear of the expansive space, but at the sheer beauty of it all. After a few minutes, her breaths came slow and even, and she allowed her eyes to open.

Carefully, she placed her phone back on the bedside table. Maybe there was a way she could investigate on her own. The *Simpson Star*, the weekly local paper, would be online at noon. She could check the section where the emergency calls and responses were posted. If a deputy had been sent to number 304, it would show up in that week's "Sheriff's Report." In the meantime, it wouldn't hurt to check if any missing-persons reports had been filed recently.

Instead of logging on to her laptop, though, she sat on her bed, shifting until her back was against the headboard. Pulling one of her pillows out from under her hip, she wrapped her arms around it. As she stared at the window across the room, she hugged the pillow and tried not to think about dead bodies, murderous deputies…or how desolate her life would be without Chris in it.

The flames followed the line of gasoline, lighting the fumes with a *whoosh*. Tyler grinned. That was his favorite part, when the fire went from the tiny flicker of a lighter to a ravenous monster intent on consuming an entire building. Heart pounding, he watched as the pile of cardboard caught fire, red and black crawling around the edges of each piece before the yellow flames appeared, growing until they almost touched the garage rafters.

Tyler coughed, eyeing the thickening layer of smoke. As much as he wanted to watch the fire close up, it was time for him to leave. Breathing was getting harder, and the owner—or a neighbor—would notice the smoke and flames. That meant the big red trucks would be arriving soon…and so would his father.

A twinge of guilt ran through him as he moved toward the side door, the one not facing the house. Tyler had promised he'd quit, and he'd tried. It was just such a rush—the roar of flames, the crash of a collapsing structure, the spreading glow as tree after tree ignited in an ever-widening circle, all because of him. *He'd* created that destruction with some accelerant and a flick of his lighter. It was tempting to tell everyone at school, all those kids who thought he was nothing— when they even thought of him at all. Tyler wouldn't tell, though. His dad had a hard enough time covering for him as it was.

Cracking open the door, he checked for any observers. A breeze brushed through the doorway, and the flames crackled and danced. After admiring the growing fire for a proud moment, Tyler slipped outside and darted for the cover of the trees.

It only took another minute or two before a cry came from the house, and the owner ran outside, wearing a coat over her pajamas. Tyler watched as she shouted into her cell phone while struggling to hook up the garden hose with her free hand.

The woman reminded him a little of Lou, and he shifted as he remembered, exhilaration and guilt surging through him. That had been the first time he'd set a fire knowing someone was inside. It had been freaky and intense to see her lying limp on the couch in a drugged sleep, to know that he was about to kill her. He'd felt a little bad, since she'd always been nice to him, but she'd been too interested in Willard Gray's death. She had to be stopped.

Tyler's dad always told him that being a man meant accepting responsibility. When Lou wouldn't stop poking around in the Gray investigation, Tyler knew he had to take action. His dad was always protecting Tyler. It'd been his turn to protect his father. He'd failed, though. Lou had lived.

A wail of a siren brought his attention back to his current creation—and destruction. The windows blew out in a shower of broken glass, and Tyler couldn't hold back an exultant laugh. *He'd* done that. The garage owner cried out and shifted away from the building, the forgotten hose still clutched in her hand. She stared at the fire, her face and body lit by the flames, as water poured from the hose and pooled uselessly around her feet.

The fire trucks pulled up to the curb just seconds before the sheriff department SUV arrived. Tyler's dad climbed out of the driver's seat, his gaze scanning the tree line. Even though Tyler knew he was hidden, he couldn't stop himself from shrinking farther behind a pine, instinctively trying to avoid that piercing gaze.

The wind picked up, making the flames shoot higher into the night sky. Since Tyler's gaze was locked on his father, he saw the sheriff's jacket flap open, revealing a black top that wasn't his uniform shirt. As if he'd felt his son's eyes on him, Rob glanced down and then zipped his coat, the tan one with "Sheriff" emblazoned on the back.

As his dad headed toward the fire chief, Tyler gave the fire one last longing glance before disappearing into the trees.

"Looking a little rough there, Dais."

Yawning, she shrugged, too sleepy to be concerned about her bed head. Once Chris was through the doorway, she allowed the door to close behind him and fumbled with the locks. Her hand-eye coordination apparently took longer to awaken than the rest of her.

"What are you doing up so early?" she asked when she eventually managed to secure the final chain.

"It's ten." He paused in the middle of untying his boots to look up at her. "That's not early. In fact, you could probably call that late."

"Not when you'll be on nights in a few days."

He shrugged. "Couldn't sleep."

"Me either. Well, until around seven this morning." Although she attempted to keep the accusation out of her tone, she didn't try *that* hard. Shuffling into the kitchen, she headed for the single-cup coffee brewer.

"Make me a hazelnut one?" Chris asked.

"Mine first," she grumbled, eyeing his obnoxiously chipper and wide-awake expression. "I need caffeine worse than you do." He'd obviously showered, since his normally unruly blond hair was behaving. His scruff was gone too, so he'd even shaved. Daisy missed the stubble. It gave a rough edge to his too-perfect handsomeness.

"Dais?" There was a note of amusement underlying his voice. "You fall back asleep?"

She blinked at him. "Huh?"

With a laugh, he reached past her and pushed the "on" button. "You zoned out on me. I figured you'd mentally gone back to bed."

"Wish I could," she grumbled, staring hard at the trickle of coffee making its way into her mug. The sleepiness faded, and the memory of what she'd witnessed in the wee hours started to loop through her mind. As she stood in the kitchen with Chris, the midmorning sunlight streaming through the window above the sink, the whole possible-dead-body incident seemed surreal.

"Any reason you were awake all night, or just the usual?" He grabbed the mug he always used, the one Daisy had painted in fifth grade. Being quite the young narcissist, she'd covered the surface in a multitude of her namesake flower.

Focusing intently on adding creamer to her cup, she mentally debated what to tell him. By the time she put her spoon in the sink, she'd decided. "I saw something really strange last night—this morning, actually."

Most of his attention on his coffee-making, Chris just gave an absent, "Hmm?"

"One of your brethren was parked in front of the white house across the street—the one that's been for sale forever?" Now that she'd had a few sips of coffee, the fog around her brain was beginning to lighten.

"My brethren?" He raised an eyebrow.

Daisy shrugged, careful not to spill her coffee. "It

was a sheriff's department squad. Not sure which deputy was on the call, though."

"At an empty house?" The brewer gave a final gurgle, and Chris pulled out the daisy mug, lifting it to his mouth in the same motion. "What was the call?"

"Since you won't get me my own emergency-services radio," she said, mostly joking, "I don't know what the call was. But it was weird."

He used the hand not holding his coffee to make a "go on" gesture.

"When I first saw the squad, I figured that Corbin was getting a stern talking-to, but the Storvicks' house was dark."

Chris groaned. "What's that little delinquent up to now?"

"Nothing that I know about…yet. I saw him arguing with someone on the phone a couple of nights ago, right before he smashed his cell against the wall."

Chris closed his eyes for a second, and his shoulders dropped in a silent sigh. "Dramatic little bastard. Thanks, Dais. I'll let the sheriff know we can expect another damage-to-property call from the girlfriend's family."

"Probably," she agreed.

"So, if it wasn't Corbin Storvick, what was a deputy doing here?"

She eyed him over her coffee mug. "It was weird."

"You said that. Weird how?"

"Before I tell you, you have to promise not to think I'm crazy." In the warm morning light, Daisy was beginning to doubt what she'd seen.

"I don't think you're crazy." He took a sip of coffee.

"Fine." She cupped her mug in both hands, since her

fingers felt cold. "I'll just tell you the facts, exactly how I saw things, and you can come to your own conclusions."

"Works for me." Setting his mug on the counter, he boosted himself up next to it. "Let's hear it."

"Okay. So, I'd just beaten the stuffing out of Max—whom I love, by the way. Thank you again for him." When Chris just waved off her thanks, she continued. "I went back to my room around three thirty, and I saw the squad parked outside. Since no one was in it, I waited for the deputy to return."

"No weirdness yet."

She frowned at him. "It's coming. Now, listen. About five or ten minutes later, I saw someone walking along the side of the house."

"Which one?"

"The for-sale one. Number 304."

"No, which side?"

"Oh! The one facing the Storvicks."

He made the "continue" flick with his hand again.

"This person is dressed all in black and is carrying a very large, tarp-wrapped object over his shoulder." It was hard to resist adding "body-shaped" to the list of adjectives. "He opens the back of the squad and puts the...*object* inside."

"Wait." Chris frowned. "The deputy was dressed in black?"

"Yep. Did I mention that this was weird?"

"Did you recognize him?"

She shook her head.

"You're sure it's a him, though?"

"Yes. Almost a hundred percent sure. Unless you have some really tall and built female deputies?"

"No. There are two women with the department, but I don't think you could mistake either for a man."

"Then he was male."

Although the frown between his eyebrows remained, he waved for her to continue.

"While the guy is putting the *object* into the back of the SUV, a boot falls out of the bottom of the tarp."

"A boot?"

"A boot." As much as she wanted to stay objective, Daisy couldn't take it anymore. "A boot! From a foot! Which is connected to the possible *dead body* that this guy was taking somewhere, probably to join the headless guy in Mission Reservoir!"

So much for sounding levelheaded. Daisy shut her mouth with a snap, but the words were out, and she couldn't suck them back in, no matter how badly she wanted to.

After staring at her for a long moment, Chris took a sip of his coffee. His maddening calm made her want to rip his mug away from him and throw it across the kitchen. Daisy reminded herself that tossing coffee around would not help the goal of making him think she *wasn't* crazy.

"A body."

"Yes." Since her attempt at a factual retelling was already blown, she figured she might as well tell him everything. "Whatever he was carrying in that tarp was shaped like a person. When he dropped it into the back, it even flopped around like a dead body would."

"Hmm."

Chris had on his cop face. He hardly ever used his cop face with her, and Daisy's chest felt tight. Beneath that mask, was he thinking about what a nut ball she was? She desperately hoped telling him this wouldn't damage their friendship—any more than it already was, at least. It was just that there was a *boot*. Surely, Chris would understand the importance of that boot.

"Where'd he go?" he asked, finally ending the silence.

"I'm...um, not sure." She made a face, not wanting to admit the less-than-brave truth. "He started looking up toward my window, and I was afraid he'd see me, so I kind of jumped back and...well, I tripped."

"You tripped." His face was blank, and she really wished he'd stop using that impassive tone of voice with her.

"I tripped," she growled, narrowing her eyes. Their stare-off continued until Daisy knew she was going to lose—she *always* did—so she started talking again to distract him. "By the time I got back to the window, he was gone."

Although he made that aggravating noncommittal sound again, his gaze was thoughtful. He focused on the mug in his hands as if his coffee were a crystal ball.

After waiting for what she felt was a more than sufficient amount of time for him to consider the situation, Daisy couldn't stay quiet any longer. "So?"

"It was dark."

It was a statement rather than a question, but she answered anyway. "Yes. The moon was bright when the clouds weren't covering it, but the streetlights out there are pretty much useless unless someone's standing directly under one."

"You're sure that he wasn't in uniform?"

"Yes." She closed her eyes to bring the memory of the scene into better focus before opening them again. "Yes. He was all in black—boots, pants, and coat with the hood up."

"What'd he look like?" The intensity of his gaze flustered her, making her feel like she was the subject of an interrogation. It was just Chris's way of asking questions, she told herself, trying to ignore her discomfort and focus on answering.

"I didn't see his face, and the angle from upstairs makes it hard to judge, but I think he was fairly tall. Not skinny, but the coat made it hard to tell if he was muscular or just chunky. I took a video, but it's really dark." Pulling out her phone, she found the video and handed her cell to Chris.

As he watched it, frowning, he asked, "Did you get the squad number off the SUV?"

"No. Sorry."

"Anything distinctive about the guy? The way he walked or held himself?" Chris held out her cell.

Accepting her phone, she closed her eyes for a moment again, but it didn't help that time. "No. He was walking through snow and carrying something heavy and dead-body-like, so…oh!" The thought made her bounce, remaining coffee sloshing around in her mug. "The snow! There'll be footprints!"

Draining his cup, he rinsed it out and left it in the sink. "I'll check it out."

Chris pulled on his outerwear and let himself out the interior door. After bolting it behind him, Daisy dashed for her bedroom window. She watched as he headed toward number 304. He took pictures of the tracks on both sides of the building with his phone before circling to the back yard.

Waiting impatiently for him to reappear, she wished she could just walk out of the house and join him. Merely catching a glimpse of the front door was enough to make her dizzy, though, so she doubted she'd be visiting the great outdoors anytime soon.

"Coward," she muttered, letting her head tilt against the chilled glass. "No wonder he won't even let you give him a hug. You're a scaredy-freak."

The glass reflected her unhappy expression. In high school—when she'd *gone* to high school—she'd been considered pretty enough. She'd been shy, though, and the attention her early developing body had attracted had made her more nervous than flattered. Her caramel-colored hair used to get blonde streaks from the sun, and her skin had tanned easily. Her mouth was full and wide, her teeth straight enough to never need braces, and dimples dented her cheeks when she smiled. She liked her eyes—greenish-gold with thick lashes.

Surely not all of that could have changed?

It was hard to look in a mirror and judge her own appearance, though. Daisy knew she was pale, and her hair was darker without help from the sun, but she didn't think she was ugly. The fitness room kept her toned and muscular. However, without outside feedback—flirty, interested looks from guys or the honest critique of a female friend—she didn't know if she'd be considered attractive. As much as she wanted him to, Chris never seemed to notice what she looked like at all.

Shaking herself out of her introspective funk, she saw Chris crossing the yard. Next door, Corbin was walking on the path that ran in front of his house. He'd almost reached the driveway where his Jeep was parked when he spotted the deputy. Although Chris wasn't in uniform, Corbin must have recognized him, because the teen lowered his head and hurried back toward the front door.

"Ooh, you've done *something* bad, baby creeper," Daisy said. "Get him, Chris!"

Chris was already striding toward Corbin, his long legs moving quickly through the snow. Before the boy could step onto the porch, the deputy was next to him. Daisy wished for binoculars once again, plus the ability to read lips, as Chris talked for several minutes. Corbin kept his head down, except for an occasional nod or head shake.

When Chris finally headed back to Daisy's front door, she scrambled off the window seat and rushed down the stairs to let him inside. Slapping the button to unlock the exterior door, she unfastened the dead bolts and chains. In her excitement to hear what he'd discovered about the mystery deputy's early morning visit—plus the smack-down he'd hopefully given Corbin—she jerked open the door without pausing to listen for the usual click of the latch.

As it swung wide, exposing the *still-open* exterior door, she felt as if all the blood drained from her body. A wide rectangle of sunlight outlined a startled-looking Chris. Her eyes fixed on that too-bright expanse over his shoulder, that yawning hole that allowed in all the dangers and horrors of the outside world. Her heart thudded in her ears, the beats so fast they started blending together. She couldn't breathe, couldn't think, couldn't do anything except stare at that terrible brightness.

Her vision blurred and tilted...right before the world went black.

Chapter 3

THERE WAS NO FUZZINESS TO SOFTEN HER HUMILIATION. As soon as Daisy opened her eyes and saw Chris's concerned face framed by her entryway ceiling, she knew what had happened. His hand was at her throat, and his cell phone was pressed to his ear.

"She's regaining consciousness. Pulse is seventy-two." His voice was clipped as he relayed the information to whoever was on the other end of the call, but it softened when he spoke to her. "Hey, Dais. You back with me?"

"No," she said. "I mean, yes. I'm fine. But you better not be calling for an ambulance, Chris Jennings, or I'm going to be super pissed."

He frowned at her. "Yes, she's conscious and alert now."

"I am. Conscious, alert, and in no need of medical assistance." She tried to sit, but he moved his hand from her throat to her upper chest to keep her lying flat. He was squatting next to her, still in his boots, coat, and hat. "Chris. I'm serious. Cancel the ambulance."

"You hit your head." Once he said it, a corresponding throb lit up the back of her skull. "I tried to catch you, but I wasn't quick enough."

She probed the lump on the back of her head, restraining a wince. "It's just a minor bump." Despite her best efforts at trying to stay calm, she could hear a hint of panic in her voice. "Please, Chris. I'll have to explain why I fainted in the first place, and what if they want to take me to the hospital?" Tears threatened to compound her humiliation as she grabbed for him, catching a handful of the BDUs covering his calf.

His silence squashed her hope, and a tear escaped. Gritting her teeth, she turned her head, burying her face against his leg in an attempt to hide.

Chris swore. "Sorry, Libby. That wasn't directed at you. Go ahead and have Med stand down."

Stupidly, relief made Daisy cry harder. Chris's hand moved from her chest to cup the back of her head. Freed, she rolled to her side, tucking her face even farther under his knee until her forehead bumped his boot.

"Appreciate it, Libby. Uh-huh." His hand stroked Daisy's hair as he spoke absently into his phone. "Okay. Thanks again." He must have ended the call, because suddenly both of his hands were free. Rocking back to sit on the tiles, Chris hauled her into his lap.

The shift in position startled her, thankfully stopping the flow of tears. She held herself stiffly for a second and then relaxed into his chest, too worn out to fight him. The material of his coat was rough against her damp cheek, but his arms were locked tightly around her, which was nice.

"Dais," he muttered, using his thumb to wipe the residual wetness from the exposed side of her face.

"Sorry." Her sigh shuddered with leftover tears. "Thanks for canceling the ambulance."

His fingers moved to feel the sore spot on the back of her head. The unexpected contact sent a throb of pain through her skull, and she couldn't help flinching away from his touch.

"I probably shouldn't have," he grumbled, his fingers returning to the aching bump. "What if your skull's fractured?"

"My skull's not fractured. Ow!" She swatted at his probing hand. "If you don't stop pushing on it, though, *yours* might be. Quit it! What are you trying to accomplish by poking at me, anyway?"

"I don't know." Thankfully, he stopped. "Just making sure you don't have brains leaking out or anything."

"Gross." She made a face and then tried to stand. As nice as it was to be in Chris's arms, she didn't want to be held because he pitied her. "I don't. My brains are all where they should be, and they're still greatly superior to whatever's in your thick skull."

At first, he resisted letting her go, but then he snorted, and his body relaxed. "Please. We both know that I'm the genius of this operation." As he climbed to his feet, he helped her stand, as well. She was grateful for his grip on her arms when the room wobbled around her. It quickly straightened, and she stepped back, slipping free of Chris's hold. After locking the interior door, she moved into the kitchen.

"Hah." She suddenly felt overwhelmingly tired and would have paid a great deal of money to be able to sit down again. She didn't trust Chris not to have Libby send the ambulance after all, though, so she feigned nonchalance and leaned against the counter, letting it support a good portion of her weight. "My brain would totally kick your brain's ass in a death match."

The worried crease between his eyebrows eased slightly. "Would not."

"Would too."

"Not."

She stuck out her tongue. "Whatever, Einstein. Tell me what you found."

"Found?"

Gesturing in the general direction of the street, she prompted, "At 304? Oh, and what'd you say to Corbin? Did you see him sprint for the house when he saw you? That boy did something naughty."

Instead of answering, he eyed her searchingly. "We can talk about this later."

"Oh, no way, Jose! I could barely wait until you got back, as evidenced by…" She trailed off, waving toward the door. "If you drag this out any longer, I'll…well, I'll think of something bad to do to you. So, spill."

After another few seconds, he caved, digging his phone out of his coat pocket. "Fine. Here. You can check out the prints while I take off my boots."

Not wanting to leave the support of the counter—since she had a feeling it was the only thing keeping her upright—Daisy held out her hand for the phone. With a shrug, he tossed it to her.

"Ack!" She fumbled but managed to catch it between her palms before it could fall onto the tile. "Careful, there. Don't you think one falling object a day is enough?"

He returned to the entryway and pulled off his boots. "I was testing your reflexes."

"Thanks, Dr. Chris," she said dryly, pulling up the most recent photos. Frowning, she flicked through them, magnifying a few to get a closer view. "What is that in some of these—a penny?"

"Yep." Having shucked his coat and hat, he moved

to stand next to her. "I didn't have my kit with me, and I needed a scale. Pennies work, since they're a standard size."

She snorted. "You just saw it in that movie we watched a few weeks ago."

"Did not. Learned that in cop school." He nudged her with his shoulder, and she caught herself before she toppled sideways. "Besides, she used a quarter in the movie."

Grinning, Daisy brought the phone closer to her face. "Can you tell anything from these? Not to knock your photography skills, but they all look like white dents in the snow to me."

"Yeah." His gloomy voice made her glance at him. "I can tell that they match my boots."

Her eyebrows shot toward her hairline. "Which means…what? That you were the one moving a body last night?"

He rolled his eyes. "Yeah, Dais. You caught me. No, these are about a size or two bigger than mine. Whoever it was walking around out there was wearing department-issued boots."

"So it was definitely a deputy."

"Unless someone just happened to get the same brand and style of boots, then yeah."

"Uh…didn't we already know that? This guy was driving a squad, after all."

Reclaiming his phone, Chris started sorting through his photos. "Not necessarily. All someone needed was access and the keys. Could've been a family member or a friend of someone on the department. Here." He handed the phone back to her, a photo of about a dozen people on the screen. "Was the person last night any of these guys?"

She looked at the picture. It must've been taken at some sort of training, because they were all in BDUs and tan T-shirts bearing the sheriff's department logo. Most of them were smiling, although a few had on their tough-guy expressions. "I didn't get a good look at his face, but we can eliminate this guy, this guy, and these two women because of their builds."

Chris scowled as she pointed.

"What's wrong?" she asked.

"Nothing," he grumbled, taking his phone again and pocketing it. "It just sucks that you took Lawrence out of the suspect pool. I wouldn't have minded arresting him."

Daisy laughed. "Sorry."

"It's premature thinking that a crime was committed, though," Chris warned. "I need to check the call log from last night and this morning to see if there was a legitimate reason for a deputy to be at that house."

"Not in uniform?" she asked doubtfully.

"There might be a good explanation for that, too."

She watched as he stared into space, obviously thinking hard. "You think it was something...not good, though."

"Maybe," he dodged. "Maybe not. I don't have enough information to determine that yet."

"Uh-huh." Daisy wasn't convinced. "But your gut tells you it wasn't just a normal response to a call. I can tell, since you have on your hunter face."

"My what?" he half laughed, losing the intent expression as he turned to face her.

"Hunter face." She shrugged. "You get this look, like you're a wolf about to take down an elk."

"Right. No more *Nature* specials for you."

She made a face at him but let it drop. "What's the next step?"

"Checking the call log, like I said." His eyebrows furrowed again as he looked at her, and Daisy met his gaze evenly, hoping she didn't look as wobbly as she felt. "I'm thinking about asking Lou if she could come over to talk to you."

"What?" That seemed to come out of the blue. Startled, she dug through her brain to remember what Chris had told her about a Lou. "You mean barista, dive team member, and stalker-killer Lou? Why?"

"That's the one." He drummed his fingers against the counter. "Because she's been looking into Willard Gray's murder."

"The guy found in the reservoir? Well," she corrected herself, wrinkling her nose, "most of him was found in the reservoir, at least."

"Yeah."

"Why should Lou come talk to me?"

Chris was still frowning, and his words came after a hesitation, as if he wasn't sure he should be saying what he was. "I can't give you details about the case, Dais. I could lose my job."

"So, you really do think what I saw this morning is related to that Gray guy's murder?"

"Probably not."

"But it might be."

Blowing out a frustrated breath, he pushed away from the counter and paced the kitchen. "The Gray case has been a complete cluster from the beginning. So many things about it don't make any sense, and it's frustrating the hell out of me. Whenever anything strange happens, I find myself trying to link it to the case. I know I'm reaching, but something's telling me not to blow off what you told me as..." He sent her an odd look, a mix of frustration and guilt.

"As the ravings of a crazy lady?" she finished for him, trying to keep her voice light even as she swallowed back bile.

"No." He stopped and scrubbed his fingers through his hair, bringing it back to its usual rumpled condition. "No. Dais, you're not crazy."

Forcing a laugh, she waved her hand in a dismissive gesture. "It's okay, Chris. I know what I am."

"Dais."

It was time to change the subject. "Tell Lou she can come over here, if she wants."

"Daisy."

"From what you've told me, she'll be fun to talk to, even if we don't unearth a countywide conspiracy." She pushed away from the counter, relieved when her legs wobbled a little but held her upright. "Did you want some coffee to take with you?"

He was watching her with a little too much intensity, so she tried to ignore him, moving over to the coffee-maker and holding up a hazelnut cup. "No," he finally said, sounding defeated. "I'm good."

They were both quiet as Chris once again donned his boots and coat. He unlocked the interior dead bolts, the heavy clicks loud in the silence, and then stilled, turning to look at her.

"You're not crazy."

Although she felt too tired to start the argument again, she couldn't make the assurances he needed to hear. Instead, she sighed. "See you later, Chris."

His face grew tight, but he finally turned away. "Bye, Dais."

After the interior door closed behind him, Daisy stared at it for a long time before moving to engage the locks.

—⁓—

Rob gave a grunt of annoyance when his phone started ringing. It always seemed to happen when his hands were full. Leaning forward, he dumped Anderson King's body onto the rocky ground and then reached for his phone, checking the caller ID before accepting the call.

"Chris," he greeted.

"Hey, Rob." A tentative note in his deputy's voice caught Rob's attention. "I've got a strange question for you. Got a minute?"

Not really. "Sure. What's up?" Holding his phone in place with his shoulder, Rob took off his backpack and pulled out the bottle of bear bait.

"Was there a call for service at 304 Alpine Lane early this morning?"

Rob froze, the bottle falling from suddenly numb fingers. He had to clear his throat before he was able to speak. "Sorry, reception got bad for a second there. Did you say 304 Alpine?"

"Yeah. It's the vacant white house that's been on the market all winter."

Shit. Shit. Shit. "There wasn't a call there as far as I know. Why do you ask?"

"My friend, Daisy, saw someone out of uniform put something into a squad." Chris hesitated a moment before he continued. "She thought it looked...suspicious."

Rob couldn't breathe.

"She got some video footage of the guy on her phone, but it was pretty dark."

Video footage? The clamp around his throat tightened.

After a few moments of silence, Chris spoke again. "There was nothing on the call log, but I figured there was some explanation other than..."

"Other than...?" Rob repeated, forcing out the words.

"Well, Daisy thought the object being put into the squad might have been a body."

Closing his eyes, Rob swallowed a frustrated grunt. Why couldn't things ever go smoothly? All he wanted to do was protect his son and the community, but it felt like roadblocks were being thrown in his way at every turn. "A body?" He put as much amused disbelief into his voice as he could manage.

"I know it sounds hard to believe," Chris said, "but if Daisy saw something she thinks is suspicious, it's worth checking out."

"Wait, is this Daisy Little you're talking about?" Recognition hit, and Rob kicked himself for not making the connection earlier. "The girl who hasn't left the house since her mom was killed in that robbery?" Some of the tension left his body. This kind of witness he could handle.

"Yes." Chris's voice was sharply defensive.

Interesting. "Daisy says there was something off about the situation, and I believe her."

"Agreed. I'll look into it." *One more clean-up job.*

"Yeah?" Chris said, sounding surprised and pleased. "Great. Thanks for taking this seriously."

"Of course. As soon as I'm done here, I'll stop by Daisy's to talk to her. We'll figure this out."

"Thanks again, Rob."

After Chris ended the call, Rob squeezed his eyes closed and allowed himself a full minute of mental cursing. Then, shaking off his frustration, he picked up the bottle of bear bait and began to pour it over Anderson's body. Once the scavengers were done with the corpse, any evidence of the bullet holes would be destroyed. In the unlikely case that his remains were found, it would be determined that Anderson had fallen prey to exposure.

Rob pushed away worries about Daisy Little. *Deal with one threat at a time*, he told himself, recapping the empty bottle and stowing it in his backpack.

A raven croaked from its perch on the blackened skeleton of a pine tree. As Rob glanced at the bird, it was joined by two more, all of them eyeing him with interest. With a grim smile, he gestured toward the bait-soaked corpse.

"Bon appétit."

―――――

The knock was different, unfamiliar, and Daisy's finger hesitated over the intercom button for a long moment. It would probably be safer to pretend she wasn't home.

The thought made her huff a humorless laugh.

Everyone in Simpson knew she was *always* home, so that probably wasn't the best and brightest plan.

When the rapping came again, louder that time, she jumped, her finger unintentionally pressing the button. Decision made for her, she leaned toward the intercom and hoped that the staticky connection would disguise the shake in her voice.

"Who is it?"

"Hi!" An unfamiliar female voice came through the speaker. "I'm Lou Sparks. Louise, actually, but you can just pretend I never told you that. Chris said he warned you I was coming."

"Warned?"

The intercom turned Lou's laugh into a buzz at the end. "Yes. He actually used the word 'warned.' I was terribly offended."

She didn't sound offended. In fact, her merry tone made Daisy smile and push the button to unlock the exterior door. "Come in."

Even after the clunk and click of the exterior door closing and locking, Daisy hesitated a few more seconds before starting on the row of dead bolts. That morning's incident had pushed her from cautious to paranoid. It was fine when she had a pane of glass separating her from the world, but the bare, wide-open doorway had brought her to her knees—or, more accurately, to her back.

She cut off that entire train of thought. It wasn't the time to analyze her issues, since she had a guest trapped between the doors.

As if to emphasize that fact, a muffled voice asked tentatively, "Should I knock again? Just let me know the procedure."

Sliding the last chain lock free, Daisy pulled open the door. A pretty blond woman in her midtwenties stood on the other side.

"No procedure. I mean, I just wait until the outside door closes before I unlock this one, but there's no other…" She shook her head, taking a step back so Lou could enter. "Sorry. I'm babbling. Come in. I'm not normally so scattered. It's just been a weird day so far."

Lou grinned. "Well, you have one up on me, then, since I do babble, pretty much constantly, and I don't need a strange day to make it happen."

Her fingers shook a little as Daisy relocked the interior door, and she tried to mentally force them to stop. Was she that far gone that a new visitor made her quiver like a Chihuahua?

"I'm okay with babbling," she…well, babbled, before she bit off the rest of the words that wanted to come pouring out of her mouth. "Would you like something to drink? Coffee or…" Mentally, Daisy inventoried the beverages in the fridge and held back a wince. "Water? I'm sorry that there's not much of a selection."

"Water would be great." Stepping out of her boots, Lou hung her jacket on the coat rack next to the door. "Today's my day off, but I normally work at a coffee shop. I don't drink coffee when I'm there, but I still think I absorb the caffeine through my pores, or something. Anyway, I'm normally wired enough that I don't need to add a stimulant to the mix."

Daisy wasn't sure how to respond to that, so she focused on digging a bottle of water out of the fridge.

"Thanks," Lou said, taking a few steps closer so she could grab the bottle. "Your kitchen is amazing."

"My dad just completed remodeling it about a year ago. It took forever for him to finish, since he kept having to leave to go to job sites. After living in half-constructed hell for that long, I'm still grateful just to have a working sink."

"Your dad lives here with you?" Lou explored the room unashamedly, running her fingers over the mosaic tiles that made up the backsplash.

"Yes. Well," Daisy corrected herself, "when he's not out of town, working on a job."

"Construction?"

"Alternative energy systems. He installs solar panels, wind turbines, things like that. His clients are really spread out, though, so he just parks the camper close to whatever job he's working on at the time. Right now, he's in Connor Springs. He's due back tonight, actually."

Lou cocked her head, giving her an unreadable look. "Connor Springs is only twenty miles away."

Dropping her gaze, Daisy busied herself with making yet another cup of coffee. "I think he likes being at the job site at night. That way, he can keep an eye on his equipment."

"Okay." Lou's voice was gentle—*too* gentle—and Daisy cleared her throat, determined to change the subject.

"Are you really a lawyer?" When Lou looked startled, Daisy explained, "Chris mentioned something about that."

"I made it through law school." Lou said "law school" with the same amount of disgust most people reserved for "cockroaches." "I even passed the bar. I never practiced, though. I decided I'd rather have the money, power, and prestige that comes from being a barista in Simpson."

Daisy snorted a laugh and was immediately embarrassed by the piglike sound. "I have you beat for least prestigious jobs."

"You work?"

She tried not to be offended at the surprise in the other woman's voice. After all, it had been a long and arduous search for a way for her to make money without leaving the house. "Yep. I sell things online. Antiques and collectables, mainly. Dad goes to the auctions and estate sales, and he brings back boxes and boxes filled with...well, mostly junk." She gave a small laugh. "Dad doesn't have a clue about old stuff, and he doesn't have any interest in learning about it, either. He texts me a lot of pictures, and I text back with a thumbs-up or thumbs-down. I clean and repair what I think will sell and then list it online."

"Nice," Lou said, playing with the cap of her water bottle. "Ingenious, really. There probably aren't that many jobs that don't require at least *some* outside time."

"Nope, there really aren't." Her smile felt a little forced as she gestured toward the living room with the hand not holding her coffee mug. "Do you want to sit down?"

"Sure." As Daisy led the way, Lou continued, "I have to say that your house is not what I expected. In fact, *you're* not what I expected."

Although she wasn't sure if she wanted to know, Daisy couldn't resist asking, "In what way?"

Lou settled on one end of the sofa, tucking her socked feet underneath her. She was so relaxed, as if she'd been there a hundred times before. Sitting on the other side of the couch, Daisy was envious, unable to even imagine possessing that kind of confidence.

"Well, you're hot, for one."

Lou's comment caught Daisy in the middle of taking a sip of coffee. It took some effort not to spray the mouthful across the room. "Excuse me?"

Her expression must have revealed her reaction, since Lou laughed. "When I think 'shut-in,' I think old and ugly, and you're definitely neither. I also imagined you dressed like an Amish woman, but I'm not sure why."

Daisy choked again. "Um...Amish?"

"You know." Lou gestured at her own thermal shirt and jeans. "Long dress, apron, funky hat."

After sitting with her mouth open for a few seconds, Daisy started laughing. "*Why?*"

"I said I didn't *know* why!" Despite her aggrieved tone, Lou was snickering, as well. "When I heard that you didn't leave the house, a picture of an Amish grandma popped into my head. It was random and weird. That happens to me a lot."

"Mental pictures of Amish grandmothers?"

"Well, sometimes. But mostly random and weird thoughts."

"I see." Taking a deep breath, Daisy got her amusement under control. "Why did the house surprise you? Did you have a mental picture of that, too?"

"Yes." Lou winced, taking a drink of her water in an obvious attempt to delay elaborating.

"Tell me. I promise I won't be offended."

"Piles of newspapers and lots of cats," Lou muttered, her gaze focused firmly on the water bottle cap she was twisting and untwisting.

"Huh." Although Daisy figured she *should* be insulted, she just found it funny. "So, I'm an elderly Amish hoarder." She frowned thoughtfully. "Wouldn't 'Amish hoarder' be some kind of oxymoron?"

Lou laughed. "I think so."

When their laughter faded, the silence reminded Daisy of the purpose of Lou's visit. "Did Chris tell you why he thought we should talk?"

"Not really," Lou said. "He called me this morning and said it would behoove me to swing by Daisy Little's house to chat, and that he'd 'warned' you I'd be coming. There were lots of meaningful pauses, but I had no clue what he was getting at. He was being very un-Chris-like in his vagueness, but he was pretty insistent about me talking to you. When I told him that Callum had the truck, Chris even picked me up from my house and drove me here."

"He told me he couldn't talk about the Willard Gray case, but that I should talk to you."

Lou's eyes lit, and she leaned toward Daisy. "Do you know something about the case? I'm doing the whole Encyclopedia Brown thing, ever since I discovered poor Willard."

"Encyclopedia...what?"

Waving off the question, Lou tilted so far forward that Daisy was afraid she'd topple over. "I've been looking into Willard Gray's murder, even before we knew who he was. Callum and I put together a murder board and everything."

The more Lou explained things, the more confused Daisy got. "A murder board?"

"It's just a whiteboard with everything we know

about the case. I snuck a couple of my less wild theories on there, too, much to Callum's dismay. He's more of a just-the-facts kind of guy."

"O-kay." Daisy took a sip of coffee to give her a chance to digest some of what Lou had just thrown at her. "So, Chris wants me to tell you what I saw this morning so you can add it to your killer board?"

"Murder board." Lou was actually bouncing on her sofa cushion. Daisy understood why she'd declined caffeine. Even without it, Lou looked about ready to rocket into space. "What did you see this morning? Did Chris actually think it was related to Willard's case? You need to start spilling immediately. I'm dying here!"

"I'm spilling! I'm spilling!" Daisy hurried to explain before Lou started levitating. "I think I saw someone moving a body."

Lou went perfectly still before shrieking, "*What?*"

Wincing, Daisy shot the other woman a look.

"Sorry," Lou mumbled through the fingers she'd clapped over her mouth. After a few deep breaths, she let her hand drop back to her lap. "I get excited when someone mentions dead bodies. Oh, wow, that just went to a really wrong place, didn't it? Okay, so forget my disturbing remark and get back to your story. I promise there will be no more screaming, unless you reveal something totally shocking. Let's just say that I will attempt to keep my verbal exclamation points to a minimum, how about that?"

"Um...sure. This morning, around three thirty, I saw someone loading what looked like a tarp-wrapped body into a sheriff's department vehicle."

Instead of screaming, Lou just stared, her mouth

open. Daisy sipped her coffee and let the other woman process the information. After several moments passed, Lou finally moved. She set her water bottle on the coffee table with the utmost care. Pulling her cell phone out of her back jeans pocket, she jabbed at the screen and then put the cell to her ear.

"Cal," Lou said into her phone, "you need to bring the whiteboard over to Daisy Little's house. I'm getting vital information here. I need my markers." Her forehead creased at his response. "The whiteboard is an important part of our investigation team, Cal. We need him here." She continued in an overly patient tone, as if the answer should've been obvious. "Of course the whiteboard is male. I named him Emerson." Lou paused again. "Because someone named Emerson has to be intelligent. So, are you up for a whiteboard delivery?"

By Lou's crestfallen expression, Daisy was pretty sure the answer was "no." "Fine. I still love you, even if you are leaving me lost and whiteboardless." She glanced at Daisy and gave her an apologetic look, mouthing *no whiteboard*. "Daisy Little's house. Uh-huh. That Daisy Little." Absently, she reached out with her free hand and started turning her water bottle in circles. "Deputy Chris drove me here. He was being really insistent in a weird and vague way about how I needed to talk to Daisy. Apparently, she saw a deputy moving a dead body really early this morning." Lou listened for a minute. "That's okay. Chris can give me a ride ho—fine! I'll call you. You know," her tone turned crafty, "if I bought that old International pickup I want, you wouldn't have to be my taxi service." Her disappointed, no-whiteboard frown returned. "But it's adorable. Who needs modern safety

features when I'm driving something so awesome? Yes.
Okay. We'll argue about this later. I need to get all the
body-moving details from Daisy now." Lou looked a
little too excited about the prospect. "Uh-huh. Love you,
too. Bye."

After poking at her phone again, Lou tucked it into
her back pocket. "No whiteboard."

Daisy snorted. "I got that."

"Do you have a notebook or a piece of paper or
something?" Lou asked. "I know I'm not going to
remember everything."

"Sure." Daisy retrieved a small notebook and a pen
from the junk drawer in the kitchen and offered them to
Lou before taking her seat on the couch again.

"Perfect. Thank you." Lou flipped open the notebook
cover. "Now tell me *everything*."

Chapter 4

THEY WENT OVER ALL THE DETAILS MULTIPLE TIMES. Instead of making Daisy more certain about what she'd seen, it only increased her doubts. Repeating the story over and over made what happened sound so outlandish and unbelievable.

"What if there's some stupidly simple and innocent explanation for this?" she finally asked Lou. "I'm going to feel so dumb that I've wasted your time and Chris's and—"

"Stop." Lou cut off her torrent of words. "If that's true, then Chris will see it in the call log, and we'll all be happy that no one is dead. But can you really think of a good reason for someone dressed in black to be shoving something shaped like a dead body—including a boot!—into a sheriff's squad at three in the morning?"

Daisy had been trying all day to come up with a logical explanation, and she hadn't succeeded. She shook her head.

"Me neither. It's not like we're going to do crazy things with this information. We're just going to add it to the other facts on the whiteboard and see if it snaps together with any of the other puzzle pieces."

"Okay." Daisy let out a long breath.

Lou's cell chirped, and she glanced at the screen. "Callum is leaving Station One right now and is headed over to pick me up. He should be here in five minutes or so."

Glancing at her watch, Daisy was shocked to see that they'd been talking for almost two hours. Now that Lou was about to leave, disappointment swept over Daisy. It had been so nice having someone new—and female—to chat with, even if that chat had been about a possible dead body. "Did you want to see the rest of the house? The quick tour takes less than five minutes."

"Definitely." Lou bounced to her feet.

As Daisy led the way through the lower level, she felt simultaneously flustered and excited. There was also a tinge of embarrassment that she was so thrilled to have found a new friend, since she probably should have outgrown that level of enthusiasm in kindergarten.

"This is the... I don't know what exactly to call it. The gym? Training room?"

Lou made a beeline to Max. "No matter what you call it, this place is awesome!" Wrapping an arm around the waist of the grappling dummy, she looked around at the rest of the equipment. "No wonder you have a body like...that." She gestured at Daisy, who flushed and resisted the self-conscious urge to wrap her arms around herself.

As she tried to look at the home gym with a stranger's eyes, Daisy had to admit it was really nice. Her dad had knocked down the wall between two rooms to give her a lot of space. She had a treadmill and an elliptical machine, free weights and benches, a pull-up bar, a variety of heavy and speed bags, and plenty of mat space for sparring. Plus, Max was pretty awesome in and of himself.

"Who trains you?" Lou asked, leaving Max with a pat on the rump to explore the rest of the room. "Or do you just use YouTube videos or something?"

"Chris, mostly, although I do have some DVDs, too." She grinned. "And maybe a few YouTube videos."

Instead of laughing, Lou gave her an interested look. "So, you and Chris…?"

"No. I mean, we're friends, but not…" Daisy waved a hand, her blush brightening. "We're friends. So…no."

"Uh-huh." Lou's voice was skeptical. To Daisy's utter relief, Lou's phone chirped, interrupting whatever else the other woman was about to say.

"Callum?" Daisy guessed.

"He's at the front door. Apparently," Lou smirked, "he's been knocking."

"Oh!" Hurrying out of the training room, Daisy said over her shoulder, "I should have a doorbell, but I normally don't get that many visitors, so it hasn't really been an issue before."

"Don't worry about Callum." After a final, longing look at the fitness equipment, Lou followed her to the front entry. "Standing outside for a few minutes won't kill him. I keep telling him that patience is a virtue."

"Um…okay." Daisy pushed the unlock button for the exterior door. There was the usual thump-click as the outside entrance relocked, and her hand moved to the first dead bolt. A heavy knock on the interior door made her jump.

"Hold your horses, Cal!" Lou bellowed right next to her ear, startling Daisy again. "There are a bazillion locks, so it's going to take a minute."

The only acknowledgment from the other side of the

door was a masculine grunt, but the knocking didn't resume, so Daisy assumed that Cal had held his horses, as requested. Her hands shook a little as she unfastened the dead bolts and chains. It seemed like a long time before she managed to open the door, revealing a big, stern-looking man wearing a baseball cap.

As his narrow-eyed gaze fixed on her, Daisy took a couple of steps back to put some space between her and the intimidating man.

"Callum!" Apparently, Lou was not at all daunted by the austere figure, judging by the way she grabbed his hand and tried to haul him into the kitchen. "You have to see this home gym. It's awesome, and there's even a naked guy in there."

That seemed to catch his attention, and his piercing gaze moved to Lou.

"I've been meaning to put some pants on him." Daisy wasn't sure why she was blushing. It wasn't like Max was anatomically correct. He was an oversized Ken doll. "I'll need to get some from Chris, since Dad's pants would be too small for him."

Callum redirected his attention back to her, making Daisy wish she hadn't said anything. There was something about the look he was giving her that made her want to prattle. "I'm Daisy."

"Oops, sorry. I'm being mannerless. Callum, this is Daisy. Daisy, Callum. As you can see, Cal, Daisy is nothing like an Amish grandma."

"Or a hoarder," Daisy added.

"Definitely not a hoarder. Come on." This time, when Lou tugged at Callum's hand, he followed her into the kitchen. A few steps in, he waved Daisy ahead of them.

She hurried to lead the way to the fitness room. Once inside, the first thing her gaze landed on was Max's Ken-doll-like crotch, and she blushed, vowing to ask Chris for some sweatpants the very next time she talked to him.

"Very nice." Callum examined the room with careful attention.

"Thank you." She could feel the babbling trying to break free, and she swallowed down the rush of words with some effort.

"Isn't this great?" Apparently, Lou was all too willing to pick up the conversational slack. "In Simpson, most of us have to make do with more natural forms of weight training, like carrying firewood and moving rocks. I'd love to learn more self-defense, though. Do you think I could invite myself to train with you and Chris sometime?"

"No," Callum said before Daisy could even open her mouth to reply. "I'll teach you self-defense if you want to learn."

"Um...I don't think so." Leaning into his side, Lou gave him a sweet smile. "When you try to teach me anything one-on-one, I end up wanting to kill you. Besides, Chris knows all the cop moves."

Callum frowned at her. "We do fine in dive training."

"That's different. There's a group of us, so it dilutes my homicidal impulses."

"I'd rather you not do any...*grappling* with Jennings."

"Fine." She turned to Daisy, who'd been watching their argument like it was a game of Ping-Pong. "Daisy, can Callum join us for our training sessions? That way, we'll have an even number of grapplers."

"Uh…sure." Daisy wasn't sure how a grappling club had just started in her fitness room, but she blamed the hurricane named Lou. "Let me talk to Chris."

"You know who else really needs to learn this stuff, especially with Anderson still out and about?" Lou had a thoughtful expression, which made Daisy worry. "Ellie Price. She probably won't be able to do much for another couple of weeks, since she's still recovering from getting shot in the chest, but she could definitely benefit from knowing a few self-defense moves."

"I think Holloway has it covered." The corner of Callum's mouth tucked in, like he was holding back a smile.

Lou shook her head. "He can't watch her twenty-four hours a day."

"He's going to try."

"I'm going to ask her anyway. George can come along, too, so the two of you can both beat your chests in a manly way."

Callum shot her a look, although he mostly seemed resigned. "Shouldn't you check with Daisy before you start inviting more people to her house?"

"Sorry, Daisy!" Lou made a face. "I didn't mean to take over your fitness room. You'll love Ellie, though. And this is right up Rory's alley, too."

"Um…okay?" Even though Daisy felt a little like she'd just been flattened by a runaway semi, there was a fizz of excitement in her stomach at the thought of having a bunch of people at her house for training. It would be the closest thing to a party she'd ever experienced, not counting birthdays when she was a kid.

"Yay! Perfect. This is going to be awesome." Lou danced over to Max and gave him a hug.

Callum watched, looking equal parts amused and appalled. "I'll bring pants for…?" He raised an eyebrow at Daisy.

"Max."

"Right." An actual smile curled his mouth, and Daisy suddenly understood why Lou could have fallen for him. "I'll bring pants for Max."

Daisy squinted at the mailing label she'd just printed and realized that the sun had almost disappeared behind the mountains. Before turning on the overhead light, she closed the shades, knowing all too well how easy it was to see into a lit room when the windows were uncovered. The office windows, as well as all the lower-level ones, were covered in metal grates. She knew it was silly to have her house fortified like she lived in the worst slums of a big city when she was actually in sleepy Simpson, but having bare windows on the first floor would have robbed her of what little sleep she managed to get.

With the light on, she could actually see the print on the mailing label. She attached it to the cardboard box containing a carefully wrapped Depression glass pitcher. As she added it to the pile of packages that were ready for the UPS driver to pick up the next day, Daisy rolled the tightness from her shoulders. Even though it was still early, she was tired. The previous almost-sleepless night, her mild concussion, and the multiple visitors were all contributing to the heavy blanket of exhaustion settling over her.

The muffled thud of a fist on her front door gave her a mild start before she remembered that it was most likely her dad. Instead of hauling around the dozen keys he'd need to gain entry, Gabe just knocked and waited for her to open the doors for him.

Daisy grinned as she hurried to the entry. He'd been gone for four days, and she'd missed him. She also had a mile-long grocery list. If she was going to start hosting training parties, she'd need snacks and beverages. Sports drinks, maybe? Daisy hoped that Gabe would be able to hit a few estate sales before he left for his next job, too. She was getting low on inventory.

Just before she pushed the unlock button, though, she caught herself. What if it wasn't her dad? She moved her finger to the intercom button instead.

"That you, Dad?"

"No." The unfamiliar voice sent a shiver through her, a mix of relief that she'd checked and horror at the thought that she'd almost let a stranger into her sanctuary. As soon as her dad returned, she was going to ask him yet again to install a camera on the porch. Maybe this time he'd actually do it. "Sheriff Rob Coughlin."

"Oh!" She'd met the Field County Sheriff once before, when she was sixteen. Most of that horrible day was blurry, thankfully, so she couldn't bring his face to mind.

Her pause must have gone on too long, since he spoke again. "Deputy Jennings mentioned that you witnessed some suspicious activity early this morning. I wanted to talk to you about it."

Once again, her finger hovered over the unlock button, but the uneasiness in her gut wouldn't let her push it. Instead, she spoke through the intercom as she pulled her cell phone out of her pocket. "I'm just going to call and confirm your identity with Dispatch."

"That's fine. Do you need the nonemergency number?"

"I have it, thanks." Chris had made sure it was one of her few preset numbers, and she tapped the contact. A woman with a squeaky cartoon voice answered and confirmed that Sheriff Coughlin was following up on a suspicious-activity call at 304 Alpine Lane.

Thanking the dispatcher, Daisy ended the call and pushed the unlock button. Despite the reassurance that the sheriff really was who he said he was, her stomach still churned. It was one thing to be visited by Chris, since she thought of him as her friend first and a law enforcement officer second. The sheriff, though, was just a cop. Taking a deep, bracing breath, she unbolted the interior door.

The sheriff stepped inside, making her scurry out of his way. His size and serious expression made him even more intimidating, and Daisy was relieved to be able to look away as she relocked the door.

"Ms. Little," he greeted when there were no more locks to secure and she had to turn around to face him.

"Sheriff." She gave an awkward bob of her head. "Would you like something to drink?" Instantly mortified that he might think she was offering him something alcoholic, like in a *flirty* way, she hurried to clarify. "Water, I mean. Or coffee, although it might be kind of late for that, since I don't have any decaf. Unless you're on the night shift?"

"No, thank you." She had to give him points for the way he didn't even blink at her awkwardness.

"Okay. Did you want to come in and sit?" Daisy didn't know the etiquette for a regular visitor, much less an official visit by a law enforcement officer who wasn't Chris.

"Here is fine." He looked around the kitchen. "This shouldn't take long."

"Okay." Hoping to put some space between her and Mr. Looming Cop, she moved to her usual spot, leaning back against the counter by the sink.

"Why don't you tell me what you saw this morning," he suggested in a way that made it more of a command than a request.

"Didn't Chris—I mean, Deputy Jennings—fill you in?"

"He did, but I'd like to hear it from you directly. Sometimes third-person reporting can turn into a game of Telephone." His smile was slight, but it still made Daisy relax a little.

"Okay. It was about three thirty this morning—"

"How did you know what time it was?"

"I looked at the clock in the training room before I went upstairs."

The way he watched her intently, as if he was memorizing every word that came out of her mouth, was unnerving. "You weren't sleeping?"

"No. Sometimes I have insomnia." Despite her nerves, she had to smile. "Plus, I was dying to try out Max."

"Max?"

"The department's old grappling dummy that Chris brought me. Thank you for letting him do that, by the way."

The sheriff's eyes widened slightly, as if in surprise.

"Of course," he said, sounding more like he was talking to himself than responding to her thanks.

Daisy eyed him curiously, which seemed to shake him out of his thoughts.

"So, you and Deputy Jennings are dating?"

She hadn't expected the question, even though it seemed to be a common assumption, at least amongst that day's visitors. "No. We're friends, but it's not…romantic."

When the sheriff eyed her for a long moment, Daisy felt her cheeks get hot. She was annoyed at herself for blushing, since it probably made Coughlin think she was lying about not being involved with Chris. Shaking off both the embarrassment and the self-directed irritation, she told herself that, even if they *had* been dating, it wasn't the sheriff's business.

"When I was in my room," she said, hoping to change the subject, "I saw a marked sheriff's department SUV in front of 304, that house that's for sale."

"Did you see the squad number on the back?"

She shook her head, regretting her silly backward lunge once again. "No. It was parked with the front end facing the Storvicks' house, and I…uh, wasn't watching when he drove away."

"He? So you saw the driver?"

"I did, but he had his coat hood up, so I couldn't see his face."

"You're sure the person was male?"

"Yes. I had a weird angle, watching from the upstairs window, but I'm pretty sure he was tall and big."

"Big?"

Under the sheriff's unwavering gaze, Daisy found herself shifting from foot to foot. Once she realized she was fidgeting, she forced herself to stop. "His coat was too bulky to really see his shape, but he wasn't a skinny guy."

"What did you see him doing that made you think it wasn't a routine call?"

"Well, he wasn't wearing a uniform. And he was carrying something over his shoulder that was wrapped in a tarp." She paused. It was one thing to sound crazy when she was talking to Chris or even to Lou, but telling the sheriff was a whole different matter. "The shape of it and the way it moved, especially when he dropped it into the back of the SUV, reminded me of a...um, a body."

The sheriff stared at her silently. She couldn't read his expression, and his silent regard made her nervous enough to drop her gaze to the tile floor.

"A body," he finally repeated, his voice flat.

"Yes." Dredging up her conviction, she met his eyes. "Especially when a boot fell out of the bottom of the tarp."

Daisy desperately wished she could tell what he was thinking, but the sheriff had that impassive look down pat.

"What kind of boot?"

It was only after she sucked in air that she realized she'd been holding her breath during the silence. "It was black, or maybe just dark-colored." She closed her eyes and tried to picture it lying on the packed snow that covered the road. "I'm pretty sure it was a man's boot because of the size."

"Can you show me where you were standing when you saw this?"

"Sure." She pushed away from the counter and led the way through the living room and up the stairs. It made her neck prickle to have a near stranger following her, even if he was the sheriff. She couldn't stop herself from glancing over her shoulder at him a few times. He looked around as they walked through the house, and his sharp gaze seemed to take in every detail.

When their silent train of two finally reached her bedroom, Coughlin moved around her and stepped toward the window. Daisy lowered her shoulders from where they'd been hunched around her ears, relieved to have his focus on something other than her.

She stood next to him, keeping as much distance as she could without seeming weird—or weird*er*. Despite his poker face, Daisy was pretty sure the sheriff thought she was an odd duck.

"The squad was parked there," she said, pointing at the spot on the street. "The deputy walked between the empty house and the Storvicks', carrying the bod—uh, the large *thing*."

"Deputy?" He turned his head to look at her. "I thought you couldn't see the person's face. Do you suspect anyone in particular?"

"No. I don't know any of the deputies—just Chris. He showed me a picture, and the only ones I could really rule out were the two women and a couple of skinny guys. Chris said one was…um…." She tried to remember his name. "Deputy Lorenzo?"

"Deputy Lawrence?"

"That's it!"

"Why do you think it's a deputy, then?"

"Because of the SUV?" It seemed so obvious to her, but just his asking the question made her doubt her logic. "Chris said it could be anyone who had temporary access to a squad car, but it just made sense that someone driving a sheriff's department vehicle would be a deputy. Oh, and Chris said the boot prints matched his."

"Deputy Jennings is right about the squad." The sheriff returned his gaze to the poorly lit scene in front of them. "If we start making assumptions, we could miss the truth just because it doesn't fit into the too-small box we've created."

She felt slightly chastised, although she did like the "we" he'd used. It made her feel included in the investigation. "I have a video of him on my phone. It's not very clear, but you're welcome to take a look at it."

He looked at her for a long, silent moment before repeating in a flat voice, "A video."

"Yes." Relieved to have an excuse for avoiding his penetrating stare, she pulled out her cell and found the video footage. Holding her phone so the sheriff could see the screen, Daisy hit play. While he watched, she eyed his face nervously, looking for his reaction, but his expression was impassive.

As the clip ended, Daisy dropped the hand holding her phone to her side. "I know it's dark, but maybe it could be enhanced and lightened with video-editing software?"

"Ms. Little." Once again, he was focused on her, and it was an effort to hold his gaze. "How long has it been since you've left this house?"

Although she'd suspected that the questions would eventually come around to that, it still took her by surprise. Daisy took a step back, feeling as though he'd punched her in the chest. "Um…almost eight years."

The assurance in his nod told her that he'd already

known, which meant he'd just asked to make a point. A flame of annoyance flickered to life inside her.

"What does that have to do with anything?" She was proud of her strong, steady voice.

He didn't answer her question but glanced toward the stack of books on her nightstand instead. "Do you read a lot of mysteries, Ms. Little?"

"Not especially." Her self-assurance was fading, and the words came out weaker than she'd hoped. "I read lots of different types of books."

"True crime?"

"They aren't my favorite. What does this have to do with anything?"

Once again, he didn't respond. "Do you watch your neighbors often?"

The earlier questions were just annoying, but that was a direct blow. Even as she tried to stop the blush, she felt her cheeks getting warm. "Yes."

His chin tipped down. "Have you ever witnessed anything else...unusual?"

Daisy couldn't stop her arms from crossing over her chest as she shook her head. The sheriff's questions made her feel naked. "Just the stuff with Corbin Storvick."

"Stuff?" he repeated, eyebrows raised.

"When he and his girlfriend have a fight, I let Chris know." She'd never seen the harm in watching the world outside her window, but admitting that to the sheriff made it sound so...slimy. Daisy dropped her eyes to the window-seat cushion. "Just so he can keep an eye out for Corbin's possible retaliation."

Coughlin made a sound between a hum and a grunt that Daisy couldn't translate. It might've been commendation or condemnation, and he made her too nervous for her to meet his eyes and try to read his expression to figure out which one it was.

"Do you receive any type of therapy for your"—he waved his hand at her room—"condition?"

Nibbling on her thumbnail, Daisy debated whether to refuse to answer him. Her emotional health didn't seem to be any of the sheriff's business. Although, she mentally conceded, if she'd witnessed a crime, her stability probably *was* an issue, especially if there was a trial. Would she be required to attend it?

At the thought, her throat closed, and her breath snagged in her throat. Logic loosened her lungs, though. There were so many other ways she could attend a trial—video conferencing, telephone, even a taped statement. They—whoever the mysterious "they" might be—wouldn't force her to leave her home. Besides, Daisy didn't think it was possible for her to exit without strong sedatives.

"Ms. Little?"

Despite her mental mutiny, Daisy folded under the heavy authority in his voice. "No. I used to have a therapist come to the house, but not anymore."

"Why not?"

That was definitely none of his business, so she gave him the short answer. "She came from Connor Springs and had a hard time getting here during the winter. Since winter makes up about eleven months of the year…" She shrugged, her words trailing away when the sheriff didn't look amused at her lame joke. "We tried phone sessions, but they didn't seem to be helping."

"I see."

Daisy doubted it. "Did you have any other questions for me? About what I saw this morning, I mean."

After eyeing her steadily for an unnerving length of time, the sheriff shook his head. "I'll call if I need anything else. Have you told anyone besides Deputy Jennings about this?"

"No." After the denial had escaped, she remembered that she'd shared the whole tale with Lou, who'd probably passed everything along to Callum. Daisy really didn't want to once again be the focus of the sheriff's reproving gaze, so she didn't correct her unintentional lie. Instead, she silently led the way back downstairs. Having the sheriff at her back was not any easier the second time.

"Your house is set up to keep out intruders." The sheriff's voice made her jump before she looked over her shoulder at him. Since that hadn't been a question, she waited for him to continue. "What happens if you need to evacuate?"

"Evacuate?" Even saying the word made her a little dizzy, but she tried to hide her overreaction. "Why would I need to do that?"

"Medical emergency, neighborhood gas leak or meth lab, fire…any number of reasons."

She paused, a little taken aback by the way he was able to casually rattle off his list of possible catastrophes. The sheriff apparently wasn't a glass-half-full kind of guy. If she had to guess, Daisy would say that Coughlin was more of a look-for-the-red-dot-from-the-sniper-rifle-on-the-half-empty-glass sort.

"Our first aid kit handles the minor medical stuff. If there was something major, I suppose I'd either be preoccupied by impending death or unconscious, so leaving the house wouldn't be a big deal." It felt like a lie on her tongue. Daisy couldn't imagine not going full-out ballistic if someone tried to force her through the door, almost dead or not. "I'd probably take my chances that you guys"—she gestured toward his badge—"and the fire department could handle the gas leak or, um, meth lab. And I have fire extinguishers all over, just in case."

He made another one of his short humming sounds, but he didn't comment on her answer, even though it sounded weak, even to her own ears. Daisy was glad he dropped the subject. She didn't need to hear about all the potential dangers that could befall her, since she had plenty of demons to deal with already.

"When's your dad getting back?"

That was a good question, since Gabe should've arrived already. She pulled her cell phone out of her pocket and saw she'd missed a text. After she pulled up the message, Daisy made a face. "Not tonight, apparently. The job is going to take an extra couple of days."

Disappointment spread through her. Not only had she been looking forward to seeing her father, but she had a bunch of out-of-the-house errands she was going to ask him to do. Daisy hated asking Chris. It made her feel so…needy.

The sheriff's gaze seemed to penetrate right into her brain and pick out her thoughts. "Will you be okay for that long? Do you need anything?"

If she wasn't going to ask Chris for help, she *definitely* wasn't about to ask his austere boss. "Thank you, but I'll be fine."

Although he looked unconvinced, he just offered her his card. "Call me if you see anything else."

"Okay," she said, although his request had been extremely vague. By "anything else," did he mean things related to a dead body, or did he want her to call every time Corbin Storvick had a tantrum? Daisy shook off her brief confusion when she realized that the sheriff was waiting for her to unlock the interior door.

"Good night, Ms. Little. I hope you're able to get some sleep tonight."

"'Night, Sheriff." As she closed the door behind him, she muttered, "After your little pep talk, I doubt I'll ever sleep again."

Chapter 5

"THE DEAD-BODY MYSTERY IS SOLVED."

Stunned into immobility, Daisy felt the jump rope smack her shins. "You've been here for twenty minutes."

"So?" Despite the speed of the rope, his voice was conversational. Daisy wondered what it would take to make him breathless and then blushed as her mind jumped right into the gutter. Clearing her throat, she refocused.

"You're just telling me this now?" She was tempted to use the jump rope to strangle the man. That might make him breathless.

He made a sound that was the verbal equivalent of a shrug. Daisy waited for a few more slaps of his rope against the floor and then demanded, "So?"

"So?" Although he turned his face to hide it, she caught a tiny grin and knew he was messing with her. She was leaning more and more toward strangling.

"Chris Jennings. Do not make me kill you."

He laughed and finally stopped jumping. "Rob called the owners of the house. They're living in Florida and said that they hired Angus Macavoy to clear out some junk in the back yard."

"Angus Macavoy?" The name didn't ring a bell. "Have you told me about him before?"

"Don't think so." Chris put both handles in his right hand and absently began swinging the rope in vertical circles. Eyeing the blurred rope, Daisy took a cautious step away from a potential unintentional slap. "He just started six months or so ago."

"That was him yesterday morning, then? Why was he doing it at three thirty?"

"According to Rob, who had a little chat with Macavoy about using a department vehicle for personal use, all the junk he'd cleared wouldn't fit in his compact car. Yesterday, after he'd worked the three-to-three swing shift, he decided to stop by and pick up the pile of stuff in the SUV. He hauled it to the junkyard and then went home to sleep."

"Why wasn't he in his uniform?"

Chris was doing figure-eight loops with the jump rope now. "He likes to change before he leaves work."

It took a few seconds to process the explanation, to make it fit with what she saw. The feeling of menace she'd experienced while watching must have been her imagination. "Of course there's a reason that doesn't involve someone dying. Sorry to drag you along on this fake mystery train, Chris."

"I'm glad you told me. It was definitely suspicious. Your neighborhood tips help a lot, especially with nipping that Corbin kid's shenanigans in the bud."

"Shenanigans? And Lou called *me* an Amish grandma?" Her smile was short-lived, and she groaned with embarrassment. "I can't believe the sheriff wasted his time on this."

"Wasn't a waste," Chris countered. "In fact, he said to thank you for giving him the heads-up that Macavoy was misusing resources. Rob'll keep a closer eye on him from now on."

Although she nodded, her face still burned at the

memory of the sheriff's sharp gaze watching her as she talked about dead bodies. "Your boss is…"

Chris picked that moment to pull up the bottom hem of his shirt to wipe his face, revealing his abs. His T-shirt still lifted, he eyed her over the fabric. "He's…what? Tenacious? Humor-free? A workaholic? A hottie?"

"Well, I was going to say intense, but now I'm more interested in discussing the fact that you're attracted to your boss."

He snorted, finally letting his shirt drop back into place, which allowed Daisy's brain to start functioning again. "I was just quoting one of the girls on a class tour a couple of weeks ago. Not the workaholic and humorless part, though. That was all me."

"Huh." During the sheriff's visit, she'd been too stressed, embarrassed, and a host of other negative emotions to rank him on the hot-or-not scale. She tried to bring up his features in her mind, but it was no use. She just couldn't get past how small and raw he'd made her feel. "I'll have to take your word for it. Do you like working for him?"

Chris's teasing expression faded as he considered the question. "Most of the time, yeah. I do. He can be rigid and rule-bound, but that's pretty common in cops. I like that he's consistent, easy to predict. Even if I know I've screwed up and am going to get my ass chewed, it's better than not knowing how he'll react. Make sense?"

After considering it for a moment, she said, "I can see that. I'm probably overreacting. He just kept looking at me like I was a bug he really wanted to squash."

Laughing, Chris said, "We call it 'going to confession.'

After a few minutes of Rob giving someone the eyeball, the suspect spills his guts about every bad thing he's ever done, even admitting to shoplifting a pack of gum when he was nine."

"I'd confess," Daisy admitted with a shiver. Talking about the sheriff was souring her stomach, so she changed the subject as she hung her jump rope on its peg. "I think we're warmed up, Yoda. What's today's lesson?"

His grin had a predatory cast that shouldn't have been as attractive as it was. "Aggression drills."

"Sounds…um, interesting?"

"It's important. You're smaller than most would-be attackers."

"I'm not *that* small." She scowled, although she couldn't force much heat into it. She was too grateful to him for the way he treated her. During training, Chris always acted like she could walk out the door anytime she wished. He never mentioned the improbability of her having to face off with anyone besides him and maybe Lou. "Oh! I almost forgot. Lou was wondering if she could join us for training sometime. And someone named Ellie, too, although she needs to recover from a bullet to the chest first?"

Her expression must have been horrified, since Chris gave an amused snort. At least, Daisy hoped he was laughing at her reaction and not at the poor woman who had been shot. "Sure. You'll get a chance to spar with someone besides me that way. And the bullet was deflected, so Ellie Price has a fractured sternum and a monster of a bruise, but she doesn't have the bloody hole in her chest that you're picturing."

"Good." She had indeed been imagining a gory

wound. "And Callum doesn't want you sparring with Lou, so he'll be here, too."

Looking perilously close to rolling his eyes, Chris said dryly, "Of course he will. There's no way George is going to let Ellie out of his sight, either, so prepare for a full house. I wouldn't be surprised if Rory joined the fun, too."

"Yeah, Lou mentioned a Rory." The name was familiar, but it took a minute for her to remember the story Chris had told her. "Isn't she the one who moved in with Ian Walsh across the street?"

"Yep. Ian'll probably tag along, too."

Daisy was quiet as she mentally inventoried food and beverages. With a group of six people coming, plus Chris, she'd definitely need to restock. As much as she didn't want to ask Chris for help, there was no other alternative unless her dad returned soon.

"Dais?" Chris's tentative tone brought her out of her contemplation. "You okay with everyone coming here?"

"Sure." She smiled at him, deciding to wait until the event was actually scheduled before worrying about training-day refreshments. "How about those anger drills?"

"*Aggression* drills," he corrected, letting it go. "We're taught to avoid acting aggressively, especially women, so we need to work on changing your initial reactions. Like this." He grabbed her forearm. "What's your instinctive response?"

Surprised at the contact, Daisy looked at his hand and then his face, not moving.

A grin started to curl up the corner of his mouth, but he quashed it, returning his expression to stern-instructor mode. "If I were a stranger, what would be your first reaction?"

"Maybe scream, depending on the situation."

"Screaming's good. What else?"

His fingers tightened, and she automatically tried to yank her arm out of his grip.

"Right!" he said, resisting her attempt at freeing herself. "Your initial instinct is to pull back. How's that working for you?"

Daisy increased her efforts, leaning back to use her body weight as well as her arm muscles to try to escape. "Not well," she gritted, her voice already a little breathless.

"Exactly. By trying to pull away, you've created a tug-of-war situation, where the one with the most brute strength wins. Which one of us will that be?"

"You," she grumbled reluctantly, giving up her attempt at freeing herself.

"Yes. Me or your probably bigger attacker. Not only have you put yourself in a contest that you won't win, but you're doing exactly what he expects." He released her arm, taking a step back, and then lunged forward to seize her again. Automatically, she tried to lurch backward, tugging against his hold. "When I grab you, I expect you to pull back."

"So I'm not supposed to try to get free?" she asked doubtfully.

He let her go again and retreated a few feet. "Grab me."

Grinning, she did, grasping his hard forearm in both hands. Daisy always liked when she got to play the attacker. It gave her a feeling of control, and, although she'd never admit it to Chris, it was a treat to be able to touch him without him trying to leap away from her.

As soon as she gripped his arm, he moved—not backward, like she had, but forward, into her space. Startled, she stumbled back a step.

"And there it is. You weren't expecting that, so it threw you off balance. Now I'm here, close to you, where I can land a knee"—he mimed the defensive movements as he named them—"an elbow or a palm heel strike." His hand brushed the side of her neck.

Trying to ignore that light contact, she frowned. "It seems wrong, though, to come closer to the bad guy when I want to get away."

"That's why it works. It's unexpected and counterintuitive. You just need to practice until it becomes second nature. Then your instinctual reaction will be to step into the assailant's space rather than trying to pull away."

"Hence aggression drills?"

He grinned. "Hence aggression drills." With his best villainous expression, he grabbed her arm.

An hour later, Daisy was clinging to the grappling dummy.

"Max! Save me from the evil drill sergeant," she groaned, her legs wobbly with fatigue.

Chris glanced at his watch. "I need to get a few things done at home anyway, so we should probably wrap things up."

"Thank you." Even to her own ears, she sounded pathetically grateful. After aggression drills, they'd done a cross-fit workout that included burpees—something

Daisy was positive had been invented by the devil in the deepest depths of hell.

He smirked, eyeing her desperate grip on Max. "You two look...cozy."

Too exhausted to care that she was hanging off a fake, naked man, Daisy just shrugged—or she would have shrugged if her deltoids hadn't stopped working twenty minutes ago.

"Don't forget to stretch," he warned as he walked to the door.

Daisy scowled at his back, annoyed at the way his legs continued to function, even though he'd worked out right alongside of her.

"Thanks, Chris!" she yelled as he headed into the hall. He disappeared, only to stick his head back in a moment later.

"Don't you need to lock the door after me?"

"Right." With a groan, she heaved herself upright. Once she was certain that her legs would support her on their own, she left Max with a grateful pat on the rear.

"You're abnormally attached to that thing," Chris said as she shuffled to the doorway.

"Max is awesome. As much as I punch him, he never holds a grudge."

"I let you punch me," Chris huffed. If she had any energy to spare, she would've laughed at his offended expression. "A lot more than Max has."

Her chuckle came out as more of a wheeze. "Yes, you're almost as awesome."

"Almost?"

"Max gets extra points for letting me cuddle him afterward." As soon as the words left her mouth, she wished she could unsay them. Although she didn't want to look at Chris, she couldn't help herself—her gaze darted to his face. Immediately, she regretted it. The teasing humor had disappeared, leaving an impassive mask that the sheriff would've envied.

The rest of their trip to the front door was silent.

"Thanks again, Chris," she finally blurted as he opened the interior door.

His nod of acknowledgment was short. "Later, Dais." Then he was gone.

Securing the locks on autopilot, she heard the clunk of the outer door closing. Her forehead made a similar sound as it hit the wood panel in front of her.

"You're a bigger dummy than Max," she muttered to herself. With a groan that was as much about disappointment as it was sore muscles, she pushed herself away from the door and shuffled toward the shower.

That night, she lay in bed, her eyes wide open. Despite the training session from hell, she couldn't sleep. The light entering her bedroom window was strange. It wasn't snowing outside, but a cloud had settled over the neighborhood like a blanket, turning everything a foggy white. The illuminated rectangle of her window called to her, but she resolutely ignored it. The memory of the sheriff's judgmental gaze still stung, and she was determined to break the habit of spying on her neighbors.

It was hard. The book she'd been reading wouldn't hold her interest, not with teenage domestic drama and furtive junk disposal happening within view. Daisy tried thinking about the upcoming training session, instead. Lou hadn't wasted any time getting it arranged, and everyone would be coming over at two o'clock on Saturday, just two days away. She glanced at the digital clock on the nightstand. When she saw that it was after one a.m., she mentally corrected herself. Saturday was only one day away.

The window beckoned. With a huff of irritation, she threw off the covers and got out of bed. "Just for a minute," she muttered, then laughed. She sounded like an addict—a spying addict.

Pulling a fleece blanket from the foot of her bed, she brought it with her to the window seat. Curling up on the cushioned bench, she wrapped the blanket around her. All the Storvicks' lights were out except for the glow of a computer screen coming from Corbin's room. It was really boring watching the kid stare at whatever website he was perusing, and Daisy reluctantly allowed her gaze to move to the vacant house next door.

She was actually relieved that everything was dark and still, with no pseudokillers or late-night handymen roaming the property. A quick glance at Ian and Rory's place showed that the shutters were firmly in place. Without anything to hold her interest within view, Daisy rested her forehead against the window and allowed her thoughts to wander.

Of course, the first person to pop into her head was Chris and his increasingly weird behavior toward her. It wasn't like she was throwing herself at him. Daisy thought she hid her feelings pretty well—at least, as long as he kept his shirt in place. She was fully aware that she wasn't girlfriend material, so, except for that one stupid attempted kiss, she tried to keep her hands and her wishes to herself. And yet, every once in a while, she'd catch him watching her with the hungriest expression. It made her wonder—

Something moved on the far side of the empty house. Jerked out of her thoughts, Daisy sucked in a breath and then groaned.

"Not again," she muttered, staring at the spot, waiting to see if there was another sign of life. After a few long minutes, her eyes were starting to burn from not blinking.

Sitting back, she dismissed the movement as her imagination. She sighed. Her brain was taking lots of trips into fantasyland lately. Maybe it was time to find another therapist like the sheriff had implied.

Yet even as she told herself there was nothing to see, her eyes remained fixed on the far side of the yard for a long time.

"Make the call."

Macavoy was breathing in short, audible gasps. "Why are you...doing this?"

"*Call.*"

With shaking fingers, Macavoy touched a number on his screen. In the following silence, broken only by the deputy's rough breathing, Rob heard two rings before the call connected with a click.

"Dispatch."

Macavoy hesitated, so Rob gave his temple a nudge with the barrel of his Beretta. "This is Angus...Macavoy."

"Angus!" The dispatcher's tone went from coolly professional to friendly. "How are you?"

"I..." Pausing, he gave Rob a pleading look, which

the sheriff answered with another, harder press of the gun to Macavoy's head. "I have...to put in...my resignation."

"Oh no! You're leaving us already? It's the snow, isn't it? Did you get a new job in California or somewhere?"

"No. Family...situation." Macavoy's breathing was worsening, each breath ending with a squeaky wheeze.

The dispatcher paused before saying, "You're sounding pretty short of breath, Angus. Are you okay?"

"Fine." The word came out as a gasp.

"You sure? Do you need me to send medical out to your place?"

Rob's hand jerked, jamming the gun barrel against Macavoy's head. The deputy winced away and then froze, as if expecting a shot.

"No!" Macavoy yelped, before he sucked in an audible breath and then continued more calmly. "No. I'm... fine. Just stress because...of the family...thing. Don't send med. I'll nebulize right after...this call."

"Okay." The dispatcher sounded reluctant to let it go, and Rob gave Macavoy's temple another shove to remind him to wrap up things. "You'll call back if things get any worse, though?"

"I...will. Have to...go now."

"Well, you have my email." The dispatcher's tone had lightened. "Let us know how things turn out for you."

With a sideways glance at Rob, Macavoy muttered agreement before ending the call. "I did...what you asked. I'll...leave. I won't tell...anyone."

"It's really too bad. You were a good deputy."

Rob pulled the trigger.

Chapter 6

T YLER MET HIM AT THE BACK DOOR WITH A BUCKET OF soapy water, a bottle of hydrogen peroxide, and a garbage bag. How had this happened, that his sixteen-year-old son knew Luminol would light up bleach residue like a Fourth-of-July sparkler? All Rob had ever wanted to do was to protect his kid, but everything had gone wrong.

"What are you doing?" Guilt leant a snap to his voice, and Tyler took a step back.

"Helping." Tyler held out the garbage bag. After a long moment, Rob sighed and accepted it.

"You shouldn't help." Rob stepped farther into the shelter of the porch before he dragged off his boots, BDUs, and sweatshirt. Although Esko Hills was a nice neighborhood, a good place to raise a family, it had more than its share of busybodies and curious gazes. "I'm your dad. It's my responsibility to take care of things like this, not yours. Your job is to go to school and not get into trouble." He gave his son a meaningful look.

Dropping his gaze to the floor, Tyler muttered, "Sorry. I couldn't help it."

"We've talked about this." In just his boxer briefs and socks, the air was cold against his skin. Rob hurried to shove his clothes into the garbage bag and yanked the drawstring. "Every time, you risk exposing yourself—and me."

His son's shoulders curled forward. "I know."

"C'mon." Rob reached to put a hand on the back of Tyler's neck, but stopped when he saw blood smeared across his thumb and index finger. "Let's go inside."

As the door closed behind them, Tyler turned. "Dad?"

"Yeah?" Rob used the soapy water to scrub at the smear on his right hand. Once the visible blood was gone, he uncapped the hydrogen peroxide and began pouring it over his hands.

"What really happened to Mom?"

He froze for a moment, watching the peroxide bubble on his skin. "What do you mean?"

"Until that day, she'd always come back. Always. And when you walked in and saw her hitting me... You looked really mad. Like, madder than I've ever seen you get."

"Why are you asking this?"

Tyler lifted one thin shoulder. "I guess because you always take care of me. That, and I wondered why she stopped coming home."

Drying his hands on a paper towel that he added to the garbage bag of clothes, Rob said, "Take these to the outdoor wood furnace, would you?" As much as he didn't want his son involved in any part of this, no matter how small that part may be, Rob needed to escape the conversation. He'd never lied to Tyler, and he wasn't about to start now.

"Sure." Taking the bag, Tyler took a few steps toward the door and then paused. "Thank you. I used to be so scared she'd come back."

Rob watched his son's back until the door closed behind Tyler.

You're welcome.

———

Her mom was sobbing. Daisy had never heard her mom cry—not like this. In her spot, crouched behind the snack-cake display, she shook and mentally called herself a coward. She should do something, help her mom somehow, but all she could do was cower and try to hold back the scream that wanted to escape. His finger tightened on the trigger—

The ringing of her cell phone brought her out of her nightmare with a jerk. Before she could figure out where she was, Daisy twisted toward the sound and fell off the window seat onto the hardwood floor.

"Ow," she groaned, crawling toward where her still-ringing phone sat on her nightstand. By the time she reached it and saw that it was her dad, the call had gone to voice mail. She tapped her screen to call him as she sat on the floor, leaning her back against the side of the bed.

"Daisy," he answered brusquely. "Let me in."

"Oh, sorry!" She scrambled to her feet and headed for the bedroom door. "Have you been knocking? I was asleep." Reaching the stairs, she flew down them two at a time.

"Yeah, I've been knocking for a while." His tone had mellowed a little, although he still sounded short. "I was worried when you didn't answer."

"Sorry," she repeated, pushing the unlock button. "I didn't think you'd be home so soon."

"Jennings called me. He told me you needed me to come home."

"Chris said what?" Daisy realized she'd been talking

and missed the sound of the exterior door latching. "Is the door locked again?"

"Yeah. Open up."

She unfastened the locks with her left hand, her right keeping her phone pressed to her ear. When she opened the door to let her dad inside, she lowered her cell and made a face at it. "Guess there's no need for these any-more. Hi, Dad."

"What's going on?" Gabe started shedding his boots and coat. He was short and wiry, and he hadn't shaved his reddish-blond winter beard yet. Ever since she was a kid, people had said she looked exactly like her mother—they used to, at least, before her mom had been killed and Daisy had disappeared inside her house. "You okay?"

"Sure. Why wouldn't I be?" After relocking the door, she headed to the coffeemaker to start a cup of French roast for her father.

"Your deputy buddy was pretty insistent that I head home immediately. I only had a day and a half left on the Connor Springs project—it'll be two days, now that I'm wasting this morning driving back and forth for no reason." He hung up his coat and followed her into the kitchen.

"Sorry." She ran through her last few conversations with Chris and shrugged. "I'm not sure why he thought you were needed here. Oh! I did mention that I wanted to have snacks when everyone comes over for training."

"Training?"

"Lou Sparks asked if she could train with me and Chris, and then it kind of snowballed. Five or six people are coming over on Saturday afternoon."

"Let me get this straight." He glowered from under his bushy, light-colored brows. "Chris sent me tearing all the way over here because you're throwing a *party*?"

It was on the tip of Daisy's tongue to remind him that Connor Springs was only twenty miles away, but she swallowed the words. Gabe was building up to one of his rages, and she'd rather not have to clean up broken coffee mugs or explain new dents in the walls to her guests the next day.

"I'm not sure why he asked you to come here," she said instead. "Did you want this coffee in a travel mug?"

His hand slapped the counter, the sound making her jump. "What do you think?" He stomped over to where he'd just left his boots. Daisy poured the French roast into a travel cup and secured the lid tightly. Her dad did not need to spill hot liquid on his lap. His head was already too close to spinning around, *Exorcist*-style.

As she waited for him to finish yanking on his coat, she debated whether she should ask him to pick up a few things before he left town again. When he turned toward her and she met his still-furious eyes, she silently held out his coffee instead. He snatched the cup and used his other hand to undo the locks, his abrupt movements testifying to his irritation. As soon as he was through the interior door, she hurried to close and relock it, knowing that he wouldn't hesitate to slam through the outer door in his current mood.

Once the locks were secured, she moved to the living room window, opening the blinds so she could watch his older blue pickup as it accelerated away from the house. He turned onto the cross street, and she gave a humorless snort of laughter. Even the jerky way he steered his truck showed his annoyance.

Heading back into the kitchen, she debated whether she wanted a cup of coffee. The caffeine would be welcome, but her stomach was churning from her dad's visit, and she didn't think acidic coffee would go down too well. Setting aside the mental debate, she called Chris.

"Daisy. What's up?"

She was a little disappointed that he sounded wide awake. It would've served him right if she'd jerked him out of a deep sleep. "Why exactly did you call my dad and tell him I needed him here?"

"Because you do."

"I do? Why?"

"You need groceries, for one."

"Seriously?" She groaned. "I make a throw-away comment about giving my training guests some munchies, and you have my dad drive all the way from Connor Springs?" Great, now she'd started with the "all the way" nonsense. It must've been catching. "That's not a necessity. I'll just tell everyone that it's BYOSD."

"Connor Springs is not that far. Also…wait. BYO-what-now?"

"Bring Your Own Sports Drink," she translated. "And I know it's not far. My dad was annoyed about losing half a day of work, though."

After a short silence, Chris spoke in a dark voice that gave her the shivers for reasons she didn't want to examine too closely. "How annoyed?"

"No crockery was broken." She tried to keep her tone light, even faintly amused. "He wasn't here long."

"He left?" Again with the growly voice. "Why'd he even come back if he wasn't going to stay?"

"After talking to you, I think he was convinced that I was dying. Once he saw that I was fine, he headed back to Connor Springs."

"Why doesn't he stay at home and commute to the job site every day? It's Connor Springs, not Alaska."

The answer to his question was something Daisy tried very hard not to think about, so she decided it was time to redirect the conversation. "Chris, I'm fine. Try to reserve the emergency calls to Dad for when I'm dying and/or dead, okay?"

"You're not fine," Chris said flatly. "Ever since you saw Macavoy moving that junk, you've been sleeping even less than usual, haven't you?"

"No." It was a lie. "In fact, Dad woke me up when he got here."

"After what? An hour of sleep? Maybe two? You can't do that to your body, Dais. You'll go nuts."

In a flare of defensive irritation, she snapped, "What does it matter, since I'm already crazy?"

There was another silence, which was finally broken by Chris's sigh. "No, you're not."

She rubbed her forehead with a hand that shook. "What do you call not being able to leave the house? I'm not exactly rational." Although she didn't mention it, it didn't seem exactly stable to mentally turn a pile of junk into a dead body, either. Maybe she was getting worse.

Instead of countering her argument, Chris suggested, "Why don't you think about starting therapy again?"

"That didn't work out so well."

"Tell Gabe he can't sleep with the new one. In fact,

you can just remove all hot shrink temptation altogether and do sessions via video on your laptop."

The thought of talking about the worst day of her life with a stranger, of admitting all her illogical yet overwhelming fears, made her wince. "I'll think about it," she lied, just so he'd drop it.

"Really think about it." Okay, so he wasn't going to drop it. "Rob said he was concerned about you, about what would happen if you were ever in a situation where you *had* to leave the house, and I agree with him. Daisy, you passed out when you just *looked* at the open door. Going on as you've been living isn't making you better."

It wasn't anything she didn't know, but it still tore up her insides to hear him talk about it. She opened her mouth to say something—she wasn't sure what—but then closed it again. If she spoke, he'd be able to tell that she was crying.

"Daisy? Dais?" She'd been quiet too long, apparently. "I don't want to hurt you, but I think you're cheating yourself by not getting help. You're—"

She couldn't listen to him any longer. Moving the phone away from her ear, Daisy ended the call. She just held the phone in front of her for a while, watching as the screen went blank. When it rang in her fingers, she jumped and then turned off the cell and left it on the kitchen counter.

Swiping at her wet cheeks, she blew out a breath. After a few more inhales, the shakiness disappeared, and she was able to stop crying. She left the phone where it was and went to go beat up Max.

It was amazing how violence could make her feel so much better. After abusing Max, she spent some time practicing with the heavy bag and the speed bag, then hopped on the treadmill for forty minutes. Afterward, she felt sweaty, disgusting, and much calmer—even a little sheepish about the way she'd hung up on Chris.

Daisy showered and then retrieved her phone, her finger hesitating over the "on" button. With a sigh, she figured she should just get it over with, so she turned on the cell. Once it came back to life, she saw that she had a dozen messages. The single one from Lou stood out amongst the eleven left by Chris. Like the chicken she was, Daisy listened to Lou's first.

"Hey, Daisy! It's Lou. I'm just checking to see if we're still on for tomorrow. I hope so, since I am so excited about learning to kick some…hang on. I'll be with you in a moment! Gotta go—customers." The way Lou growled the word made Daisy smile. *"Let me know if anything changes. Otherwise I'll see you tomor— Just a minute! I'll be right there to take your order!"* Her voice dropped to a mutter. *"Seriously? They can't wait two seconds for their lattes? I tell you what, Daisy— I'm going to have some major aggression to work out tomorrow, so you'd better hope we don't get paired up. Otherwise, it's pow! And wham! And—Coming! Jeez Louise, Callum isn't the only one who needs to learn patience. See you tomorrow!"*

Daisy was laughing by the time Lou's message ended, making it easier to listen to Chris's. All of his were short, consisting of some variation of *"Dais. Call me."* With a grimace, she tapped his name on her screen. He answered after a single ring.

"Daisy. Finally."

"Hey, Chris. Sorry I hung up on you earlier, but I really don't want to talk about that anymore."

"Fine." His heavy exhale was audible. "Just don't turn off your phone like that. What if you needed to call for help?"

"Then I'd turn it back on?"

She was pretty sure that was a growl she heard. "What if I needed to reach you urgently?"

"Okay, Chris. I promise I won't turn it off because I'm in a snit."

"Thank you." He paused for a few seconds. "You okay?"

Daisy felt a small surge of irritation. It felt like he was always asking her that. "Yes. I assaulted Max and took a shower, so I feel much better."

"Good." There was another un-Chris-like hesitation. "Can I do anything for the training tomorrow? Maybe pick up some things on my way to your house?"

"Since you're the one doing the training, I think your contribution is big enough without supplying snacks."

"Okay." This time, the silence stretched until she checked to make sure the call hadn't been dropped. "Do you need anything?"

"Some strong sedatives, if you don't stop treating me like your invalid aunt." She immediately felt bad about her sharpness. "No, Chris. I'm stocked like a good prepper. Dad could stay away for another six months, and I'd still have enough to eat." She'd be out of chocolate long before then, though, and that could lead to severe crankiness.

"I'll see you tomorrow, then."

"Bye." The word was more of a sigh. This Chris was

nowhere near as fun to talk to as her friend used to be before some alien performed a personality transplant on him.

———⚡———

"Gabe," Rob called over the construction noise. "Got a minute?"

Gabe Little scowled. "No. Not after your deputy wasted my entire morning."

Raising his eyebrows, Rob waited.

"Chris Jennings called me and told me Daisy needed me at home." His frown deepened with each word. "Thought she was in trouble or something. When I drove all the way home, she was fine. Said she had no idea why Jennings dragged me to Simpson. I ended up turning around and driving right back to Connor Springs. What a waste of time."

"Hmm..." Rob was beginning to realize just how attached Chris was. He should've known something was up when Jennings bought a new grappling dummy for the department, when their "old" one had barely been used a year. "Sorry you were inconvenienced, but I have to admit that I'm concerned about Daisy, as well."

"What?" His surly expression faded, and concern seeped into his tone. "Why? What's wrong?"

"Has she shown any signs of improvement since her mother...passed? Any attempts at leaving the house?"

The final traces of annoyance disappeared as Gabe deflated, sitting heavily on a concrete block. "Not really. She had a therapist for a while, but that didn't...well, it didn't pan out."

"Why not?"

Guilt flashed over Gabe's expression, and the defensive scowl returned. "What's this all about, Sheriff?"

"Like I told you," Rob said evenly, allowing sympathy to color his voice, "I'm concerned. What would happen if there was a structure fire? Or if she was injured or ill, and no one could get to her?"

Holding his hands palms-up in a gesture of helpless anger, Gabe demanded, "You think I don't ask myself those questions every day? You think I don't worry about her in that house?"

"I know you do," Rob said soothingly. "I'm a father, too. I understand about worrying all the time. I'm not here to add to your problems. I'm here to offer to help—as much as I'm able, at least."

Gabe slumped, and Rob knew he had him. "Thanks, Sheriff. Sorry. It's just...hard."

"I know." Reaching out, Rob clasped the other man's curled shoulder. "If something were to happen, is there any way I could reach her? Is there a key?"

"No." Gabe didn't raise his gaze. "There are too many locks on that inside door. My key chain would look like a janitor's."

Holding back a frustrated scowl, Rob asked, "Is there any other way into the house, any way to get to Daisy if she needed help?"

Gabe started to shake his head but then stopped, his expression brightening. "Yeah, there is. I'd almost forgotten about that."

Rob listened intently, not allowing his satisfaction to show.

———

Her shaky hands had returned for the stupidest reason.

"Yes?" she said into the intercom mic, glad she could at least keep her voice steady.

"It's me."

"Oh, thank God! I mean, come on in, Chris." She unlocked the outer door.

Once he was in the kitchen, she realized he hadn't been wearing a coat. "Is spring finally here?"

"For now." He leaned against the counter and crossed his arms, watching as she dropped spoonfuls of dough on a cookie sheet. "Are you making those cheese-and-sausage biscuits?"

"Yes. I forgot to ask if anyone's a vegetarian, so I tried to cover all my bases. There's artichoke dip with chips, hummus with pita squares, these biscuits—even if they are greasy heart attacks waiting to happen—and I wanted to have a vegetable tray, but I only have frozen veggies, and those would be limp and soggy and gross, so I'm thinking about mini-pizzas, but there's only water and coffee to drink, and I—"

"Daisy." He crossed the kitchen and put his hands on her shoulders, the unexpected contact cutting off her flow of words. "Breathe."

"I know." She knew it would make him squirrelly again, but she couldn't help it. Her head dropped forward to rest against his chest. "I'm being an idiot, but this is my first…thing. I haven't even been to a party, or a get-together, or any kind of social gathering in years. I don't know what I'm doing!" The last came out as a wail.

"Dais." He sounded amused. Scowling, she raised her head to check.

"Are you laughing at me?" she demanded.

"No. At least, I'm trying really hard not to."

She smacked him on the upper arm. "I'm having a nervous breakdown, and you think it's hilarious."

"It'll be fine, Dais." He gave her shoulders a pat and then dropped his hands. Daisy tried not to miss the contact. "They're coming to train. They won't be expecting any of this"—he gestured at the array of ingredients she had strewn across the counters—"so they'll appreciate whatever you offer them. Okay?"

Daisy took a deep breath and then let it out. "Okay." She turned back to her biscuit-making. "Why are you here so early anyway? You just about gave me a heart attack, thinking everyone was arriving already when the kitchen looked like this." She gestured at the chaos with her spoon.

He grinned. "Figured you might be freaking out, so I thought I'd get here early and see if you needed help with anything."

"Thanks." She put the cookie sheet in the fridge, along with the remaining dough. "I think I'm good, though. I just need to clean up and calm down."

Chris moved to help. "I saw Lou yesterday when I stopped at the Coffee Spot. She's beyond excited about this."

Daisy laughed as she loaded the dishwasher. Just chatting with Chris was relaxing her. She could almost feel her blood pressure dropping as they worked side by side in easy harmony, as if the argument and subsequent awkwardness of the day before hadn't happened. "I know. She left me a message yesterday."

"Makes me a little nervous," he said, and she looked at him skeptically. Daisy doubted he'd ever been nervous in his life. "They're expecting a lot from this training. Hope I can live up to that."

"Please," she scoffed, smacking him on the rear with the rubber spatula she'd just rinsed. "Don't even pretend to be humble. You just want some ego stroking."

Mouth open, he stared at her. "Did you just *spank* me with that thing?"

She shrugged. "It was handy."

"You know what else is handy?" He grabbed a wooden spoon off the counter and swung it toward her posterior. Twisting around, she parried with the spatula. They dodged and danced around the kitchen in a kitchen-utensil swordfight. Taking advantage of his superior weapon and Daisy's ill-timed attack of the giggles, Chris drove her back toward the sink. As she tried to hold him off with the spatula in her right hand, she turned the water on with her left and grabbed the spray nozzle.

"Ahh!" Chris yelled, holding up his free hand to ward off the jets of water. "Twenty penalty points for using unauthorized weapons!"

"All kitchen contents and appliances are weapon-use approved. That's the official Swordfight Code Section 136.8." Daisy released the sprayer anyway, since she was laughing too hard to stand up straight.

"Who brings a water sprayer to a spoon fight, anyway?" he teased, pulling at his wet T-shirt. It clung to his sculpted chest in a way that made Daisy glad she'd decided to turn their battle into a water fight.

She pretended to ponder the question. "Um…the winner?"

With a snort, Chris swung the spoon he still held toward her rear, but she dodged easily and pretended to reach for the sprayer again.

"Truce?" Chris wiped a droplet of water from his cheek.

"Truce." Even as she pretended nonchalance, Daisy decided that soaking wet was a good look for Chris…a very good look. As they finished tidying the kitchen, she kept a wary eye out for possible retaliation, but he behaved himself.

As Daisy started the dishwasher, Chris said in a too-casual voice, "Lou also mentioned wanting to talk more about the Willard Gray case with you."

"Okay?" She didn't understand why that merited his odd delivery.

"If you don't want to discuss it with her, she'll understand."

Now Daisy was really confused. "Why wouldn't I want to talk to her about that? It's fun—okay, that sounded weird, since we're talking about some poor murdered guy, but it's interesting. A real-life mystery."

"She could use someone new to bounce ideas off of. I can't talk to her about it, and I think she and Callum are both at the point where they're running around in circles."

She frowned at Chris. "Why are you trying to talk me into this when I already said I'd do it? The cows are in the corral already, cowboy. You can stop the round-up."

He gave an amused snort. "Did you just refer to yourself as a cow?"

Waving that off, she said, "I want to talk to Lou about the Gray case. Why are you being weird?"

"I just didn't want it to, I don't know, stress you out or anything."

"Chris Jennings." Her hands planted on her hips. "Quit treating me like I'm fragile. Don't make me get the spatula."

"Just try it." He smirked. "I'm prepared for your assault now."

A knock at the door made her fly toward the stairs. "Can you let them in?" she asked over her shoulder. "I have to change."

"Why change?" His gaze ran over her current outfit of yoga pants and a baggy T-shirt. "What you're wearing is fine."

It would take too long to explain the rules of fitness fashion to him, especially since she was fairly fuzzy on them, herself. All she knew was that her clothes were shapeless, smeared with various food items, and smelled like sausage. "Door?"

Although he rolled his eyes, he turned toward the entrance.

"Thank you!" she yelled as she dashed up the stairs.

After a quick change, Daisy hurried out of her bedroom. An attack of nerves hit at the top of the stairs, and she came to a screeching halt. Despite no longer smelling like pork products, Daisy regretted not being the one to answer the door. She hovered for a moment before forcing herself to descend to the first level. From the sound of the voices, Chris had already escorted them to the training room, so at least she didn't have to worry about everyone watching her come down the stairs, debutante-style.

The mental image made her giggle, but she cut off her laughter as soon as she heard how nervous she sounded. Not allowing herself to hesitate at the bottom of the stairs, she marched through the open gym door.

The room went quiet as soon as she entered, and Daisy hid her cringe, forcing a smile instead. There were a lot of people, and they were all staring at her.

"Daisy!" Of course Lou was the one to speak. Just in the short time she'd known Lou, Daisy had already realized that silence was the other woman's nemesis. "I know I've already seen this place, but I'd forgotten exactly how awesome it really is. Thanks for letting us do this."

"No problem." Her voice cracked in the middle and squeaked at the end, so she cleared her throat, hoping her next attempt wouldn't make her sound like a pubescent boy. "It'll be fun to have new sparring partners." Even as she said it, though, doubt filled her as her eyes settled on a bearded giant. Despite her years of training with Chris, there was no way she could take on that one. She'd have to go with flight, rather than fight, if he got hostile.

"The big guy you're really hoping not to go up against is George Holloway." Lou's mind-reading made Daisy blush as she nodded to the oversized man. "Next to him is his girlfriend, Ellie. You probably know Ian and Rory, since they're your neighbors." Daisy did kind of know them, although they looked different close up. "And you've already met me and Callum, so I think the introductions are done, and we're ready to be turned into human weapons."

Ellie laughed at that, and a few of the others smiled. When Chris stepped forward, drawing everyone's attention, Daisy gave a silent sigh of relief.

"Sorry, Lou. No human-weapon creation today. I need to get a sense of what each person's conditioning and skill levels are, so we're going to do some circuit training. Ellie, I know you're still recovering, so just do what you can. If something hurts, stop." She nodded, her hand raising to hover above her breastbone.

As he explained each station, Daisy listened with half an ear, sneaking glances at the visitors. Ellie and George were a mismatched pair—her so slight and elegant and him such a typical mountain man. Although the two weren't touching, they stood close. One of George's hands held the pull-up bar above their heads, tilting his body forward slightly and giving the impression that he was hovering over his girlfriend.

Turning her attention to Ian and Rory, she marveled at how striking they were. Ian could've been a fitness-apparel model dropped into her home gym, and although Rory wasn't traditionally beautiful, there was something about her bearing that demanded attention. Her face serious, Rory was listening intently to Chris's instructions, but Ian caught Daisy's look and raised his eyebrows in question.

Embarrassed to be caught gawking, she shook her head and focused on Chris, knowing she was red from her forehead to her upper chest. Daisy was aware she was an antisocial recluse, but she didn't have to *prove* it to everyone in the first ten minutes of them meeting her.

With a clap of his hands, Chris sent them to their stations. Seeing that the treadmill was free, Daisy hopped on and arrowed up the speed. Once she was running at her usual warm-up pace, she was free to look around again, although she tried to be more discreet about it this time.

Standing next to the heavy bag, Lou and Callum were

chatting with Chris as they wrapped their hands. Rory and Ian had chosen the jump ropes. As Daisy watched enviously, they competed with each other to see who could do the most doubles in a row.

At the pull-up bar, Ellie was struggling to raise her chin over the top when she winced and lowered herself until she was hanging from the bar with her arms fully extended. Grabbing either side of her waist, George lifted her until her face and most of her chest was above the bar. At first, Ellie's eyes rounded in surprise, but then she started laughing.

"That's one way to do assisted pull-ups," Chris said wryly before turning back to Lou. He watched her throw a straight punch and then corrected her form.

An uncomfortable feeling built inside Daisy as she watched them—watched everyone, in fact. It wasn't envy of their comfortable twosomes, but more a longing, a wistfulness, as if she were looking at a picture of something she would never have. Her foot caught on the edge of the belt, making her trip. She caught herself before falling, but it reminded her to pay attention before she ate the floor and experienced true humiliation.

"You okay?" Chris called from across the room, where he'd moved next to Ellie, George, and the pull-up bar. She gave him a wave, wishing he hadn't called attention to her little bobble. Unable to keep her attention away from Chris for very long, she kept darting glances in his direction. Daisy frowned. There seemed to be some tension between Chris, Ellie, and George. She made a mental note to ask Chris for the story later.

Pulling her attention away from the threesome, Daisy increased the speed to her normal running pace. When she looked up from the digital display, she almost tripped again. Callum was standing right next to the treadmill.

"Hi?" Her voice was uncertain.

He nodded toward the display. "Good pace. Do you swim?"

That was random. "Um...not really. I took lessons when I was a kid, but I don't have much opportunity now."

"Huh," he grunted.

"Why?"

"Your fitness is impressive. You'd make a good candidate for the rescue dive team."

Daisy was glad her legs were running on autopilot, since she would've stopped and been dumped off the back of the treadmill otherwise. "I don't really...well, leave the house. Ever."

His next grunt was dismissive, as if she'd just told him she couldn't dive because she had a head cold. "Too bad." With a final lift of his chin, he returned to where Lou was practicing uppercuts.

"Don't listen to him, Daisy." Ian's raised voice brought her gaze to him, where he was still jumping rope with the ease of an expert. "Fire is better than the dive team. Who wants to jump into icy water?"

"Please. Fire, schmire. Who wants to run into a burning building?" Lou countered, sounding breathless. Her fist connected with the heavy bag. "Daisy would only join Fire if she were a gossipy old woman, which she's not."

"Everyone knows that firefighters are at the top of the first-responder food chain." Ian threw in a couple of crisscrosses, just, Daisy was sure, to show off. "I don't see a calendar featuring rescue divers. Help me out here, Ror."

"I don't know." Rory's expression was completely deadpan. "I was thinking about quitting the fire department and joining the dive team."

There was a moment of shocked silence. In the middle of throwing a straight punch, Lou turned toward Rory, so her fist missed the bag altogether. Thrown off balance, Lou fell, grabbing the bag on her way down. Callum lunged to catch her, but she was already sitting on the floor, laughing, by the time he reached her.

Ian stared at Rory, eyes wide, until a tiny smile tugged up one corner of her mouth. Eyes narrowing, he gave her a light push on the shoulder, just hard enough to knock her off balance so she missed her jump.

"Hey!" she complained, untangling her jump rope from her legs. "I was going for a record there."

"Just wait," he said in a mock growl. "I'll get you back for that, sometime when you're not expecting it."

Resuming her jumping, Rory rolled her eyes without missing a beat. Daisy was impressed. "I think you're overestimating your stealth."

In response, Ian waited until the rope was swinging over her head and then poked her in the side. It must have been a ticklish spot, since Rory yanked her arms down, dropping the jump rope onto her head. She glared at him while he grinned.

"I'm plenty stealthy."

A "whoa" from Lou caught Daisy's attention, and she followed the other woman's gaze to where George was doing pull-ups. Despite his loose-fitting sweatpants and T-shirt, his muscles stood out in obvious relief. Even though Daisy thought Chris was about as perfect as a guy could get, she had to admit that George's body was incredible. The sheer power of his arms as he flexed and extended them was truly awe-inspiring.

Mesmerized by the show of male strength and beauty, Daisy lost count of how many times George's chin rose above the bar before he dropped to the floor.

"That was...*nice*, honey." Ellie's gaze was fixed on George like he was a piece of chocolate cake, and he smiled at her.

"I'm next." Callum sounded cranky as he jumped to grab the bar.

Lou snickered. "Sorry I was ogling another guy, Cal. You know you're my favorite man candy." She paused as Callum pulled his body upward. "Oh my. Yes, you're definitely my favorite."

Chris and Ian jostled to be next at the bar when Callum finished after an unreal number of pull-ups. A well-placed elbow knocked Ian back just long enough for Chris to jump for the bar. Not to be deterred, Ian grabbed the section of bar next to Chris, and they pulled themselves up in tandem.

"I feel like we're remiss in not recording this," Ellie breathed, her eyes fixed on the show until George stepped in front of her, blocking her view. "Hey!"

Although Daisy knew Chris was in good shape, she always tried not to stare at him too long, in case it got weird. She couldn't take her eyes off him now, though. As she watched his biceps stretch his sleeves and his shirt cling to his contracting chest, her legs moved slower and slower until the treadmill belt kicked her off the back. She stumbled, regaining her balance without dropping her gaze from Chris.

Because there were two of them, the competition was

intense, and neither wanted to be the first to drop off the bar. With their teeth showing in tight grimaces and the veins bulging in their arms, they grunted with each raise. Chris got stuck two-thirds of the way up, his arms shaking with effort, but he held the position for a fraction of a second longer than Ian.

Their feet hit the floor at almost the same time, and Chris looked over at Daisy. She knew she should look away, but someone else was apparently controlling her body, since it was impossible. It took Rory's voice to break their connected gaze.

"I'm not sure what the protocol is on this," she said, idly running the rope through her hands as she watched a panting Ian shake out his arms. "Should I run to you and throw myself into your arms, overwhelmed by your display of masculine power?" Her flat delivery struck Daisy as funny, and she started to laugh. Instead of taking offense, Ian grinned.

"Yes. That is the correct protocol," he said, holding out his arms.

Blushing, Rory shook her head at him. He walked over to rejoin her, sliding an arm around her waist and saying something in her ear that made her blush even harder. That same wistful feeling she'd had earlier slid through Daisy, and she looked away from the pair. Climbing back onto the treadmill, her feet straddling the belt, she picked up her run again.

"Unless you've wrecked yourself trying to show off," Chris said to Ian, "get over here and let's see if you can throw a punch. You too, Rory."

"*I* was the one trying to show off?" Ian smirked at Chris, throwing a glance toward Daisy that she couldn't interpret. Despite his words, he followed Rory to the heavy bag.

Daisy increased her speed, hoping that would take her mind off the too-tempting display of masculine power still running on a loop in her mind. It was so unfair for Chris to look as good as he did and act as sweet as he could. Sadly, she knew that, no matter how fast she ran, she couldn't escape her unrequited feelings for Chris.

Chapter 7

DAISY GLANCED AT THE CLOCK HANGING ON THE WALL and was shocked that almost two hours had passed. It was amazing how fast the time went when there were people training with her. The others had also taken Chris's focus off Daisy, so she could grab quick breaks when he wasn't looking, something that was impossible when it was just the two of them. She looked around the room, which had started to resemble a battlefield, thanks to the slumped and limp bodies scattered around.

"Are you guys ready to quit?"

Ellie, lying flat on her back on the sparring mats, groaned. Daisy took that as a yes. The rest of them chorused their agreement.

From her position sitting next to Max's feet, one arm wrapped around his knees, Lou extended her other hand for her water bottle. It was six inches past her reach.

"My most wonderful and loving Callum, could you kick my water bottle a little closer?"

He looked up from where he leaned heavily against the wall. "You've almost got it. Just put a little effort into it."

"I'm out of effort," she whined. "There's no effort left in me. If I lean over to get it, I'll have to let go of darling Max, and then I'll fall over and look like Ellie."

Ellie groaned.

Realizing that it might be hours if she waited for the

others to regain their feet, Daisy said, "I'll just go put the sausage biscuits in the oven."

As she headed toward the door, Lou grumbled, "How are you still walking?"

Daisy laughed. "Chris's been torturing me a lot longer than you. I'm used to it."

"Hey!" Chris didn't sound too offended, though. He moved from where he was talking to Ian, who was either being held up by or holding up Rory—probably both. "I'll go with you."

When they got to the kitchen, Daisy turned on the oven and then looked up to see Chris opening the interior door. Her first thought was that he was going to leave her with six almost-strangers to entertain, and panic made her eyes go wide.

"I just need to grab something from my truck," he said. Her worry must have been obvious, since he made soothing motions with his hands. "Can you get the door behind me?"

"Sure." Before the door shut all the way behind him, she grabbed it. "Swear you're coming back?"

There was laughter in his voice when he promised, "Thirty seconds."

He was as good as his word. Daisy pretended like she hadn't been leaning against the door, counting, when he returned at the twenty-three second mark. After the outside door locked behind him, she opened the interior door to see that he had a case of sports drinks and several grocery bags of snacks piled in his arms.

"I was kidding about the BYOSD part." She tried to take some of his load, but he twisted away from her.

"I've got this. Just get the door."

She hurried to relock it, returning to the kitchen to find him unpacking the bags. "Thanks, Chris. You didn't have to do this, especially after being everyone's personal trainer."

He shrugged. "Figured more food is always a good thing. And"—he shook a package of cookies at her and grinned—"while everyone else is distracted by this stuff, I'll grab all the sausage-and-cheese biscuits."

With a laugh, she tore open the case of sports drinks and started pulling out bottles. "Ah, I see. It's all an evil plot."

He gave his best villain laugh, which sounded more like an asthmatic donkey, and she cringed.

"No, Chris. Just...no." She paused, a bottle in each hand, as she remembered something. Lowering her voice, she asked, "What's the tension between you and George and Ellie all about?"

His happy expression faded, making her regret asking. "They're pissed at me—as they should be. I was supposed to be watching Ellie the night she got shot."

Daisy sucked in a breath. There had to be more to the story, she knew. Chris was the most conscientious person she'd ever met—not that she'd met a huge number of people, but still. Chris wouldn't have neglected his duties without a good reason. "What happened?"

Grimacing, he glanced toward the doorway, as if hoping the others would come traipsing in and save him from explaining. "There isn't a landline or cell coverage at George's house. My radio battery was dying, so I ran out to the squad to switch it out for a spare. The reception out there is crap, but I thought I heard Rob asking for my status. I had to drive all the way to the county road before I could talk to Dispatch. On the way, I passed Joseph Acconcio's car." He gave a humorless laugh. "I was stupidly grateful he was there, that he'd watch her while I was gone. I didn't know what he…"

He broke off with a single shake of his head. "Never mind. There's no excuse for having left Ellie alone. So that's why George wants to throw me through a wall, and Ellie doesn't trust me. I'm actually surprised they came."

"Oh." Daisy blinked. "Wow." Even as isolated as she was, she'd heard of the search and rescue leader who'd been killed by a drug dealer. She just hadn't realized it had happened at George and Ellie's house, or that Ellie had been Anderson King's other victim that night. Daisy tried to process that information while thinking of something she could tell him that would erase Chris's grim, guilty look. Before she could say anything else, though, she heard the rest of the group approaching. With a final, worried glance at Chris's averted face, she turned toward Rory and Lou, sports drinks extended. Later, once she thought of the right words, she'd reassure him that Ellie's injury wasn't his fault. In the meantime, she offered him a sports drink, which he accepted with a small but genuine smile.

Sitting back with a sigh, Ellie patted her stomach. "There's nothing like pigging out after working out. All the pleasure with none of that nasty guilt."

"I hear you," Lou agreed, grabbing another cookie. "Daisy, those biscuit things were awesome."

"Thanks." Daisy heard Chris grumble under his

breath, and she held back a smile. Rather than the entire batch, Chris had managed to grab only two of the biscuits before the ravening horde had made them disappear.

"Now that our mouths aren't full…" Lou regarded her half-eaten cookie and shrugged. "Well, now that *most* of us are done eating, can we talk about dead people?"

"I won't be able to contribute," Chris warned. "I'll listen, but I can't give out information about an active case."

"Understood." Callum gave him a brisk nod.

"Do you mind starting from the beginning?" Daisy asked, playing with the cap on her sports-drink bottle. "Lou gave me the basics the other day, but mostly we talked about my"—she made a face—"dead body."

"What?" asked a chorus of voices, as almost everyone sitting around the dining room table stared at her.

Daisy flushed. "I saw someone putting…something into the back of a sheriff's department SUV really early one morning. It ended up being a deputy who was hired to clear junk out of the empty house. His car was too small, so he used a sheriff's department vehicle." She turned to Chris. "Will you have any trouble with the deputy for getting him in trouble with the sheriff?"

"No." Chris shook his head. "Rob said he didn't tell Macavoy who'd reported seeing him."

"Good." She'd worried about it causing an issue, especially since Chris's job could be a lot more dangerous if his backup was holding a grudge.

"Why was he moving junk at—what was it, Daisy? Three in the morning?" Lou asked.

"He'd just gotten off a swing shift."

Callum's grunt was skeptical as he looked at Chris. "How well do you know this guy?"

"Not that well," Chris said, frowning thoughtfully. "He started last fall, so he's still the new guy. He's pretty quiet, keeps his head down. A lot of deputies don't last a year out here, so it takes a while for them to…integrate, I guess. Why do you ask?"

"When you're moving a bunch of junk, how do you carry it?" Callum asked instead of answering.

Lou made an amused sound. "Here we go with the Socratic method again."

Ignoring her, he just waited for Chris to answer.

"Depends on what I'm moving. I'd try to make as few trips as possible. Big, heavy pieces, though, I'm going to have to move one at a time."

"Small stuff, I'll throw in a box or wheelbarrow." George's contribution made everyone jump. Daisy was pretty sure that was the first time she'd heard the man speak.

Callum nodded. "This guy was carrying something wrapped in a tarp, right, Daisy?"

She sat up straight in her chair. Callum's stern tone made her feel like she was back in school being called on by the teacher. "Yes."

"If you're using a tarp, let's say in place of Holloway's box, how do you load up the junk?"

It was Ian's turn to contribute. "I'd stretch the tarp out flat, pile everything in the middle, and wrap it up like Santa's bag of toys."

Turning to Daisy again, Callum asked, "Is that how he was carrying it?"

"No." The image was still clear in her mind. "It was rolled, like a rug or a burrito. The ends were open, since the boot fell out of the bottom."

"A boot?" Ian frowned. "Is that why you thought it was a body?"

"Yes. It came out when he was putting the tarp in the back of the squad SUV." Now that they were talking about it, she couldn't see how the bundle Macavoy had been carrying could have been a pile of junk. "Plus, it just *acted* like a dead body. That sounds crazy, I know, especially since I'm not an expert in any way, but he had it over his shoulder, and it hung. Lumber or metal or whatever would've stuck out straight. When he dumped it in the back of the SUV, he kind of bent over and dropped it, like it was really heavy." She made a frustrated sound. "I'm not explaining this right."

"You're doing fine, Daisy." Callum's voice was gentle. "We're thinking along the same lines. What kind of junk can you roll up in a tarp, hinges at the waist, is heavy, and sheds a boot?"

"Holy monkeys, it *was* a body!" Lou started to bounce in her chair, but then winced and sat still.

"That is why I asked if you know this deputy well," Callum said to Chris, leaning back in his chair.

Chris didn't look convinced. "If Macavoy was moving a corpse, why admit to Rob that he was at the house at all?"

"If he thought he'd been spotted and identified, he probably didn't think he could deny it," Lou offered.

"I'm confused." Ellie frowned, absently picking at her cuticles. When George put a hand over hers, stilling her fingers, she gave him a grateful smile and then turned back to the group. "If it is a body, it's a new one, right? So who is it?"

There were a few moments of silence before Lou

broke it. "Argh! Nothing fits together. We keep getting new information, but it just leads to more questions."

"Has anyone been reported missing?" Rory asked Chris, who shook his head.

Ellie made a pained sound. "Just my dad."

Daisy stared at her. "Your dad's missing?"

As Ellie nodded, close to tears, George released her hands so he could rub her back. "Anderson King was hunting him—hunting both of us—and I don't know where either my dad or Anderson is."

Although she leaned into George's touch, Ellie still looked miserable. Daisy had to glance away. It had been one thing to speculate on whether she'd seen an actual body or not, but thinking that there was even a possibility it could be sweet Ellie's father made her stomach curdle. She was glad she'd been too nervous to eat much. Otherwise, she'd have been sprinting for the bathroom.

"El." George's voice was low. "Remember."

She sighed, the exhale shivering with imminent tears. "I know. Dad can take care of himself. It's just hard not to imagine the worst."

"It probably wasn't even a body," Daisy blurted, needing to say *something* to make Ellie's lost look go away. "Even if it was, there'd be no way Anderson King would be driving around in a sheriff's squad. I'm sure it wasn't your dad—if it *was* someone, I mean, and not a tarp full of scraps." She stopped talking abruptly, aware that her words were just getting more and more muddled.

Ellie didn't seem to mind the convoluted logic, though. She gave Daisy a shaky smile. "Thank you."

"Your dad will be calling soon," Lou assured her.

"He's safe in Mexico or Canada or Cleveland or some-where." The rest of the group added their reassur-ances, until Ellie looked, if not completely convinced, at least a little farther from tears than she had a few minutes earlier.

Ian glanced at his watch and stood. "Shift tonight. I'd better get home and shower first, or no one's going to want to ride in the truck with me."

As if that was a signal, everyone else started to rise, gathering the remains of the improvised feast and bring-ing it to the kitchen.

"You can just leave it," Daisy protested. "I'll clean it up later."

Everyone just ignored her, though, and the kitchen and dining room were spotless less than ten minutes later.

"What are you doing Monday morning?" Lou asked Daisy.

"Nothing special. Why?"

"I still want to talk to you about the Gray case. Are you up for it?"

"Sure."

"Wait." Rory frowned at them. "I want to be in on that, but the shop's open until six. Can we meet here Monday evening, instead?"

"At eight?" Lou suggested, looking at Daisy for confirmation.

"Can I come, too?" Ellie asked, then laughed. "That made me sound like a preschooler, but I really would like to join you guys, if that's okay?"

"Of course," Daisy said, answering all their questions at once.

"Sure?" Lou asked. "That won't be too late?"

Daisy gave the other woman a look. "I thought we'd decided that I *wasn't* an Amish grandmother. Besides, I don't really sleep much. We could meet at midnight, for all I care." An unhappy sound to her left made her turn her head and catch Chris's frown. After giving him a reassuring smile, she turned back to the women. "Eight is fine."

With that settled, everyone except Daisy and Chris said their good-byes and clustered into the small space between the interior and outer doors. Six people made it a fairly tight fit, but Daisy could hear them chatting and jostling each other good-naturedly, so no one seemed to mind waiting to exit until she'd secured the inner door.

When the locks were refastened, Chris reached over her shoulder and slapped the door with his open palm a couple of times. The voices faded as the group left, and the outside door cut them off completely when it closed behind them. Daisy looked over her shoulder at Chris.

"That went well, don't you think?" Without giving him a chance to answer, she added, "It felt like it went well. At least, I'm pretty sure it did. Right?"

He waited until she fell silent. "You done?" She glared at him, but he just looked amused. "It went very well."

Slumping back against the wall, Daisy felt suddenly exhausted—happy, but exhausted. "It was nice of you to lead the training."

He shrugged off her thanks. "I enjoyed it. If I ever get sick of being a cop, I might become a personal trainer."

"You can practice on us, then." She smiled at him. "We'll give you good references when you start training the rich snow bunnies who want to improve their skiing."

Making a face, he admitted, "That doesn't sound appealing. Maybe I'll stick with training cops instead."

"And me," Daisy said on a yawn.

"And you, snoozy. Go take a nap."

Surprisingly, she felt like she could sleep for a week. "Are you taking off, then?"

"Yes, if you can pry yourself off the door." His smile was teasing.

"I suppose." With put-on reluctance, she straightened and stepped to the side. "Thanks again, Chris."

He was watching her in an odd way, but he just said, "You're welcome, Dais. Sleep well."

She couldn't take her eyes off the gun. Even when she heard the sheriff's deputy yelling at him to drop his weapon, and she knew that help had arrived, her gaze remained fixed on the matte black surface of the pistol. She saw his finger, curled around the trigger, pull tighter and tighter until—

Something woke her abruptly. Sitting up quickly before she was fully awake, she swayed a little as she listened for whatever noise had disturbed her sleep. All was quiet, though, and she eventually relaxed.

The clock on her nightstand glowed, showing that it was close to ten p.m. With a yawn, she relaxed back against the pillows, but the spurt of adrenaline that had shot through her veins when she startled awake kept her heart beating quickly and her eyelids open. With a sigh, she resigned herself to being awake for at least a few hours.

Kicking off the covers, she slid out of bed. If she

wasn't going to sleep, there was no sense in wasting time lying there and staring at the dark ceiling. She might as well be productive.

Daisy cleaned the training room first, snickering to herself at the sight of Max's now-covered lower half. As promised, Callum had brought a pair of sweatpants and had even dressed the dummy himself. While she stood on a bench so she could wipe down the pull-up bar, the memory of the guys having their impromptu competition made her smile again.

It had been a fun day. Before the group training session, Daisy had been worried that she'd accidentally do something or say something that would drive them away, never to return again. As much as she loved her books and computer time, it would've been hard to go back to seeing only Chris and her father occasionally. Now, she had Monday night's get-together to look forward to, plus they'd been talking about making the training sessions a regular, couple-times-a-week thing.

As she moved the mats so she could vacuum, she did a mental inventory of the pantry and freezer. The Monday evening meeting would be held too late for a big meal, but she had the ingredients to make teriyaki meatballs and crab wontons. She wished she had eggs, so she could make some brownies, too.

"What do you think, Max?" she asked over the whine of the vacuum. "Would it be crossing a line to ask Chris to pick up a few things at the store?"

The dummy dangled silently on his hook, his new sweatpants hanging low on his hips.

"I know he brought groceries today without me asking, but it's different when I request it. It changes it from a favor between friends to, I don't know, a duty for the poor housebound girl, I guess. I don't want him to see me as helpless and needy."

Max's silence felt slightly judgmental.

"I know, I know. I *am* needy and kind of helpless. It's stupid, but I want Chris to look at me and see a whole person, not just this living ghost haunting my house."

Turning off the vacuum, she gave Max an accusatory glare.

"It's a good thing you're useful in other ways, Sir Maximillian, because as a therapist? You kind of suck."

By the time she finished with the training room, Daisy was in full-on cleaning mode, so she decided to tackle the rest of the house. Her dad's room had a slightly stale smell from disuse, and she left the door open to let it air. It was close to one in the morning by the time the house was done.

Feeling grubby, Daisy took a shower and then crawled back into bed. She knew she wasn't tired enough to sleep, so she grabbed a book off her nightstand. It was by one of her favorite urban fantasy authors, and it was a sign of how crazy her life had gotten over the past few days that she hadn't finished it yet. It had been a long time since her real life was as interesting as what happened in her books.

After rereading the same page over and over for a half-hour, she gave up on the book. Her brain was spinning with so many things—the training session, Chris's recent weirdness contrasted with his consideration, the renewed possibility that Deputy Macavoy might actually *have* been hauling a dead body around at three thirty in the morning, the Gray case and the fact that the other women were interested in getting her, Crazy Daisy's, opinion about it, and even the pros and cons to making brownies for Monday night, *if* her dad returned in time to make an egg run. How could a book, even a good one, compete with all that?

Daisy sighed. Since she wasn't going to be able to sleep or read with all the thoughts crowding into her brain, she didn't want to stay in bed. She turned off the bedside lamp and moved to the window seat, once again feeling that twinge of guilt. It wasn't a strong enough pang to keep her from opening and raising the blinds, however.

As usual, Ian and Rory's house was shuttered, with no hint of light showing. Daisy waved at the dark building, feeling a glow of pleasure that she'd actually met them, worked out with them, laughed at their jokes. The Storvicks' place was dark as well, but Daisy had no urge to meet any of those family members.

As if magnetized, her gaze moved to the white house with the for-sale sign in the yard. She wished it would sell, so she'd have a new family to watch, rather than scouring the darkness for the possibility of a second body removal. Shaking her head, Daisy reminded herself that there was a very, very slim chance that Macavoy's burden had been a person.

Leaning against the window, Daisy shivered at the touch of the cold glass. She debated whether to take the ten steps it would require to fetch a blanket, but pulled her knees to her chest instead. It was a poor substitute, but she was feeling lazy.

The clouds were moving quickly, and Daisy watched, mesmerized, as they scurried through the night sky. She quit trying to control her thoughts and just let them run through her brain. Chris popped up more than she'd hoped, but, for once, she didn't fight it. Ever since she'd stopped leaving the house when she was sixteen, he'd been a regular visitor. He'd always acted like an older brother, teasing and overprotective, but she'd never felt like his sister.

Thinking about the early days of their friendship made her mind drift toward thoughts of her mom. She slammed a mental door, blocking any memories of that day. Shifting on the window seat, she hugged her legs harder and replayed the training session in her head again instead.

A shadow shifted, moving from the trees to the far side of the empty house. Daisy straightened so quickly, she knocked her head against the wall. Absently rubbing the back of her skull, she peered into the blackness.

Before she could even begin to blame her imagination and the poor illumination, the shadow moved again. The light from the closest streetlamp reflected off a pale face.

"Should've worn face paint, whoever you are," she muttered, moving to her knees and leaning close to the window. When her breath started fogging the glass, she reluctantly shifted back a few inches and used her sleeve to clear the condensation. "Or one of those black bank-robber face masks."

The figure disappeared, and Daisy made a sound of annoyance. She didn't move, as if a shift in position would ensure that she didn't see the trespasser again. She stared so hard at the spot where she'd last seen the shadow that her eyes began to itch and burn. When she finally allowed herself to blink, her vision blurred with tears, and Daisy hurried to rub away the wetness.

It took her a few seconds to catch the motion on the near side of the house, since she was concentrating so hard on the other. The figure stood out against the white of the house and the remaining snow, showing the differences between the current intruder and Macavoy. This one was lanky and not quite as tall as the deputy. That, and the way he moved, made her think he was a teenager.

Daisy squinted, trying to bring the kid's uncovered face into focus. "Corbin, is that you? What are you up to this time?" She wondered if he was trying to sneak inside so he didn't get in trouble with his parents for breaking curfew. Instead of looking at his home, though, possibly-Corbin was peering into one of the side windows of the white house.

That wasn't going to lead to anything good. Although she hated taking her eyes off the skulking kid, she made a quick dash to grab her phone off the nightstand where it'd been charging. Returning to the window seat, she saw that maybe-Corbin was still in the same place. He'd grown bolder, though, and had cupped both hands around his face to better see into the dark room.

Daisy's finger hovered over Chris's name, but it was his last day off before he started on nights. Instead, she found the nonemergency number for Dispatch and tapped it. Whoever was manning the phones would be up already—hopefully—so she wouldn't be waking someone to report some bored, trespassing kid.

"Communications."

"Hi," Daisy said awkwardly. "This is Daisy Little,

and there's what looks like a teenager sneaking around outside the empty house across the street from me. It's 304 Alpine Lane."

"Daisy Little?" the dispatcher repeated. "The sheriff wanted to talk to you directly if something else happened involving that house. Can he give you a call on this number?"

"Oh," Daisy said, flustered. "I'm pretty sure it's just a bored kid, so you don't have to wake up the sheriff for something so minor. I just don't want any damage to be done to the house. Could you just have one of the on-duty deputies do a drive-by?"

"Sheriff Coughlin was insistent," the dispatcher told her apologetically. "Is this number the best one for him to use? I'm sure he'll call you immediately."

"This number is fine," she said reluctantly. If she'd known it was going to require a conversation with Sheriff Judge-y-pants, Daisy would've woken Chris, instead. "Could you let him know that it's definitely not an emergency, though, and that I don't require a call back?"

"I'll tell him."

"Thanks." After she ended the call, Daisy stared at her cell phone in dread for a few seconds before remembering the trespasser. When she looked at the white house, the kid was gone—or out of her sight, at least. She watched the property, alternating between the near and far sides of the house, but no one was skulking in the shadows.

The sound of her ringtone made her jump. In her attempt to get another glimpse of the intruder, the sheriff's call had slipped her mind. With the kid gone, she was even more reluctant to answer. Daisy was afraid if she didn't, though, the sheriff would send someone to her front door to check on her. Over-the-phone embarrassment was preferable to in-person embarrassment, so she accepted the call.

"Hi, Sheriff."

"Ms. Little." He sounded alert, so hopefully the dispatcher hadn't woken him. "More trouble in the neighborhood?"

"Nothing major," she said. "I didn't mean to bother you with this, but the dispatcher insisted you'd want to talk to me."

"It's fine. What's going on?"

"Someone was sneaking around outside the for-sale house. It looked like a teenager. He went around the back and then looked in a side window. I just called Dispatch in case he was thinking about doing some vandalism or wanted to break in or something."

"Is he still there?"

"I don't think so." Her eyes were glued on the empty house, and everything was still. "He slipped away while I was talking to the dispatcher."

"I'll stop by in the morning," the sheriff said, making Daisy wince.

"You really don't have to do that, Sheriff." She tried to sound grateful and discouraging at the same time. "I just thought a squad passing through the neighborhood would drive the kid away. He's gone now, and you don't need to waste your time—"

"Seeing to your peace of mind isn't a waste of time, Ms. Little," Coughlin interrupted. "I'll be by around six thirty tomorrow morning, if you'll be awake by then?"

"I'll be up," she said faintly.

"Good. Sleep well, Ms. Little." He ended the call.

Daisy brought her phone to her lap and stared at it absently. Why had he mentioned her peace of mind? She'd told him flat-out that she didn't think the teenager would be a danger, except maybe to one of the house's windows. The way he said it made her feel like he was coming over to pat her hand and assure the weak-minded girl that the bogeymen wasn't real.

With a mental shake, she stood and took her phone to the nightstand. While she plugged in the charger again, she told herself she was being too sensitive. The sheriff didn't have the best bedside manner, at least not with her, but he was trying to help. She should be pleased that he was taking her concerns seriously—more seriously than she thought they warranted, in fact.

As she settled back onto the window seat, she gave a humorless laugh. Being awake in time for the sheriff's visit wouldn't be a problem, since she was fairly sure she wouldn't be sleeping any more that night. There was something about conversations with Coughlin that kept her awake.

It was worse than she'd expected.

"None?" she asked.

"No fresh boot prints anywhere around the perimeter of the house," Sheriff Coughlin confirmed.

"It was windy last night. Maybe the drifting snow filled in the prints?" Even before she finished speaking, the sheriff was shaking his head.

"With the warm temperatures we've been having, the snow is either frozen or wet and heavy. If someone had walked through that yard last night, there would've been prints."

Daisy hid her wince at his words, even though they hit as hard as an elbow to the gut, and struggled to keep her voice firm. "There was someone walking around the outside of that house last night, Sheriff. I don't know why there aren't any boot prints, but I definitely saw someone."

He was giving her that look again, but it was worse, because she saw a thread of pity mixed in with the condescension. "Have you given more thought to starting therapy again?"

The question surprised her. "Not really. What does that have to do...?" As comprehension dawned, a surge of rage shoved out her bewilderment. "I didn't *imagine* that I saw someone last night. There really was a person there, looking in the side window."

All her protest did was increase the pity in his expression. "It must get lonely here by yourself."

"I'm not making things up to get attention!" Her voice had gotten shrill, so she took a deep breath. "I even said there was no need for you to get involved. I only suggested one of the on-duty deputies drive past to scare away the kid."

"Ms. Little." His tone made it clear that impatience had drowned out any feelings of sympathy. "Physical evidence doesn't lie. No one was in that yard last night."

"I know what I saw."

The sheriff took a step closer. Daisy hated how she had to crane her neck back to look at him. It made her feel so small and vulnerable. "Do you really?" he asked. "Eyewitness accounts are notoriously unreliable. Even people without your issues misinterpret what they see all the time. The brain is a tricky thing."

Daisy set her jaw as she stared back at the sheriff, fighting the urge to step back, to retreat from the man looming over her. There *had* been someone there, footprints or no footprints. She couldn't start doubting what she'd witnessed the night before. If she did, then that meant she'd gone from mildly, can't-leave-the-house crazy, to the kind of crazy that involved hallucinations, medications, and institutionalization. There had to be some other explanation, because she wasn't going to accept that. Not when her life was getting so much better.

She could tell by looking at his expression that she wasn't going to convince Coughlin of anything. "Thank you for checking on it, Sheriff. I promise not to bother you again."

Although he kept his face impassive, his eyes narrowed slightly. "If you...see anything else, Ms. Little, please call me."

That wasn't going to happen, especially when he put that meaningful pause in front of "see" that just screamed "delusional." Trying to mask her true feelings, she plastered on a smile and turned her body toward the door in a not-so-subtle hint for him to leave. "Of course."

Apparently, she needed some lessons in deception, since the sheriff frowned, unconvinced. Daisy met his eyes with as much calmness as she could muster, dropping the fake smile because she could feel it shifting into manic territory. She'd lost enough credibility with the sheriff as it was.

The silence stretched until Daisy wanted to run away and hide in a closet, but she managed to continue holding his gaze. The memory of Chris telling her about the sheriff using his "going to confession" stare-down on suspects helped her to stay quiet.

Finally, Coughlin turned toward the door. Daisy barely managed to keep her sigh of relief silent.

"Ms. Little," he said with a short nod, which she returned.

"Sheriff."

Only when he was through the doorway with the door locked behind him did Daisy's knees start to shake.

Chapter 8

DAISY PASSED THE TIME FROM THE SHERIFF'S DEPARTURE until noon alternating between pacing, one-sided conversations with Max, and chewing her thumbnails down to nothingness. Since Chris would be on duty, working the six-to-six shift that night, she knew he'd try to sleep as late as possible. It probably would've been safer to call him midafternoon, but Daisy was afraid she wouldn't have thumbs left if she had to fret for another three hours.

"What's up, Dais?" he asked, sounding awake and fairly cheerful, thankfully.

"I'm not crazy, right? I mean, I am about the whole not-going-outside thing, but I'm not loony tunes, seeing-things-that-aren't-there, get-thee-to-a-nuthouse type of crazy, am I?" After the words rushed out of her like verbal vomit, Daisy rested her head against the training room wall. Even if she had *planned* the most insane way of starting the conversation with Chris, she couldn't have sounded more cracked.

"What's this about?"

Her stomach clenched. "Did you just avoid answering the question?"

"You're not crazy. Now what's going on?"

The whole story spilled from her. Hearing it out loud made it seem even more insane, and she cringed several times during the retelling. It didn't help that Chris was silent for a long time after she stopped talking.

"Chris?" Although she'd been determined to let him be the one to speak first, she couldn't stand not knowing what he was thinking. Daisy could stand up to the sheriff's suspect-cracking stare, but Chris's ambiguous silence broke her easily.

"I'll be over in ten minutes."

That wasn't any clearer than his silence had been. "Okay."

"Dais?"

"Yeah?"

"You're not crazy."

After he ended the call, she hovered by the door. Only seven minutes had passed when she heard his distinctive knock. Once he was inside and the doors relocked, she moved to the coffeemaker. It was as good an excuse as any to avoid looking directly at him.

"Want some?" she asked, already reaching for his daisy cup.

"Sure. Before you make it, though, show me exactly where you saw this kid last night."

Leaving the cup on the counter, she led the way upstairs and into her bedroom. It was strange having Chris there, and her skin prickled with an odd combination of heat and goose bumps. She firmly ignored both reactions.

Kneeling on the window seat, she felt him behind her, close enough for his body heat to warm her back through her shirt.

"I saw someone move from those trees"—she pointed—"to the far side of the house. He kind of peeked around the corner, like he was checking to see if anyone was watching, and then he must've gone around the back of the house. The next time I saw him, he was on that side"—her pointing finger shifted—"looking in the window."

"Did he touch the glass, could you tell?"

As she nodded, her hair brushed against his chest, catching on the buttons of his flannel shirt. "He cupped his hands on either side of his face, like he was trying to see inside better."

"Okay." He gathered her hair and tucked it over her shoulder, away from the snagging buttons. She turned her face toward him in surprise. "I'm going to go check things out over there."

Daisy nodded again, her voice stuck in her throat. Chris was leaning forward slightly, his head tipped down, his eyes on hers, and he had an unreadable look on his face. It wasn't the *bad* sort of unreadable, like the sheriff tended to wear. Chris looked…hungry and sad and the same sort of wistful as she'd felt the day before as she watched the three happy couples. Then he stepped away, and the look disappeared, making Daisy wonder if she'd imagined it.

After all, she'd apparently been imagining all sorts of things lately.

⚬⚬⚬

As Chris walked around the for-sale house, peering intently at the snow-covered ground, Daisy tried unsuccessfully not to obsess over what he was seeing. After catching herself wandering into the living room to stare at him through the window for the hundredth time, she decided that, if she was going to watch Chris anyway, she might as well have a good view. Taking the stairs two at a time, she hurried to her bedroom window.

While she'd been switching locations, Chris had stopped focusing on the ground and had turned his attention to the window the prowler had been looking through the night before. The distance made it hard to see details, but Chris had some sort of black case, about the size of a shaving kit, open on the ground next to him.

Leaning farther and farther forward, she tried to make out what he was doing. Chris was holding something dark and was moving his hand in back and forth motions over the window. It almost looked like he was painting, although, from Daisy's vantage point, it didn't appear that the brush was leaving anything behind on the glass.

After he finished his brushwork, he pulled a sheet of clear film off its white backing and pressed it to the glass. Peeling it off the window, he returned it to the backing, using the side of the house as a work surface. He repeated this one more time before packing up his kit and walking to his squad where it was parked in front of her house.

Daisy rushed downstairs to meet him at the door, although she was careful this time not to open the inner door too early in her excitement. Impatiently, she waited for the thud-click of the exterior door lock before untwisting the locks and freeing the chains.

"Well?" she asked as she pulled open the door.

He raised an eyebrow. "Are you going to let me in? Maybe make me that coffee you promised?"

Stepping back, she waved him inside. This time, she waited until the door was relocked and he'd stepped out of his boots before demanding, "What did you find?"

"The yard's a mess," he said, looking at the coffeemaker and back at her.

"What does that mean?" When he continued eyeing the brewer like it was a water fountain in the desert, she sighed and popped a hazelnut cup into the machine. "You know, you're welcome to help yourself."

"It tastes better when you make it."

"That makes no sense."

"Do you want to hear what I found over there or not?"

"Yes, please." She put the daisy mug in place to catch the coffee and turned back toward Chris, making the "get on with it" gesture that she'd stolen from him.

"There are boot prints everywhere. Some I could tell were old, since they'd gone through some melting and refreezing cycles. The new ones were mostly similar to mine, so I'm assuming those are Rob's from this morning."

"Mostly?" Her pulse accelerated. Despite Chris's insistence that she wasn't crazy, the incident with the sheriff had allowed doubts to creep into her head.

"Hard to tell, but I thought I saw a few partials—very partial—of a different style of boot. The other prints almost completely covered them, though."

"Covered them?" Daisy frowned, confused. "Like the sheriff walked on them? Why would he do that?"

Chris shrugged, his brows drawn together. "Not sure. I haven't talked to him about this yet."

Her stomach dipped. "Is this going to cause a problem

for you? I mean, I basically shooed him away and called you to tattle. Will he be pissed?"

Scowling, Chris said, "*I'm* pissed. If he trampled evidence because he was determined you were imagining things, he deserves to be called out on it."

"How do you know I wasn't?" Although she tried to keep her voice casual, Daisy couldn't quite manage it. "Imagining things?"

"First of all, I know you. If you said you saw someone, then there was someone there." His matter-of-fact tone calmed her. "Secondly, I lifted a couple of handprints from the window."

It took a second for the information to sink in. "*That's* what you were doing to the window! Really? There were prints?"

He grinned as he nodded. "Both sides, as if someone had cupped his hands against the glass to look inside. *And* I lifted a beautiful, crystal-clear print of his right pinkie finger. He must have rolled his right hand as he took it off the glass."

Relief flooded through her, the feeling so intense that she couldn't breathe for a second. When her lungs started working again, she blew out a long exhale. "I'm not crazy."

"You are not crazy. The handprints won't be much use unless we have a suspect in custody so we can do a comparison, but I'll send the fingerprint to the Colorado Bureau of Criminal Apprehension and have them...*oof*."

Daisy looked up at his stunned face, her arms wrapped tightly around his middle. "Sorry. I know you hate it when I touch you, but I'm just so *relieved* that I couldn't

help myself. I'm letting you go and backing away now."
She retreated to the other side of the kitchen, unable to
stop grinning, even when Chris's surprised expression
turned into a scowl.

"What do you mean?"

"What do you mean, what do I mean?" It wasn't that
funny, but she started giggling as she offered the filled
coffee mug to Chris. He accepted it absently but didn't
take a drink, all his attention still focused on her.

"I don't hate it when you touch me. What makes you
think that?"

She shrugged. "Whenever I try to give you a hug, you
jump away like you're a cat and I'm an ocean wave."

"No, I don't."

"Please." The complete and total lie made her smirk
at him. "The last time I tried to hug you, after you gave
me Max, you couldn't run away fast enough. Admit it—
you're a total hug-blocker."

His mouth hung open. Daisy was tempted to close it
with a finger on his chin, but she supposed she'd pushed
him far enough for the day, especially since he'd come
running over when she'd needed help.

"There are so many things wrong with what you just
said. I've never run away from anything," Chris said.
Daisy hid another grin. Of course, accusing him of running off was what had tweaked him the worst. "And I'm
not a hug-blocker, whatever that is."

"Yeah, you kind of are."

"I'm not—are you laughing?"

"Sorry. I'm not laughing at you. Well, maybe a
little, but I'm mostly really happy that I'm not having
hallucinations."

His outraged expression softened. "You're as sane as I am, Dais." He finally took a sip of his coffee, his eyes fixed on something over her shoulder as he thought. "What's Rob's deal, I wonder?"

The thought of the sheriff made her stomach start churning again, in a mix of anger and apprehension. "The dispatcher said he wanted to know if I called. Isn't that...weird?"

"It is unusual." His thoughtful frown deepened. "I'll check with...do you know which dispatcher you talked to last night?"

"I didn't get a name, but she had a squeaky voice."

Chris's mouth quirked up in a smile. "Libby. I'll see if she's working tonight. Maybe she'll know why Rob's fixated on you."

Her stomach lurched. "Fixated?"

Refocusing on her face, Chris shook his head. "Wrong word, sorry. I'm wondering if he's thinking Macavoy's going to try some moonlighting again, so Rob's using you as his security system."

Although she tried to smile at his weak joke, Daisy wasn't very successful. The idea of having the sheriff's focus on her for whatever reason was not a pleasant thought.

"Isn't Gabe back yet?" Chris's scowl had returned.

"Nope." She kept her voice light. "The Connor Springs job must've hit a snag."

His grunt was skeptical. "I'm back on nights now, so call me if anything comes up."

"Will do."

"Good." Grabbing one of Gabe's travel mugs from the cupboard, Chris dumped the remaining coffee from his cup into the to-go mug. "And I don't hate it when you touch me."

"Uh-huh."

He rinsed the daisy mug and put it in the dishwasher. "I don't. It just makes it…harder."

Since his back was turned, he couldn't see her confused expression. "What does that mean?"

"Nothing." He blew out a breath and headed for the door. "Never mind. See you later, Dais."

As she locked the inside door behind him, she yelled through the wood, "You are so weird, Deputy Jennings!"

If he responded, she didn't hear him.

--***--

"He did what?!" Lou leaned forward, a teriyaki meatball hovering inches from her mouth.

Hearing the horror in the other woman's voice made Daisy hedge her words. "It could've just been a case of not watching where he was stepping, I suppose."

"He's the sheriff," Lou said flatly. "He was looking for evidence. That's pretty sad if he trampled on the very boot prints he was looking for by *accident*." Eyeing the meatball in front of her face as if trying to figure out how it got there, she popped it into her mouth.

"It does seem strangely incompetent of him," Rory agreed. "He can be hard-edged, but I've never found Rob to be inept."

Ellie frowned. "You don't think Rob did that on *purpose*, do you? But he's such a sweetheart. Since this whole Anderson King thing started, he's been wonderful about lending me his deputies every time George gets called away. Plus, he organized that search for my father. I just can't imagine him hiding evidence."

"He's always been upfront with me, too," Lou added. As silence filled the room, Daisy shifted uncomfortably. These women didn't know her very well at all. To them, she was probably still that weird shut-in. If she kept pushing, insisting that the sheriff had covered up evidence—either by accident or on purpose—Daisy would not only lose the argument, but she'd probably lose her only chance at friends, too. In a determinedly cheerful voice, she said, "Let's talk about the Gray case."

"Okay." Lou hopped up from the couch and hurried over to the pile of stuff she'd dumped in the corner of Daisy's living room. Daisy got up to help, but Lou already had an easel set up and an oversized pad of paper propped on it before Daisy even reached her.

"Is this the substitute whiteboard?" Ellie asked, smiling.

"It is." Lou pulled out a set of markers. "Cal volunteered to bring the real one here in the back of the pickup, but with the sleeting-raining thing it's doing outside, I didn't want to risk having the whole thing erased by the time we got here. I needed something whiteboard-like, though. It helps me to see things written down when I'm trying to figure something out."

"Where is Callum?" Ellie asked.

"City Council meeting."

That was met with a chorus of groans from everyone except Daisy.

"I assume that's bad?" she guessed.

"So boring," Lou agreed. "If I hadn't already had

this planned, I would've had to make up something so I could get out of going. Speaking of that, Ellie, don't you have search and rescue training tonight?"

"Nope. That's George's thing. I'd just get myself lost if I tried to find someone in the wilderness. I help him with his reports, but that's about it."

"Does Ian have night shift tonight?" Lou asked Rory, who nodded.

"Where's your guy?" Ellie asked Daisy.

She blinked at the woman in confusion. "My...guy?"

"Please." Lou chucked a marker at her, and Daisy ducked out of the projectile's path just before it connected with her forehead. "We all saw how Deputy Chris was showing off for you on Saturday." Her voice lowered. "'Me big strong man, do many pull-ups.'" She finished her imitation with a grunt.

"Oh no!" Despite herself, Daisy felt her cheeks getting red. "We're not... Chris and I are just friends." Ellie and Lou snorted laughter, making her face even hotter. Even Rory looked like she was holding back a smile.

"*Friends*," Lou said, "do not look at their *friends* like your cop looks at you."

"She's right." Ellie reached over from where she was sitting in one of the armchairs and squeezed Daisy's hand. "Chris couldn't keep his eyes off of you. And his expression goes all...smooshy when he's looking at you."

Daisy was pretty sure she'd be able to toast a marshmallow on her face, it was burning so hotly. "No, really. We've never stepped out of the 'friends' box. He doesn't even like it when I give him a hug."

"Maybe he likes it too much." Lou was doing something weird with her eyebrows as she said it.

"What's wrong with your face?" Rory asked, squinting at Lou.

"Can we talk about dead people now?" Daisy asked quickly.

"Fine." Lou didn't sound happy about it. "But trust us on this—Deputy Chris wants you."

Shaking her head, Daisy let it drop. It was too embarrassing to tell them about all the times Chris refused to let her touch him. A subject change was definitely in order. Besides, it would be nice to think about something other than her own drama for a while. "Could you recap what you've learned so far? Chris gave me the highlights, but he's not really able to share much."

Lou grabbed a blue marker and uncapped it with a flourish. "Sure. It helps to go over everything again, anyway. I see new connections that way." She sketched a line of blue spikes.

"What are those?" Rory asked.

"Waves." She drew some stick people next to the squiggly lines.

"Really?"

Lou glared at Rory. "Yes. I accept that I am not an artist, okay? If you are going to be judgmental, then you can be the draw-er."

"Why are you drawing pictures?" Ellie asked. "We're all literate. You can use, you know, *words*."

"Fine." Lou sighed, scribbling beneath the feet of the stick people. "Everyone's a critic. So, Willard Gray was a Vietnam vet who lived by himself in a run-down cabin at the edge of Simpson. According to town gossip—which is kind of hit-and-miss as far as accuracy—he kept to himself, except when the Esko Hills home

development was about to be built next to his property a
few years ago. He de-hermit-ified long enough to attend
a few City Council meetings to protest the new construction, but the homes were built, and he retreated back to
his cabin, shaking his angry fists." Lou picked up her
glass from the coffee table and took a drink. Placing the
water back on its coaster, she looked around at the other
women. "How am I doing so far?"

"This matches what I've heard about him," Rory said.

"Good. So, sometime between last fall and this past
January, someone kills Willard, cuts off his head and
hands, and tosses him into Mission Reservoir. In early
March, a lucky, lucky dive team volunteer manages to
find the body during an ice-rescue training exercise."

With a cough that might have been disguising a
laugh, Rory interjected, "She kicked him."

Frowning, Lou turned her glare onto Rory. "Ian is
rubbing off on you, and not in a good way."

Widening her eyes in mock-innocence, Ellie asked,
"So, you *didn't* kick poor Willard's corpse?"

"Not really relevant." Lou sent all three women a
warning look, which Daisy didn't feel she deserved. Until
that moment, she hadn't known about Lou's method of
corpse-discovery. "Moving on. We didn't have a name
for the victim at first, since his…um, missing parts made
identification tricky. I felt sort of responsible for the poor
dead guy, since I…*discovered* him—don't say it!"

Ellie and Rory gave her innocent looks.

"So, I started trying to find out who this guy was.
Once Cal and I figured out the 'Willard' part, Chris
was able to ID him as Willard Gray, Simpson's resident
grumpy hermit."

"I think more than one person qualifies for that position," Rory said dryly. "The town is made up of about seventy percent grumpy hermits."

Lou laughed. "True. Once we knew who the victim was, though, we couldn't figure out a possible motive, much less narrow down the suspect pool. No one knew Willard well enough to hate him, at least that we've been able to find out. I mean, his Esko development protests were really minor, as far as irritations go."

"So there haven't been any suspects at all?" The Gray case was much more interesting than the tiny bit of information that Chris had given her had suggested.

"A few." Lou shot an amused glance at Rory. "Ian was arrested for a minute."

"It felt like much longer than a 'minute' at the time," Rory grumbled.

"Ian?" It shocked Daisy to think that her neighbor had been a suspect.

"His pendant," Lou said, "which is *not* to be called a necklace—at least not in front of Ian or he'll get pissy—was found in the reservoir, attached to the weight holding down the body. The cops theorized that he'd lost it while disposing of the evidence, but Rory managed to prove that he'd still had possession of his pendant long after the body was dumped."

Scowling, Rory added, "Someone stole the pendant while he was showering at the clubhouse, then planted the evidence."

"Whoa." This was better than any mystery novel.

Ellie gave her a wide-eyed look. "I know, right? Isn't this just crazy?" Daisy nodded before turning back to Lou, who'd flipped to the next sheet of paper on the oversized pad and seemed to be scribbling some sort of timeline.

As she wrote, she kept talking. "The main suspect right now is Anderson King, a local drug dealer."

Rory explained, "When the Liverton Riders—the local motorcycle club—started falling apart, Anderson was right there trying to fill the criminal void. He came to talk to me at my shop one day about buying—" She stopped abruptly, swallowing the rest of what she'd been about to say and looking so discomfited that Daisy's curiosity shot through the roof. "Uh, buying guns. He killed the guy who headed up search and rescue, and now Anderson is after Ellie and her dad."

"I was just getting to that part," Lou jumped in. "Willard's one friend, Baxter Price—"

"My dad," Ellie interrupted.

"The one who's missing?" Daisy instantly regretted asking when the woman's face dropped.

"Yes. He checked himself out of a mental-health facility north of Denver almost a month ago. I haven't heard from him since then, though we've been looking everywhere. He's schizophrenic."

It was Daisy's turn to reach for Ellie's hand. "I'm sorry."

Ellie gave her a watery smile before turning back to Lou.

"He's okay, El," Lou said firmly, as if she could will her words into being. "He's tough and wily."

"I know." Ellie gave a quick nod and then gestured for Lou to continue.

"When Baxter doesn't hear from his friend, Willard, for a while, he comes to Simpson to investigate." Lou frowned. "Ellie, this part gets a little confusing. Would you mind taking over?"

Ellie's laugh was a little shaky. "Sure, although I don't know if I can make it any less confusing. My dad called me out of the blue one night and told me that someone was after him, so he was headed to my grandpa's old cabin to hide. I didn't take him seriously about the someone's-after-him part, but I didn't want him wandering around the mountains alone, so I went searching. It ended up that two men *were* trying to kill him—Anderson King and his...uh, his brother." She ducked her head for a moment, her expression tight with what looked like sadness and guilt. Before Daisy could ask Ellie what was wrong, she continued. "They are—were—local meth dealers who were informed by someone else that Dad had witnessed a sale. I overheard Dad saying the informant had lied to the dealers, sending them after him because Dad knew this person had killed Willard."

"Chris really *has* been holding out on me," Daisy breathed, trying to take in the story. All this had been happening while she was shut up in the house, unaware of the drama. Frustration surged through her, surprising her with its strength. She wished so badly to be normal, to be able to grocery shop and visit someone else's house and follow the local gossip and date...

Shutting the mental door on the unexpected flood of self-pity, she refocused on Ellie. "What happened?"

"Anderson's brother was killed"—Ellie swallowed, her gaze dropping to her lap again—"and Anderson... got away. He tracked me down in the woods outside of George's cabin. That's how I got this." She tugged at the top of her thermal shirt, revealing a bruise in various shades of green, yellow, and purple. Daisy winced in sympathy. "They're still hunting for him, but the sheriff's pretty sure he headed to Mexico and won't be seen again."

Just that quick mention of the sheriff made Daisy shiver, and she quickly refocused her attention on Ellie.

"With my dad, it's hard to know what's real and what's not. Plus, I think he was trying to protect me by not telling me who Willard's murderer was. We thought Joseph—the search and rescue guy who was killed—might be involved." She shot Daisy an apologetic look. "Or maybe even Chris."

"What?!" Daisy straightened abruptly. "Chris? Why? He's the most ethical, kindhearted, nonmurderous—"

"I know! I know!" Ellie waved her hands as if trying to calm Daisy. "*Now*, at least. Once I spent time with Chris, I knew he couldn't have been involved. It was just, after he left me alone at the cabin right before Anderson arrived…"

The conversation with Chris replayed in her head. "Oh, when you were shot! Chris told me about it. He feels so awful that you were hurt on his watch."

"That's what he said," Ellie agreed. "He explained about the lack of radio and cell reception, and he apologized to me and George."

Although Daisy still felt prickly at any suggestion Chris could be a bad guy, she turned her attention to a different question niggling at her brain. "So did your dad say anything, or give any hints as to who it might be?"

Ellie bit the side of her thumbnail. "Not really. The last time I talked to him, before he left Armstrong, all he said was something about 'the fires.' We were interrupted before he could explain what he meant, and he checked himself out that afternoon."

"The fires?" Lou and Rory chorused.

"You didn't mention that before," Lou said, scribbling "Fires" on the paper and underlining it several times. "What'd he say about them?"

"Sorry," Ellie said, looking back and forth between Lou and Rory. "I figured it was just in his mind, especially after the explosion at the cabin. He didn't say much, just mentioned 'the fires.'"

"The cabin exploded?" Daisy repeated, her eyes widening, but the others weren't listening to her.

"Rory," Lou said, "could you ask Ian if there were any unusual fires last fall or winter, around the time that Willard was killed?"

"Sure. There've been some intentionally set fires since I started volunteering with the department," Rory said. "Just small structures, like tool sheds. Plus, there were those wildland fires last fall."

"Oh!" Ellie sat up straight. "I saw those burned areas when we were hiking to the cabin. George said those were probably arson, too."

"Derek told me that he and Artie found accelerants and other suspicious fire-starting stuff in a forest service cabin," Lou added as she wrote nearly illegible notes under the "Fires" heading. "Did Rob and the fire chief think they were used to start those wildland fires?"

"I don't know, but Ian will." She pulled out her cell phone. "As long as he's not on a call, he'll answer."

No one spoke as they waited, but Rory eventually shook her head as she ended the call. "Voice mail," she explained. "I'll try him a little later."

"Lou," Daisy said a little tentatively. As the new-comer to the group, she didn't want to bring up a suggestion that had already been discussed or, even worse, was so illogical that it didn't need to be discussed. "Wasn't your cabin intentionally set on fire?"

"Yes." Lou's jaw tightened at the memory. "But that was my nutso stalker. He was in Connecticut when Willard was killed."

"Oh." Something didn't seem right, though. "Isn't it strange that your stalker burned down your house at the same time there was an arsonist loose in Simpson?"

The other three women went quiet, staring at Daisy.

"I did wonder why Clay went from thinking he loved me to full-on homicidal," Lou said, finally breaking the silence. "He—or whoever it was—actually kicked me back into a burning building. That doesn't really say 'come back East with me and be my wife.'"

"But Rory said all the other fires have been small buildings," Ellie said.

Lou winced. "My cabin wasn't very big."

"'Shack-like' was the word someone used to describe it," Rory said.

"Hey! Watch the cabin smack-talk, bunker dweller." Despite her words, Lou was laughing. "Wait…did that 'someone' happen to be Callum?"

Rory's phone rang, saving her from having to answer Lou.

"Hi." Just in the short time Daisy had known her, she'd noticed how much Rory's voice softened when she was talking to Ian. "You're at Letty's? She okay? Well, as okay as she gets?" Daisy watched Rory's face with interest. Her expression was open and happy—very unlike the Rory Daisy was familiar with. "Good. Who took over my dog-tending duties?" She laughed. "Poor guy. Is my favorite paramedic there this time?"

Her laughter faded into a teasing smile. "Yeah, I know. That's why I said it. Listen, we have a question for you." She broke off as if Ian had interrupted her. "Yep, I'm still at Daisy's. No, no sausage biscuits this time. The meatballs and wontons were just as good, though." Her grin widened, and Daisy found herself smiling as well. Rory's happiness was contagious. "Can't. We ate them all. Can I ask my question now? Thanks. How long have the arsons been going on?" At Ian's response, her expression grew serious. "That often? And all small structures, right? Any chance Lou's cabin could've been considered a small structure?"

There was a long pause as Rory listened intently, her frown deepening. "Do you know anything about those accelerants Derek found in the forest service cabin? Okay. Let me know what the chief says. See you tomorrow morning." Rory tipped her head away from the others, as if trying to hide her returning smile. "No, I don't think I'll be hungry for breakfast after eating all of these delicious snacks of Daisy's." Her laugh was soft. "Fine. See you then. Be safe."

By the time she'd ended the call, her poker face was back in place. "Ian said these fires have been happening about every month or two for over a year. He'll look up when the first report was when he gets back to the station. Once Chief Early arrives tomorrow morning, Ian will talk to him about whether Lou's house could've been the work of the arsonist, rather than her stalker, and Ian will check on what they found out about the accelerants. In return for the information, Ian requested that I bring home a doggie bag of snacks for him."

Lou winced. "So good to know it could've been *two* homicidal crazy people gunning for me."

"At least one's dead now," Rory said, making Daisy cover her eyes and groan. "What?"

Luckily, Lou just laughed. "Thanks, Rory. That does help."

After another hour of brainstorming possible links between the arsons and Willard Gray's murder, they called it a night.

"Should we meet again in a couple of days?" Lou asked as the group headed for the front doors. "We made so much progress—*and* you three don't shut down my wild theories like Callum does."

As the others agreed enthusiastically to a second meeting and exchanged phone numbers, Daisy was positively giddy with excitement. Once everyone had exited and silence returned to her world, Daisy slid down to sit with her back against the door and pulled out her phone. Her thumb automatically found the tiny dent in the back where it had connected with the granite counter a few months back. Smiling, she scrolled through her contact list. So what if there might have been a dead-body removal across the street or that the sheriff had a strange obsession with making her think she was delusional? He was just one man, and her group of friends had expanded to the point that everyone couldn't fit on the screen anymore. The sight of the lengthened list of names made her...not content, but closer to it than she'd been since her mom's murder.

——∾——

The crawl space access panel was right where Gabe Little had said it would be. Finally, something was going right.

Rob silently belly-crawled farther under the porch, his penlight gripped between his teeth. With his right hand, he reached down and worked a Phillips-head screwdriver out of the side pocket of his BDUs. The screws holding the access panel in place were corroded and rusty, and Rob gave a soundless huff of aggravation as he worked the first one loose.

It had been a long time since he'd done an unauthorized entry. If Daisy Little had been compliant, he wouldn't have to be lying in who-knows-what under a porch at two in the morning, fighting with decades-old hardware. Instead, he could be home with his sleeping son. Rob couldn't have her making Chris suspicious, though. The department was already down a deputy. They couldn't afford to lose another.

By the time he'd worked out the final screw, Rob was sweating and more than a little annoyed. He held his temper and carefully lifted the access panel away from the foundation. His tiny flashlight wasn't much help in cutting the thick darkness of the crawl space, but now wasn't the time to get hesitant. Unpleasant as it was, this had to be done.

Rob slid headfirst through the opening.

———

Daisy woke with a start.

Her heart was pounding, but she hadn't had a nightmare—that she could remember, at least. Lying perfectly still, staring through the darkness, Daisy listened. It was quiet. So quiet, in fact, that it was almost eerie. Her heart rate took off at a gallop again, and she slid out of bed. Glancing at the glowing clock numbers, she sighed. She hadn't even been asleep for an hour. Tomorrow was going to be painful.

Her bare feet were silent as she padded toward the window, listening for a repeat of whatever sound had woken her. There was nothing, though. Even the wind had taken a short, rare hiatus. It was strange not hearing the howling gusts battering at the house. Daisy had become so accustomed to that sound that the absence of it made her feel like the world was holding its breath.

With one knee on the window seat, she leaned forward and looked outside. Fog spread over the neighborhood, hiding all but the most basic shapes of the houses across the street. With a shiver, she moved away from the window. Trying to guess what might be out there, hiding in the mist, would only make her nerves worse.

She stood in the middle of her bedroom. If she tried to go back to bed, she'd just lie awake and jump at every faint sound. There'd be no way she could concentrate on a book, either, so reading was out. A run it was, then.

After turning on her bedside lamp, she moved over to her dresser and picked out a sports bra and some shorts. As she started pulling the oversized sleep shirt over her head, a muffled thump from downstairs made her freeze.

The fabric was still bunched around her face, blinding her, and she yanked it back into place. If she was going to be investigating mysterious noises, she wasn't about to do it almost naked.

I imagined it, she tried to reassure her frantic brain. *No one is downstairs. The windows are sealed shut, and the door has a bazillion locks on it. There's no way someone could be downstairs. If someone's here, then that means this house isn't safe, and that means...* The floor tilted, and she swayed as her room began to gray around the edges.

"Stop!" she whispered fiercely. It wouldn't help anything if she talked herself into a panic attack. She started to move toward her bedside table, where her phone sat, but then she paused. Who would she call? Chris, to tell him she *might* have heard a noise? The sheriff? Daisy actually snorted out loud, imagining Rob Coughlin's reaction.

Before she called in reinforcements, she needed to make sure there really had been a noise, and that the noise had been caused by something dangerous. Tentatively, Daisy moved toward the hall, stopping in the doorway to try to peer through the darkness. All she saw were shadows.

Her heart tripped faster as she made her way to the stairs, carefully lowering her weight on each step so as not to make a noise. At the bottom, the doorway into the exercise room loomed. This was her sanctuary, her safe place. Tonight, though, it didn't feel safe.

Forcing herself to move, she pushed open the exercise room door and stopped abruptly. The windowless space wasn't shadowed and dim like the hall and the stairs—it was pure blackness.

Cursing herself for not grabbing the flashlight out of her nightstand, she reached along the wall and switched on the lights. The overheads blinded her for a few seconds, turning the exercise equipment into strange, overexposed shapes. Daisy blinked rapidly, twisting so she could see all corners, and the room came into focus. Her gaze darted around, searching for anything out of place—or anyone, full stop. Everything looked as it always did, but something made the room seem wrong. The equipment was too still, too quiet, and the light too bright, casting harsh shadows. She'd always loved this room, and its unexpected eeriness felt like the betrayal of a close friend.

Giving in to the growing urge to escape, she returned to the hall. As she checked each area, she continued turning on lights—the study, living room, dining room, and kitchen. With each flick of a switch, she held her breath until the new room came into focus and proved to be intruder-free. Every window was secured, and the front door locks were fully engaged. Despite all that, Daisy couldn't relax. The house, this home in which she'd spent so many years, was suddenly a hostile stranger.

Trying to rein in her runaway imagination, she returned to the kitchen. The house was an inanimate building, she reminded herself firmly. Any emotions she felt from it came from her own mind. She leaned against the counter, suddenly and completely exhausted as the adrenaline started to leave her system. The sound hadn't been an intruder. It could've come from outside or from her stressed, overtired brain. As soon as that thought occurred to her, she pushed it away, not willing to accept that she was hearing sounds that weren't there.

Despite the limp-noodle state of her limbs, she knew sleep would be elusive. Instead of doing her planned run, she headed for the bathroom and skipped straight to the post-workout shower. The water was almost painfully hot as it needled her scalp. Tilting her head back,

Daisy closed her eyes and tried to let all the residual fear
run down the drain.

After he heard the shower start, Rob slipped out of his
hiding spot in the pantry. He was completely silent as he
made his way up the stairs and into her bedroom.

Chapter 9

"So...?"

"So...?" Daisy echoed absently as she examined her phone. Something was bugging her about it, but she couldn't figure out what. It just seemed *off*. It was definitely her phone—all her new contacts were still in there, plus her apps and email—but it just didn't feel right.

"Hey." A single-serve packet of coffee grounds bounced harmlessly off her head, making her look up from her phone to see Chris watching her curiously. "Pay attention to me. It's too early to be texting."

Although she shot him a mock-scowl, she placed her not-right phone on the kitchen counter next to her. "I'm not texting. And most people would think six is too early for friendly visits, too."

Chris just waved that off. He'd come to her house right from work. Even if he hadn't mentioned it, she would've known from the bouncy energy he always radiated immediately after a shift. "How'd last night go?"

"Great." She smiled at the memory of the evening. "Fun."

He grinned broadly. "Good. Did you figure out anything about the case?"

"Nothing definite. We mostly talked about the fires."

"Fires?"

"The arsons—the ones around town as well as the

forest fires. Ellie's dad thinks they're related to Willard Gray's murder."

"Related how?" All teasing was gone from his expression as he shifted into professional mode.

"We're not sure. Ellie's dad only said, 'the fires,' and then he took off."

"Hmm."

Daisy felt a smile starting. That hum was so Chris. "You're going to look into that more, aren't you?"

"Probably."

"And you're going to tell me what you find out?" She wasn't honestly that hopeful, but she figured she'd give it a shot.

"No."

Accepting that with a shrug, she was surprised when Chris frowned deeply.

"What?"

"I talked to Rob about yesterday morning."

"Yeah?" Daisy gave him her full attention.

"Yeah." Now he wasn't just serious—he looked positively *grim*.

"What'd he say about the boot prints?"

Chris started to pace the width of the kitchen. "It was...weird. I figured he'd say he'd been hurrying through the investigation, since he didn't really believe anyone had been there, so he was trying to pacify you in the quickest way possible."

"But..." His upheld hand stopped her.

"He shut me down. Wouldn't discuss it. Point-blank refused to send the fingerprint to the BCA for analysis. He turned it around on me."

"On you? How?"

"Said I wasn't thinking clearly when it came to you. He implied that you were... I don't know, unbalanced or attention-seeking or something."

At Daisy's flinch, he took a step closer to her and then stopped, thrusting his hand through his hair and making it stick up even more wildly than normal.

"You know I don't think that. I *know* you, Dais. None of the things he was saying were even close to reality, which is what made it so..."

"Weird?" she said softly.

He looked tired. "Weird."

"So what's the next step?"

Chris resumed his pacing. "Rob pretty much banned me from having anything else to do with that empty house or any future calls from you."

Sucking in a harsh breath as the implication hit her, Daisy whispered, "So you can't visit anymore?"

"No!" He'd been pacing away from her, but he whirled around to face her. "Of course not! Even if he could control who I see in my personal life, I wouldn't listen to him."

Her shoulders sagged as the panic drained out of her. The thought of losing Chris had almost brought her to her knees.

Chris was still talking. "If you see that kid again, though, don't call Dispatch. Call me—I don't care what time it is—and I'll have one of the other deputies come out and do a thorough investigation."

"Why is the sheriff so anti-me? Did he say anything?"

"Not about that." His face was set in frustrated lines. "I talked to Libby last night, and Rob didn't mention to her why he wanted a heads-up if you called.

She said he's done that with a couple of other people, but only the real"—his gaze shifted off to the side for a moment, like he was searching for a word with a PG-rating—"dirtbags."

Squishing up her face, Daisy said, "Well, that makes me feel good."

"Sorry, Dais." He moved so he was standing in front of her. "I don't know why he's acting like this. It makes me wonder…"

"Wonder?" If he didn't finish his sentence, she'd die of curiosity.

To her relief, he continued, "If he thinks that Gray's murderer is with the department."

Her eyes widened. "The sheriff suspects the killer is a *deputy*?"

"Possibly. That would explain why Rob's being so secretive, withholding information from us, like about Baxter Price. After the whole thing with Macavoy's early morning 'junk pickup,' it made me start wondering."

The thought that she might have witnessed the murderer in action punched her in the stomach. "Do you think Macavoy…?"

"He couldn't have killed Willard Gray, because he hasn't been here long enough, but he's involved somehow. I can't even talk to him about it, though, since he quit."

"He quit?"

"Yeah." Chris looked frustrated. "Called Dispatch, said he was quitting, and then he just left. He won't even answer his phone—at least not when I'm calling him. I wanted to talk to him about this whole thing, plus now we're shorthanded. We're running from call to call like a bunch of headless chickens."

"But...he can't just leave!" Daisy sputtered. "He put a body—well, a possible body—in a squad car. Shouldn't the sheriff have told him not to leave town or something?"

Amusement lightened Chris's expression for a moment. "Cops don't actually say that in real life, you know. Besides, Rob is certain that it was junk, not a dead body, being put in the squad. If Rob suspects one of us, it isn't Macavoy."

Daisy hummed, not liking that Macavoy could skip town so easily. Rob might think his former deputy was just hauling junk, but the sheriff hadn't seen it like Daisy had, hadn't watched the weight and movement of the corpse-like bundle.

She was still trying to absorb the possibility that a *cop* might have killed Willard Gray. Whether it was Macavoy or some other deputy, the idea was just wrong. The good guys should be just that—good. Not decapitating, cold-blooded murderers. Some of the deputies sounded better than others, but it was terrifying to consider that the very guy they were hunting could be the one who was supposed to provide Chris with backup on a dangerous domestic call. "Maybe the sheriff doesn't think it's someone in the department. Could he be trying to keep the information from some of the looser-lipped deputies so that it doesn't leak?"

"Like Lawrence?" Chris said thoughtfully. "Could be, but we already only give him information on a need-to-know basis. After the last time his brain took a vacation and he spilled confidential info to Lou, Rob's had him on a tight leash."

"It could've made him paranoid about another leak—
the sheriff, I mean." As the theory took shape in her
mind, she let the words leave her mouth unfiltered. It
could be completely bogus, but Daisy realized she was
slightly desperate to move away from the idea that a
deputy was responsible for Gray's death. "Or he suspects someone in the outer circle."

"Outer circle?"

"Medical, Fire, Search and Rescue," she clarified.
"From what the training group said, it's a complete
gossip-fest. Is that true with the sheriff's department,
too? I mean, would deputies talk to the EMTs or firefighters about details on the case and not think they were
doing something wrong?"

"Could be." His eyebrows pulled together as he
thought. "I try to keep my mouth shut around anyone
who isn't a cop—and not assigned to the case I'm talking about—but I know that some of the guys are a little
more casual about it."

"That's so spooky." She shivered, wrapping her
arms around her middle. "One of the good guys might
be a killer."

Chris didn't respond beyond a slight tip of his head,
but his mouth turned down at the corners.

As she studied him—her handsome, wonderful,
loveable Chris—she mirrored his frown. She hated this
uncertainty, not knowing whom they could trust. "Be
careful out there."

Meeting her gaze, he held it for several beats.
"Always."

—⁓—

Only an hour had passed after Chris left when there was a knock on the door. It was actually more of a series of heavy thuds, rather than an actual knocking sound, and she pressed the intercom button tentatively.

"Hello?"

"Daisy, let me in."

Her eyes widening with surprise, she pushed the unlock button. When she opened the inner door, her dad came inside, his forearms and wrists strapped with grocery bag handles. He was juggling a couple of cardboard boxes, as well, and she hurried to grab one from him. Daisy grunted at the unexpected weight.

Setting it on the floor by her feet so she could secure the interior door locks, she eyed the box, but the flaps had been folded over so it was impossible to see what was inside. As soon as the last chain was in place, she scooped up the mystery package and followed her dad into the kitchen.

"Hi, Dad," she said, putting the box on the counter so she could help put away the groceries. "You got eggs! Thank you. I've been wanting to make some brownies."

Bent over as he placed something in the vegetable-crisper drawer, he responded, "Figured you'd gotten low, so I stopped by the Connor Springs grocery store before heading home."

"Oh, good." As she reached over him to put away the milk, she craned her neck to see what vegetables he'd gotten. "Their produce is always so much better than the stuff from Melcher's."

He made a sound of agreement.

"Watch your head when you stand," she warned as she opened the freezer door. "Was chicken on sale? I think you bought out the store."

"No." He carefully retreated, ducking his head until he could straighten without braining himself. "I just know you like it, so…" He shrugged, not meeting her eyes.

"I do. Thank you." She finished stacking the packages in the freezer. Picking up a pound of ground beef, she hesitated and then put it in the fridge, instead. "I'll use that to make your favorite meatloaf, as long as you picked up some jalapeños?" She glanced down, loving how the fruit and veggie drawers were full of colorful things. Frozen vegetables and canned fruit were fine, but nothing like fresh ones.

"No." Her dad gathered the empty bags, still avoiding eye contact. "I mean, I did get jalapeños, but I won't be here for dinner tonight."

"Hot date?" Although she felt mild disappointment, it was nothing like she would've felt even a week ago. She still missed her dad, but she'd been having plenty of company, and that seemed to have filled the usual void of loneliness.

He shook his head. "New job."

"Oh." That was quick. Typically, he stayed several days or even a week before heading off to the site of a new project. "Another one in Connor Springs?"

"This one is south of Parker. Huge new house with ground-source heating and cooling, PV and passive solar, wind—pretty much every alternative-energy system they could think of, except for conservation. Ten thousand square feet, including a turret. Rich people are nuts."

Her smile was slightly forced. "It's going to be a long one, then, huh?"

He shot her a sharp look. "Don't be laying a guilt trip on me for working."

"I'm not." She focused on smoothing a bag of Tropical Skittles. He'd gotten all her favorites. "I'm not. I'll miss you, but I made some new friends."

"Yeah? That's good." His expression softened slightly, although it remained wary. He nodded toward the box she'd carried inside and its slightly bigger mate. "Come see what else I found for you."

She'd forgotten about the mystery boxes, and she made an excited sound that was embarrassingly close to a squeal. She loved presents. Unfolding the flaps on the box she'd left on the counter, she sucked in a breath.

"Oh, Dad! These are awesome!" Daisy carefully pulled out one of the vintage children's books that filled the box. "Where'd you find these?"

"The Connor Springs library had one of those fund-raising sales, where people can donate books." She nodded, still focused on the box's contents. From her first quick peek, the books looked to be in great condition. Daisy couldn't wait to list them online. "That box was five bucks. I was going to text you a picture to see if you'd be interested, but I wanted to surprise you."

"These are perfect—thank you!"

"There's another box, too."

"Oh!" Daisy quickly returned the books she'd pulled out of the box and headed for the second one. "I totally forgot about Box Number Two." She used her game-show announcer voice, but her dad just looked confused.

Shrugging off her failed joke, she opened the flaps on the second box. Peering inside, she had to fight the urge to jump back in horror. "Oh...wow." Inside was the creepiest pair of dolls she'd ever seen.

"Those were at the junk store on Evergreen Street.

They looked really old, so I figured you might be able to get lots of money for them." He sounded so proud that Daisy stifled the need to reclose the flaps and send the box with Gabe to Parker. If they were in another town, they couldn't kill her in her sleep.

The one with the wonky eye was staring at her as if it were plotting her murder. Daisy already had possible dead-body shuffling going on outside her bedroom window. She didn't need a pair of hell dolls adding to her nightmares. Her dad looked so pleased with himself, though, that she couldn't crush him.

"These are…great, Dad. I'll have to do some research so I know what I'm selling. Dolls are new to me."

"Yeah." He laughed. "Even as a little girl, you'd pick a stuffed animal over a doll every time."

She smiled back, quickly folding the flaps closed to break the dolls' unwavering stares. "Thank you again, Dad. That was really thoughtful of you."

Brushing off her thanks uncomfortably, he turned toward the garbage can. "I'd better head out. I'll take out the trash on my way." Pulling a handful of mail from his coat pocket, he laid it on the counter. "I stopped by the post office, too."

"Thanks." Her stomach twisted a little. "Want me to make you a sandwich for the road?"

"No, I'll just stop somewhere. Coffee'd be good, though."

Daisy didn't hesitate to move toward the brewer. It was a relief to have something to do so she didn't have to stand there and watch him scramble to leave as fast as possible. She focused on the *drip, drip* of the brewing coffee until it gurgled to a stop. After she transferred it to a travel mug, she saw he was by the door, ready to go.

Her smile was forced, but it didn't matter, since he was careful not to make eye contact with her.

"Travel safe," she said, trying to keep her voice light. "Thanks again for the books and the dolls." Daisy was proud at how the word "dolls" came out with barely a pause. Maybe Chris would take them with him next time he stopped by to visit. They could ride shotgun in the squad and terrify criminals into surrendering.

"Bye, Daisy."

She carefully fastened the locks, one by one, until she was secure again. Alone, but secure.

She could hear her mom sobbing, pleading, but Daisy couldn't see her face. Everything was blurry except for the gun in his black-gloved hand. Daisy shook so hard that her tremors rattled the snack-cake display she was hiding behind. Although she desperately tried to be quiet, the scream built up inside of her, pressing against her lungs until she had to let it out or she would suffocate. The shrill sound escaped, filling her ears and drowning out everything—her mother's cries, the stranger's threats, the sirens outside. Where was Chris? Chris always came at this point. He wasn't there, though. No one was there. The gun flashed, and Daisy knew her mom was gone. Grief blended with fear, and her scream grew louder and louder until the gun pointed straight at Daisy's face.

She jerked awake with a gasp. As soon as she realized it had been a dream, she scooted to the edge of the bed. The sheets were damp from sweat, and they clung to her skin, slowing her progress.

With a small noise of disgust, Daisy yanked at the material. In her half-awake panic, she just managed to tangle herself further. Her feet caught the edge of her blankets, tripping her as she lurched out of bed. She landed on her hands and knees, the hardwood floor connecting painfully, the throb telling her she'd have bruises later. Twisting so she was sitting on the floor, she kicked her way free of the covers that still managed to cling to her feet.

Finally free, she scrambled to her feet and hurried toward the stairs, whacking her shoulder on her bedroom doorframe as she passed through it. She grimaced, rubbing the spot where yet another bruise would appear. It was like the house itself was punishing her for what she'd done that day eight years ago.

Although she hadn't had a destination in mind when she'd fled her bedroom, her legs carried her automatically to the training room. Ignoring the creeping feeling of menace emanating from the immobile equipment, she jumped onto the treadmill. Daisy arrowed up the speed past her usual warm-up, needing to run fast enough to get away from the nightmares and the memories and her stupid, panicky, shut-away life.

Running was too monotonous, though, giving her too much time to think. She kept thinking she heard things over the steady *burr* of the treadmill—a creak of a floorboard or the click of a latch. Every imaginary sound made her jump and flinch so strongly that, several times, she stepped on the edge of the belt and almost fell. Running wasn't enough to kill her past and present ghosts, so she started a circuit, moving from pull-ups to leg-lifts to jump-ups to burpees to sit-ups to punching the heavy bag to push-ups and back to the treadmill for more sprints. She lost track of how many rotations she'd done, her muscles burning until they finally just went numb.

Numb was good, she decided, as the feeling disappeared from her body and then her brain. She stopped hearing the phantom intruder, her mother's sobs, a gun firing. All she knew was her feet pounding on the treadmill or her fists smacking against the bag, until either she tripped or her legs decided they were done, and she sprawled on the floor.

That didn't hurt as much as it should have, either, so there was another benefit to the numbness. With the current noodle-like state of her muscles, she barely managed to roll over onto her back. The high ceiling was white and bumpy, and Daisy stared at it until her eyes grew fuzzy and she had to close them.

She wondered if she'd really damaged her body, if the lack of feeling was disguising a serious injury. With her phone upstairs, Daisy would have no way to call for help. She'd be trapped in the exercise room, possibly for days, until Chris decided to visit. Or maybe he'd never come. He'd decide she was too much trouble, or the sheriff would order him to stay away, or Chris would find a girlfriend who could actually leave the house and go on a date, and he'd marry this non-messed-up woman, and they'd have adorable blond babies who'd wear Chris's charming grin.

Daisy knew she was wallowing in self-pity, but she couldn't stop. Her muscles and her mind had nothing left to give, no reserves of emotion or energy to help her bounce out of her funk. She could only lie there, tears seeping from under her eyelids and tracking over her temples. Finally, she took the only escape she had open to her—unconsciousness.

The pounding woke her. It was faint, but persistent, and it seemed to be growing louder. She rolled onto her side and groaned when every piece of her shrieked in agony. The floor was hard underneath her, and she reluctantly opened her eyes to see the legs of a weight bench in front of her face.

Painfully, she hauled herself to a sitting position, blinking a few times to orientate herself.

"You couldn't have made it to the mats before you passed out?" Daisy muttered. She'd never been drunk, so she'd never been hungover, but she wondered if it felt anything like her current state. If so, she'd continue abstaining for reasons other than just because her dad refused to buy her alcohol.

The pounding was getting ferocious, so Daisy stumbled to her feet, straightening her body with a whimper. Her first steps were stilted and uneven, although moving helped the stiffness in her muscles. By the time she reached the front door, she was walking almost normally—normally, at least, for a ninety-year-old woman.

She jabbed at the intercom button. "What?"

There was a pause before Chris's voice came through the speaker. "What do you mean 'what'? Why didn't you answer?" He sounded pissed.

"I was sleeping," she snapped, feeling a little cranky herself. "Why didn't—this is dumb." Releasing the intercom button, she buzzed Chris in and then leaned against the door, taking some of her weight off her complaining legs.

The exterior door closed with a harder thud than usual, meaning Chris had helped it along. For some reason, the idea of him slamming doors like a hormonal thirteen-year-old girl made her snicker as she unfastened the interior door locks.

When she saw his face, her initial theory was confirmed. He was indeed pissed.

Although she expected him to tear into her as soon as he was inside, Chris remained silent until she'd locked the door and made her stumbling way into the kitchen.

"What's wrong with you?" he finally demanded, following her. Instead of heading to the coffeemaker, he stood stiffly by the far counter, his arms crossed over his chest. As always, it really did nice things to his muscles when he stood that way.

Daisy shook off the lecherous thoughts, trying to focus. "What's wrong with me?" she repeated. "You're going to have to be more specific."

His scowl deepened, and Daisy didn't have the heart to tell him it made him more attractive rather than intimidating. "You're limping. Are you hurt?"

"Just sore." With a yawn, she figured she might as well take advantage of the brewer if Chris wasn't interested. "I worked out pretty hard last night." She started a cup of coffee and grabbed a glass for water. From the way her head was pounding, she knew she had to be dehydrated. She downed two glassfuls while Chris glared at her.

"Why didn't you answer your phone?"

Apparently, it was going to take a few more minutes for Chris to get over his snit. "My phone's in my bedroom."

For a moment, he looked more confused than angry. "You just said you couldn't hear me knock because you were sleeping."

"I *was* sleeping." She traded her water glass for the coffee mug. Between the water and the caffeine, one or both should help with her headache. "Just not in bed." A yawn interrupted her explanation. "I fell asleep in the training room."

"Why were you sleeping in the training room?"

Sometimes it was a pain to be friends with a cop. "It wasn't really a planned decision. I was tired after working out, so I lay down and dozed off."

"On the floor of the training room."

Since her mouth was full of coffee, she just gave an affirmative shrug.

"How long did you work out?"

Seriously, he was a bulldog. "I don't know. A while."

"A while." He'd talked about the sheriff's confession-winning stare, but his wasn't too shabby. "Did you fall asleep or did you pass out?"

"Does it matter?" She couldn't hold his gaze. Instead, she focused on tracing the rim of her mug. "Did you want some coffee?"

"Yes, it matters." He ignored her other question. "What happened? Was it hearing about the Gray case?" His arms uncrossed so he could scrub his hands over his face. "I knew I shouldn't have gotten you involved."

"No!" she yelped, panicked at the thought of her new friends disappearing as quickly as they'd entered her life. "It's not that. I like hearing about the case. I just had a nightmare. It was probably from eating too many brownies."

"Brownies." His tone was skeptical, but he let it go as he connected the brownies-to-eggs-to-father dots. "Your dad's here?"

She shook her head, glad to be focusing on something other than the possibility of getting kicked out of the Nancy Drew club. It wasn't Chris's decision, but she didn't know the women well enough to determine if they'd stay away if he asked. "He stopped by with groceries and demon dolls, but he left right away for a new job."

"A new job? He didn't even stay one night?" The muscle on the side of his jaw was doing a weird twitchy thing. "Wait. Demon dolls?"

"Yes. I guess it's a huge new house going up outside of Parker. And wait until you see these creepy things." She hurried over to where the box was still sitting on the counter. She'd brought the kids' books into the study but left the dolls, since the kitchen was the room farthest from her bedroom.

"Daisy. We're not done talking about... What the hell?"

"Hell." Daisy moved the box closer to Chris so he could get the full creepy impact. "Exactly. Because that is where they are from and where they want to drag us all."

"Your dad brought those?" He glanced at her in disbelief and then returned his focus to the dolls, as if he couldn't stop himself. "Why?"

"He found them at the junk store in Connor Springs."

Feeling she'd tortured Chris enough—even as high-handed and bossy as he was currently being—she returned the box to its place on the counter and closed the flaps before reaching for her coffee again. "He said they looked old, so he thought I could sell them online."

"Someone would buy those?"

She shrugged and gave him a small grin. "My dad did."

His snort was more than half a laugh, and he moved to the coffeemaker, so Daisy assumed lecture time was over. "They look like something we'd find in a serial killer's house."

"Exactly." She eyed him over the top of her mug. "And it was the dolls that made him do it."

That time, Chris really did laugh. "No wonder you had nightmares last night." The reminder sobered him. "Was it the usual?"

"Yeah." Her hands were suddenly shaky, and she put her mug on the counter so the hot coffee didn't slosh over the sides onto her fingers. "Mom. You weren't there, though."

His head whipped around so he could stare at her, his expression stricken. "I'm usually in your nightmares?"

He looked so upset at the thought that she hurried to reassure him. "No. It just normally follows what really happened." Her hands were sweating now, as well as trembling, so she rubbed them on her pajama-slash-workout pants. "Last night, after Mom…fell, he looked at me. The gun…the gun was…" Her throat closed, not permitting her to speak, barely allowing her to breathe. Even though her palms were dry, she kept rubbing them up and down her thighs.

"Hey." Chris was suddenly right in front of her, holding her wrists and keeping her hands still. "I *was* there. I shot him before he could even *think* about doing anything to you, okay? I just wish…"

"I know." Leaning forward, she let her forehead rest against his chest. "I wish that, too."

His thumbs stroked the inside of her wrists as they just stood silently for a while. Daisy basked in the rare contact of his skin against hers. She was tempted—so tempted—to raise her head, to bring her lips to his. The only thing that allowed her to resist was the memory of his appalled reaction the last time she'd attempted to kiss him. If she tried again, would he stop visiting her altogether? The thought was so terrifying, she felt the prickle of anxious sweat.

"Next time you have that nightmare—any nightmare," he said quietly, "don't work out until you're unconscious. Just call me, okay?"

With her forehead still pressed to the front of his shirt, not wanting to give up the contact, as little as it was, she said, "You do enough for me, Chris. I'm not waking you up at two in the morning because I'm scared of a bad dream."

"Yes, you are. And half the time, I'm awake at two a.m."

"Because you're working." She lifted her head so she could give him a stern look. "I'd probably call you in the middle of some sort of sting operation, and the ring of your phone would give you away, so the bad guys would scatter before you could bust them."

He stared at her and then started laughing. His hands slipped away from her wrists as he retreated to the coffeemaker, and Daisy swallowed hard with disappointment.

"You do realize I work for the Field County Sheriff's Department, right? At two this morning, I was helping Ian Walsh and some other guys from Fire drag a bull elk off the road after a semi hit it. After that, I directed traffic for a while so some dumbass who was moving and didn't secure his things in the back of his truck could pick up the remains of his possessions. He'd been losing chairs and boxes and even a mattress for several miles before he realized he was leaving a trail. Let's see...then I had a quiet half hour to write reports, which ended when I was sent on a domestic call."

His monolog had allowed her to push the memories of her nightmare and the triggering event to the back of her mind where it belonged. Since her hands were steady again, she retrieved her coffee and leaned against the counter to enjoy Chris's story.

"Everyone okay on the domestic?"

He snorted. "They were uninjured, but I don't know if you could call them 'okay.' For some reason, whenever those two start fighting, they take it to their front yard. The neighbors don't appreciate the screaming, so they call us. The only actual violence was when the woman threw their daughter's doll against the garage door. It knocked off the head completely."

"Poor kid. Do you think she'd like a replacement...or two?" Her gaze flicked over to the box.

Chris gave her a chastising frown. "Why would you want to traumatize an innocent child like that? Besides, I managed a pretty good repair job after we got the parents to stop yelling at each other."

"That was nice of you." The mental image of Chris, the doll doctor, made her smile. She hid it behind her mug.

He shrugged, focusing on his coffee. "Didn't want the kid to find her doll decapitated. That'd require a lot of future therapy."

"True. Busy night."

"I'd rather have that than a slow shift. Lots of action makes the time go by faster, and it keeps me awake. I did have a minute to read the transcripts of the interviews with Ellie's dad. Looks like he wouldn't say a word, either time. If he knows who Gray's murderer is, he's not telling."

Her legs were still tired from her workout, so she placed her coffee mug down and attempted to boost herself up to sit on the counter. Unfortunately, her arms had suffered as much as her lower half, so they refused to support her weight. Daisy's feet returned to the floor with an ungraceful thump.

Without even trying to hide his amusement, Chris put his coffee aside and moved toward her. Not sure what he was planning, Daisy eyed his approach warily. He grabbed either side of her waist and lifted her, making her squawk in surprise, and then deposited her onto the counter. The unexpected assistance made her wobble, and he waited in front of her, his hands still at her waist, until she steadied.

"Good?" he asked, retreating a step, although he kept his arms extended as if to catch her if she fell.

"Uh…yes?"

Chris returned to his corner and his coffee, leaving her feeling off balance in a couple of ways. That was twice in five minutes that he'd voluntarily touched her, and any Chris contact, no matter how fleeting, had the power to destroy her equilibrium.

"So..." It took her a second to pick up the conversation where they'd left off. "Did you get a chance to look into the arsons?"

That made him scowl at his mug. "No. For some reason, the arson reports aren't filed with the rest. I couldn't find the call notes in the computer system, either. I'm going to have to stop by during nonvampire hours and talk to Stacy in Records to see if she knows where they're stored."

"Why would the reports on those calls be treated differently?" Daisy wasn't familiar with the department's record-keeping system, but it seemed strange to her that one type of report would be kept elsewhere.

"Could be because Fire's involved," Chris offered. "Rob and Chief Early are both responsible for the suspected arson investigations. With interagency cases, the paperwork's gotta be a beast."

She nodded, took a sip of her coffee, and then asked, "Not that I'm complaining, since I'm always happy to see you, even in the predawn darkness—"

"The sun's been up for hours." When she looked skeptical, he amended his statement. "Well, maybe not *hours*, but it's definitely not predawn."

"Anyway..." She stretched out the word. Although Chris rolled his eyes, he stayed quiet. "Is there any reason for your daily visits to Daisyville?"

He choked a little on his coffee. When she looked at him questioningly, he just shook his head, declining to explain his reaction. Instead, he coughed and said in a slightly strangled voice, "A lot's been happening lately. I get worried."

That wasn't a very satisfying answer. "You can't just text? If you abbreviate obnoxiously, it's only four letters—*R*, *U*, *O*, and *K*."

"Doesn't work when you don't answer your phone."

"Hey, I take sleep where I can get it, even if it's the hard floor of the training room." Swinging a leg, she tried to kick him, but the kitchen was too wide. "And quit dodging the question."

"Why didn't you...never mind." He shook his head. "I'm not dodging the question. I already answered it. Stuff's been going on around here, and there's been a lot to discuss." Glaring at his coffee a lot harder than it probably deserved, he was quiet for a few moments. "I like talking things out with you. I'll be in the middle of a call where something crazy is happening, and I'll think, 'I can't wait to tell Dais about this.'"

His admission made her stomach warmer than the coffee had. "I like talking to you, too. It wasn't a complaint. I was just curious."

"And I promised I'd look at your stove."

They were both quiet for several sips until Chris spoke again.

"So...you made brownies?"

After she and Chris ate two-thirds of the pan of brownies for breakfast, she grabbed her laptop and settled on the kitchen floor to keep him company while he checked out the recalcitrant burner.

"Looking at porn?" he asked, lifting the grates off the top of the stove.

"Not unless there's such a thing as antique doll porn."

Before he could respond, she hurried to add, "And if there is, I don't want to know. There are some things you can't unlearn."

He raised the top of the stove and propped it on the bracing rod. "If you can think of it, there's porn related to it. People have dirty, dirty minds."

"Chris. What did I just say about wanting to remain blissfully ignorant?"

With a snort, he asked, "So you're actually going to try to sell those things?"

"Figured it was the quickest way to get them out of the house, unless I can convince you to take them to give away to kids."

"Absolutely not."

"Firefighters do it."

Turning away from whatever he was messing with, he gave her a look. "Fire gives kids cute little stuffed animals, not one of those…things." He gestured toward the box. "People already love firefighters more than cops. I don't need to make it worse."

"*Some* people," Daisy corrected, and he gave her a grin before turning back to the stove. Even using a lighter, he didn't seem to be having any luck getting the burner to work. Since watching him wave an open flame around a gas appliance—even if that appliance involved fire on a regular basis—made her nerves twitch, Daisy turned her attention back to her laptop.

She frowned at a photo, trying to recall if the doll in the picture matched either of the ones her dad had given her. The few times she'd opened the box, she hadn't wanted to look too closely, so she couldn't recall any distinguishing features. With a groan, she put her laptop aside and climbed to her feet. Her sound of dread shifted to a grunt of effort as her muscles protested.

"What's wrong?"

She grabbed the box and returned to her spot on the floor. "I have to actually *look* at the freaky things."

He laughed and lowered the top of the stove. "I have more bad news, too."

She made a face. "Hit me."

"The problem doesn't seem to be the igniter, so it's most likely the gas line. Since that's beyond my handyman skills, we'll need to call in a professional."

While she was still processing that information, Chris's cell phone rang. After glancing at the screen, he answered. "Hey, Rob. What's up?"

Whatever the sheriff's answer was, it made Chris glance at his watch, flinch, and then hurry to replace the grills on top of the stove. "Sorry about that, sir. I didn't realize it was so late."

"Leave those," Daisy whispered. "I'll get them if you need to go."

With a shake of his head, he replaced the rest of the grills before moving to the door. "I'll be home in four minutes. I'm leaving Daisy's now."

Climbing to her feet again with more determination than grace, she followed him to the entrance so she could secure the door after he left.

"No new trouble," Chris said. "Well, except with her stove."

From the half of the conversation Daisy could hear, it sounded as if Chris was late meeting the sheriff, so she was surprised that he didn't leave, but stood by the door instead.

"Don't worry about that," he told the sheriff with a laugh. "I know my limitations, especially when it comes to things that could explode. I'll give the repair guy from Connor Springs a call and have him come out and take a look."

After another short pause, Chris started opening the interior door locks. "See you in a few. Sorry again." He ended the call. "I forgot to bring in my old portable radio—the one that doesn't hold a charge—last night. Rob said he'd swing by my house on his way in to work this morning to grab it. I lost track of time, so he's standing on my porch, wondering where I am."

"Sorry for delaying you," Daisy said. "And thanks for looking at the stove."

"Not your fault I blew off my boss." With a grin, he ducked through the interior door and then looked at her over his shoulder. "And I didn't do much. Don't use it until we get someone out to fix it."

"I won't. Go on—you told the sheriff four minutes. You know he has the stopwatch running."

"Bye, Dais." Her name was muffled as the door swung shut behind him.

After refastening the locks, she returned to the kitchen. Gathering her laptop and the dolls' box, she headed for the study. The house seemed too quiet in Chris's absence. Strangely, the increased frequency of his visits was making it harder when he wasn't there, instead of easier.

Although she tried to return to her research, she found herself staring blankly at the computer screen. Without Chris there to joke with about the dolls, she couldn't work up any enthusiasm for the project. Normally, she liked learning new things, but too many thoughts were currently taking up space in her brain. The differences between composition and leather doll bodies just wasn't holding her attention.

Leaning back in her desk chair, she spun in a circle. Daisy stared at the ceiling, trying to figure out what the deal was with her growing dissatisfaction. Before, she'd had moments of melancholy or loneliness, especially during sleepless nights, but she'd bounced out of it quickly. Her life wasn't exciting—well, it *hadn't* been until recently—but she'd been content...sort of.

It wasn't just Chris's weirdness, his switching back and forth between pushing her away and being Mr. I-Was-Worried-About-You. The walls of the house, which had always felt safe and protective, were beginning to chafe. More and more, her sanctuary felt like a trap.

After spending time with Lou, Rory, Ellie, and their respective men, Daisy wanted more. She was starting to feel like she could *have* more, too. They'd argued over if she was going to volunteer for the fire department or the dive team, as if it wasn't an impossibility.

Hearing that had woken a tiny voice in the back of her mind, one that whispered how it *might* be conceivable, that she might not have to be trapped in her house for the rest of her life. It was a seductive glut of possibilities—getting a real job and learning how to drive and being able to make brownies whenever she got a craving, because she could pick up the eggs herself, instead of waiting until guilt drove her dad to stop by with groceries. Maybe, if she really wanted to put the cherry on the top of her fantasy, she could even go on an out-of-the-house date with Chris.

It was a wonderful dream, but it would never become reality if she fainted every time she saw an open door.

"Okay," she said, the loudness of her voice startling her a little. She sounded almost fierce. "That's what I want. Now how do I get that?"

Adjusting her computer so the screen faced her, Daisy opened a new browser window. After taking a deep breath and letting it out again, she began to search.

Chapter 10

LETTING OUT A GRUNT, RORY STUMBLED BACK A FEW STEPS.

Daisy cringed. At least the other woman hadn't landed on her butt like the last two times Daisy's kicks had knocked Rory over. "Sorry! I keep forgetting you're not Chris."

"Dais!" Chris snapped. "Hands up. Don't drop your guard."

Her fists lifted in front of her face. "I just feel bad for assaulting Rory."

"Don't." Rory returned to her original position and adjusted the kick shield. "I need to learn this, just in case I don't have a gun at exactly the wrong moment. Besides"—her teeth bared in more of a snarl than a smile—"I want to be able to take Ian down eventually. It'll be useful for keeping him in line."

"Heard that," Ian called from his spot by the heavy bag.

Daisy's laugh took the power out of her next side kick, and she had to hop on her standing left leg to keep her balance as her right barely brushed Rory's shield.

"Daisy. Focus." Chris was crabbier than usual. She wondered if it was just the night shift taking its toll, or if he'd had a bad call. The thought kept her from making a smart-ass response. Instead, she concentrated on the target, and her foot connected solidly with the shield. Although Rory's breath left her in an audible huff, she kept her position.

"Nice, Ror!" Daisy grinned at her and was rewarded by one of Rory's brief smiles.

Quickly regaining her serious mien, Rory ordered, "Again."

"Great," Daisy muttered, although she obediently sent her foot toward the shield again. "She's turning into Chris the Dictator's mini-me."

Rory gave her another one of her pseudo grins that Daisy thought were just an excuse to bare her teeth. "Just wait until I teach you to shoot."

"How can you do that?" The next kick connected solidly. Daisy loved that feeling. "It's not like I can shoot up the living room. Well"—her foot hit the shield again—"I *could*, but my dad would probably be annoyed when he saw the damage."

Rory tilted her head in thought, not looking discouraged. "We could shoot through a window."

"No," Chris said flatly, without looking away from his attempt to correct Lou's form.

"It'd need to be an upstairs window." As always, George's deep voice came as a surprise. Pausing in the middle of a push-up, he braced his arms and held his body weight off the floor with an effortlessness that Daisy envied. "Metal grates on the ones down here. You'd have to angle the target to adjust for the shooter's height if she was on the second story." Shifting to one arm, he illustrated his words by lifting his hand and holding it at a diagonal. The ease with which he supported his body with one arm and his toes made Daisy stare.

"No shooting out the windows." Ian put a hand on the heavy bag to steady it while he sent a warning glare over his shoulder at Rory. "This is not the Old West, and our homestead is not under attack."

"It'd be good practice for defending the house from zombies." Since Rory was the queen of deadpan humor, Daisy wasn't sure if she was serious or not.

"Can I practice shooting from the window, too?" Lou asked, exertion making her breathless. "I'll bring my new gun. This'll be so much fun."

"We'll only aim at the annoying neighbors," Rory promised. That time, Daisy was sure she was kidding. Fairly sure.

"No." Callum added his voice to the chorus that time.

Rory rolled her eyes, as if the guys' protests were ridiculous. "Fine. No shooting the obnoxious neighbors. I'm sure there's at least one window in this place that faces an unpopulated area. Daisy, again."

As Daisy obeyed, she tried to decide if training-tyrant Rory or gun-toting Rory was scarier.

"Have her dry fire at a target," Ellie suggested from her spot on the elliptical machine. "When do I get to kick people?"

Looking at Ellie with surprise and, Daisy was pretty sure, dawning respect, Rory nodded. "Good idea. Get her comfortable with it until we figure out how to work around the not-leaving-the-house thing. I'll bring a couple of handguns for you on Saturday."

"And you get to kick people when the doctor clears you to kick people," Chris answered Ellie. George, apparently done talking for the day, grunted. Although Daisy was still learning to interpret George-speak, she was pretty sure it translated as something like, "What he said."

Ellie grinned. "Should I ask the doctor to write me a note specifically stating that I am healed enough to kick, knee, elbow, and punch others?"

"I have to get to work." Callum extended the kick shield toward George. "Mind taking my spot?"

With a nod, George rolled to his feet and moved to stand opposite Lou, who appeared to be taking full advantage of her break. Her hands were braced above her knees as she panted for breath.

Dropping a kiss on Lou's cheek, Callum asked, "Sure you don't need the truck today? You could drop me off at the station."

"Nope, I'll be fine. We're going to have some breakfast here while we talk about death."

"Okay. Call me if you need anything." Callum headed for the door.

"Don't I always?" Lou called after him. "Have a nice day at work, honey!"

Turning away from her departing boyfriend, Lou eyed George's massive form. "I'm glad I'm the one doing the kicking."

"Be right back," Daisy told Rory, who looked a little relieved to drop the shield and shake out her arms.

"Callum." Daisy hurried after him. "I'll let you out."

Pausing just outside of the training room, he nodded and stepped back so she could lead the way. When they reached the entry, she unfastened the locks and opened the inner door for him. With a nod of thanks, he started to pass through the doorway, but then he paused.

"Don't let them start shooting," he said quietly, "from *anywhere* in your house."

Daisy laughed. "I'm pretty sure Rory and Lou were kidding about that."

"Probably." Despite his words, his frown said clearly that he doubted it. "Thank you for letting us use your gym."

"Anytime. It's fun. I like having people to train with—besides Chris, I mean." She kept her focus on Callum and off the exterior door. Her hands were sweating, and she wanted to dry them on her pants, but she didn't want to give away her nervousness.

"We appreciate it." His expression was analytical, and she knew he noticed the signs of her anxiety, even though she tried to hide them. "Take care, Daisy."

"Bye." She forced herself to count to five in her head before she allowed herself to close the inner door behind him and start locking the dead bolts. Her impulse had been to slam the door as soon as he was through, but she managed to quietly shut it and not embarrass herself by smacking him in the backside with the door. Even the thought of the potential humiliation that could have occurred made her squeeze her eyes closed.

Resting her forehead against the door, she took a minute to compose herself before heading back to the training room.

—~~~—

Since Ian had grabbed five doughnuts and headed home to sleep, only the four women, George, and Chris gathered around the dining room table for coffee, water, and breakfast pastries. Chris pulled out a chair, preparing to sit, but Daisy shook her head at him.

"I'm staying." The stubborn set of his jaw made Daisy roll her eyes.

"You can if you want to," she said, "but you look ready to fall asleep standing up. Why don't you go home and rest? I promise to take really good notes."

"My time off starts tonight. It's better if I stay up as long as possible to transition over to days." Despite his words, he remained standing, showing that he was at least thinking about his bed.

"Just sleep for a couple of hours, then, to keep you from being a complete zombie. You can't violate confidentiality, anyway, so you'd only be listening. And snoring." Encouraged by the upward quirk of his mouth, she continued. "If you have a digital recorder handy, we could use that. It'd be even more accurate than my notes, and you could listen to it after you get some sleep."

It only took him a few seconds to consider it before he nodded. "Good idea. I'll run out and see if I have a recorder in my squad."

"Actually, now that I think about it, there's no need." Daisy nodded at her phone sitting in front of her on the table. "I can record our conversation using this."

"Good idea. Thanks. I'll take off then." He leaned toward her, and she automatically turned her face toward his. His lips were just inches from hers when she realized what was happening and froze, staring at him. For a moment, it had felt like they were an old married couple, and he was about to kiss her good-bye. Her throat tightened with almost painful longing. How much she would love to have that easy, comfortable, *content* life with him. She wanted that good-bye kiss and all it represented so badly that her chest ached with it. It was just a daydream, though. She would never have that, not if Chris's startled expression was anything to go by.

His eyes widened as he took a step back, bumping into a wall with an un-Chris-like lack of coordination. "Right. See you later." Turning, he hurried out of the room.

His exit caught the others' attention. "Is Chris leaving?" Lou asked—or Daisy *thought* she asked. It was hard to understand her exact words, since Lou's mouth was full of doughnut.

"Yeah." Daisy stood and followed the fleeing deputy to the door. "He's following Ian's example and getting some sleep."

"Night shifts are tough," Lou said, and Rory made a sound of agreement. "It's hard enough dragging myself out of a warm bed to go on a dive team call."

When Daisy caught up with Chris at the door, he was focused on unfastening the locks, not even glancing at her when she stopped next to him. Apparently, squirrelly-acting Chris had returned. Daisy hadn't missed him.

"After you get a nap in, want to come over for a matinee?" she asked, deciding that at least one of them should try to act normal. "Dad picked up the mail, and *Brutal Fists* finally arrived." His hand paused on the first chain lock. "C'mon. You know you want to make fun of their technique in the cage-fighting scenes."

His exhale was audible, and his shoulders relaxed slightly. "Sounds good. I have a couple of errands to run first, so I'll be here around five or so."

"Perfect." She knew her grin was too wide, but she couldn't do anything about it. "I'll make some cornmeal-crust pizza and a salad, and we can finish off the brownies."

Smiling slightly, he finally made eye contact. "You'd better hide them from the sugar vultures in there, or there won't be any left for tonight."

With a snort, she waved off his warning. "Did you *see* how many doughnuts Ellie and George brought? Everyone's going to inhale about ten each before slipping into diabetic comas. No one will even want to hear the word 'brownies.'"

"Brownies?" Lou's excited voice chirped from the dining room, and Chris gave Daisy an I-told-you-so smirk.

Closing her eyes, Daisy shook her head. "I'll hide the brownies."

He chuckled and slipped out the door. After securing it behind him, Daisy hurried into the kitchen to start another cup of coffee and to slip the covered pan of brownies into a cupboard behind a salad spinner and her Crock-Pot.

"Daisy!" Lou shouted. "Get your toned little butt in here. And don't forget those brownies."

"Give me a minute, and I'll bring some more coffee," she yelled back. "But there aren't any brownies."

There were a few seconds of silence before a scowling Lou strode into the kitchen. "Daisy Little. Are you hiding brownies?"

"What brownies?" She widened her eyes in her best innocent expression.

"Fine. Be that way, B. H." Lou's sigh was heavy. "We'll just have to make do with the gazillion doughnuts in there. Now hurry up. Ian gave Rory the arson scoop."

"B. H.?"

"Brownie hoarder."

As silly and most likely temporary as it was, it still

made Daisy smile that she'd been given a nickname. "Just a few more seconds…"

The brewer gave its final gurgle, and Daisy grabbed the mug. With all the company she'd been having lately, she was going to have to get a coffeemaker that produced more than a single cup at a time.

"Ready! Let's talk about fires."

Rory's scowl was so severe that it made Daisy stop abruptly as she entered the dining room.

"What's wrong?" she asked, setting down the mug and carefully nudging it in Rory's direction.

"I feel like I have to give an oral report," Rory grumbled, playing with the notepad in front of her. "I'm supposed to tell you what Ian found out about the arsons."

"It's just us," Ellie said. "We won't judge. Besides, Lou won't let you get out a full sentence before she interrupts, so your oral report will be a very short one."

"Hey!" Lou protested.

Uncrossing her arms, Rory picked up the notepad and frowned at it. Daisy tapped her screen to start recording, resisting the urge to examine it, to try to figure out exactly why her phone *still* felt so strangely wrong. Corralling her straying thoughts, she focused on Rory.

"The first of this string of arsons was—"

"Hold up!" Lou jumped out of her chair and retrieved the oversized notepad that Daisy had propped against the dining room wall. "We need to do a timeline."

Ellie started giggling so hard that she would've fallen off her chair if George hadn't grabbed her and hoisted her upright again. Her laugh was so infectious that Daisy couldn't help but join in.

"Did I call that or what?" Ellie asked when she'd

recovered enough to speak, holding up her fist toward George. When he stared at it and then looked at Ellie, she sighed. "Don't leave me hanging. Fist-bump me."

Tentatively, George touched his knuckles against hers, although it was more of a nudge than a bump. Instead of withdrawing, he closed his fingers over her fist, his huge hand completely enveloping her small one. Bringing their hands to his mouth, he slid his down toward her wrist so he could kiss her fingers before lowering their hands into his lap.

Ellie gave him a tender look, and it was obvious that both had completely forgotten that they weren't the only ones in the room. Despite the usual pang in her belly that she felt as she watched their sweet couple-y-ness, Daisy had to smile.

When they finally broke eye contact and turned their heads to see the other three women eyeing them with varying degrees of amusement, Ellie visibly jumped before blushing.

"Sorry." Clearing her throat, she focused her gaze on the oversized pad. "What were you saying?"

"What was Rory saying before you mocked me, taught George of the Jungle here a native greeting, indulged in some googly eyes, and then returned to Earth?" Lou recapped cheerfully as she looked around the room in search of something. "B.H., where'd you hide the markers? Is it the same place you're hiding the brownies?"

Three pairs of eyes fastened on Daisy, who tried not to flinch.

"Brownies?" Ellie repeated, her eyes wide and hopeful.

"No brownies." To hide the fact that she was lying so badly her pants were most likely going to spontaneously combust, Daisy hurried into the living room. "The markers are still in here."

She grabbed them off the coffee table and returned to the dining table, where everyone was still staring at her.

"Why are you all looking at me like a bunch of half-starved puppies?" she asked, sliding the markers across the table to Lou. "Eat another doughnut."

"They're gone," Ellie said mournfully, tipping the container so Daisy could see the few scattered crumbs of icing that remained.

"But…how?" Daisy blinked at the empty box. "You guys must have bought every doughnut at the Gas and Guzzle. How are they all gone?"

Rory shrugged. "I was hungry."

"Me too." Lou didn't look too concerned as she sorted through the markers, as if choosing the correct color would solve the case immediately.

Ellie said earnestly, "We had to eat as many doughnuts as possible before the post-workout, guilt-free window closed."

"Wow," was all Daisy could say.

George cleared his throat and tipped his head toward Rory.

"He's right," Lou said. "We only have an hour before Rory has to open the shop, so let's get cracking. When was the first arson?" She drew a horizontal line across the top of the paper and then poised the marker on the left side of the line as she waited for the answer.

"About eleven months ago, on May thirtieth. It was the remains of a run-in shed in that field off of Easton Road."

"Run-in shed?" Daisy repeated. "As in a shelter for horses and cows and things?"

Rory nodded. "The field hadn't held any livestock for years before that, though. The shed had partially collapsed."

"Well, I'm glad no animals were singed," Daisy said as Lou scribbled below the timeline.

"Not to be the dumb out-of-towner," Ellie said, "but where's Easton Road?"

George looked at Daisy. "Map?"

She shook her head, but then reconsidered her answer, hopping up from her chair and heading into the kitchen. "Wait. I think I do. Hang on."

In one of the drawers she hardly ever opened, she dug through a couple of emergency candles, a pair of scissors, and a calendar from several years back to unearth a Simpson phone book. She would have just recycled it, since she found everything she needed online, but her dad had insisted on keeping it, just in case. She'd have to remember to thank him the next time he was home.

As she returned to the dining room, she flipped to the back and found a map of Simpson. Bracing the phone book on the table, she carefully tore out the sheet and handed it to George.

"Would you mind doing the mapping?" she asked, and he nodded, holding out an open hand to Lou.

"Marker?" she asked, picking up the set. "What color?"

He didn't answer, just gave a silent sigh and continued to hold out his hand.

"Purple," Ellie answered for him.

He accepted the marker and started examining the map. He made a small circle and added a "1" next to it before sliding it closer to Ellie. She studied the map for a few moments, tracing a few streets in an attempt to get her bearings.

"Okay," she finally said, returning the map to its original location in front of George. "I've never been there, but I have an idea of the general area. Where was the second one?"

"Eighty-one Bluebird Court." Rory grimaced. "Those Esko Hills street names are obnoxious."

Lou looked up from her timeline. "Esko Hills? Why does that subdivision keep popping up?"

"Could be a coincidence," Daisy said, leaning forward to get a better look at the map as George added another circle with a "2" next to it. "Simpson isn't that big, after all. There aren't that many neighborhoods."

"Maybe," Lou said, but her tone was skeptical. "When was that?"

"July 4th. Ian put a question mark next to this one, since they were pretty sure it was kids messing around with fireworks who started it."

Adding the date to the timeline, Lou asked, "What kind of structure?"

"Detached garage."

"Okay. Next?"

Rory detailed the where, what, and when of the eleven arson cases. By the time she'd worked her way through all of her notes, George's map had a cluster of purple numbers and circles, and Lou's timeline covered three sheets of paper. Frowning, she flipped back and forth.

"Do you mind if I take this home with me so I can transfer it to the whiteboard?" Lou asked. "Not to borrow Callum's OCDish tendencies, but this is a mess."

"Of course," Daisy said. "I'll just get some pictures of it first, so I can show Chris. Oh, and the map, too."

"Speaking of the map," Ellie said, sliding it to the center of the table so everyone could see it, "any obvious patterns?"

The five of them studied it for a quiet minute.

"They're all in town." Daisy was the first to speak.

"What about the wildland fires?" Rory asked. "Shouldn't we include those?"

Lou frowned thoughtfully. "Not yet. I think we need more information about those first. We don't know the ignition points or dates or really anything about them. Did Ian talk to the chief?" She glanced at Rory, who shook her head. "Okay, so until we learn more about the wildland fires, we'll just say that all the arsons were in Simpson."

Everyone except for Rory nodded in agreement. "Unless Lou's place should be on here, too."

Daisy had forgotten that possibility. Darting a look toward Lou, who appeared a little grim, Daisy suggested, "Maybe we should add her place—former place—to the map."

"Use a different color, though." Lou's tone was a little too casual. "I'm still not convinced that it wasn't loony Clay."

When George held out a hand, Lou slapped an orange marker in it. They all watched as he marked a "12" with a question mark and added an arrow pointing off the edge of the map.

Ellie tilted the map toward her when George had finished writing on it. "These two were really close to Willard Gray's cabin."

"What do you think the connection between Gray and the fires is?" Daisy asked, tilting her head to see the map at a different angle, as if the answer would jump out at her if she only looked at it in the right way. "We've already agreed that he couldn't have been the arsonist, since more than half of the fires were after his death."

"Could he have witnessed something?" Lou reached to tap the cluster of numbers closest to Gray's cabin.

Rory hummed, but it was an unconvinced sound. "Would someone really have committed murder to hide burning down a few sheds? Seems like overkill to me."

When Lou snorted, everyone looked at her. "Over*kill*? To commit murder? Never mind."

Glancing at her watch, Rory rose abruptly, gathering the sheets of paper holding her notes. "I have to go open the shop."

"We should probably get going, as well." Ellie and George rose, followed by Lou.

"Can I get some pictures of the timeline?" Daisy asked, turning off the recording on her phone and opening the camera app. When Lou held up the notepad and flipped to the first sheet, Daisy took a picture and then nodded for Lou to turn the page. Once she had taken photos of all three sheets containing parts of the timeline, she gave Lou a smile of thanks. When Daisy held up her phone to George, he slid the map in front of her so she could get a shot of that, too.

"Oh!" As she lowered the phone after taking the picture, she realized what had seemed so strange. The dent was gone. Her fingers ran over the too-smooth surface, finding nothing. Her eyebrows drew together. It had to be her phone; it had all her stuff on it. But how did a dent just disappear?

"Daisy?" Lou's voice drew her out of her confused thoughts. "You okay?"

"Sure." She forced a smile. If she tried to explain, she was going to sound completely paranoid. Nodding toward the notes in Rory's hand, Daisy asked, "Would you mind leaving those? Chris would probably like to see them."

In response, Rory held the stack of paper toward Daisy.

"Thanks."

She followed the last of her guests to the front door and ushered them into the entry as everyone said their good-byes. After securing the locks behind them, Daisy headed for the study, trying to understand how the dent in her phone could have just disappeared—unless there'd never been a dent in the first place, and she'd just imagined it. Why, though? Why would she remember a nonexistent dent? Was her brain that scattered, that unreliable? If she was wrong about that, what else could she have been wrong about?

Shoving the unanswerable question out of her mind, Daisy decided to do some doll research and stop obsessing.

As she waited for her laptop to boot up, she settled into her chair, resisting the urge to spin. That would just lead to more thinking about Chris and phones and dead guys and fires and the call she had to make that afternoon. Since her phone appointment was at one p.m., she had just over three hours to finish her research and list the dolls for sale.

It struck her how full her day was, and she realized that it must be how most people's regular schedules were. Normally, she had to search for things to do to fill the days between Chris's visits and her dad's time between jobs. Daisy decided she liked being busy. Time flew, and she didn't spend as many hours fighting off things she didn't want in her head.

Pulling up an Internet browser window, she forced herself to go to the antique doll site she'd been looking at earlier. The lure of other, more entertaining and less profitable web pages called to her, but she was determined to get some work done. To give her motivation, she opened the box and carefully extracted one of the dolls, placing it on the desk to the left of her computer. Pulling out the second, Daisy laid it on her right. She started to look away from the second doll but then did a double take, leaning closer to the thing's face.

"Are those…teeth?" she muttered. "That is so creepy. Great. Now I know this one can bite."

Dragging her brain away from the mental image of an army of attacking zombie dolls, Daisy turned back to her computer screen. Having them staring at her—and one baring its two little teeth—was definitely giving her incentive to get them listed and sold.

Tyler leaned his head against the cool glass, eyeing the frozen meal options and trying to work up some enthusiasm. It was hard to care what he'd have for his solitary meal that night though, when his dad would be out doing what he needed to do.

His huff of annoyance made a foggy spot on the door. He'd caused the mess. Tyler should be allowed to help clean it up, but his dad insisted on treating him like he was still a kid.

"Is there any way you'd reconsider? It'd really help out Daisy. I'd be happy to pay extra for the service."

Tyler lifted his head at the sound of Chris Jennings's voice coming from the grocery-store owner's office. Although Tyler had never had a problem with Chris, his nutso girlfriend was a different story, with her late-night spying and video-taking and trying to turn Chris against Tyler's dad. He wished there was something he could do about her.

"I can't," Mr. Lee, the store owner, said. "If I offer delivery to one customer, everyone is going to want it, and that would be a mess. I'd have to buy a snow-mobile—or a dog sled. Why don't you just bring her groceries to her yourself? Heard that you're over there just about every day."

"Who'd you hear that from?" Chris's voice had an undertone that was chillier than the freezer Tyler was leaning against.

"Uh...can't remember," Mr. Lee stammered. "But, anyway, there's no way I can do the delivery. Maybe there's some neighborhood kid who'd be willing to do it?"

Wheels started turning in Tyler's mind, and he tuned out the rest of the conversation. Reaching into the freezer, he grabbed the first thing that came to hand and hurried through the store, finally finding his dad in the produce section. Tyler dropped his frozen selection into the cart.

"Black-bean burgers?" His father raised his eye-brows. "That's a first. Are you going vegetarian on me?"

Tyler restrained a wince at his absentminded dinner choice. He wasn't a big fan of beans. "No. Just didn't notice they weren't beef. I was thinking about something else."

"Yeah?" Keeping his attention on Tyler, he started pushing the cart toward the registers. "What about?"

Trying to keep the excited smile off his face, Tyler pretended to be interested in a display of tomatoes. "I was thinking about getting a job."

Chapter 11

A KNOCK ON THE FRONT DOOR MADE HER START. AFTER the one o'clock call, she'd worked off her nervous energy on the treadmill for an hour before showering and returning to the computer just five minutes ago to dive back into research.

As she got up from her chair, her eyes flicked toward the clock in the corner of her laptop screen. It was still pretty early for Chris, and he would've texted her before showing up an hour and a half ahead of time. Walking to the front door, she pressed the intercom button.

"Hello?" She half expected to hear the voice of one of her recent guests, asking about some forgotten item. A young, unknown male answered, instead.

"Hi. Um...Ms. Little?"

"Yes?" Her tone was cautious. It was unusual for strangers to come to the door—not counting new friends recruited by Chris.

"I'm Tyler Coughlin. I work for Melcher's?"

"The grocery store?" Her unease faded to puzzlement.

"Yes, ma'am. I'm going to be delivering your groceries from now on."

"You are?" She knew she sounded like a clueless idiot, but that was basically how she felt.

"Yes, ma'am. So...uh, can I come in?" Strangely enough, the hesitation in the kid's voice made her relax.

He'd probably be shocked to know that he'd made her even more nervous than he was.

"Okay." Her finger hovered over the unlock button for a long moment before she mentally told herself to stop being paranoid and just let the poor kid inside. He sounded like he couldn't be over sixteen. If she started being afraid of *children*, then she might as well give up and become a full-fledged Amish hoarding grandmother. With a resolute poke of her finger, she unlocked the exterior door.

Her hands were sweating as she unfastened the dead bolts. Taking a deep breath, she tried to rearrange her expression to something that didn't scream "terror" before opening the door.

As Tyler stepped into her entryway, she let out the air she'd been holding. Her initial estimate of his age looked to be right. He was tall, but gangly, and he had an ungainly puppy look, as if he hadn't completely finished growing into his body yet.

"Hi." Giving her an uncertain smile, he tossed his too-long bangs out of his eyes. His gaze flickered up and down her body in a clumsily obvious attempt at secretly checking her out, before he blushed and turned his eyes toward the floor.

"Hi." As she relocked the door, Daisy noted that her hands had quit sweating once she'd confirmed it was, indeed, just a kid. "What's this about groceries?"

His smile fell away, making room for confusion. "Uh, didn't you talk to Mr. Lee?"

"Mr. Lee?" The name sounded vaguely familiar.

"The owner of Melcher's?"

Daisy had to smile at the way their conversation

seemed to be made up of questions, and she waved toward the kitchen doorway. "Want to come in?"

With a nod, he followed her. Automatically, she headed for the coffeemaker, but then she paused. Was sixteenish too young for coffee? The teenagers on TV seemed to drink an awful lot of it, but Daisy didn't want to stunt the kid's growth or anything.

"Are you old enough for coffee?" she asked, almost laughing at his startled expression.

His shoulders pulled back as he answered, "Sure. I drink it all the time." His too-casual tone gave away the lie, but Daisy just shrugged. A cup of coffee wasn't going to kill him, and he was plenty tall already, so the threat of growth-stunting was minimal.

"Go ahead and pick one." She gestured toward the round-robin display of different coffee flavors, all packaged in single-serving cups, sitting next to the brewer.

After a glance at her, as if checking to make sure she'd been serious about the offer, Tyler hurried toward the coffee. He examined the options with a gravity that made Daisy swallow a smile. It had been a long time since she'd been around any kids his age, and it was different because she'd been a teenager back then, too.

When he finally decided on mocha and held it up as if asking for her approval, Daisy nodded and held out her hand. Placing his chosen cup in her palm, he stepped back so she could reach the brewer.

As she popped it into the coffeemaker and got a mug out of the cupboard, she prompted, "Groceries?"

"Um...I'm not sure what's going on. Mr. Lee just told me I'd be bringing them to you every week. They don't do deliveries usually—or, like, ever, at least not in the month I've been working there—so I wasn't sure if you were going to text me with your list or what. That's why I stopped by here."

Daisy only had to think about it for a few seconds before the Chris-shaped lightbulb turned on. "Excuse me," she said to Tyler as she pulled her phone out of her hoodie pocket, found Chris's name in her contacts—her *two* pages of contacts—and tapped the screen.

"What's up, Dais?" He'd answered after only a single ring.

"Um…the grocery deliverer is here."

"Really? That's great! I didn't think Mr. Lee was going to do it."

Daisy opened her mouth, but then glanced at Tyler and closed it again, remembering that anything she said would be all over Simpson High School within a few hours. Scratch that—it would be all over Field County, if teenaged Simpsonites were as gossipy as their fully grown relatives.

"Dais? You there?"

"Yes." She was still trying to figure out how to argue with him without giving Tyler a show. It seemed rude to go to another room and leave him alone in a stranger's house, especially when she was the one who'd made the call.

"What's wrong?"

Daisy gave up trying to figure out how to yell at Chris in code. "I'll talk to you about it when you're here later."

"Are you mad?"

Since she was feeling more irritation than anger, but she couldn't explain without also saying it to Tyler—who wasn't even trying to hide the fact that he was avidly listening to every word of her side of the conversation—she just said, "Later, Chris."

"You shouldn't have to wait for fresh food, Dais. If you want to make brownies, you should be able to fucking make them without having to wait for Gabe to wander into town."

Daisy blinked in surprise. Chris hardly ever swore—at least, not in front of her.

"You can be mad at me if you want, Dais, but fresh vegetables and milk shouldn't be a special treat, for God's sake. I'm just—"

"Chris," Daisy interrupted, since he was getting louder and louder, and soon both she and Tyler would be able to hear everything Chris was saying. "I'll talk to you when you get here."

Ending the call, she forced a smile. "Your coffee's ready."

He gave the mug a wary look before picking it up, making Daisy fairly sure he didn't actually drink coffee. The way he winced at the first bitter sip confirmed it. Hiding her amusement, she pulled out the sugar bowl, a spoon, and some milk, placing everything on the counter next to Tyler.

"Would it be easiest if I just texted you my grocery list?" she asked as he poured enough milk in his coffee to turn it tan.

"Sure." He paused between adding his fifth and sixth spoonful of sugar to his mug in order to tug his phone out of the back pocket of his jeans and extend it toward her. As he finished adding sugar and then stirred the milky syrup that used to be coffee, she added her name and number to his phone and then called it so she'd have his number. Although she wasn't trying to pry, Daisy couldn't help but notice that his contact list was even shorter than hers.

Sympathy made her smile at him a little too warmly as she returned his phone. When his surprise turned into a mix of interest and hope, she realized her mistake. It wouldn't be good to make her new grocery-delivery boy think she was hitting on him.

"What grade are you in?" she asked, trying to think of questions she could ask that would emphasize the enormous, unsurmountable eight years or so that stretched between them without hurting the kid's feelings.

"I'll be a junior this fall." His attempt at rounding up made her feel another surge of compassion for the boy. Despite that, she tried to keep her expression muted as she nodded.

"Do you have your license yet?" A quick glance at his mug showed that he'd barely made a dent in his coffee. Daisy held back a sigh. She was almost out of age-appropriate questions, and then there would be awkward silence. She just knew it.

"Not yet." His mouth twisted. "I have my permit, but I still need to get more practice hours in, and my dad works a lot."

The mention of his father made her realize something. "Oh! You said your last name is Coughlin. Your dad is the sheriff, then?" Now that she'd made the connection, Daisy could see the resemblance.

"Yes," Tyler said, almost reluctantly.

She wondered why he didn't want to admit who his father was, but then she figured that it was a typical teen reaction to be embarrassed by his parents.

Also, Sheriff Coughlin probably cast a pretty long shadow, making it easy for Tyler to disappear in it, especially in such a small town. Instead of commenting, she just nodded. After all, what was she supposed to say? *Your dad thinks I'm crazy* would probably not be appropriate.

Her silence apparently made Tyler nervous, though, since he rushed to speak. "What do you... I mean, do you need anything right away? Groceries, that is."

"No, thanks. I'm actually fully stocked right now." Despite her irritation with Chris for his high-handedness, Daisy felt a trill of excitement at the thought of having weekly groceries. Although she told herself to be grateful she wasn't going hungry, she always hated when she only had the canned and frozen options but was craving fresh food. Plus, with weekly deliveries, her chocolate stash would never be depleted. The thought killed any lingering annoyance with Chris. "How about next week? What's a good day?"

"Friday? I almost always work on Fridays. I don't have school, so I could get them to you earlier."

"I'll text you Friday, then."

"Okay." Shifting his weight, he looked at his mug and then toward the sink, as if he wasn't sure what to do with his coffee.

"Here," she said and held out a hand. "I'll take that. You probably need to get back to work."

With an affirmative shrug, he handed her the coffee. "See you next week."

"Bye, Tyler."

He was still hesitating, so she moved toward the door and unfastened the dead bolts and chains. "Wait to go through the outer door until I have this one relocked, okay?"

"Okay. Bye, Ms. Little."

"You can call me Daisy," she said, and he flushed and dropped his gaze.

"Thanks…Daisy." His voice was just a mumble as he slipped through the doorway.

She quickly refastened the locks. Even though she'd asked him to wait, she wasn't sure if she trusted him to remember. Once the last chain was in place, she thumped the door, and she heard the exterior door open.

"Good kid," she said under her breath and then snorted a laugh. She needed to hang out with teenagers more often. Tyler's awkwardness made her feel pretty proud of her social skills, despite having been locked away from almost everyone for eight years.

She turned away from the door. A pounding stopped her before she could go two steps. It was Chris's knock, and she frowned as she pushed the speaker button and the unlock button at the same time.

"You're early," she said.

"You're mad," was his response.

Rolling her eyes, she waited until the exterior door locked behind him and then undid the locks for what felt like the hundredth time that day.

Pulling open the door, she stepped back so Chris could step inside. "I'm not mad."

She might not be, but from the way a scowl rumpled his forehead, it looked like *he* was.

"It was the logical thing to do," he said.

"I know." She headed toward the study. Since she was pretty sure work was over for the day, she wanted to put a layer of cardboard between her and the one doll's teeth.

"If you know," Chris said, following her, "then why are you mad?"

"I'm not," she said over her shoulder. "Honestly. I'm irritated that you didn't talk to me about it first, but it's a good idea."

"Oh." That seemed to have knocked all the indignation out of him. "Why'd you hang up on me then?"

"Because Tyler was listening to everything I said, and I didn't want our business being discussed by a bunch of high schoolers." She carefully returned the first doll to its box.

"Tyler? Rob's kid?"

"Yes." Picking up the second doll, she held it closer to Chris. "Look. This one has teeth. Doesn't that make it just exponentially creepier?"

"Yes. Get that thing away from me." Despite his words, he looked more relaxed than when he'd arrived. "So you're not mad."

"I'm not mad," she agreed, "although I might start getting annoyed if you keep asking me that."

"I'll quit then." His mouth relaxed into a little smile. "What was Tyler doing here?"

"He's going to be my grocery-delivery boy." Folding down the box flaps, she frowned. "If he doesn't have his license, how's he going to deliver my groceries?"

Chris shrugged. "Bike maybe, or on a sled after it snows. You don't get much, so he could even carry them. It's less than a mile to the grocery store. I didn't know he was working at Melcher's."

"Tyler said it's only been for a month." She shut down

her laptop. "I feel bad for the kid. He seems lonely. Even *I* have more contacts in my cell than he does."

While he waited for her to finish, Chris leaned against the wall, his arms crossed over his chest. "Why were you looking at his phone?"

"Putting my number in there," she said, just to watch his eyebrows shoot toward his hairline. She wasn't disappointed. "So I can text him my grocery list."

He grunted. "Why does he need *your* number for that?"

"So he knows who's texting him? Why are you being so weird about it?"

"I'm not being weird."

"Right." With a shrug, she dropped the subject and headed toward the living room. "You hungry? We could do the early-bird-special dinner, or we could watch a movie first and then break out the pizza."

"I can wait."

"Okay." Turning to face him, Daisy walked backward and grinned. "You just can't wait to watch *Brutal Fists*, can you?"

As soon as she reversed direction, Chris's gaze shot up to meet hers. "Uh...right."

A little confused by the guilt in his expression, she continued to walk backward, frowning at him. "What'd you do?"

His answer came too fast. "Nothing."

"Your lying skills could use some work. Don't they teach you that in cop school?"

"No. Watch where you're going, or you're going to run into something."

Cocking her head to the side, she stopped so she could study him. The obvious answer was too ludicrous to consider, but it popped out of her mouth anyway. "Were you looking at my butt?"

"No." That time, the quick denial was paired with a dark red flush across his cheekbones.

"Liar." She turned away from him to hide her pleased smile. "Do you want something to drink? Besides coffee, I have…well, water. Or milk."

"I need to actually sleep tonight, so I'll have some water." He sounded like he'd regained his equilibrium. "I'll get it though. Want some?"

"Sure. Thanks." As she set up the DVD, she couldn't stop grinning. Deputy Chris Jennings had been checking out her butt. Once she had everything ready to go for the movie, she pulled off her hoodie. Although she told herself it was only because she'd get too warm otherwise, Daisy knew she was lying to herself as she smoothed the soft material of her newly revealed fitted shirt. When Chris returned bearing two water glasses, she quickly dropped her hand and took a seat on the couch.

"Guess what?"

"What?" he responded absently, placing the water on the coffee table in front of them.

"I have a new therapist."

His head jerked up, and he stared at her for a moment before a grin stretched across his face. "Hey, that's great, Dais!"

"Yeah." Her face was flushed with excitement and embarrassment. "We had our first session over the phone this afternoon, and we're going to do a video conference on Monday. Dr. Fagin is in Denver, so he's going to come here eventually, but I told him I'd feel more comfortable doing the phone and video thing first."

"He?" Chris seemed to lose a little of his enthusiasm.

"Yes." Making a face, Daisy explained, "I figured that might keep Dad from sleeping with this one." Chris laughed. "And this guy was really highly recommended."

"Do you like him?" he asked, sitting on the other side of the couch and angling his body so he could look at her.

"I do." Daisy tucked her bare feet underneath her. "We didn't talk about anything too intense today, since it was kind of a get-to-know-you session, but he seemed really relaxed and laid-back. He didn't have that condescending psychiatrist thing going, either."

"That's great." His grin was open, without even a hint of the weirdness that had been popping up lately. "I'm proud of you, Dais."

"Thanks." She bounced a little. "Ready for *Fists*?"

With a mock-groan, Chris turned toward the flat-screen mounted on the wall. "Am I ready for horrible fighting technique and cheesy dialog? Sure. Hit me. I mean it. Hit me hard enough that I pass out and miss this movie."

With an amused snort, Daisy ignored his moaning and started the DVD. "Whatever. I know you're dying to see it."

Although he gave a huff of denial, she noticed that Chris's eyes were already fixed on the screen. Grinning, she settled back to watch the movie.

———

"I'm feeling a violent need to punch her." Daisy jammed a spoonful of brownie sundae into her mouth. "Why is she just standing there while her boyfriend is pummeled?"

Chris smirked at her. "Pummeled?"

"Yes, pummeled. Thrashed, beaten, ganged-up on, smacked-down, trampled." With a groan, she closed her eyes. "And now she's screaming. Great. That's really helpful."

"Why are you acting like you've never seen this movie before?" He bit into his brownie. Unlike Daisy, he preferred to have his dessert straight, without ice cream and hot fudge. "We must've watched this fifty times."

She shrugged. "I always forget how useless Taylor is until her stupid screams remind me. I mean, look." Daisy pointed at the screen. "Those three guys have their backs to her. No one's paying attention to her. She could take those guys out easily."

"Easy for you, maybe," Chris said mildly. "But you have skills."

"Mad skills," she agreed, making him laugh. "Even if she's clueless, though, she should at least try *something*. Call for help, even. I know she has that stupid bejeweled cell phone in her pocket, since she was just texting her friend in the last scene."

"Don't judge until you've been there," he said, focusing on the still-screaming woman on the screen. "You never know how you'll react until you're in the middle of a life-threatening situation. Your brain and body do some crazy stuff in crisis mode—most of it not helpful."

"I know." Putting her bowl on the coffee table, she tucked herself into the corner of the couch and hugged her knees. Although she was sure Chris hadn't meant them to hurt, his words gutted her with their accuracy. When it had mattered, when she could've acted and saved her mom, she'd been just like Taylor—useless. Maybe that was why she hated the character so much.

Daisy stared at the screen as the attackers fled and Taylor threw herself on her boyfriend's limp body. Normally, this was the point where Daisy mocked the woman's lack of first-aid skills and ranted to Chris about how her clutching the semiconscious man had probably just aggravated a spinal injury, but Daisy wasn't seeing the movie anymore. She was sixteen and huddled in the corner of Miller's Convenience Store, trying to hide behind a display of individually wrapped Little Debbie snack cakes.

"Dais." Chris must have moved, since he was right next to her. Cupping her face with both of his hands, he tipped her head so she had to look at him. "I'm sorry. That was a stupid thing to say."

"No. You're right. I just sat there and did nothing to help her." It was too hard to keep eye contact when Chris looked at her like that, with so much kindness and sympathy that she didn't deserve. Her gaze shifted to his left eyebrow. "I even screamed at exactly the wrong time. I wasn't just useless like Taylor; I was destructive."

Despite her effort to avoid his eyes, he moved his head slightly so she couldn't help but meet them. His fingers tightened, not quite enough to hurt. "Your mom was just shot in front of you. I think you're allowed to scream." His voice was rough, as if something was caught in his throat.

"No." Since he wasn't letting her dodge his gaze, she closed her eyes completely. She'd held these words inside of her for eight years and, now that she'd started letting them out, she couldn't seem to stop. "It was a second before he pulled the trigger. I startled him. I screamed, and he shot, and she fell. That's how it went."

"*No*. No, that's not how it went. Daisy, look at me." Although she really didn't want to open her eyes, it was hard for her to deny him anything, especially when he was being so serious, so intense. She met his gaze. "I was there, Dais. I was there, and that's not how things went down."

A remote part of her brain was touched that Chris would lie to try to make her feel better, but she couldn't duck the responsibility of what she'd done. "It was, Chris. I see it happen every night."

"Oh, Dais." It was Chris's turn to close his eyes, and when he opened them again, his expression was fierce. "You're not the only one watching the reruns. I was the first deputy on scene after the call went out."

"Did someone outside see what was going on?" she asked. "I always wondered how you got there so fast."

He frowned. "Didn't anyone tell you what happened?"

She tugged on his wrists, and he released her. It felt good to be touching him, though, so she shifted her hands and tangled her fingers with his. "I never wanted to discuss it—or even *think* about it. Besides, people probably figured I already knew, since I was there." There in the corner, screaming at just the wrong time.

Her explanation didn't seem to placate him. "I'm sorry, Dais. I should've told you a long time ago, but you always used to walk away when I tried to bring it up, and I…well, I hated talking about it, too. I didn't realize you were blaming yourself all these years. The clerk pushed the emergency button under the counter, and Dispatch sent out the call that an alarm had been triggered at Miller's Convenience Store. I was only a block away, so I was the first deputy on scene. Almost all of those types of calls end up being false alarms, but I'd only been working as a deputy for six months, so my heart started beating fast. I'd been on my own for just three weeks after finishing my probationary training period, and I hadn't had time to get bitter and jaded yet."

As he paused, she watched the muscles in his jaw work. Listening to him tell the story made her feel disconnected from it, as if everything that had happened that day had ruined someone else's life, not her own. It was completely different from her nightmares, which allowed her to say fairly calmly, "I can't imagine you ever getting bitter and jaded."

Chris smiled, but it was faint and disappeared quickly. "Miller always had those promo posters hanging in the windows, so I couldn't see what was going on inside. I had my gun out, and I was worried that would scare people in the store if it was just a false alarm. As soon as I entered, though, I saw him, saw them both…him and your mom."

"You yelled, 'Sheriff's department! Drop your weapon!' over and over." She squeezed his hands. "I was so relieved to hear that. I hadn't thought that help would ever come, and then there you were."

His lips pressed together until they almost disappeared. "I didn't see you at first. All I could see was a man with a gun pointed at a woman's skull. She looked so scared."

"Yeah, she did." The story had become hers again, and tears rushed to fill her eyes. Daisy clenched her teeth to try to hold them back, but there were too many, and they flowed over her cheeks and dripped off her jaw. Chris's eyes focused on her face, bringing him back from that convenience store eight years ago, and he tugged his hands free from her grip.

"I'm sorry, Dais." He wiped at her cheeks with the backs of his fingers, but tears just kept coming.

"Not your fault," she said, hating the hiccup that interrupted her words.

Apparently giving up on drying her face, he wrapped his arms around her and pulled her into him. Daisy rested her forehead against his shoulder and tried to concentrate on how good Chris smelled, like wood smoke and brownies, rather than remembering the acrid tang of urine when she'd wet herself in fear. Even dumb and useless movie-Taylor hadn't peed her pants like a baby.

"It was, though." It took a moment for Daisy to figure out what he was referring to. When she finally did, she shook her head against his shirt. Before she could protest, he continued. "When I was in law-enforcement training, we were required to take a basic firearms class. It was the same drills, over and over, and I got bored. Instead of aiming for center mass like we were supposed to, I'd pick some other body part, like the forehead or the crotch, and I'd see how tight I could make the pattern."

Since she wasn't sure how to respond to that, Daisy stayed quiet, waiting for him to continue.

"Your mom was small, smaller than you, even," he eventually said. "He had his arm around her neck and had pulled her up on her toes, and the top of her head still only reached his collarbone."

As she listened, Daisy grabbed his shirt with both hands, wadding the material in her fists. She'd been focused on the gun, her mother's sobs, her own terror. That's what came back to her night after night. The details he'd remembered were different, changing the scene in her head for the first time in eight years. Daisy wasn't sure if that made it more terrifying or less, but she did know that she had to hold on to something, and Chris's shirt was the closest grabable thing.

"I aimed at his head. It's funny that you remember me yelling at him to drop his weapon, since I didn't even realize I was saying it. It was really quiet for me—quiet and slow and clear. He looked at me, and I saw him decide. I saw it in his eyes that he was going to kill this woman. I saw that, recognized it, and I still hesitated."

Daisy stopped breathing, her fingers clenching so tightly around the flannel fabric that her hands went numb.

"He pulled the trigger, and she just...dropped. Her expression was so surprised. It wasn't until then that I shot him. I waited until it was too late, and then I finally acted—no." Chris blew out a hard breath. "I *re*acted. And action beats reaction every time."

"No. No, no, no." When she realized she was chanting the word over and over, she clamped her teeth together. Even though hearing about it, talking about it, was as painful as having her guts scooped out with an ice-cream spoon, Daisy didn't want to stop. She had to know, had to have those details, and she was positive Chris would stop talking about it if she got hysterical on him. She forced herself to breathe. "It was me. I screamed. It was my fault."

"It wasn't you, Dais." His hand stroked over the back of her head. One or both of them was shaking. "He decided, and I knew, but I didn't shoot him until it was too late to save her. And I never heard you scream."

It was overwhelming—too many new details that

didn't mesh with the old memories, the ones she'd always assumed were right. She thought she should reassure Chris, should tell him it wasn't his fault, but words weren't lining up in her head right. Instead of saying anything, she just leaned her head on his shoulder and clutched his shirt. For the moment, breathing was all she could manage.

Chapter 12

DAISY DIDN'T KNOW HOW LONG THEY SAT THERE BEFORE she relaxed her grip on Chris's shirt and turned her head to the side. Enough time had gone by for the movie to finish and start looping through the opening sequence.

"I'm going to donate that movie to the library." Her voice sounded rusty. "I might not be able to blame Taylor for being useless without being a hypocrite, but she still pisses me off."

His chest moved with a laugh that was more of a hard exhale. "I'll take it with me and drop it off."

He shifted, and she forced her fingers to release him completely. She felt too raw to meet his gaze, so she studied the mess of melted ice cream and brownie goo left in her bowl.

"Did you..." Chris cleared his throat. "Do you want me to leave?"

"Leave?" Her eyes snapped to his. "No. Definitely not. I was trying to think of a not-awkward way of asking if you'd stay tonight." At his shocked expression, she shook her head, hating the blush that invaded her cheeks. "Not, like, in a dirty way. And now I'm talking like I'm Tyler's age. Sorry." Taking a deep breath, she started again. "There's a lot happening in my brain right now, so I know I won't sleep. If I'm here by myself, I'm going to end up in the training room, beating up on poor Max until I pass out. You don't have to stay up or anything. I just don't want to be alone."

His expression unreadable, he eyed her for a long time.

Daisy finally couldn't hold back the prattle. "Don't feel obligated to stay, though. Max will eventually forgive me for pulverizing his internal organs. I'm used to staying awake."

"I'll stay." He was still looking at her oddly, though.

"What?"

"What what?"

"You're acting weird."

He gave a short bark of laughter. "Sorry. I'll try to normalize."

"I'd rather you just tell me what the problem is."

"It's not a problem, really." He stood and gathered the abandoned desserts, as if he needed to move. "I'm just surprised you want me here, that's all."

"Why is that surprising?" She followed him into the kitchen. "I like having you around. Well, most of the time. You do have those occasional annoying moments, but they're rare, and I'm forgiving."

Dropping the bowls on the counter, he turned toward her so quickly that Daisy took a step back. "Are you?"

"Am I what?"

"Forgiving."

"Yes." The word came out slowly and a little warily.

"I guess you'd have to be." That time, his laugh had no humor in it.

"You're being weird again."

"Sorry." He stared at her. "Do you think you could forgive me?"

"For what?"

Bracing his hands on the counter to either side of him, he stared at the tile floor. Finally raising his eyes to meet hers, he said quietly, "Hesitating."

It took her a moment to figure out what he was saying. When realization struck, her whole body jerked with shock. Her mouth opened, but there was no air for speech.

"Never mind." He turned away from her, but Daisy lunged forward, grabbing his arm to spin him around.

"Chris…" Even though the words in her brain weren't any more ordered than they had been earlier, she knew she couldn't stay silent. "It wasn't your fault."

His blank expression didn't change. "I had the shot, but I didn't take it."

"He *decided*, you said," she argued. "He'd made the decision to kill my mom."

"If I'd made the shot before he did—"

"She'd probably still be dead!" Her voice had gotten loud, so she brought it down a few decibels. "His finger was on the trigger. I remember. I was staring at it, praying that he didn't pull it. If you'd put a bullet in his head that half-second earlier, what would've happened? I don't know what a body's reaction to being shot would be, but if his hand had tightened, even a little bit, he would've killed her anyway."

"We don't know that!" Now he was yelling. "We don't know what would've happened!"

"No." For some reason, his frenzy was making it easier for her to be calm. "We don't. If I hadn't screamed, if you'd shot a tiny bit sooner, if another deputy had needed a bag of potato chips and happened to be in the store, if my mom would've misplaced her car keys and been five minutes later getting there… I've thought all of these things. Every time I rewrite it in my mind, though, it doesn't help. My mom's still dead, and I'm too messed up in the head to leave the house."

Breathing hard, he stared at her. His face was pulled tight, his eyes almost wild, and he looked like a stranger. Deciding she needed to fix that, Daisy closed the gap between them and took his face in her hands, just like he'd done for her earlier.

"I'm alive because you shot him. You're alive because you shot him. The other deputies who arrived to back you up are alive because you shot him. I know you wish you could've saved my mom, too, but it didn't work out that way. You need to make your peace with that, or you'll end up as crazy as I am."

"You're not crazy."

Her laugh was more of a sob. "Oh, Chris. I do love you." The words were out, raw and honest. His reaction when she'd tried to kiss him was bad enough, but now, if he rejected her… It was too horrible to think about. But no matter what he said or did, it wouldn't change the truth about her feelings. She did love him. She'd loved him since that awful day, and she'd keep loving him for the rest of her life. A sense of resigned peace filled her, and she slid her arms around his middle. It was a long time before he relaxed enough to hug her back.

"I love you, too, Dais." His hold on her tightened. "You're my best friend."

Joy flooded her for just a moment before the truth soured her happiness. Chris was right—they were friends. No matter how much she might wish for more, friends were all they ever could be. Shoving away the melancholy cloud that settled over her at the thought, she hugged him tighter. If friendship was all he could offer, she'd hold onto that with both hands. He was *her* best friend, too, and that was precious and wonderful. Daisy wasn't about to ruin that by sulking because Chris didn't have a romantic interest in her. She could do the just-friends thing, she decided, even as her heart twisted painfully in protest.

With a sigh, she disentangled herself from Chris's hold. "My brain is tired. Can we watch something stupid and mindless?"

"Sure." He sounded relieved, which made Daisy duck her head to hide a smile.

"Or we could talk about our feelings for another couple of hours." She tried to make her tone as earnest as possible as she sent him a sideways glance. "Then we could braid each other's hair and talk about cute boys."

His expression of horror faded as his eyes narrowed, and he lunged for her. With a squeal of laughter, Daisy ducked under his arm and dashed for the living room. She'd almost made it to the couch when he caught her and lifted her off her feet. Chris spun her around before tossing her into the air. Weightless for a moment, she landed on the couch with a grunt.

When she saw Chris start to hurdle the couch, she hurried to pull her legs clear of his landing zone, but he skipped the cushions completely and landed on his feet in front of the sofa. He examined her DVD collection for a while, and Daisy studied him. After their gut-ripping conversation, she felt surprisingly lighter. There was a possibility that she *hadn't* caused her mom's death, and that was a huge relief.

"How about this one?" He held up a goofy comedy with no redeeming intellectual qualities at all.

Daisy grinned. "Perfect."

Her eyes still closed against the invasive early morning light, Daisy shifted and held back a groan. Waking wasn't as uncomfortable as it had been after the night on the training room floor, but her muscles protested the awkward sleeping position. Her neck, especially, was twisted in an uncomfortable way, with her temple resting on something too hard to be even the worst of pillows.

As she slowly returned to consciousness, she frowned. In addition to her rocklike pillow, there was also a heavy weight over her side, and the back of her shirt was damp with sweat, thanks to the heater behind her. Everything combined was odd enough to make her open her eyes.

Blinking a few times until her gaze focused, she saw the coffee table and the TV beyond it. From that, she determined that she'd fallen asleep on the living room couch. It didn't explain the source of heat behind her or the weight pressing on her lower ribs, however.

Lifting her head and wincing at the stiff muscles in her neck, she saw the male hand resting on her belly. Her body jerked in surprise, and the radiator behind her gave a sleepy, masculine grunt. Daisy turned her head the other way and saw that his arm, the one not draped over her waist, was the hard pillow.

Racking her brain, she remembered getting drowsy during movie number three. At that time, she'd been curled up in her corner of the couch, while Chris had been sitting on the middle cushion, just close enough that she'd been able to touch his leg with her drawn-up toes. Sometime during the night, they must've shifted into this position.

Before she could wrap her brain around the fact that she was *spooning* with *Chris*, the big spoon himself stirred behind her.

"'Morning," he rumbled, and Daisy tried not to fixate on how raspy and deep his just-woken voice was.

"'Morning," she echoed. Her voice, in contrast, was slightly shrill, and she buried her face into the cushion to prevent herself from saying anything else. Unfortunately, she ended up grinding her forehead against his arm. As soon as she realized what she was doing, she pulled up her head. For good measure, she rolled away from him. Unfortunately, the couch wasn't that wide, and she toppled onto the floor.

As she lay on her back, blinking at yet another ceiling, she was thankful she at least hadn't hit her head on the coffee table when she went over the edge. She'd rather not be unconscious in front of Chris again—or be unconscious at all, really.

His blond head appeared, blocking her view of the ceiling. His hair was flattened on the right side of his head, and a slight scruff had grown in overnight. It didn't seem quite fair that his sleep-mussed state made him more attractive, rather than less. Daisy was pretty sure her current look was more "hot mess" than "hot."

"You okay?" he asked, still with that gravelly voice.

"Yeah." She smiled at him. "Just used to a wider bed."

His lips curled in response. "Me too." He pushed himself off the couch and stood, carefully placing his feet so he straddled her legs before he extended both arms. When she placed her hands in his, he pulled her to her feet. Once she was upright, he kept hold of her until she was steady. In fact, he didn't let go until she squeezed his hands and gently pulled hers free so she could reach over her head to try to loosen up her stiff muscles.

"Thanks." Her full-body stretch was accompanied by a yawn. "Want to hit the gym before breakfast?"

"No." His newly awake expression had been replaced by his bossy one. "And neither are you. It's a rest day."

She folded forward to stretch her hamstrings and her back, hiding her face against her knees. Despite her position, Chris must have caught her grimace, since he continued lecturing—either that, or he just liked to lecture her.

"You need to let the muscle fibers repair themselves. That's the only way you'll grow stronger." She'd heard this so many times, she could've mouthed the words along with him, but she didn't. He'd just spent the night with her because she'd asked, and he was training her *and* her new entourage without complaint, so he didn't deserve her teasing. Besides, she knew he was right. "If you work out every day, you're not getting the full benefit of your training, and you're just asking for an injury."

Straightening, she couldn't help giving him a mock-pout. "I hate rest days. They make me antsy."

"I know." To her shock, he wrapped an arm around her shoulders to steer her to the kitchen. Spooning and now side hugging—Chris had gotten oddly touchy-feely in the past twelve hours. Daisy figured she might as well take advantage of it while it lasted, so she leaned into his side, surprised once again when he didn't pull away. "But just think how antsy you'd get if you couldn't work out for weeks because you'd injured something by overtraining."

"Yes, boss." She sighed, pretending like her interest in working out hadn't flown right out the window the minute he'd put his arm around her. "Breakfast then?"

"Sure."

Since the stove was out of commission until the gas-line issue was worked out, they ended up eating cold cereal while sitting on the kitchen counter. Instead of his usual position across the room from her, Chris had hopped up next to her, adding to the morning's oddities. Daisy wasn't complaining, though—she'd take this relaxed, affectionate mood over weird Chris any day.

"I love milk," she said, adding more to her bowl. "I think that's what I miss the most when Dad's delayed. No, lettuce. All fresh veggies, actually."

He frowned. "That's why I talked to Mr. Lee about getting your groceries delivered. If you want milk, then you should have milk."

"I told you," she said, poking him with the handle of her spoon, "I think it's a great idea. I just wish you'd talked to me about it first. When you make decisions for me, it makes me feel like a kid—a stupid kid who needs to be taken care of."

After a short pause as he chewed, he nodded. "Sorry. I'll work on that. I'm just used to doing what needs to be done. Hazard of the job."

"So, what you're saying is that I'm basically just another dead elk in the road you need to deal with?" She tried to narrow her eyes in warning, but her mouth kept wanting to curl upward.

"Sometimes. Other times, you're a domestic. Occasionally, you're a disorderly conduct."

Instead of her spoon, she used her fist to connect with his arm that time. Her fingers stung at the contact, but she refused to shake them and show it, especially when he just laughed.

"Speaking of disorderly conduct," she said, "has the psycho-in-training across the street taken his revenge on the red-haired girlfriend yet?"

"Not yet." He chewed with more force than the cereal required. "Her parents called a couple of nights ago when they heard voices outside. By the time I got there, the daughter was in the tree outside her bedroom window, hysterical. She'd been trying to sneak out to meet the Storvick kid but hadn't thought through her escape route."

Since her mouth was full of cereal, Daisy just raised her eyebrows in a request for him to continue.

"There weren't any branches lower than twelve feet off the ground, so she was stuck."

Her laugh came out as a snort. It took an effort to hold in her amusement until she'd swallowed. "How'd you get her down?"

"I couldn't. She was screaming and clinging to the trunk. Her parents' tallest ladder was only six feet, so I climbed up on that, but she was still above me. If she'd cooperated, I could've managed it, but I ended up having to call Fire."

"So they took a break from getting cats out of trees to get a girl out of a tree. Were Rory and Ian there?"

"Yeah. They weren't the ones to climb up and get her, though. Those two aren't the most..." He paused, as if thinking of the right way to put it. "They don't have the most...delicate touch of the firefighters, especially Rory. She would've been more likely to tell the girl to knock off the crying and get her butt out of the tree or else Rory was going to go get the tranquilizer gun." The image made Daisy laugh again. "Two other firemen, Soup and Steve, were elected. Steve has two girls of his own, and Soup—I don't know why Soup was picked. Maybe because of his teasing big-brother vibe? Whatever the reason, it worked. They eventually calmed her down enough to get her to release her death-grip, and then it was pretty easy from there—at least as far as I could tell. I was on the other side of the yard, talking with Ian and Rory."

"Did that convince her to dump Corbin for good?" Daisy's bowl just held milk, so she dumped in some more cereal.

Chris's shrug was doubtful. "Hope so. That kid is a problem."

"Do you think he was the one looking in the windows of the empty house?"

"Probably." He lifted his shoulders again. "There are a couple of other kids he hangs out with who cause just as much trouble as he does. It could've been one of them, too."

"Or a completely random kid who was bored and in the area."

"Yep."

Thinking of the teenaged trespasser made her brain jump to the possible dead-body disposal and then to the murder case. "Did you find out anything new about Willard Gray?"

He absently tapped his spoon against the rim of his empty bowl. "Just more questions, especially if the arsons are somehow connected. Thanks for recording your meeting yesterday—and for the pictures and notes. I'm planning on going through all that and trying to put it together in a somewhat coherent report before presenting it to Rob."

"Do you..." Feeling awkward about broaching the issue, since she knew her feelings about Chris's boss were much different than his, she hesitated. Curiosity made her finally just ask. "Do you have any idea who the sheriff suspects? Or if he even has a specific person in mind?"

"No." He reached to place his spoon and bowl next to the sink, and then he did the same with Daisy's. "It's making me crazy and paranoid, though. I'm looking at everyone suspiciously."

Since Chris was the only deputy she knew, Daisy didn't feel like she could be much help pinpointing who at the sheriff's department might be the murderer. "Any luck getting ahold of Macavoy?"

His mouth went tight and flat with frustration. "None. He won't return any of my calls or texts. Even though he said he was quitting because of a family issue, I called his mom—his emergency contact—and she didn't know of any 'family issue.' Also, she hasn't heard from him since he quit and took off. She gave me some names of friends and relatives of his, but they've all been dead ends so far."

"I'm sorry." She gave him a sympathetic grimace. "I wish I could help more."

Hopping off the counter, he looked at her in surprise. "You are helping, Dais. We've gotten more new information from you and your training buddies than we've found in weeks." He helped her down and stayed standing in front of her, close enough to make her breathe faster than normal. "It helps to talk to you, too, especially now that I have to keep my mouth shut at work, just in case the wrong person is listening."

His proximity was shutting down her brain, so she just bobbed her head like a dummy. "Good. I mean, I'm glad I can help."

"More than you know, Dais." He leaned closer, his gaze flicking from her eyes to her lips and back. Her stomach tightened in anticipation, but he turned his head slightly and pressed a kiss to her cheek. Even as the contact of his lips against her skin made her blood buzz with excitement, disappointment flooded her. She'd wanted a real kiss, not something a sister or grandma would receive. Shoving down her dissatisfaction, she told herself to enjoy their restored camaraderie and quit wanting more from him than he wanted to give. That was the road to becoming an angry, bitter old lady.

Chris pulled away and headed for the door. "I'm going to go home and grab a shower."

Lifting the collar of her shirt so she could sniff it, she nodded, scrunching her face to make Chris laugh. "Me too."

Her efforts were successful, and he chuckled as he unbolted the door. "Remember, it's a rest day, so no exercise of any kind."

"I might need to climb the stairs occasionally," she said, trying to keep her expression serious.

"If you absolutely have to go upstairs, then do it slowly." He winked at her as he left. "Bye, Dais."

"Later, Chris." Closing the door behind him, she started to turn the dead bolts, beginning at the bottom as she always did. When she reached the two chain locks, she fastened the first, but her hand stilled on the second one. Daisy'd had enough of longing and wishing for things to be different. To change, she needed to act. No matter how terrifying it was, the thought of a life trapped in her house, a life without Chris, was even scarier. With her heart pounding in her ears, she released the chain, letting it swing loosely against the door.

She took a step back, and then two, her eyes locked on the dangling, unsecured chain. The floor tilted beneath her, and she sat abruptly, not wanting to fall and hit her head if she fainted again. Her breath came fast and shallow, and her skin switched between hot and sweaty and clammy. To her relief, though, she stayed conscious.

Daisy wasn't sure how long she stared at that one unfastened chain lock before her body stopped freaking out and returned to normal—seminormal, at least. Her hands still shook slightly, and her stomach felt raw and sore, as if she were recovering from the flu. The sweating had stopped, though, and her heartbeat, although elevated, had slowed from its initial hummingbird speed.

With her hands pressed to the floor, she shifted to her hands and knees. When that didn't bring any waves of dizziness, she pushed herself to an upright kneeling position. Her vision blurred a little around the edges, so she waited until she was seeing clearly again before climbing to her feet.

Once she was up, she focused on the open lock again. It looked wrong, hanging there when the door was closed, and her fingers itched to secure it. Daisy resisted, though, turning to face the kitchen. She found it was easier when she wasn't looking at the chain, so she took a step away from the door and then another.

When she reached the study, Daisy lowered herself to sit in the chair. There was an anxious buzz in the back of her mind, telling her that something wasn't right. She could ignore it, though. She wasn't fainting or sweating or hyperventilating, so she could handle the slight uneasiness that urged her to run to the door and fasten the lock.

"I did it," she said quietly to the demon doll with teeth. A laugh bubbled out of her, unexpected and loud. "I did it!" Reaching for the doll, she almost grabbed it and hugged it, but then she pulled back her hand. It probably wouldn't be wise to let the toy of the devil that close to her jugular. The thought made her laugh again, and she spun her chair in a circle.

It was a single lock on a single door, but for today, it was enough.

As soon as it got dark, Tyler slipped through the trees to his favorite watching spot. All her blinds were pulled, blocking his view, but he still stared at the house. Anger surged through him at the thought of how much trouble and worry she was causing. There had to be something Tyler could do to help his dad.

Absently, he pulled his favorite Zippo lighter out of his pocket and began flicking it open and closed in a steady rhythm. His dad always told him he needed to think things through before acting. Tyler could manage that. He'd wait and watch and eventually know what he had to do to keep their tiny family of two safe—and he'd do anything necessary.

His gaze dropped to the lighter as the tiny flame flared to life.

Anything.

Chapter 13

"DID YOU FORGET ONE?" ELLIE ASKED, NODDING TOWARD the dangling chain.

"No." Daisy had been waiting for someone to notice. It seemed too small a thing to announce out of the blue, but she'd hoped someone would ask so she could share her tiny victory. "I'm leaving it open. It's been that way since yesterday morning."

Ellie's eyes widened along with her smile as she grabbed Daisy's arm and jumped up and down. "Daisy!" Her name was an excited shriek that brought the others rushing back through the kitchen in a stampeding herd.

"What's wrong?" Chris asked sharply, his cop eyes raking over them.

"Nothing's wrong." Like Ellie, Daisy couldn't stop smiling. The night had been hard—really hard. The open lock had haunted her, demanding that she go downstairs to fasten it, but she'd resisted. It had made it worse that she couldn't kick the stuffing out of Max to relieve some of her nervous tension, but she'd promised Chris to take a day of rest. Instead, she'd cleaned and paced and listed the dolls for sale and tried unsuccessfully to read and stared blankly at the television. It had been miserable, but she'd done it, and she was very, very proud of herself.

"Look!" Ellie gestured toward the door with a game-show-hostess flourish. Everyone stared at the unfastened lock except for Daisy. She'd found it was better if she kept her gaze away from it.

Lou was the first to react. With a high-pitched scream that put Ellie's earlier exclamation to shame, she lunged forward and grabbed Daisy in a tight hug.

"That's so awesome, Daisy," she said, finally releasing her so that Daisy could breathe. For a small woman, Lou was surprisingly strong. The others gathered around and gave her their sincere but more subdued congratulations. Chris stayed back, though, and Daisy sent him a worried look. She'd expected that he'd be the first to share her excitement.

"How long have you had that open?" His tone was even, but there was something in it that made the others come to a silent agreement to head toward the training room after a final round of pats and accolades.

Now that it was just her and an impassive Chris, insecurity began bleaching out Daisy's excitement. "I never latched it after you left yesterday."

He stared at the lock a long time before meeting her eyes again. "Daisy."

"What?" Her nervousness bubbled over, mixing with hurt. "I thought you'd be happy for me."

In two strides, he was right in front of her. "I am." He glanced at the lock again and blew out a hard breath as his gaze returned to her. "Dais. This is…incredible." Finally, he started to smile.

"Yeah?"

"Hell yeah!" With a whoop, he scooped her up into a hug and swung them in a circle. When he returned her feet to the floor, he kept one arm around her shoulders. "That's great, Dais. I'm so proud of you."

"I know." She laughed from sheer happiness. "I'm proud of me, too."

Shaking his head, he looked at the dangling chain again. "I can't believe it only took one session with the new therapist."

"It wasn't just that." Their conversation two nights earlier had been more of an impetus than the phone call with the psychiatrist, but she kept that to herself, not wanting to squash Chris's good mood with the reminder. "I was just...ready."

His arm tightened around her, squeezing her against his side. "Whatever the reason was, I'm just *glad*."

She smiled at the unfastened lock, happy that he'd realized such a small thing was actually a huge deal for her. "We'd better get to the training room. The others will be waiting."

"Sure." He steered her through the kitchen without releasing his hold on her shoulders. "I bet you're going to be bouncing off the walls in there."

"Finally!" Although she pretended to be annoyed, she couldn't stop grinning. "I've been dying to work out since yesterday."

With a fake gasp, he flattened his free hand over his heart. "Did you actually take an entire rest day?"

"I did." Ducking out from under his arm, she entered the training room first. "It nearly drove me bonkers, but I did it. Well, unless manic cleaning counts as exercising."

He frowned, considering that. "It probably does, but we'll give it a pass this time." His mock-serious expression melted into a smile. "Grab a jump rope."

"Yes, coach!" she barked, attracting everyone else's

attention. For once, she didn't mind having all eyes on her. She was too happy for anything to kill her mood. When she headed across the room toward the hook holding the jump ropes, she was practically skipping.

"Great," Lou groaned from the treadmill. "With Daisy all cracked out with excitement, she's going to be running circles around us today."

"She always runs circles around us," Rory corrected.

"True." Despite her resigned sigh, Lou grinned at Daisy.

Adding an extra hop as she crossed the rope in front of her, Daisy laughed.

Her sleepless night had an upside—she'd cooked enough food for an army. The training group demolished everything she'd made, plus the burritos and cookies that had been Lou and Callum's contribution, in under ten minutes. It was impressive and a little scary.

"Why burritos and cookies?" Ian asked. He'd won a battle with Chris over the final peanut butter one, and he held it close to his chest to protect it. "They don't really go together."

Lou shrugged. "I like burritos, and I like cookies. Therefore, burritos and cookies."

"But there's no theme."

"Are you going to eat that or just cuddle it?" Rory asked. Widening her eyes, she glanced between the treat and his face. His shoulders lowered in defeat as he held out the cookie toward her. Rory pounced on it with glee.

Chris gave an amused snort. "She just played you,

buddy. You're helpless when she puts on her big-eyed, starving-kitten-in-the-rain face."

Instead of getting offended, Ian just stretched an arm over the back of Rory's chair. "Pretty much. I like making her happy."

The responding "oohs" varied in tone from sweet to mocking, but Daisy was pretty sure all the guys in the room would give up their last cookie to make their women happy, even Chris—not that she was his woman. Despite his recent behavior, she tried to keep her hope under control. The last thing she wanted to do was drive him away by pushing for more than he had to give.

"Any new Willard updates?" she asked, changing the subject to derail her dangerous line of thinking.

"Thanks for reminding me, Dais," Chris said. "Walsh, would it be possible for me to get copies of those arson reports—and the wildland fire ones—from Chief Early? I went through Rory's notes, but I have some questions."

"Sure, I can get you copies, but not from the chief. He said his reports on the arson calls are kept in Records at the sheriff's department."

Chris's eyebrows snapped together. "What? No, they're not. Stacy even double-checked the files, and she couldn't find anything."

"That's strange." Frowning, Ian absently massaged the back of Rory's neck. Chewing the last bite of her cookie, Rory looked too blissed out to focus on the conversation. "I always keep a copy of all my reports, so that's where Rory got her notes. I can get you copies of those. They're just the ones for the calls I was on, though. It's not all of the arsons."

"It's not?" Lou sat forward in her chair. "If they're

not at either place, where do you think those reports ended up?"

"No idea." Chris's expression contradicted his words. He looked like he *did* have an idea, but it wasn't one that was easy to swallow. "Who has access to Fire's records?"

"Just the Chief has direct access, but anyone can request a copy. What about yours?"

"Anyone with a key card can get into the Records room."

"Which means all the deputies," Daisy clarified. It was looking more and more like Ellie's father had put them on the right track regarding Willard's death being linked to the arsons.

Chris nodded. "Plus Stacy, the records manager, and Paul, who does maintenance."

"What's your gut telling you?" Callum asked, looking at Chris, who twisted his mouth in a grimace.

"It's not being too specific."

"My vote would be Deputy Lawrence," Lou said, and then looked around the table at the surprised faces. "I'm just saying what everyone else is thinking."

"He doesn't fit Daisy's description." It was a testament to how bothered Chris was that he was so easily discussing the case with them. "She said that guy was bigger. Dais, can you show everyone that video you took?"

"Sure." She took her phone from her pocket.

"Video?" Lou repeated. "Of what?"

"Macavoy that night," Daisy answered absently as she pulled up her videos.

"Wait," Lou said. "You had video of the dead-body-toting deputy this whole time and didn't share? Daisy!"

Daisy wasn't paying attention to Lou's scolding,

because the video was missing. It had been the last thing she'd recorded, so it should've been right there. Frowning, she flicked through the thumbnails, checking her small collection of saved videos several times. "It's not here."

"What do you mean?" Chris asked. "I watched it. It was on there—what happened to it?"

Making a sound of frustration, Daisy scanned her videos again. "I don't know. It's just not on here anymore."

"Could you have deleted it by accident?"

Although Daisy started to protest, to say that there was no way she could have done something so careless, she stopped. No one else had access to her phone. It had to have been her. "I guess I must have. Sorry, everyone. It was really dark, though, so I don't think it would've helped much."

"You thought he looked taller than Deputy Lawrence?" Lou asked, still sounding hopeful that he could be a viable suspect.

"Yes, but don't assume what I saw had anything to do with the Gray case," Daisy warned. "For all we know, it was Macavoy doing exactly what he said he was doing. Have you had any luck tracking him down?"

"Not yet. It's like he just fell off the planet. None of the other deputies were close with him. Angel, one of the dispatchers, said she sent a couple of how-are-you messages to his personal email, but he didn't respond. The guy's disappeared. The way he ran and hid makes me pretty certain he's involved in *something* illegal." Blowing out a hard breath, Chris stood, looking at Ian. "Can I get copies of your reports on the arsons?"

"Sure. But since they're my reports, they won't have

the law enforcement angle. Most of them will read, 'Got there, dumped some water, went home.' You're welcome to look them over, though." He stood, as well. "I'll talk to the chief, too, and see if we can get some information on the arsons that happened when I wasn't on duty."

"No." Ian had barely gotten out the offer before Chris sharply shut him down. "Don't talk to Early about this yet."

His eyes narrowing, Ian leveled a hard glare at the deputy. "You think the *chief's* involved?"

Pacing parallel to the table, Chris shoved a hand into his hair and tugged. "Honestly, no. This whole thing is making me doubt everyone, though, so I can't discount the possibility. I just would rather you not tip him off that we're looking for a connection between the arsons and the Gray case. Not until we get a better handle on this."

After a pause, Ian gave a tight nod. "Fine. For now. I don't like keeping things from the chief, though."

"I know," Chris said. "So thank you."

"It's probably best if we don't share this with anyone beyond this room, then," Lou said. "You know how fast gossip spreads around here, especially among the emergency services groups. If this leaks out, the chief will definitely hear about it."

Ellie looked around their circle and snorted. "I think we have the only nongossipers in Simpson here."

"I'm probably the loosest lips of all of us," Lou agreed, "and I can keep my mouth shut." Callum gave her a teasing look of doubt, and she smacked his arm. "I can!"

"You know I won't be blabbing to anyone," Daisy said dryly. "Except for my dad, you guys are pretty much my entire social circle."

"Not for long." Lou bounced a little in her seat. "You already have one of the locks undone. Pretty soon, you're going to be visiting me at The Coffee Spot."

"And you can come to the range at my shop, so we don't have to shoot out of your upstairs window," Rory added.

"Road trip to Denver!" Ellie almost shrieked, flushing when everyone stared at her. "Sorry. I got excited." With a small smile, George rubbed her back.

Hearing the possibilities out loud made Daisy simultaneously terrified and thrilled. It could actually happen. Until she'd made a step toward going outside, she hadn't realized how resigned she'd been to never leaving the house again. With that one tiny unfastened lock, she'd relit a flame of hope in her chest. Daisy rubbed the spot, almost feeling the physical burn, and jumped when a hand landed on her shoulder.

"You okay?" Chris bent over so he could speak quietly in her ear.

She nodded, feeling the fire in her chest growing stronger. "I'm wonderful."

When everyone gathered by the door in preparation for leaving, Ellie pulled her back. Surprised, Daisy allowed the other woman to tow her to a corner of the kitchen. After a quick glance at them, George kept his distance, even if that distance was only ten feet.

"I just wanted to tell you how brave I think you're being." Ellie rushed the whispered words, as if she knew they'd have only a minute of privacy before someone crashed their conversation. "When George has to go on a search and rescue call during the night"—she took a quick glance over Daisy's shoulder, presumably to make sure he wasn't in hearing distance—"I get so scared when I'm alone out there, even with a deputy sitting in a squad car outside. Instead of sleeping, I prowl around the house, checking the door lock for the millionth time. George doesn't know it bothers me. If I told him, he wouldn't leave, and then whoever was lost in the wilderness wouldn't get George's help. They might die, all because I'm a chicken."

Daisy had no idea what the right thing to say was. It wasn't like she was the best person to be giving advice about anxiety. "I'm sorry."

Her mouth turning down at the corners, Ellie admitted, "I didn't used to be like this. I used to love being alone, until…" With a small shrug, she gestured toward the center of her chest.

"You were shot," Daisy said. "I think you have the right to be scared."

"I just wish they'd catch him. Not knowing if he's in Mexico or watching me from the trees outside my bedroom window is making me crazy."

Grabbing her hand, Daisy gave it a comforting squeeze. "I never sleep." When Ellie just blinked at that, she clarified, "I mean, I have insomnia. Next time George has to go on a call at night, give me a buzz. If you think it would help, I mean. That way, we can talk about something completely unrelated to murder or gun-toting psychos. Okay?"

Ellie's eyes got a little glassy with tears, but she smiled. "Okay. That sounds…good. There's something about being up at two in the morning that makes me feel like the only person on Earth, you know?"

"Oh, I know."

When Ellie focused on something over her shoulder, Daisy knew their private time was done. This was confirmed by George's rumbling voice.

"Ready?"

Her smile broadening, Ellie nodded. "Bye, Daisy. *Thank you.*"

"Anytime." As she followed them to the door, Daisy tried to analyze the odd—but good—sensation she was experiencing. She finally realized that she felt *helpful*. It had been so long since she'd offered a hand, rather than always being the one accepting it. Excitement fizzed through her, carbonating her blood. It almost felt like she was floating.

Everyone made their way through the interior doorway, chatting and shouting final good-byes to Daisy.

"I'll call you later," Chris said quietly in her ear. "I'm so proud of you."

When she turned to smile at him, their gazes clung. The voices in the background faded until it was just the two of them. When Chris stepped back, breaking the moment, Daisy had to resist reaching out to him, grabbing him and keeping him with her. Instead, she contained herself and just watched as he joined the others.

Once everyone was cleared from the entryway, she gave a last wave and closed the inner door. Each dead bolt slid home with a thud, and then she reached for the bottom chain lock. Before she could touch it, her fingers stopped in midair. Instead of latching it, she left both chains hanging uselessly against the door.

Raising her fist, she gave her usual "good to go" pound. She heard the exterior door open and her friends as they spilled out, talking and laughing as they headed to all the places she couldn't go.

Yet. She looked at the two unlatched chains and smiled. She couldn't go *yet*.

Chapter 14

THE KNOCK WAS SO HESITANT THAT DAISY ONLY HEARD it because she was standing by the door. She'd been staring at the final dead bolt for an embarrassing amount of time. Her hand kept creeping toward it, but she'd been successful so far in not touching it. The interior door was completely unlocked, and she would've been excited and proud if she hadn't been so close to screaming hysterically and possibly fainting.

At the hesitant tap, tap, tap, she jumped as high as if someone had slammed into the door with a battering ram. Her finger fumbled for the intercom button, but she hit the unlock one instead. Her entire body went rigid. Illogically, her main source of panic was not that she'd just let who-knows-whom into her house, but that there were no locks between her and the open door.

The edges of her vision went gray, making her only able to focus on that bottom, unfastened dead bolt. She was frozen, not even capable of reaching forward and locking the single barrier between her and the outdoors. The outer door resettled into place with a thud, followed by the click of the lock.

That tiny sound released her from her terror-induced paralysis, and she grabbed at the door. Before she could reach the dead bolt, though, reason wormed its way through her panicky thoughts and reminded her that the outer door was now closed. Compared to her recent overwhelming surge of fear, her twinge of nervousness at not knowing who was waiting between the doors felt inconsequential.

Another timid knock, on the closer door that time, had her turning the doorknob before she'd even thought it through. As she opened the door, Daisy saw a woman who couldn't have been an inch over five feet tall. Her strawberry-blond hair was in a pixie cut, and she was wearing black-framed glasses and a peach-colored pantsuit.

"Hello." The woman's voice was as tentative as her knock had been. "I'm so sorry to bother you, but I'm Natalie Sharp, with Mintle Real Estate?" Her voice went up at the end, as if asking Daisy if she recognized the name.

Daisy shook her head. The unexpected appearance of her visitor had knocked the panic right out of her, so she was able to function like a seminormal person. "Sorry. It's not familiar, but then I don't get out much. I'm Daisy Little."

"Nice to meet you." Natalie's hesitation faded, as if the polite exchange had allowed her to regain her composure. Stepping through the doorway, she held out her hand. As Daisy shook it, she reached over with her other arm to shove the inner door closed. Despite the lack of fastened locks, it was nice having a solid obstacle between her and the outer door.

The realtor peered around as if she was checking out what parts of the house she could see. Daisy figured it was probably a professional hazard.

"Did you need something?" Daisy asked when the woman had been silently looking around for a while. "We aren't interested in selling the house, I'm afraid."

"Oh, no." Natalie pulled her attention back to Daisy's face. "Although it's a beautiful place. If you ever are considering selling, here's my card." She pulled out a white rectangle and handed it to Daisy.

"Okay…?" Bemused, she accepted the business card.

Natalie gave a small laugh. "Oh, I'm sorry again. Your gorgeous ceramic tile floors distracted me. I just finished showing the house right across the street to a couple, and I was hoping you could answer a few questions for me about the neighborhood and…well, some other things."

The mention of the place Daisy had mentally been referring to as—in a rather morbid and not very creative way—the dead-body house brought all her attention to the realtor. Her near-mental breakdown was temporarily forgotten as curiosity took precedence.

"Did you want to come inside?" Daisy asked, gesturing toward the archway into the kitchen.

"Oh, I'd love to." Natalie was already heading into the kitchen. Giving the unlocked inner door a single glance, Daisy hurried after her guest.

"Would you like some coffee?" she asked. Although she was dying to know about the house across the street, she figured she should be polite. The realtor's questions would probably just be the standard and boring ones, like whether there were many children in the area or if anyone threw loud parties late at night. Daisy wondered if she should let Natalie know about Corbin and his destructive tendencies.

"No, thank you. I'm not really a coffee drinker." Natalie was closely examining the cupboard doors. "Did you recently remodel?"

"Yes." Since Daisy had a feeling that a conversation about home renovations could go on for hours with Natalie, she prompted, "You mentioned you had some questions about the neighborhood?"

"Oh, yes." Turning away from studying the countertops, she gave Daisy a wide smile. Despite the realtor's attempt at pretending to be at ease, she seemed nervous, which was strange. "As I mentioned, I showed the house to a young couple this morning. Very nice pair. They'd been looking in Connor Springs, but places in this area are a bit closer to their price range."

Daisy nodded, still trying to figure out what was making Natalie so tense.

"Do you know why the owners are selling?"

"They moved to Florida about eight months ago," Daisy said. "I wasn't...um, close with them, but I heard they were sick of the cold and snow. They were travel agents, so they switched from arranging ski vacations to beach trips. There were two kids, a boy and a girl, about ten or twelve? I'm not really good at guessing kids' ages." She didn't mention that it was especially difficult when you only had an oblique view of the children from an upstairs window. When they'd moved, Daisy hadn't been too sad, since the parents hadn't provided much entertainment, and the kids had liked to knock on her door and run away.

"Did anything...well, *unusual* happen there?"

Cocking her head to the side, Daisy repeated, "Unusual?"

"The husband noticed something on the ceiling of the living room." The realtor shifted her gaze from Daisy to the sink. "Very nice fixtures, dear."

"Um...thank you." This was an odd conversation. "What was on the ceiling?"

"Well, it was just a few dark-colored spots, and I didn't think anything of it. He became rather interested, since he was determined that it was...well, blood. He mentioned being an avid hunter, and said that he knew what dried blood looked like. Since it was such a small amount, just a few drops, I didn't think it was worth focusing on, even if he was right about it being blood."

Natalie paused, her eyes narrowing on Daisy's face. Daisy wasn't sure if the realtor was checking to see if she believed her story, or looking for signs of murderous guilt. Either way, Daisy kept her expression blank, and Natalie resumed her story.

"I pointed out the lovely stone fireplace and the two-year-old windows, but he wasn't paying attention. Instead, he was checking the floor and the walls — looking for more blood. He thought he found it, just a light pink swipe on one wall and a few traces on the floor. It didn't look like anything to get excited about to me. He kept asking what had happened, if someone had been seriously injured in that room, and if that's why the owners were selling. I told him it had been a relocation, but he'd already made up his mind that it was...well."

Natalie paused, looking flustered. Not breathing, Daisy waited for her to continue.

"He was talking as if it was a *murder* house or something equally ridiculous."

The word "murder" made the image of the deputy carrying the tarp-wrapped, body-shaped bundle resurface, and Daisy sucked in a breath.

The realtor stared at her. "Do you know something?"

"No." It wasn't really a lie, since Daisy didn't know anything for sure. "You should tell the sheriff's department, though, so they can check it out."

Natalie shook her head, her hands coming up as if to ward off any oncoming deputies. "Oh, no! I couldn't bother them with something so…silly. It was such a tiny bit of blood—if it *is* blood—that I would look like a hysterical fool if I told them about this. The client just made me paranoid with his theories of bloodshed and murder, so I knocked on your door on a whim. Since nothing actually happened there…"

"But what if something did?" Daisy asked. The tarp-covered form wouldn't leave her head. "Better it be a false alarm than have them miss an actual crime scene."

Her eyes widening at the phrase "crime scene," Natalie all but ran toward the door, skirting Daisy as if *she* were the killer. "It's a small community. I can't be known as the realtor who calls the cops on her clients. Please just forget what I told you. I'm sure it's nothing. Have a nice day! You have a beautiful home!" As she spoke, Natalie grabbed for the door and yanked it open, diving through it as if escaping from a haunted house.

"Wait!" Daisy lunged for the inner door, trying to close it before Natalie opened the exterior door. Her fingers fumbled, and the door banged against her hip before heading back to the wall. Self-preservation peeked out from her overwhelming panic and sent her to her knees so she would be closer to the ground in case she fainted. Her position made it harder to get out of the way of the door, though, and then it was too late. Natalie shoved open the exterior door.

Daisy's throat closed, making breathing impossible.

The rectangle of light burned its image against her eyes. She could hear the strange noises coming from her throat, but she couldn't get herself to stop making them. The usual darkness ringed her vision, shrinking her field of view until just a small circle of light remained.

That small bit of illumination disappeared. It took Daisy a few seconds to realize that she hadn't fainted. She blinked a few times, ignoring the burn as a droplet of sweat touched the corner of her eye. The light was gone because the door had closed. Just as that thought occurred to her, the sharp click of the exterior lock made the world return in a rush.

Shuffling backward on her knees, she got her body out of the way of the inner door and slammed it shut. As soon as it latched, Daisy twisted around to sit on the floor, leaning against the blessedly closed entrance. Her head fell back, landing against the wood panel with a thump. She didn't mind the slight ache, though. It actually felt kind of good, showing her that she was alive and she was conscious. She'd looked directly at the outside world, and she hadn't fainted. Sure, she'd freaked out a bit, but she'd survived.

Her fingers didn't seem to be working as she fumbled her phone out of her hoodie pocket. Daisy felt like she was wearing thick gloves as she tried to bring up Chris's contact and tap the screen to call him. On her first try, she dialed her dad's number by mistake, and she quickly ended the call. Her second attempt was more successful, and she raised her phone to her ear with shaking hands.

She laughed, too loudly, as the cell rang on Chris's end. Her hands weren't the only part of her that was shaking. In fact, her whole body was vibrating like she was a human earthquake.

"What's up, Dais?"

His usual greeting had her laughing again. It wasn't that she found anything funny, but she was just filled with such *relief* and the residue of her earlier terror that she had to laugh. There must have been an edge of hysteria remaining in the sound, though, because Chris's voice sharpened.

"Daisy? You okay? Talk to me."

"I'm good." Her teeth had started chattering, apparently feeling left out when all her other body parts were shuddering. "Both doors were open, Chris, and I was right there. It's okay, though. I'm okay. I didn't pass out."

"Dais, I can't understand you." There was a pause and some background noise before he returned. "I'm headed your way. Now tell me what's going on. Talk slowly."

"No, you don't have to come," she protested, but then her jumbled brain cleared enough for her to change her mind. "Actually, it's good you'll be here. You can check out the blood."

"Blood?" The tension in Chris's voice ratcheted up several notches. "What blood? Do you need Medical?"

"No!" She needed to immediately become more coherent, or Chris would send Fire, Med, and every on-shift deputy to her house. "I'm fine. Really. Mentally and physically. Especially mentally. Chris, I didn't faint!" Okay, maybe that wasn't quite as comprehensible as she would've liked.

"That's…good, I guess." It seemed to have helped a little, at least, since he was no longer threatening her with ambulances. "Whose blood are you talking about, then?"

"A realtor stopped by my house." Daisy was relieved that her words were coming in a more logical order. "She said there was blood on the ceiling of number 304."

In the following silence, Daisy could hear chatter from the squad radio in the background, although she couldn't make out any of the words. "How much blood? And why didn't she call it in? Hang on. I'm pulling up in front of your house now."

"Okay. I'll see you in a minute." She ended the call and scrambled to her feet, feeling like a newborn foal as she swayed, forcing herself to brace her weight against the door. By the time she'd managed to get upright, Chris's fist hit the outer door. Daisy pushed the unlock button and, before she could think about it too hard, yanked open the interior door.

"Daisy!" Chris's eyes went wide as he reached for her, his movement distracting her from the opening behind him. Her knees, which had just recovered, went wobbly again, and she clutched the edge of the inner door for support. Even through the haze of panic, she could feel it was easier that time.

The outside door closed just as Chris reached her, wrapping his arms around her in a half-hug, half-lift. Moving them both into the entry, he kicked the interior door closed behind them.

"Shit! What were you thinking?" His hands moved over her, as if checking for injuries. The idea that he thought she could get hurt by getting a glimpse of the outdoors made her laugh. Her amusement didn't seem to calm Chris, judging by the way his arms tightened around her.

"I'm okay, Chris." Her words were muffled by his chest, where her face was mashed against him. She tilted her head back to get some space between his shirt and her mouth. Having Chris's arms around her made her feel so safe and protected that she felt like she could do *anything*. "I didn't pass out the first time, and I just wanted to see if I could do it again."

"The first time?" He frowned, examining her face.

"When the realtor left in a hurry, I couldn't get this door closed quickly enough." She tilted her head toward it. "I freaked when she opened the other door, but I didn't faint or, you know, *die* or anything." Grinning at him, she felt his tight muscles ease slightly. It also brought her attention to the fact that the full length of her body was pressed against his. Her skin warmed at the front-to-front contact, and she knew her face was turning pink.

"Warn me first next time," he grumbled, although his hands had stilled on her back. "I almost had a heart attack."

"Me too." Although she tried to hold her serious expression, a giggle slipped out. "I did it, Chris."

"Yeah, you did." He spun her around, making her laugh harder and press her forehead against his chest so she didn't get dizzy. Being that close to him made her loopy enough. "That therapist you found must be a genius. You've had, what? Three sessions with him? Four? And you're about two steps away from walking out the door."

The idea of actually leaving the house cut off her laughter. "Not quite," she managed to squeeze out of her suddenly tight throat. "And it's not all Dr. Fagin's doing. When we talked about…Mom last week, and you told me your version of what happened, it just… knocked something loose in my head." Chris raised his eyebrows, and she shook her head. "In a good way. It was like I'd been in this loop, with my memories and nightmares and everything, and you shoved me out of it. I'm not explaining this well."

He smiled. "No, I get it. I think you knocked me loose, too." Instead of putting her down, he carried her into the kitchen with her feet dangling several inches off the floor. She laughed as he hoisted her to sit on the counter, giddy from excitement and triumph and being held so close to Chris for so long. "Now tell me about the blood."

Daisy repeated everything Natalie had told her, while Chris scribbled in his small notepad.

"Natalie…what did you say her last name was?"

Making a face, she admitted, "I don't remember it. Sorry. Oh, wait!" She dug into her sweatshirt pocket, pulling out the realtor's business card and glancing at it before handing it to Chris. "Here. It's Natalie Sharp."

"Thanks." Accepting the card, he slipped it into the notepad, which he then tucked into one of his BDU pockets. "I'm going to call Rob. He's talked to the owners recently, so he might be able to get them to allow us to search the place. If not, we'll need to get a warrant."

"Want me to go find somewhere else to hang out while you talk to him?" she asked, starting to move toward the edge of the counter in preparation of hopping down. With a shake of his head, Chris stopped her with a hand on her knee. He left it there, warm and heavy, and Daisy couldn't stop staring at it as he pulled out his phone.

"Rob. I'm here at Daisy Little's place." He frowned slightly at whatever the sheriff had said, and Daisy wished she had superhero hearing so that she could listen to both sides of the phone conversation. "That place across the street that's for sale? A realtor was showing it this morning and noticed some blood in the living room." Pausing, he gave a small shake of his head. "No, not much, just traces on the ceiling, wall, and floor. After that weird thing with Macavoy, I thought—"

He cut off abruptly, as if the sheriff had interrupted, and his frown deepened. "If you spoke to the owners again, and they gave permission for a search, then we wouldn't need to get a warrant." It was obvious, from Chris's scowl and the way his fingers were digging into her leg, that he was not pleased. "After what Daisy saw, we should at least—" The vein in his temple began throbbing in time to the muscle clenching in his jaw. He glanced at her and then looked away, his tone becoming stiff. "No, sir, she *is* a credible witness."

With a final quick squeeze of her knee, he moved into the living room. Daisy managed to stay where she was for almost three seconds before slipping off the counter as quietly as she could manage. Peeking through the doorway, she saw Chris's back as he headed down the hallway toward the training room.

Although she felt a slight pang of guilt, it wasn't strong enough to keep her from following. He'd closed the door, but it hadn't latched, so she eased it open just enough to hear. Chris's voice boomed through the space, making her jump.

"She's not delusional!" Even his pause vibrated with anger. "She has some anxiety issues. Her mom was shot in front of her when she was sixteen. I think that would mess up anyone." She heard his boots thump against the floor as he paced. "She's never been an attention seeker, and she's never had a problem separating reality from fiction. Besides, *she's* not the one who saw the blood." His footsteps got faster and hit harder. "Why not check it out? It'll only take me an hour to process the scene. If the owners give their permission—" The next pause was short. "But—" After another silence, his exhale came out like a growl. "I don't understand why—"

He'd stopped pacing, and the echoes against the high ceiling faded. "Yes, sir." His voice was stiff, almost robotic. "Of course, sir." There was another moment of quiet before an enormous crash made her nearly jump out of her socks. "*Fuck!*"

Unable to resist seeing what, exactly, Chris had killed in his fit of rage, Daisy pushed open the door and cautiously poked her head inside. He whipped around to look at her, and his expression was ferocious enough to make her want to duck right back out of there. Instead, she raised her eyebrows.

"All that noise from just a weight bench going over?" she asked, taking a step into the room.

He stared at her a long moment, his chest moving quickly with his breath, before he gave a short shake of his head. "The bench hit the weight rack."

As she moved closer to Chris and the overturned bench, she saw the hand weights scattered over the floor. "Ah."

"Sorry." The apology came from between still-gritted teeth. "I'll clean it up."

"Don't worry about it. It'll just give me more to do

at two a.m. when I can't sleep." She smiled, but he didn't return it, so she settled on another, upright bench. "What'd the sheriff have to say?"

The question made him start pacing again. "No."

"Just no? That was it?"

"Pretty much." He stomped over and straddled the bench so he sat facing her. "Well, that and I'm supposed to turn on my portable. Apparently, Dispatch has been trying to get ahold of me. Deputy Lawrence needs assistance with his current call."

"Oh!" Drawing her knee onto the bench, she turned toward him, surprised he wasn't hurrying out the door. "Shouldn't you go, then, if he needs help?"

Chris snorted. "I heard Dispatch send the call to him when I was headed over here. Some tourists are missing the spare-tire cover off their Jeep. They think it was stolen while they were at The Coffee Spot."

"Why would anyone want to steal a tire cover?" she asked, confused.

"No one would. It probably fell off somewhere, and they just noticed it now."

The conversation still wasn't making any sense to her. "So, why does Lawrence need your help with something so stupid?"

"He doesn't." Chris's smile held no amusement. "This is my punishment."

"Your punishment? For what?" Indignation raised her voice an octave.

Although he didn't get up and start pacing again, Chris did begin jiggling his knee up and down. "I don't get it. This isn't like him. If anything, Rob sticks *too* closely to the rules. Everything is black and white with him. He's a bulldog, too, about solving cases and enforcing the law. Why doesn't he want to search the house?"

"Could he be protecting Deputy Macavoy?" Daisy guessed. "Or maybe the sheriff just really doesn't like me, and it's clouding his judgment."

"That's another thing." He frowned, his leg still bouncing. It was strange to see calm Chris so agitated. Usually, he never had nervous tics. Daisy had always figured that she had enough anxiety for the pair of them. The more wound up Chris got, the calmer Daisy felt, as if there wasn't room for her neuroses anymore. It was an unfamiliar sensation to be the sane one, but Daisy kind of liked it.

"What is?" she asked.

"Rob's problem with you. Everyone else who's met you falls in love within five minutes, but Rob's determined that you're some delusional, attention-seeking psychopath." He gave her an apologetic glance. "Sorry. I didn't mean to tell you all of that."

"It's fine." She tried to force a smile, but his unhappy look deepened, so she couldn't have been very successful. "I figured as much, especially after listening in to your side of the conversation just now."

Chris gave her a brief, chiding look but let her admission of eavesdropping go surprisingly easily. She supposed they had more important things to discuss than her lack of manners. It baffled her how loyal Chris was to the sheriff, how he and Daisy's new circle of friends all thought Rob was a wonderful guy. It was as if he was a completely different person around Daisy than with everyone else. Was she seeing the real Sheriff Coughlin, or was he truly a stand-up guy, and she was just blinded by her resentment?

With a groan, Chris stood, interrupting her frustrated thoughts.

"I'd better go help Laurie with his tire-cover theft ring." He rolled his neck, as if stretching out the kinks of annoyance. "With Rob acting so out of character, I don't want to push him too far. If I get fired, the only job I'll be able to get around here is with Lou at The Coffee Spot."

"You could work for Highway Patrol," she suggested, taking his proffered hands and allowing him to help her to her feet. "I like their squad cars. Very sporty."

His laugh was a little rusty, but at least it was there. "I don't know if I could do traffic all day. I like my job—at least I *did*, before my boss went nuts on me."

"Why doesn't Simpson have a police department?" she asked, leading the way out of the training room. "Is it too small?"

"It's big enough to have one if they wanted, but the city council has always contracted with Field County. I think the idea of starting up a city law-enforcement agency is intimidating, and Rob's always done a good job covering Simpson, as well as the county."

They reached the front door, and Daisy turned, intending to say something, but the awed look on his face stopped her.

"Look at that," he said, running his fingers over the vertical column of locks, all unlatched. "I'm so proud of you, Dais." His gaze shifted to her face, and his expression of fierce pride made her feel like the most amazing woman in the world.

"Thank you." She turned her head to look at the door so she didn't give in to the temptation to blurt out how much she loved him and hurl herself into his arms. When her gaze settled on the unsecured inner door, she smiled broadly. *She*, Daisy Little, hoarding Amish grandma, had done that. It made her think that maybe, just maybe, she could have a future with Chris.

Right now, she felt like anything was possible.

Chapter 15

IT WAS HARDER THAN THE NIGHT SHE'D LEFT THE FIRST chain lock undone. Daisy couldn't stay still, much less sleep. Every time she paused, even for a second, she was overwhelmed with the knowledge that the inner door was completely unlocked. It didn't matter that the exterior door was locked, or that she lived in the tiny, mostly crime-free town of Simpson, or that she had a deputy on speed-dial. The unsecured door made her feel as vulnerable as if she were lying naked in the front yard.

She tried to think of something she could bake that didn't require eggs, but she was too distracted to do more than pull a few ingredients out of the cupboards. When she caught herself staring blankly into the sugar canister, Daisy decided that attempting to prepare edible food when she couldn't concentrate for more than two seconds at a time was probably a dangerous idea.

After putting away the items and cleaning the kitchen, she wandered into the study. Although the dolls still freaked her out, they were growing on her a little. It might have been because both were doing so well in their online auctions. Apparently, there were a lot of people who didn't feel that the antique dolls were toys of the devil.

She booted up her laptop. After deleting a few junk emails, she opened up an Internet browser. Only two minutes later, she shut down her computer, unable to sit still.

Checking the clock on the desk, she groaned. It wasn't even one yet, and it felt like an entire week had gone by since Chris had left to help Lawrence with the missing tire cover. He'd called her after he'd gotten off work, but he'd been distracted, so they'd ended the call shortly after she'd confirmed that she was doing fine.

Daisy wandered into the training room. Friday was officially her rest day, but she figured it could still be considered Thursday night, if she really wanted to lie to herself. She jumped and grabbed the pull-up bar, swinging back and forth like a kid on the monkey bars. When her hands started to sting from the friction, she lifted her legs up and over the bar, releasing the grip of her fingers so she hung upside-down by her knees.

Her spine popped as she dangled from the bar, and she thought of how different the room looked from her inverted position. When her face burned from too much blood flowing into it and her eyes felt like they were about to pop out of her head, she swung back and forth, flipping her legs off of the bar to land on her feet. Unfortunately, she couldn't stick the landing, and she fell back on her butt with a grunt.

Glad that she didn't have an audience for that ungraceful maneuver, she scrambled to her feet and headed for the treadmill. If she didn't do *something* physical, she was going to lose the battle raging in her head, run to the door, and fasten every single lock, erasing all of her progress.

As she settled into her warm-up jog, she thought about how Lou had mentioned at their last training session that she wanted to set up Daisy with a fireman named Steve. The thought of dating someone hadn't really occurred to her, except for her daydreams about Chris during unguarded moments. Lou's mention of the fireman, though, had her actually considering the idea.

The thought of dating a stranger made her stomach churn with a mixture of excitement and nerves. She tried to picture someone next to her on the couch while they watched a movie, or someone across from her at the dining room table as just the two of them shared a meal, or someone next to her in bed… Her insides clenched, and she shoved the last thought away. Even considering it felt like cheating.

Daisy growled as she increased the treadmill's speed, annoyed that she couldn't even think about dating someone who wasn't Chris without feeling guilty. They were only friends—friends who, up until a week or so ago, hardly even touched in a friendly way.

After they'd talked about her mom, though, Chris had touched her…a lot. Daisy reminded herself sharply not to read too much into the hugs and pats and knee-squeezing. They were still strictly friends, just huggier than they had been, and she was asking for awkwardness and long absences if she tried to push them into more.

Even her father didn't want to be in the same house with her, so Daisy wasn't sure why anyone else would, either.

"Stop," she said out loud, annoyed with her angst and self-pity. She hit the button to increase the speed several times, until all she could think about was moving her feet and trying to breathe.

Working out killed an hour of the endless night, and a shower used up another twenty minutes by the time she was moisturized and dressed. She was exhausted, having finally crashed from her adrenaline surge, so she decided to attempt sleeping.

"This is probably a bad idea," she muttered, pulling down the covers. She stared at the sheet-covered mattress for a while, but she just couldn't bring herself to lie down. As much as she longed for sleep, to be unconscious and oblivious until she woke refreshed in time for Chris's six a.m. breakfast visit, Daisy knew it wasn't going to happen. With a sigh, she headed for the window seat.

The second she sat, she was tempted to pop right back up again. Irritation with her restlessness kept her in place. Automatically, she checked each house across the street for any signs of movement. Ian and Rory's house was dark, with no light peeking around the shutters. Daisy couldn't remember if Ian was on duty or not. There was a reassurance to the idea that Ian and Rory were sleeping across the street, so she decided to pretend that Ian had the night off, and his house was not as empty as it looked.

The Storvicks' was almost equally dark, except for the dimmest glow from the younger daughter's bedroom. She always slept with a night-light. Corbin's computer must have been off or sleeping, since his window was pitch-black.

Almost reluctantly, Daisy shifted her gaze to number 304. Now that she knew there was blood in the living room, the building felt almost menacing. Had it really been a body Macavoy had been hauling out of the house that early, early morning? Was that where the blood had come from? If so, who was the poor dead person?

Her brain spun. No wonder Lou needed a whiteboard

or an oversized pad of paper to organize her facts and theories. Keeping everything in her head was overwhelming and confusing. Daisy felt like she was thinking the same thoughts, the same questions, over and over. She looked at her phone where it was sitting quietly on her nightstand, and she was tempted to call someone.

Ellie had said she had trouble sleeping, but only when George was on a search and rescue call. Daisy had no way of knowing when and if he'd be gone, and she didn't want to wake up anyone in the middle of the night. Just because she couldn't sleep didn't mean she should share her misery.

An odd glow in one of the upper windows of the vacant house caught her attention. She stared, thinking she had imagined it at first, but then it got stronger. The light reminded her of the Storvick girl's night-light, just a muted illumination that was almost lost in the ambient light from the streetlamps.

The color was more orange than the night-light, though, almost an eerie red. Scooting closer to the window, Daisy stared at the odd glow, trying to puzzle out the source. It wasn't right for a flashlight, although it might be if someone had a hand in front of the beam.

Although she didn't want to take her eyes off the mysterious light, she needed to let someone know about it. She jumped off the window seat, grabbed her cell phone, and returned. Instead of sitting, she put one knee on the cushions and leaned forward.

The light was brighter, flickering and dancing, and Daisy sucked in a breath as she recognized the motion.

Fire.

The house was on fire. Fumbling a little, she pulled

up the screen, planning to dial 9-1-1…but then she hesitated. If Libby or another dispatcher wanted her to talk
to the sheriff before they sent the call to the fire department, the house could be burnt to the ground before
anyone with hoses arrived. Instead, she pulled up her
contacts and tapped on Ian's number.

The ringing felt like it continued forever, and she
wanted to cry when Ian's recorded voice told her to
leave a message. "Hi, Ian, it's Daisy. The white house
that's for sale—the place two down from yours?—is on
fire. I'm going to call Rory. Oh, it's about two forty-five
in the morning."

She ended the call and called Rory. This time, there
were only three rings before she answered. Although
the other woman's voice was a little gravelly, she
sounded surprisingly alert, considering the time.
"Daisy. What's wrong?"

"The house across the street is on fire."

Daisy heard a sucked-in breath. "Ian's house?"

"No." Even though Rory couldn't see her, Daisy
shook her head. "Sorry. No. It's number 304. I see
flames in the upstairs window."

"Anyone inside?"

"I don't think so."

"Did you call Dispatch?"

"No. The sheriff—" Daisy cut herself off. It would take
too long to explain, and the orange-and-red flickering was
getting brighter. "I'll explain later. Can you call it in?"

"I'm on it." When Rory's voice came again, it was
muted, like her head was turned away from the phone.
Daisy figured she was giving the information to Dispatch
over her radio. "Daisy?"

"Yes?"

"Libby's sending out the call. I'm at the shop, so I'm going to grab my gear and head out, but Ian and the other guys should beat me there. We'll get there soon, okay?"

"Okay." Daisy wasn't sure why *she* was shaking. It wasn't like she was the one who'd be fighting the fire. "Thanks, Rory."

"Thank *you*, Daisy, for spotting it."

It was terrible, watching the flames get brighter as she sat there and did nothing. She couldn't take it any longer, so she focused her gaze on her phone. Chris would want to know, she decided, so she tapped his number. Like Rory, he answered quickly and sounded wide awake.

"Daisy. What's going on?"

"Hey, Chris. Sorry to wake you, but the house with the blood is on fire." She lowered her forehead to her palm. She'd been halfway coherent when she'd talked to Rory, so why had she gone into babbleland as soon as Chris picked up the phone?

"What? Did you call Dispatch?" he asked.

"No, because of the whole sheriff thing, but I got ahold of Rory, and she called it in." She heard the faint wail of sirens. "I hear them coming."

"Good. That was smart." His last words were muffled, and the phone crackled.

"Chris? Are you still there?"

"I'm here." The line sounded clear again. "I'm getting dressed. I'll call you when I'm in the squad, okay?"

"Okay."

The call ended, and she was back to being useless as the house burned. She looked away from the flames, trying to see if the fire had spread, but the other windows still looked dark. A shadow shifted on the far side of the house, grabbing her attention. She stared at the trees, trying to catch any other movement, but everything was still.

Deciding that it must have been her imagination, she returned her gaze to the glowing window. The sirens were getting louder, and the first engine turned into view, its flashing overhead lights blinding. To her relief, they cut the sirens as they pulled up in front of number 304.

The truck had barely stopped before three firefighters jumped out of the cab. Daisy recognized Ian, but the other two men were unfamiliar. They all seemed to know their individual tasks and moved with quick efficiency.

Lights turned on in the Storvicks' house. A second engine arrived, as well as a smaller truck. Daisy's cell phone rang in her lap, making her jump and hit her nose against the window. The screen showed it was Chris calling.

"Ow. Hi."

"Are you hurt?"

"No." Her voice sounded a little nasally as she rubbed the throb out of her nose. "Just bumped the glass. I'm fine. Fire's here."

"Good. I'm less than a minute out." His words were clipped like they got when he was in cop mode. "Did you see anyone in the house before the fire started?"

"No, but I thought I saw something moving by the far side of the house right after I called you. It could've been anything."

"I'll check it out." His squad flew around the corner

and stopped abruptly in front of her house. Daisy hurried downstairs, but he was already knocking by the time she reached the door. After she pushed the unlock button, she opened the inner door, focusing on Chris's large form rather than the gaping hole letting in the flashing lights from outside.

As he'd done before, he moved her bodily out of the way before closing the interior door. "It still blows my mind when you do that, Dais." His crisp cop-voice had softened. "You okay?"

"I'm fine."

His eyes did their own check, quickly sweeping her from head to feet. "Good. Show me where you saw the movement."

She hurried upstairs, Chris following close behind, and led him through her bedroom to the window seat. The area lights mounted on one of the fire trucks had been raised and illuminated, so the entire property was almost as bright as it would've been in daylight. "It was on the far side of the house, next to that squatty-looking pine tree. I just caught a flicker in the corner of my eye, so it could've been my imagination."

"Worth checking it out." He headed toward the bedroom door. "Call if you need anything."

"Okay," she agreed, although she wasn't sure what she might need while the neighbors' house was on fire. She watched him leave, thinking of how strange it was to not follow him. Since he was capable of closing the interior door, and the outer one locked on its own, she wasn't needed for exits anymore. The change was equal parts freeing and terrifying.

While Chris had been distracting Daisy, Rory had

arrived and was talking to the firefighter in the white helmet. From the way he was shouting orders and gesturing, Daisy guessed he was Chief Early. They'd gotten the front door open somehow, and Ian and another fireman—masks covering their faces and oxygen tanks strapped to their backs—were hauling hoses inside.

Rory was working on something by one of the engines, although she kept glancing at the entrance where Ian had just disappeared. Daisy tried to imagine watching Chris walk into a burning building, and her stomach cramped at the thought. Although she knew that his job was dangerous, it would be so much harder to actually watch him in action. Her gaze found her deputy making his way around the trucks and firefighters to the far side of the yard.

She watched Chris examine the area, squatting down at one point next to the pine tree she'd indicated. There was a flash of light in front of him, and she was confused for a second before she figured out that he was taking pictures. Another Field County squad pulled up behind the one already parked in front of Daisy's house, and the sheriff climbed out of the driver's seat.

After scanning the scene, he strode over to where the man Daisy presumed was Chief Early directed the other firefighters. The two spoke briefly before the sheriff's head snapped in Chris's direction. When Coughlin started toward where the deputy was still taking pictures, Daisy hurried to tap out a text to Chris, letting him know that the sheriff was headed his way.

Even though his back was toward her, Daisy knew when he read the text, since he turned around and waited for the sheriff to reach him. Despite the distance between Chris and her viewing perch, she could tell that his entire body was tense.

Their conversation was short, and it ended with Chris retracing his steps around the firefighters toward her house. After a cursory look around the area Chris had been examining, the sheriff returned to the fire chief's side.

Although Chris was clearly stalking toward her front door, Daisy was reluctant to stop watching the activity outside long enough to run downstairs and let him in. She knew she wasn't helping, but it still felt like she'd be abandoning the firefighters if she looked away for even a second.

Tamping down that illogical compulsion, she forced herself to tear her gaze from the window and hurry down the stairs. Even competing with all the other noise from outside, Chris's knock was loud.

Daisy pushed the button and opened the inside door. By the time the night was over, she figured she'd be completely comfortable with seeing the open exterior door.

Well, at least *more* comfortable.

"What's up?"

Apparently, she wasn't the only one becoming accustomed to her newfound bravery, since he didn't pick her up and move her out of the way that time. Instead, he stepped around her as he entered, allowing her to close the door on her own.

"I've been grounded," he gritted, heading for the stairs.

"Grounded?" Daisy followed him to her bedroom, where he alternated between pacing and watching out the window. Unwilling to give up her view, she ducked under the arm he'd braced against the wall and reclaimed her spot on the window seat. Chris didn't seem to notice and just watched the scene below them over her shoulder.

"Sent away like a kid who was acting up. I managed to get a few pictures of a partial shoe print in the mud by that tree you pointed out before Rob arrived. Good thing, too, since he ordered me back here after a verbal spanking."

"But..." With an effort, Daisy looked away from the hole being chopped in the roof of the burning house and focused on Chris's profile. "That makes no sense. You're just doing your job."

"Trying to, at least." His jaw muscles were flexing again. "He's got to be protecting Macavoy. I just don't get why he's covering for someone he's known less than a year. Blackmail, maybe? Could Macavoy have some kind of dirt on Rob?"

Turning her attention back to the window, she watched the action blindly as her thoughts spun on the hamster wheel. "We just assumed it was Macavoy because of the way he quit and ran. What if it wasn't? What if it's someone else?"

In her peripheral vision, Daisy saw him turn his head so he could look at her. "But he admitted to Rob that...shit."

As she met his gaze, she saw the dawning horror in his face. "Did you ever talk to Macavoy about it before he quit?"

"No." He shook his head, as if to deny the suspicions that had just popped into his brain.

Daisy hesitated before asking, "Is the sheriff close with any of the other deputies?"

His laugh had a bitter edge. "If you'd asked me that last week, I would've answered, 'me.' Rob's pretty remote. He keeps his work and personal lives separate."

"Who are his friends, then, off the department?" she asked. "Do you know?"

Shaking his head, he moved away from the window and started pacing again.

"This is small-town, gossip-fueled Simpson," she said when he didn't respond. "Someone has to know the sheriff's personal friends."

"I don't think he has any." When he reached her bed, he pivoted and reversed his course back to the window. "He works such long hours that he doesn't even have time for his son."

Remembering Tyler's comment about his dad not teaching him to drive, she grimaced in sympathy. "Poor kid. What about a girlfriend?" When Chris shook his head again, she made a sound of frustration. "Isn't there *anyone* he gets along with?"

Instead of answering, he paced in silence for a few minutes. "This isn't like Rob," he finally burst out, startling Daisy. "I've worked with him for over eight years. He's not—" Chris cut off his words as he made another pass across her bedroom. "He's one of the good guys."

Daisy hadn't gotten a good-guy vibe off the sheriff, but she kept that to herself. "We're just speculating," she said instead. "You know him much better than I do. What is your gut telling you about how he's been acting?"

He finally came to a halt behind her. Craning her neck, Daisy watched him settle his shoulder against the wall so he could stare out the window over her head.

"He's been...strange. Distracted. Evasive." Pausing,

Chris let out a deep breath, sagging a little harder against the wall. He looked tired. "Acting like he's hiding something."

Reaching behind her, she caught his hand and pulled it over her shoulder so she could hold it. "Whatever's going on, we'll figure it out." She injected as much confidence as she could into her words.

He shifted so he was standing close enough for her to feel his body heat against her back. Holding her breath, she eased back the half inch it took to make contact. When he didn't move away from her, she exhaled and leaned a little harder against him. Instead of jerking back, he wrapped his free arm around her upper chest. Despite her worry about what was going on outside, she was glad to be in his arms. Being held against Chris always made her feel so safe, even as the fire raged across the street.

They stayed like that, silently watching, until the firefighters put away their hoses and someone pounded on Daisy's front door.

Chapter 16

WHEN DAISY, FLANKED BY CHRIS, PUSHED THE INTERCOM button, it turned out that the "someone" was actually two "someones."

The fire chief, Winston Early, was an older man wearing bunker gear, minus the gloves and helmet. After she invited him and the sheriff into the kitchen, he introduced himself. His wide, beaming smile made her automatically return it. "Mind if we ask you a few questions, Daisy?"

"Sure." She kept her gaze on the friendly face of Chief Early. The sheriff loomed in her peripheral vision, and she was afraid she'd show her nervousness if she looked directly at Coughlin. "Was there much damage to the house?"

"The one bedroom is pretty much gutted, and there's a ventilation hole in the roof, but the rest of the house is salvageable. If you hadn't called Rory, we probably could've only saved the basement." The chief's smile widened.

"Jennings." The sheriff looked pointedly at Chris and then at the door. "Why don't you wait outside? I'll talk to you as soon as we're done in here."

Chris looked like he wanted to object, but he just nodded stiffly at Coughlin, squeezed Daisy's shoulder, and left the kitchen. Daisy watched him go. From the set of his shoulders, she could tell that he was unhappy about being dismissed.

"Okay, Daisy," the fire chief said, giving her another smile. "We'll make this quick. Why don't you tell us what happened tonight."

"There's not much to tell." She shifted her weight, wishing she could sit. Since she didn't want this interview to last any longer than it had to, though, she ignored her ingrained manners and didn't ask if the two men wanted to go into the living room. If they weren't sitting, then she didn't want to be, either. It would make her feel too...vulnerable or something.

"I couldn't sleep, so I was at my window seat at about two thirty. I saw an odd light coming from the left top window of the empty house across the street, number 304, and I realized it was flames. I called Ian, but he didn't answer, so I tried Rory, who called it in. After that, I called Chris. Right after I got done talking to him, I saw something move on the far side of the burning house."

That got both men's attention. "What exactly did you see?" the sheriff asked.

"Not much," she admitted. "Just something moving next to that funny-looking, squatty pine tree. I kept watching the area after I saw it, but that was it. Chris was taking pictures over there, though, of someone's shoe print in the mud."

The two men glanced at each other, and Daisy locked her teeth together so she didn't start defending herself. She'd seen what she'd seen, and there was nothing she could do if they didn't believe her.

"Ms. Little," Coughlin said, "how much sleep have you gotten over the past few nights?"

"About the usual amount," she lied. "Why?"

Instead of answering, he asked another question. "When you saw the flames, why didn't you call 9-1-1?"

Since she didn't think it was a good idea to tell them that the sheriff would have wasted too much time if she'd called Dispatch directly, she shrugged. "I was a little frantic, so I just started going down my recent calls list. Ian didn't answer, so I called Rory."

"Why have you been calling Walsh?" Coughlin really knew how to inject accusation into his even tone. "Aren't you and Deputy Jennings a couple?"

Her tired brain couldn't make the connection of why he was asking her that. She was tempted to say that she'd tell him the answer as soon as she'd figured it out herself, but she reminded herself that smart-assery was not going shorten this interview.

"Ian called to see if our training group was meeting last Wednesday," she said instead.

Both men looked at her blankly.

"There's a group of"—she counted quickly in her head—"eight of us. We work out in my home gym a couple of times a week." Shaking her head in a futile attempt to clear it, she shifted her weight again. Her legs were so tired that they were starting to feel rubbery. "I'm sorry, but what does that have to do with the fire?"

"Just trying to get all of our facts straight," Chief Early nonanswered. "Did you see anyone before you saw the fire?"

"No." She mentally reprimanded herself for not paying more attention, instead of freaking out about the unlocked door. "Sorry."

"Not your fault." The chief smiled at her again.

"Thanks to you, we were able to save most of the house, so it was a good night."

Although she returned his smile, the very last of her adrenaline was leaving her, and she was starting to sway. "Is that everything you needed?"

The two men exchanged another one of their cryptic glances, and she resisted rolling her eyes.

"That should do it." The fire chief was the one who answered. "We'll stop by or call if we think of anything else."

"Okay." When they didn't move, she turned and walked to the door, hoping they'd follow. They did, although they stayed several steps behind, talking in low voices that she couldn't overhear. "Do you think this is the work of the arsonist?" she asked, glancing over her shoulder.

Coughlin's eyebrows drew together in a fierce scowl. "How did you know about the arsons? Did Jennings tell you?"

"Just because I'm stuck in here," she said with attempted ease, trying to pretend that her stomach wasn't jumping around like crazy at his menacing look, "doesn't mean I'm not still in Simpson. Everyone gossips here, except for Chris. He never shares the details of his cases with me." That wasn't quite the truth, but he'd only told her about the minor, harmless calls, like the missing tire cover, and he never mentioned anyone's name. Besides, he wasn't the one who'd brought up the arson cases. The information had flowed *to* him, but not from him.

Early gave a wry grimace when she mentioned the gossiping, but the sheriff returned his expression to his typical emotionless mask, which gave Daisy the impression that he didn't believe her. Mentally apologizing to Chris for even bringing up the arsons, she opened the door, hoping to encourage the two men to leave before she said anything else that caused more trouble.

"Next time something happens"—the sheriff stepped close to her—too close—"call 9-1-1. That system is in place for a reason."

"I'm hoping this is the last time I'll need emergency services," she said, intentionally not agreeing to his command. "At least for a while."

"We hope so, too," the fire chief said. "Be safe, Daisy."

"Thank you."

After a final hard glance, Coughlin followed the other man out. Closing the door behind them, Daisy fought the urge to throw every last lock and then hide under her bed. Before she could follow the impulse, though, her cell chirped. When she dug the phone out of her pocket, she saw it was a text from Chris.

OK if I stay over tonight?

Without hesitating, she sent back a *yes*. It would be a relief to have his company, even if they didn't end up spooning on the couch again. The memory of waking up with him pressed to her back and his arm over her waist made her flush with heat. The phone chirped again.

Need to talk to Rob, then I'll knock.

Her thumbs flew over the screen, and she sent the text without thinking about it too hard. If she allowed herself to dissect everything she sent to him, each text would take an hour of agonizing.

    Great. I'll be waiting.

———

It wasn't very long before Chris knocked, but she'd still managed to doze off while she waited, sitting on the tile with her back against the door. Her body wasn't very cooperative, and it took her a few tries before she could scramble to her feet and reach the unlock button.

Turning the doorknob, she pulled it toward her as she backed against the wall, letting the position of her body and the door block any sight of the outside world. She wasn't going to start backsliding and locking the door again, but her tired brain had had enough shocks for the night…or day or whatever. She yawned so widely that her jaw cracked.

The knob was pulled gently from her grip as Chris stuck his head around the door. "You all right back here?"

Since she was in the middle of another yawn and couldn't talk, she just nodded, making him laugh.

"Okay, sleepyhead." He pushed the door closed and took her hand, tugging her away from her leaning position. "It's bedtime." When she resisted, not wanting to leave the support of the wall behind her, he grabbed her other hand and pulled. "C'mon. You look ready to fall over."

That's how she felt, too. With a groan that made him laugh again, Daisy peeled herself off the wall and allowed him to tow her toward the stairs.

"What'd the sheriff have to say?" she asked through yet another yawn.

"More of the same." The amusement slipped from his expression as grimness replaced it.

"Sorry." She squeezed his hands.

"Not your fault." Shifting around behind her, he urged her up the steps with a hand on her lower back. "I'm just glad my days off start tomorrow so I have some time to try to figure this out. If I'd been sent on one more bullshit—sorry, Dais—call, there's a good chance I would've punched Rob in the throat."

"Not a good thing to do to your boss," she mumbled, weaving a little as he steered her into her bedroom.

He gave a short laugh. "Not if I want to keep him as my boss, or if I want to stay in law enforcement instead of becoming a mall cop." His hand fell away from her back as she turned to face him. "What's that look?"

"I'm trying to picture you as a mall cop." Shaking her head, she frowned. "Sorry. I just can't see you in anything but this uniform."

His grin was a little crooked. "Good thing I kept my fists to myself, then."

Her response was interrupted by a yawn.

"Bed," he ordered, pointing.

"Fine," she grumbled, putting her phone on the nightstand before pulling her hoodie over her head. The tank underneath started to come along for the ride, and she grabbed it, tugging it to cover her belly again. The neck of the sweatshirt was narrow, and it caught around her face.

"Problems?" Along with amusement, Chris's voice also held something deeper. When she answered with a bad-tempered grunt, he laughed, and then his hands were there, easing the hoodie off her head.

"I forgot how much I don't like that sweatshirt." She glared at it balefully as she tossed it over her desk chair. "It's for laundry-day-only use."

Without thinking anything except how tired she was, she shoved her yoga pants over her hips and let them drop to the floor. It took Chris's harsh inhale for her exhausted brain to realize that she'd just stripped her lower half to her *underwear* in front of him.

"Sorry!" she yelped, diving for the bed. Her coordination was off, thanks to exhaustion and half-naked panic, so she tumbled onto the mattress in an ungraceful heap. As she tried to pry the top sheet out from underneath her, she babbled. "I don't like to sleep in pants, since they tend to wrap around my legs if they're loose, but I don't like leggings, either, so that's why I—what is wrong with this sheet?!"

"Lift up." When she obeyed, he yanked the recalcitrant bedcovers back far enough for her to finally get her legs under them. Even with her bare lower limbs hidden, she still felt exposed, so Daisy pulled the covers up to her chin. Chris stood by the bed, an unreadable expression on his face.

"Sorry," she said, a little more calmly now that she was buried in blankets. "I didn't mean to flash you."

To her surprise, he grinned at her. "You still had too many clothes on for flashing. It wasn't even indecent exposure yet."

"It felt indecent," she grumbled, although his laugh forced her to smile. "And I'm a terrible hostess. Did you want to sleep in Dad's room? The sheets are clean."

"The couch is fine." He sat by her hip, and she could feel the heat of him, even through the covers. "It's comfortable."

"Okay." Her eyes couldn't stay open anymore. "I'll get you some blankets."

He snorted. "You're not going anywhere except la-la-land. I'll get my own blankets."

"Mm-kay." Any plan that didn't involve her getting out of her warming nest of a bed was fine with her. "Linen closet's by the bathroom."

"Got it." Something brushed her forehead, but her eyelids refused to lift so she could see what it was. "Good night, Dais."

"'Night, Chris."

Chapter 17

SOMEONE WAS IN THE HOUSE. IT WAS TOO DARK TO SEE, but Daisy could feel the staring eyes, hear the raspy breathing. Her shaking hand reached for the bedroom lamp, and she turned the switch, but nothing happened. The room stayed draped in blackness. Sliding out of bed, the floor cold against her bare feet, she crept toward the door. The shadows moved, shifting into menacing shapes. She had to get downstairs, but the doorway kept sliding farther away, as if the house was taunting her, trapping her. When she tried to run, it felt like she was moving in slow motion. He was going to catch her, hurt her. She needed to get away, but she couldn't. She couldn't stay, couldn't leave, couldn't run, couldn't scream—

"Daisy!"

Her eyes popped open, and she sat up abruptly. Chris jerked out of the way, barely avoiding a clash of foreheads. It took a moment to adjust to reality, but then the familiar shapes of her bedroom stood out in the gray dawn light. Her first breath hurt her throat, before her breathing slowed, as did her heart rate.

"Chris? What are you doing in here?" He was sitting on her bed again, almost exactly where he'd been when she fell asleep. If not for his crazy bed head and the fact that he was wearing fewer clothes than he had been earlier, she would've thought he'd been sitting there the whole time.

"I heard you." He pushed some stray strands of hair out of her face. "I figured you were having a nightmare. Your mom?"

"No." She blinked. "No. It wasn't my mom. Wow. This is the first nightmare I've had in years that wasn't about her."

"What was it about?" His hand brushed her hair again, but she didn't think he was dealing with unruly strands anymore. Instead, it was almost like he was stroking her.

"Someone was in the house." When he lifted his eyebrows, she shook her head, starting to smile. "Not you. Someone...scary. I wasn't screaming, was I?"

"No. It was more like whimpering."

When she eyed his face and saw no signs of teasing, she groaned in embarrassment. Falling back so her head hit the pillows, she pulled the covers over her face. Despite the muffling effects of the blankets, she heard him laugh as he tugged them from her grip.

"Shove over," he ordered. "It's only been an hour since everyone left. That's not enough rest to keep from going insane from sleep deprivation."

Too startled to protest, she scooted to the side as he slid into bed with her. Even with a few inches between them, she felt his warmth, and it was tempting to curl into his side and use him as an oversized heating pad.

"What are you doing?" she finally organized her half-awake and scattered thoughts enough to ask.

"Trying to sleep," he grumped. "If I'm here, maybe you won't wake me up with your sad little noises."

"Sad little..." She poked him in the side, hard. "Soon you'll be the one whimpering." She jabbed him again. Laughing, he caught her hand.

"I don't whimper," he said, making her even more determined to reduce him to tears. He reversed the assault, though, finding all her ticklish spots and showing no mercy, even as she shrieked with laughter. He rolled her beneath him, holding her down with his body weight as his fingers dug into the sensitive places on her sides.

"Okay," she panted, an occasional hitch of leftover giggles interrupting her words. "You win. No more. I give up." Obviously, she wasn't going to win in a tickle fight with Chris. She vowed to find his weakness eventually, though, and fully exploit it.

Although she'd expected triumphant crowing from Chris, he'd gone serious. His breath was coming fast—she could see his chest move—and his expression was intent. The look in his eyes made her heartbeat speed up from something other than exertion, even before his gaze dropped to her lips.

He lowered his head slowly, checking her expression every few seconds, as if expecting her to protest. All she could manage to do was lie still and wait for his mouth to descend to hers. For a second, she wondered if her dream had just shifted topics, since she'd never truly believed her relationship with Chris would reach this point.

When his lips touched hers, however, she knew she was awake. It was too intense, too incredible, too *real* for something created by her imagination. Even though he kept the contact light, the sensations radiating from her mouth made her dizzy. She slid her fingers into his hair. That way, she could play with the silky strands while also making sure his lips didn't leave hers.

The kiss got a little deeper, a little harder, and Daisy discovered that his hair was just long enough to grab. From his heavy breathing, she was pretty sure he didn't mind the light tugs on his scalp. It had been a long time since she'd been kissed, since the fumbling experiments in high school, but she didn't worry about her technique. Her brain was completely occupied with feeling, so there was no room to think.

When he nipped on her bottom lip, she sucked in a quick breath. Chris took advantage of her parted lips, invading her mouth with his tongue, and she groaned. As if that sound was a trigger, he went wild. Rolling them so they were on their sides, he freed his hands to roam—and roam they did. Despite being distracted by his lips and teeth making their way down the side of her throat, Daisy was intensely aware of the placement of those hands.

With her head tilted back to give his mouth access to her neck, she moaned as both of his palms slid under the hem of her tank top. That motion gave her hands the green light to explore, and she slid them over the back of his head and down his neck. His bare back was hot beneath her touch. She was fascinated by the shifting of his muscles under his skin.

She stroked his shoulder blades, making him shiver as he nipped right above her collarbone. Jerking in his hold, she unintentionally dug her short nails into his back, and he made a hungry noise in response. Surprised by his reaction, she curled her fingers again, and he made the same sound. Daisy smiled, liking that she could drive him just as crazy as he'd been making her for *years*.

His head rose, and her happy expression changed to

a frown. "Why are you stopping?" She cringed at the slight whine in her voice, but it couldn't be over so soon. She'd waited such a long time for Chris to make a move, and they'd barely started kissing. Daisy wanted more time—much more. Even if her issues meant they would never have a future together, she at least wanted the present.

"You okay?" His voice was hoarse and breathless, his pupils dilated more than the dim room required.

"Not if we're stopping," she said.

He laughed, just a short huff. "You're sure you want this?"

"Yes. Now quit trying to talk it to death and get back down here." Both of her hands returned to his head so she could pull his mouth down to hers. His chuckle was cut off abruptly, but she still felt it against her lips. Then the intensity returned, and neither of them were laughing.

He pulled back, attempting to peel her tank top over her head. Once she figured out what he was trying to do, she quit chasing his lips and pushed up to a sitting position. His expression turned wary, as if he thought she might be pulling away, but he relaxed when she grabbed her bottom hem and yanked it up and off.

Chris made another one of his wordless sounds. "You're beautiful."

The cool air hitting her skin made her realize how exposed she was, sitting in just her panties, but the feeling was short-lived. Chris grabbed her, pulling her over him as he turned onto his back so their bare chests were pressed together. It felt like an electric shock when their skin connected, only without the pain.

Daisy sucked in a breath, her eyes closing as she absorbed the unfamiliar sensation.

"Okay?" Chris asked, and she nodded, her eyes still shut.

"Mm."

"Is that a good 'mm' or a bad 'mm'?" Although he still sounded breathless, there was a thread of humor running through his words.

Opening her eyes, she lifted off him enough to glare. "Well, it *was* a good 'mm' until you got the giggles."

"I don't *giggle*." He sounded quite offended, which, contrarily enough, made Daisy want to laugh. She kept her expression serious with an effort.

"Or whimper."

"Exactly." His eyes narrowed in a way that made her shiver. "Were you planning on talking some more, or can I kiss you again?"

She made the motion of zipping her lips. With a growl, he lunged up to meet her mouth, pulling her head down at the same time. Flipping her onto her back, he straddled her with his knees on either side of her hips. His hands stroked over her shoulders and cupped her breasts. The heat that ran through her almost brought her off the mattress.

His mouth followed his hands, and that was even better. As he kissed and nipped over the sensitive skin of her belly, his fingers hooked into the sides of her panties. He skimmed them down her legs and off, and Daisy tensed when she realized she was completely naked.

"Wait…" she started, but then his fingers and his mouth landed between her legs. "Oh! I changed my mind. Don't wait! Please, don't wait."

The vibration of his chuckles against her made her squirm and clutch handfuls of his hair again. As the tension built, she tugged harder. A tiny part of her worried that she was hurting him, but she was too caught up in the new and crazily intense pleasure to let go.

"Am I—oh!" She jolted at an especially electric touch of his tongue.

He lifted his head just enough to ask, "Are you... what?"

As his breath blew against her most sensitive spot, she forgot for a moment what she was about to say. "Am I pulling too—mm, that's nice—hard?"

The feel of his husky laughter almost made her levitate. "No." His teeth lightly scored her inner thigh, and she sucked in an audible breath. "It's making me hot."

She liked that, liked that she was doing something to turn him on. It was wonderful being on the receiving end of his ministrations, but she wanted to give, too. Knowing that he was just as excited added to her pleasure, and soon she was lost again to sensation.

Chris seemed to know exactly what to do, where and how to touch her in the best way. Pressure built inside her as her blood rushed faster and her skin heated. She couldn't keep still, but twisted and writhed underneath him, tugging at his hair. Her body bowed upward as she came, pleasure surging through her until it was her entire world. Eventually, she collapsed back onto the bed in a boneless heap.

Her fingers ached as she released his hair, petting the strands in remorse. "Sorry I pulled your hair so hard." Even to her own ears, she sounded a little drunk.

He crawled to lie next to her, propping himself up on

an elbow. To her relief, he was smiling. "I told you it didn't hurt." Leaning down, he kissed the corner of her mouth. "I liked it."

"You're weird." She smiled back. As her body recovered, she expected Chris to start kissing and touching her again, but he just played with a strand of her hair and occasionally kissed odd places, like the bridge of her nose or her chin. When she shivered, he went hunting for the covers that had gotten tossed aside in the excitement and pulled them over both of them.

Turning onto her side, Daisy looked at him, a little confused. "Um...is that it?"

His grin was devilish. "What's wrong? Did I leave you unsatisfied?" The last word was almost a purr, and it made her clench her thighs together.

"No. *I'm* very satisfied." Her glance darted to approximately midway down his covered body. "But you weren't."

That time, his kiss glanced off her ear. "I'm fine. Next time, I'll come prepared."

"Prepared?" It took her a few seconds before she figured it out, which made her feel a little slow. "Oh! Right. Sorry. I'm not prepared either."

He grinned. "Yeah, I didn't expect you'd be."

For some reason, his assumption annoyed her a little. "Don't worry about it, though. I'll add it to the grocery list I send to Tyler."

It was gratifying how wide Chris's eyes went. "What? No, don't do that. I'll just bring them next time."

"That's okay." She bit the inside of her lip to keep from smiling. "It'll be good to have a supply around. I mean, what if I do have an at-home date with Fireman

Steve? He sounds like a nice guy. It's probably good to have a stash, just in ca—"

His mouth came down roughly, cutting off the rest of her words. Daisy didn't mind being interrupted.

"Just to be clear," he said when he finally lifted his head, his voice an odd mix of hoarse and stern, "we're dating. As in, *exclusively* dating. So, no Fireman Steve."

She smiled, cupping his face with one hand, just because she could, because they were *dating*. Finally. "No Fireman Steve."

"Good." He settled onto his back next to her.

After a few minutes of silence, she asked, "Why now?"

"Why now what?"

"You've had eight years to make your move." She stared up at the ceiling. "Why didn't you do anything before this? I mean, you didn't even want me to touch you up until a few weeks ago."

Rustling noises told her he was shifting, but her focus stayed on the ceiling until his face blocked her view, forcing her to meet his gaze. "First of all, if I'd made any kind of move during those first two years, it would've been creepy. And illegal. You were *sixteen*. The next three or four years after that, it would've still felt wrong. The last few years, I couldn't stop thinking about it. That's why I didn't want you hugging me. I was so wound up that any contact would've destroyed my willpower. It was pretty shaky as it was."

"So? Why not act on those thoughts once I was old enough?"

With a groan, he rolled over to his back again. "I figured you wouldn't be interested."

"Not interested?" She turned onto her side so she

could see his face. "Are you kidding? I was practically screaming my interest. I tried to *kiss* you."

The vein in his temple started throbbing. "I figured you were just lonely, and I was handy. I mean…" His jaw flexed, making his next words come out tightly. "Why would you be interested in the guy who got your mom killed?"

All of Daisy's breath left her in a whoosh, leaving her unable to speak for a full minute. She finally managed to force out the words. "What? I never blamed you."

"Yeah." He glanced at her quickly and then returned his gaze to the ceiling. "When we talked about it that night, I finally got that. After all these years, it was just hard to change my thinking, you know?"

"I know." Tucking her body close to his side, she laid her cheek on his shoulder and stretched her arm across his chest. It felt strange to be lying there like that with Chris, but it also felt right. Even though she didn't expect it to last—how could it when she couldn't leave her house?—she was going to enjoy every second of this closeness with Chris. "Just so we're clear, my mom's death wasn't your fault."

He burrowed his arm underneath her so he could wrap it around her. "I shouldn't have hesitated."

"Not your fault."

The silence continued for so long that Daisy began to doze.

"Okay, Dais," he said quietly, the air from his words warm against her head. "Okay."

A sleepy smile touched her face as she closed her eyes again. He'd sounded as if he was starting to believe it.

"Sorry I texted my list to you so late," Daisy said, opening the interior door to let Tyler inside. Each time she got a glimpse of the outside, it got easier. Her next plan was to have someone hold the door open while she took a step toward it, but that would wait. She wanted to savor the day, to enjoy the knowledge that she and Chris were actually dating, without dealing with a potential anxiety attack.

"That's okay." Holding two grocery bags in each hand, he flicked his head to the side, tossing his bangs out of his eyes. His gaze was focused on her shoulder. "You probably were up pretty late. I heard about the fire."

Daisy reached for the bags, but he turned, holding them out of reach.

"I'm supposed to put everything away," he said, still not meeting her eyes. "It's part of my job."

She studied him for a few seconds. "Okay." Although she really didn't want someone else putting away her groceries, since it was a good way to lose the peanut butter in a cupboard she never opened, Tyler appeared determined. Something was off about him. He seemed unhappy, and she didn't want to make his day worse. Maybe she could turn her search for her missing groceries into a treasure hunt. It could be fun.

Leading Tyler into the kitchen, she asked over her shoulder, "Did you want a coffee?" From the distaste he'd tried to hide the last time he'd had it, she expected him to decline, but he nodded, instead.

As she started his mocha-flavored coffee, he began putting her groceries away in sullen silence.

"You okay?" she asked.

One of his shoulders lifted in a shrug.

"Trouble at school?" She didn't know if she should pry, but the quiet was uncomfortable, especially since he'd been chatty last time. Besides, she felt bad for the kid, apparently friendless and with the sheriff for a father.

"No. It's almost done for the year, anyway." His mournful tone didn't match his words. Weren't kids supposed to be excited about summer?

"Everything okay with your dad?"

"Why?" He almost dropped the milk, barely catching it before the glass bottle hit the floor.

"Just trying to guess what's wrong." And succeeding, judging by his reaction. "When I was your age and something was bothering me, it was usually something at school, or my parents were driving me crazy." Her smile slipped away. "After my mom...died, it was a different story."

"Your mom died?" He finally met her gaze.

She nodded. "She was shot during a gas station robbery."

"Shit! How old were you?"

Daisy wondered if she was supposed to reprimand him for swearing, but then she just shrugged it off. "Sixteen."

With his hip propping open the refrigerator door, he focused on the egg carton he was holding. "That sucks."

"Yeah." The understatement almost made her laugh. "It does."

"My mom's crazy." Meeting her eyes briefly, he dropped them to the eggs again. "Full-on wacko. Not, like, a little bit crazy, like you." His head came up, and he stared at her, stricken. "I...I mean..."

Taking pity on his obvious consternation, she smiled. "I know what you mean. Don't worry about it. I'm fully aware I'm not juggling with a full set of balls." When she heard the words as they left her mouth, she frowned. That seemed like an inappropriate thing to say to a teenager.

Tyler didn't appear to be offended. "She left. My mom, I mean. She used to come back once in a while, but then, one day, she was gone for good."

"I'm sorry." Daisy felt like a self-pitying ass. She'd had a great mom for sixteen years, and now Daisy couldn't leave the house. This poor kid had a messed-up mother who'd left him, and Tyler seemed to function just fine. She even felt a spark of sympathy for the sheriff.

"It was better, actually, when she left." If he squeezed the carton any harder, he was going to crush her eggs. "She could be...mean."

Overwhelmed with pity for the kid, she took a step closer to him. She wasn't sure if she was planning to hug him or what, but he turned around before she could do anything.

"Sorry," he said to the interior of the fridge. "I'll just get your groceries put away."

"Thanks, Tyler." She stared at his back for a moment, wishing she could do something for the poor kid. A knock drew her attention to the door, and she hurried over to push the intercom button. "Hello?"

"It's Bill," the familiar voice of the package delivery service answered. It was strange that Daisy knew his voice so well, but she'd never seen him. Their routine was for her to leave any shipments between the doors, but that was one more thing she'd forgotten during her discombobulated morning.

"Hey, Bill. Give me a minute, would you? I need to grab the boxes from the study."

"No problem."

As she moved through the kitchen, she said, "I'm sending out a few packages, Tyler. Help yourself to milk and sugar for your coffee, and I'll be right back."

"Sure." Tyler sounded depressed again. Obviously, she'd done the wrong thing by discussing their dead and insane mothers to try to cheer him. Grimacing, she hurried to the study, trying to think of different conversational directions that might make Tyler feel better, instead of worse.

The grimace turned into a smile as she toted a stack of carefully wrapped packages toward the front door. "Good-bye, demon dolls." They'd both sold for much higher than she'd expected, and now they were leaving the house. It was a good day. "Soon you'll have brand-new families to terrorize—especially you, Fangs."

Shifting the boxes around to free up one hand, she pushed the unlock button. Bill's eyes went wide when he saw her standing there, holding open the inner door.

"Daisy! Nice to meet you in person, finally." He looked pretty much how she'd pictured him, with a graying goatee and a good-sized belly. His smile was warm and wide.

"You too." She grinned back at him. "Pretty soon, I'll be meeting you at the curb."

"Can't wait." He took the boxes from her and retreated through the outside door. "See you next time!"

"See you." Giving him a wave, she made herself wait

until the outer door had closed completely before shutting the inside one. As she headed back for the kitchen, she turned one of her steps into a skip. It really was a good day.

"So, Tyler—" Her words stopped as he brushed by her, almost running toward the front door.

"Gotta get back to work." He didn't look at her as he yanked open the inside door.

"Okay. Bye," she called after him. The door closed with a thud, and she stared at it for a moment. "Weird kid."

With a shrug, she headed into the kitchen to see if she could find all of her groceries. Two and a half bags were on the counter, waiting to be put away.

"What was his hurry?" She unpacked the bags and stashed the food, a little relieved that she could put everything where it usually went with the care it deserved. Her poor eggs had almost gone the way of Humpty Dumpty in Tyler's hands. Daisy hoped he hadn't gotten a bad-news text that had made him fly out of her house like his jeans were on fire.

Once she'd unpacked, she headed to the study to sort the children's books she'd gotten from her dad. As she crouched by the box, she realized that she hadn't heard from Gabe in a while, so she sent him a cheerful text letting him know she'd sold both dolls. After a few minutes, her phone chirped with his return text consisting of one word—*good*. Shaking her head, she returned her phone to her sweatshirt pocket. At least she knew he was still alive.

The books only held her interest long enough to pull them out of the box and stack them on her desk. Buzzing with energy from the whole Chris thing, she decided she needed to do something more active. Since she'd already worked out very, very early that morning, exercising twice in one day would reveal her to be the training-obsessed person she was. Besides, it was officially supposed to be her rest day.

"Rest day, schmest day," she muttered, and then laughed at her immature pouting. The training group was coming as usual the next day for their Saturday session, so Daisy figured she should probably clean the equipment in preparation for that. She walked into the gym, groping for the light switch next to the door. Ever since that strange night when she'd thought she'd heard someone in the house, the windowless training room had seemed almost menacing, especially when it was dark and she was alone.

She paused with her finger on the switch, feeling the usual prickle of unease as she glanced around the heavily shadowed room. Although she told herself she was being silly, a part of her didn't want to stay in the gym.

"I'll just grab some water first," she said, knowing it was just a stall. Leaving the room in darkness, she headed for the kitchen. Once in the doorway, she stopped, her nose wrinkling. Something was wrong. There was a bad smell, one that made alarm bells go off in her brain.

It was gas.

HURRYING TOWARD THE STOVE, SHE CHECKED ALL THE burners, but they were solidly in the "off" position. The odor was stronger there. Daisy looked more closely at the stove, but everything appeared normal. Her appliance knowledge was pretty much limited to turning things on and calling a repair person if it stopped working, so she wasn't sure if she'd even recognize the problem if she saw it. She definitely wouldn't know how to fix it.

"Think, Daisy. Think." She tried, but all that came into her head was the exploding-house scene from a movie she'd seen with Chris the week before. "Okay. I need to stop the gas. There has to be a main valve that'll turn it off. Where would that be?"

As she searched inside the cabinets on either side of the oven, she continued her monologue. Talking kept her breathing without hyperventilating. When she couldn't find any gas valve around the stove, though, she felt her heart start beating double-time.

"Next step." It was harder to smell the gas, but she figured that was just her nose getting tired, rather than the leak stopping. "Okay. I need help."

Pulling out her phone, she retreated to the living room and then continued all the way up the stairs. She figured it would probably be best to get as far away from the gas leak as possible, since breathing the fumes couldn't be good. Neither could getting blown up, but she couldn't start thinking about that, or she'd be too scared to function.

Her fingers shook as she tapped at her phone, but she managed to call Chris on her first try.

"Hey." Instead of his usual casual friendliness, his tone was warmer, more intimate. If there hadn't been such a strong likelihood of her house exploding in the immediate future, she would've taken a moment to revel in it.

"Hi. How do I stop a gas leak?"

"Gas leak?" The boyfriendy tone changed to his cop voice. "From the stove?"

"I think so. It smells the strongest there."

"Can you hear it escaping?"

She thought back, but all she remembered hearing was the thunder of her heartbeat. "No. I can just smell it."

"Have you turned off the main supply valve?"

"I can't find it." Her voice shook, and she squeezed her eyes closed, trying to regain her calm—or at least the illusion of it. Hysterics were not going to help the situation.

He swore, making her jump. He hardly ever cursed in front of her, so he had to be freaked out. "It's probably outside. Okay, Dais. I'm going to relay this to Dispatch. Don't call anyone else. I don't want you using your cell."

Her hand tightened around the phone. She hadn't thought about her cell triggering an explosion. It suddenly felt like she had a stick of lit dynamite in her hand. Shoving the thought away, she forced herself to focus on what Chris was saying.

"Don't turn on any lights or start a fire or anything."

Despite the situation, she gave a strangled laugh. "I'm not going to start any fires, Chris."

Her sarcasm flew right over his head. "Good. I'm on my way, but I'm at least twenty minutes out. I had to serve papers at a place south of Liverton, and I just left. Open all your windows, and I'll call this in. Fire will be there in five minutes—less if Ian and Rory are home."

"I can't open the windows," she said quietly, but Chris was already gone. She stared at the phone for a moment, tempted to put it somewhere far away from her body, but she didn't want to lose her only line of communication with the outside world. Tucking it back in her pocket as gingerly as if it were a bomb, she turned to face her bedroom window.

None of the downstairs ones could open. When her dad had installed the metal grates, she'd asked him to permanently secure the windows as well. It had been just a short time after her mom had been killed, so Gabe had been in a haze of grief and guilt. He'd done what she'd asked.

Although Daisy hadn't opened a single upstairs window in those eight years since, she was pretty sure it could be done—physically, at least. All she had to do was break through the paralysis that was gluing her feet to the floor.

"Daisy," she said sharply, glad that no one was there to listen to her give herself a talking-to. "Get your butt over there and do it. If you die before you get to have sex with Chris, all because you were too chicken to open a stupid window, I'll never forgive you."

As silly as her self-directed lecture was, it allowed

her to move her feet. By the time her knees bumped the window seat, her entire body was shaking, but she was doing it. Her brain refused to focus as she stared at the angled glass that made up the right side of the window. The center portion didn't open, but both sides did. She just needed to figure out how to make her hands work.

Since talking out loud had helped before, she tried it again. "Okay, Dais. This isn't rocket science. First, unlock the window."

Ignoring the very large portion of her mind screaming at her that it was a bad, bad idea to open the window, she reached out a shaking hand and thumbed back the latch. Without allowing herself to pause, afraid that any hesitation would give her fears the chance to take over, she turned the crank that pushed out the vinyl-edged pane.

It resisted at first, before giving way with a harsh creak. Daisy focused on the end of the crank protruding from her clenched fist. If she didn't look at the gaping window, then she could pretend it wasn't opening. She kept turning until the crank resisted going any farther, and then she repeated the process on the second side of the window.

Breathing hard, she closed her eyes. Although her legs were going soft at the knees, and she wanted nothing more than to crumple to the floor, there were more windows to open. Plus, firefighters would be banging on her door soon, for the second time in twelve hours. Her laugh came out as a gasp. When had it become a common occurrence for firefighters to come to her house?

"Right." She opened her eyes, staring straight ahead at the center portion of the window—the one that didn't open. "Let's go." As she turned toward the door, she stifled another strangled laugh. If she survived, she'd probably end up with multiple personalities, judging by the way she was ordering herself around.

Once she was in the upstairs hallway and out of sight of the opened windows, moving was easier. She hurried to Gabe's bedroom, not letting herself slow, so momentum drove her to the first window. His were flat, latching at the top and sliding upward.

She bit the inside of her cheek and tasted blood as she used both hands to turn the two locks. Bracing the heels of her palms against the top edge, she shoved open the window.

There was nowhere to look but straight ahead, at the vulnerable screen. A breeze blew against her skin, and she was shocked into stillness. How could she have forgotten what the wind felt like? Her nerves were raw, and she'd raised the window expecting only terror. The air, cool but hinting of spring, felt wonderful. For a second, she forgot her fear and the gas filling the house below her. She closed her eyes and smiled.

The sirens jerked her back to reality. Rushing to the second window, she unlocked it and pushed it open on autopilot before darting out of the room. In the hallway, she stopped, trying to slow her rushing thoughts. The bathroom didn't have an operable window, and the third upstairs bedroom was used for storage. To reach the far wall, she'd have to dig her way through unused furniture and stacks of boxes.

Judging by the volume of the sirens, the fire trucks would be arriving very soon. She hesitated at the top of the stairs, not wanting to go back to the source of the gas leak. Daisy wondered if the fumes rose, like helium, or if they hung heavy, close to the floor. It was stupid of her not to have planned for something like that. She should have at least known where the main gas shut-off was.

The sirens were really loud now. If her windows hadn't been open, she would have run into her bedroom to watch the trucks' approach. Instead, feeling blinded, she forced her feet to descend the stairs.

The smell of the gas was stronger, or else her nose had had a chance to rest in the cleaner air upstairs. She waited by the front door, trying to keep her breathing shallow, although she had no idea if that would help keep the gas out of her lungs.

Even though she'd been expecting it, the urgent pounding made her jump. As she depressed the unlock button, she had a moment of panic that it would create a spark and set off an explosion. If a light switch could do it, why wouldn't an electric lock? She sucked in a harsh breath, not releasing it until Ian had pushed open the inner door and took her arm. Two other firefighters headed for the kitchen.

"Outside, Daisy," Ian ordered.

The panic surged again. "No," she tried to say, but her lungs weren't working, so only her mouth moved.

"Yes." His expression behind his face shield and mask was sympathetic, but his hold on her arm was firm. "Med's on their way, and a paramedic can give you a sedative, but you have to get out of this house until we can clear out this gas."

She couldn't stop shaking her head. "I opened the windows." When he glanced through the arched doorway at the still-closed kitchen window and then back at her, she clarified, "Upstairs. The downstairs ones don't open."

Pressing his free hand on the top of his helmet, he groaned. "Jesus, Daisy. You've trapped yourself in this place. What if there'd been a fire?"

"I have extinguishers!" Her voice was getting too high-pitched, and she couldn't seem to breathe.

"Doesn't matter right now. I'm getting you out." His mouth tightened as he took a step closer, shifting into position to put her over his shoulder. Daisy knew she'd be helpless once he picked her up, helpless as he carried her through the doors, helpless as he took her outside. She couldn't let it get to that point or else she'd die of fear once he dragged her out of the house.

Pivoting into position, she raised her knee, connecting with the side of his thigh, right where the peroneal bundle of nerves was located. The heavy material of his pants absorbed some of the blow's force, but the hit was sufficient to loosen his grip enough for her to break free.

Daisy scrambled back, putting a few feet of space between them. Her training told her to land a couple of kicks, to disable her opponent so she could escape, but it was *Ian*. Even in her frantic state, she knew he was trying to help her, to save her. He didn't realize that taking her outside would end her just as quickly as an explosion.

Instead of continuing to fight, she whirled and ran. She heard him behind her, too close behind her. Afraid that he would catch her if she took the stairs, she sprinted to the training room, slamming the door just before his bulk connected with a thud. Twisting the dead bolt, she thanked her paranoia that had made her add locks to every door, even the interior ones.

It wasn't enough, though. Ian was a firefighter, and they had ways of getting into locked rooms, she was sure. It was dark, but she knew the gym so well that she made her way to one of the weight racks without crashing into any of the other equipment. Once her hands closed on the rack, she knocked it over, letting the weights hit the floor. Just the rack alone was too heavy for her to lift, but she managed to drag it in front of the door.

"Daisy!" Ian yelled. "You need to get out of here! It's not safe!"

She knew it wasn't safe. The house was filling with gas. The smallest spark could ignite an explosion that would destroy the entire neighborhood—and anyone in it. The thought was so frightening that her entire body shook. It was still not as terrifying as going outside.

Running to where she'd dumped the rack, her breath catching with every inhale, she got down on her hands and knees to feel for the abandoned weights. With sweating, trembling hands, she piled the ones she found onto a mat, using it as a sled to slide the weights over to the door. As she returned them to the rack, her tremors making them knock loudly against the metal, Ian continued yelling.

Soon, though, he went quiet. That was scarier than his shouts. Had he been overcome by the gas? Had he left her to be blown to bits, alone in death as she'd been so much of her life?

When she heard the muffled sound of his voice, relief poured over her, quickly followed by guilt. He shouldn't be in here. He shouldn't have to die because of Daisy's mixed-up mind. His unclear words continued, and she assumed he was talking on the radio. When even that stopped, she drew in a shaky breath.

"Ian?" she called through the door, his name cracking in the middle. "I'm sorry for the knee strike."

"It's okay, Daisy." His voice was still loud enough to reach her, but he'd quit shouting. "You really need to leave."

"I can't." With all the weights she found back on the rack, she sat heavily on the mat. The air around her felt weighted, thick with anticipation, ready to explode at any second. "I'm sorry."

"C'mon, Daisy," he coaxed. "I like you. Even Rory likes you, and she has a very limited number of people she can tolerate. We don't want you to be blown to bits."

His words reminded her that she wasn't the only one in danger, that she'd be responsible for this brave, beautiful man's death. Because she was a coward, Ian could die. That seemed so wrong. "Please go, Ian. I don't want you to be in bits, either."

"You'll just be outside for a little while," he said, ignoring her plea. "They've shut off the main line, and they're setting up the ventilator fan to exhaust the house. As soon as it's clear, you can come back inside."

Instead of answering, she drew her legs to her chest and rested her cheek on her knee. How could she explain the mind-erasing terror that took over when she thought about stepping outside? It wasn't rational, wasn't logical, but it was real, and it just might kill her and Ian.

"Jennings is worried about you. He wants you out of here, too."

Just the mention of Chris broke something inside her, and she started to cry. Daisy tried very hard to keep silent, grateful for the muffling effects of the door between them. She'd been so proud of her baby steps, of the unlocked inner door and of staying conscious despite her glimpse of the outside. It had given her hope that she'd eventually get better.

Now, though, curled in a ball and sitting in a dark gym, a dead bolt and a rack of weights separating her from the fireman who was risking his life trying to save her, she didn't see how she'd ever be worthy of someone like Chris, a hero who ran toward danger. All she did was hide from imaginary bogeymen.

"Daisy? You still conscious in there?"

If she didn't talk, he'd think she was passed out—or dead. "Yeah." It was impossible to hide the tears in her voice, and she flushed with that additional shame.

"Did you hear me before? About Jennings?"

"Yeah." She wiped her cheek on the knee of her pants. "He deserves better."

There was a pause, and then he groaned. "Are you serious? You're going to make me do this?"

"Do what?"

"Have this conversation."

"What conversation?"

"This conversation. The one where you make something simple complicated."

"What do you mean?" She scooted over next to the door so she could lean against the wall and hear Ian better. As much as she didn't want him to risk his life by staying with her, it was so comforting to have him there.

"If you want to be together, be together. Stop making it so complicated."

"Does Rory make things complicated?" Daisy knew she was changing the subject, but she didn't want to talk about Chris, not when she was on the verge of being blown up and never seeing him again. The thought made her want to bawl like a baby, and she'd just managed to control her tears.

"Nope." His tone was positively smug. "That's one of the reasons I'm marrying her."

"Marrying her?" she echoed. "You two are engaged? Congratulations!" It occurred to her that it was a strange conversation to be having in a gas-filled house while barricaded in her training room. The fear eased when she talked to him, though.

"Don't tell her yet," he warned as his radio chattered faintly in the background. "I want it to be a surprise."

"Surprise? You're not going to put the ring in her pulled pork at Levi's or something equally cheesy and public, are you? Because I think Rory would hate that. Plus, she might break a tooth or swallow it or something. I've never understood how burying a diamond in food is romantic." Granted, all of her experience with proposals had been from watching TV or movies or reading about them in books.

"No." By the heaping amount of defensiveness he managed to pack into that one-word denial, Daisy was pretty sure he'd been planning something close. "Nothing like that. I just want it to be a surprise."

"I won't tell."

"Thanks." There was a pause before he spoke again. "Do you seriously think that Jennings isn't full-out panting for you?"

The change of topic threw her. "What? No, I...I mean...what?"

"Because if you even glance in his direction during training, he starts flexing."

"He does not!" She choked on a laugh. "I thought you didn't want to have this conversation."

His sigh was so exaggerated that she could hear it through the door. "I'll suffer through it, as long as you and Jennings finally get together and stop with the fake just-friends deal."

"It's not fake!" When he didn't respond, it was her turn to sigh. "We are friends. And Chris wants to be more than friends."

"Finally," Ian muttered just loud enough for her to hear.

Letting her head tip back against the wall, she ignored his comment. "I want that, too—so much—but I can't do that to him."

"Do what to him?" He sounded cranky. "See, this is why I hate these conversations. There are always these vague reasons why you have to make things complicated. Things are not complicated. You want him. He wants you. Therefore, you f—uh, date."

"Ian!" A flare of anger burned through her misery. "I just beat you up for trying to save my life. I've locked myself in a room in a house that could explode at any second, and you think I should inflict this mess on Chris? He doesn't deserve that."

"You didn't beat me up." Of course that was what he focused on. "It was one lucky hit that took me by surprise."

"Whatever. That doesn't change the fact that I'm a crazy person who doesn't leave her house."

When he spoke, his tone was gentle. "Daisy. We're all messes, just in different ways. I dragged Rory into my mess, and she dragged me into hers. It's kind of the definition of a relationship. Besides, you're getting better."

She didn't feel like she was better. The unlocked door seemed so small a step compared to her freak-out over leaving the house—a dangerous, gas-filled house. The reminder made her turn toward the door so quickly that her elbow hit the weight rack.

"Ow," she yelped, cupping the throbbing joint with her other hand.

"You okay, Daisy?" His voice had sharpened. "What's wrong?"

"Nothing." Although she grimaced, she swallowed any other sounds of pain. "I'm fine. You need to leave, Ian. If the house explodes, I don't want you in it."

"It's fine." Daisy opened her mouth to protest, but he continued. "I've been listening to the other guys' progress on the radio. The gas levels are almost down to nothing. That new ventilator we just got is kick ass."

"You shouldn't have stayed with me." Now that the fear had ebbed, guilt was taking its place. "I would've felt so bad if you'd been blown up because of me."

"No, you wouldn't have, since you'd have been just as dead as me." His matter-of-fact tone almost made her laugh. "You might want to start moving whatever you piled in front of the door out of the way, since they're going to be letting people back into the area soon. That includes your man, who's going to be charging in here as soon as they stop restraining him."

Although she grimaced at the thought of facing

everyone after the cowardly way she'd scurried to a dark corner, she started moving weights off the rack and back onto the mat. When Ian's final couple of words belatedly sank in, she repeated, "Restraining him?"

"Yeah. Whenever the chief was talking, I could hear Jennings yelling in the background. I'm guessing it took at least a couple of guys to keep him out of here. Maybe handcuffs, too." It sounded like the idea amused him.

"See," she said, all desire to laugh gone, "all I do is cause problems for him."

"Quit the whiny, self-pitying sh—crap and grow a pair, Daisy. If you dump him, you're going to make him miserable. He loves you, and that includes your hatred of the great outdoors. So zip it."

Her mouth hung open as she stared at the door. "I should grow a pair?"

"I didn't mean that literally," he grumbled. "Although, even if you actually did, Jennings would probably *still* follow you around like a puppy."

Her laugh returned at that, and she started moving weights again. "Thanks, Ian."

"Anytime, Daisy."

Chapter 19

IT WAS HARD FOR HER TO UNLOCK THE TRAINING ROOM door, but it wasn't because of fear that time. She was embarrassed and didn't want to face the people she'd made worry. Ian's words about growing a pair rang in her head, giving her the strength to stiffen her shoulders and twist the dead bolt.

With the weights moved and the rack dragged off to one side, all she had to do was twist the knob and pull. Daisy decided she was sick of standing on the wrong side of doors because she was too scared to step through them. Blowing out a hard breath, she closed her fingers around the knob and opened the door.

Ian, looking extra-large in his bunker gear, was leaning one shoulder against the hallway wall. He'd removed his mask and pushed up the clear face shield onto his helmet. Reluctantly, she met his gaze and was surprised he didn't look angry.

"Aren't you mad?" she asked.

He seemed honestly confused by her question. "No. Why should I be?"

Before she could answer, Chris came barreling toward them. The force of his hug lifted her feet off the ground and squeezed the air out of her lungs.

"Dais!" His voice was rough. "Jesus, Dais. You scared the shit out of me."

She wrapped her arms around him, feeling his heart

hammering against her. The realization of how scared he'd been brought another rush of guilt. *She*'d done that to him. What kind of horrible, selfish person was she, to endanger Ian's life and to terrify the man she loved?

"They wouldn't let me past the perimeter." His arms tightened even more, and she squeezed him in return, trying to apologize without words. "All I could do was stare at the house, just waiting for the explosion."

He took a step back, although he kept hold of her shoulders. With a little space between them, she could see Chris's face and the destroyed look on it.

"I'm sorry," she said. "It was my fault. I'm the one who scared everyone."

"Fuck." He moved his hands from her shoulders to her face, cupping it gently. His fingers were shaking. "I thought I'd lose you."

She grabbed his wrists, not to pull his hands away, but because she needed to touch him. Opening her mouth, she wanted to tell him how much he meant to her, how much she regretted putting that tortured look on his face, but what came out was something different. "I did a peroneal strike on Ian."

Chris blinked. "What?"

His hands prevented her from turning her head toward him, but she could see enough of Ian in her peripheral vision to tell that he looked amused. "I'm sorry. It was just instinct. He was going to do the fireman's carry and take me outside, and I just couldn't go." Dropping her gaze, she stared at Chris's chin. "Not yet. I'll do it, I promise. Just…not yet."

Chris was quiet for too long of a time. Although she wanted to check out his expression, to see if he looked

mad or exasperated or impatient or exhausted, she just
couldn't bring herself to look any higher than his chin.
It was a nice chin, strong and square with a hint of
stubble, but it didn't give her much feedback as to what
he was feeling.

"Knee strike?" he finally asked, and surprise allowed
her to meet his eyes. His expression didn't show any
of the emotions she'd been expecting. Instead, he
looked...blank.

She nodded slowly, wondering what was behind his
impassive mask.

"Nice. You took him down with one knee strike?"
His mouth curled up in a proud smile. "Look at you,
warrior woman."

There was the sound of a throat clearing from Ian's
direction. "I wouldn't say she took me down."

"Not all the way," Daisy agreed, feeling a little
light-headed from relief that neither Chris nor Ian was
furious with her. "He just sort of sagged a little, and
I was able to pull my arm free. I was going to land a
couple more kicks, just to make sure he stayed down,
but then I remembered he was Ian, not a bad guy, so I
just ran."

"That's the whole point of our training," Chris said,
his eyes warm as they fixed on hers. "Getting away. Not
that I don't wish Walsh had managed to catch you and
drag you out of this house."

The thought of what might have happened if she'd
been a little slower still had the ability to turn her legs
into rubber. The logical portion of her brain scoffed at
her for fearing going outside more than being inside
a gas-filled house, but it couldn't change her body's

conviction that terrible things would happen once she stepped through her front door.

"Hey, Jennings. Can you let go of your lady long enough for me to do a quick check?" a male voice behind Daisy asked. When Daisy turned to see who'd spoken, Chris's hands dropped away from her face and landed on her shoulders again. He tugged her closer, so her back pressed against his front.

"Junior," he greeted the firefighter, who was already pulling out a blood-pressure cuff from his medical bag.

"Why don't we take this party into another room?" Ian suggested. "It's getting crowded in this hallway."

"Things are a little busy back there." Junior jerked his head in the direction of the living room. "The repair guy's here fixing the leak, with the sheriff hovering over him asking questions about what caused it. That, and the windows wouldn't open, so we had to break some of them when we were ventilating. They're boarding them up now."

"The windows are broken?" Her stomach jumped at the thought of the open spaces that would surround her without the protective glass barriers.

Chris's hands started to massage her shoulders as he moved his mouth close to her ear. "I'll call Lenny over at the hardware store and see how soon he can get here. Until then, they'll be covered in plywood."

Although she nodded, her insides were still unhappy.

"The training room, then?" Ian asked, reminding her of the direction the conversation had been headed before she'd been distracted by broken windows.

"Sure." It wasn't until she was leading the three men into the gym that she remembered the mess she'd made with her improvised barricade. When Junior gave a low whistle, she cringed. "Sorry about this." She waved her hand at the scattered weights. "I usually keep it neater."

"This is awesome." Apparently, the whistle had been in admiration of the room, not condemnation of its untidiness. "Man, I'm jealous. If I had this nice of a gym in my house, I probably wouldn't leave either."

Chris, who'd dropped his hands from her shoulders when they'd moved into the training room, stiffened and put a hand on her lower back. Daisy gave him a reassuring smile. Junior's comment was probably the least upsetting thing that had happened in the past few hours.

Oblivious to Chris's irritation, Junior grinned as he waved her toward a weight bench. "Your throne, gym princess."

She smiled and took a seat, but Ian cuffed the back of the other fireman's helmet.

"Watch it," Ian growled. "Jennings is ready to rip off your"—he paused with a quick glance at Daisy—"face."

She ducked her head to hide her amusement. Hovering behind her, Chris made a wordless sound confirming Ian's warning.

Junior didn't seem too concerned, judging by the wink he gave her as he wrapped the blood-pressure cuff around her upper arm. He did keep his comments to himself while he took her vitals, although that might have been his professionalism kicking in.

"Everything's within normal range," he told her as he unclipped the oximeter from her finger. "I'm assuming you don't want to visit the hospital?" When she shook her head, he continued, "Medical's outside, so I can have the paramedics come in and check you out, if you want."

"Won't they just check the same things?" she asked.

He grinned at her. "Pretty much, yeah."

"They don't need to come in, then. I'm fine."

"Daisy…" Chris said in his *I-know-better-than-you* tone, and she turned her head to give him her best *no-you-don't* glare.

"I'm fine," she said firmly. "Thank you, Junior."

"Anytime." As he put his equipment away, his eyes roamed the room. "Although if you really want to show your gratitude, you could let me use your gym once in a while."

"Of course." She frowned. "Although we might have to start a new training group, since it's already a pretty tight fit with eight people."

"Eight?"

"Yes." She ticked each person off on her fingers as she named them. "Me, Chris, Ian, Rory, Lou, Callum, George, and Ellie."

Junior whipped around to scowl at Ian. "You've been working out here with a bunch of hot chicks and haven't invited any of the rest of us? Way to hold out on your fire brothers, Beauty."

"Thanks, Daisy," Ian groaned. "Now we'll never keep him out of here. There's a gym at Station One, Junior."

"Yeah, with crappy equipment and zero hot chicks. I want to come here."

"We could have firefighter training days," Daisy suggested, twisting to look at Chris. "They could just come and use the equipment, so you wouldn't have to give up more of your time to coach."

"Nuh-uh." Junior shook his head. "I want the coed training time."

"Don't make me have to smack you again." Ian raised a hand, but he grabbed the back of Junior's coat instead of hitting him that time. "Get your bag. Let's go."

"You okay, Daisy?" Rory's voice brought everyone's attention to the doorway where she stood.

When she saw the other woman, Daisy felt her earlier guilt resurface. "I'm sorry."

"For what?" Rory took a few steps into the room. Her bunker gear was obviously new, almost painfully clean compared to the guys' soot-darkened coats and pants.

"For beating up Ian and almost getting him blown up," she admitted in a rush, swallowing back the tears that wanted to break free.

"You beat up Beauty?" Junior asked, his glee obvious.

At the same time, Ian protested, "You didn't beat me up."

Ignoring both men, Daisy focused on Rory. "I'm sorry. When he tried to make me go outside, I panicked. I didn't think he'd stay in here with me."

"Tell us about the beat down," Junior urged, "in very specific detail. Did you make Ian cry like a tiny baby?"

Daisy didn't even glance at him, too worried about Rory hating her for endangering her soon-to-be fiancé. Well, soon-to-be fiancé if Ian didn't screw it up by burying the engagement ring in shredded meat slathered with barbeque sauce. Corralling her straying brain, she watched Rory's face for any hint of loathing.

"His hero complex isn't your fault," Rory said, sending a quick smile in Ian's direction. "He'd never leave someone in danger. That's just who he is."

"If I would've just let him carry me outside instead

of doing that knee strike…" Even just saying the words made sweat dampen her palms.

"It worked out, Dais." Chris had been standing quietly behind her, but now he wrapped an arm around her upper chest in a backward hug. "Everyone's okay, and you can work on getting out of the house in your own time."

"You need to make some changes, though," Ian said, crossing the room to stand next to Rory. "If you can't leave, you need to make this house as safe as possible. A sprinkler system would be a good start."

"Oh!" Rory's normally grave face lit with enthusiasm. "A panic room. Fireproof, explosion-proof, with a separate ventilation system, so you'd be safe from smoke inhalation or gas leaks. It'd also protect you during a home invasion."

"Or a zombie attack," Ian teased, giving her an affectionate bump with his shoulder. Even though she rolled her eyes, Rory couldn't hide the smile that was trying to break free.

"Thanks." Daisy suddenly felt exhausted. "But I really just want to leave the house. Then, I won't need a panic room, since I can panic outside."

"Everyone can use a panic room," Rory said with a sideways glance at Ian. "If you have one, I could run across the street and use yours, since we don't have one."

It was Ian's turn to roll his eyes. "Maybe, if you're a very good girl, Santa will bring you a panic room for Christmas."

"Really?" Her eyes grew wide as she turned to Ian. "We're getting a safe room?"

Daisy was starting to think that Ian should propose with a panic room instead of a ring.

"Possibly." He grimaced. "I might have to win the lottery first."

"Everyone okay in here?" Once again, a voice from the doorway drew everyone's attention. That time, it was Chief Early entering the training room. "Whoa. This is a nice set-up."

"Daisy invited everyone from Fire to use it," Junior piped up. "She's going to have coed training sessions, too."

The sound that came from Chris was a strange combination of a laugh and a growl. "You just make up whatever reality you want, don't you?"

"Yep." Junior grinned, as if he'd been complimented.

The chief cleared his throat.

"Daisy's fine," Ian belatedly answered.

"Good." After giving Daisy a nod, the chief turned a stern face toward Ian. "A word?" Even though it was phrased as a question, there was no hiding the command in his voice.

Looking resigned, Ian gave Rory's arm a squeeze before following Chief Early out of the room.

"What was that about?" Daisy asked.

Junior looked serious for the first time since she'd met him. "Ian disobeyed a direct order. Not sure what the repercussions will be. Could be he just gets chewed out." His doubtful tone indicated that he didn't think Ian would get off so lightly.

"What order did he disobey?" Her gaze darted from person to person. From their grim expressions, everyone knew what was going on except for Daisy. None of them answered, so she tried to work it out in her mind. When he'd talked on the radio, his words had been muffled, so she hadn't been able to understand what he'd said until he raised his voice loud enough for her to hear through the door.

From the other three's reluctance to answer her, she had to assume his refusal had something to do with her. Had the chief ordered him to take her out of the house? Ian shouldn't be blamed for her actions, and she'd made it impossible for him to force her to leave. What else would the chief have ordered Ian to do?

Her breath caught as the answer popped into her head—so obvious that she was angry with herself for taking so long to figure it out.

"He was ordered to evacuate." Her voice was flat as another layer of guilt settled over her. "Chief Early told Ian to get out of the house, but he wouldn't because I wouldn't leave."

"It's not the first time." Junior reached a hand toward her, as if to give her a consoling pat on the shoulder, but he withdrew it without touching her after a wary glance at Chris. "Not even the tenth. Walsh has some issues with the command structure. Chief says, 'Get your ass out of there *now*,' and Ian's brain adds, 'Unless you have a better idea.'"

"He won't leave anyone behind." Although Rory was frowning as she watched the door, she didn't seem angry at Daisy. "Much less a friend."

"Should I talk to the chief?" Daisy asked, leaning back against Chris. His arms tightened around her, and she felt even guiltier for receiving comfort that she didn't deserve. All of this had been her stupid fault. "If anyone is reprimanded, it should be me. Ian probably won't even tell him about the knee strike."

"I'm still waiting to hear about that." Although Junior's tone was light, there was still tension underneath his teasing. Like Rory, his gaze was fixed on the door.

Daisy smiled halfheartedly. "I think I've done enough damage to Ian today. You don't need more ammunition."

"But it's important to give Beauty a hard time," Junior protested, his amusement becoming more genuine. "If we don't shrink that head of his, it'll explode. The dude is seriously too hot for his own good."

Opening her mouth, Daisy closed it again without speaking, not sure how to respond to that. When she glanced at Rory, she saw the other woman roll her eyes and look briefly amused. Daisy decided to change the subject for the good of them all.

"Who's watching the gun store?" she asked Rory.

"No one." Rory turned her attention away from the door as she answered. "When the call came through, I stuck my 'Back Later' sign on the door and headed this way. Ian beat me here, though, since he was already at the Simpson grocery store when he heard the call. He left his basket of food and ran outside. When he heard the sirens of Rescue One approaching, he realized they'd go right by the store, so he grabbed his bunker gear from his Bronco, flagged them down, and hitched a ride."

"Should we see if they're done boarding up the windows?" If they weren't, she'd rather not wander into the kitchen or living room and face the gaping holes, but her phobia had caused enough issues for the day. She was going to pretend to be a normal person, just for a while.

"I'll go check," Rory volunteered, darting out the door even before she finished saying the words.

"And I'll make sure Rory doesn't decide to defend

her man by shooting the chief or something." Grabbing his medical bag, Junior followed her into the hall.

When they were alone, Daisy craned her neck to look up at Chris. At that oblique angle, all she could really see was the underside of his jaw—his very tense jaw.

"You okay?" she asked, trying to pull away so she could look more directly at his face.

"No." His other arm joined the first, so she was doubly locked to his chest.

Giving up on her escape attempt, she relaxed in his hold, feeling the usual rush of security and desire. She'd happily spend the rest of her life in Chris's arms.

"You could've *died*, Dais," he said, his voice rough. "I couldn't do anything out there, except watch your house and pray it didn't explode."

"I'm sorry." Patting his arm, she winced. Her apology seemed so...paltry in response to the residual terror she could hear in his words.

"I know." His lips pressed against the top of her head. "And I know there's nothing you can do, except continue what you've been doing. It's just that I've always thought you were safe in your house. Now, with the fire across the street and this gas leak... It feels like you're stuck in a trap."

"Yeah." The same thought had occurred to her, and she shivered. "My thinking brain knows that, but the rest of me is determined that outside is the scariest place." That time, when she pulled away, Chris let her go. She stood and turned to face him full-on, so he could see how serious she was about her next words. "I'm going to do it, Chris. I'm going to get out of here."

"Yeah, you will." She could tell he truly believed it,

and her chest warmed. Having Chris on her side made everything seem possible, and it made her even more determined to become the partner he deserved. It was terrifying, the thought of leaving the house, but the idea of continuing her lonely, trapped life was even more frightening. She stood on her toes, stretching up to meet him as he bent to kiss her.

Their lips had barely made contact when Junior's voice made them jerk apart. "Yo. Windows are done, and you're needed in the kitchen."

"Which 'you'?" Chris asked, not hiding his irritation at the interruption very well.

Junior shrugged with a grin and then disappeared from the doorway.

His chest lifting and then falling again in a silent sigh, Chris pressed his lips to her temple and then took a step back. "Ready?"

He didn't specify what exactly he was asking. Was she ready to face the broken windows, the other fire-fighters, the chief, Ian, or her stove? Except for the last one, the honest answer was "no." But when Chris held out a hand, his smile closer now to his usual happy one, she interlaced her fingers with his.

"Let's do this."

Chapter 20

"Sorry I wasn't able to get here before this."
Guilt made the lines in the stove repairman's leprechaun-
like face droop. Apparently, there was a lot of that emotion being passed around. "Seemed like everyone and
his brother needed repairs done this past week." Wally
gave her newly fixed stove a glare. "I didn't think this
was going to turn into a real emergency, though."

"I didn't either," Chris told him, giving Wally's
shoulder a friendly slap. "If I'd thought it was going
to be a problem, I would've been harassing you to get
over here."

The repairman frowned. "Like I told the sheriff, it
was a freak thing the way it started leaking. I've never
seen anything like it."

Chris's cop-face settled into place. "What do you
think caused it?"

Lifting his hands in an I-don't-know gesture, Wally
shook his mostly bald head. "No idea how the line
could've been damaged like that."

"Do you think it was intentional?"

Until Chris asked that question, Daisy's attention
had been only half-focused on the guys' discussion. She
hadn't been able to keep her gaze from drifting to the
sheets of plywood hiding the empty window frames.
Once she heard the word "intentional," however, she
jerked her head around so she could stare at them.

Wally gave a hoot of laughter. "You cops, always looking for foul play. Who'd want to hurt this nice lady?" He bobbed his head in Daisy's direction.

"There's no way the damage could've been deliberate, then?" Chris pushed, not sharing the repairman's amusement.

"Well, I wouldn't say there was 'no way' someone did this on purpose." Wally smoothed the white fringe that circled his bald spot. "Just doubtful, that's all. You done with this witness, Deputy?" Without waiting for an answer, he started collecting his tools. Chris ignored the sarcastic remark and stared at the stove.

"Thanks for coming over so quickly," Daisy said when it became evident that Chris was too wrapped up in his thoughts to continue the conversation.

Wally waved off her thanks. "I'm just sorry I didn't get here before all of this"—he gestured toward the wood-covered kitchen window—"happened."

With a nod, she escorted the repairman to the door. He lifted his cowboy hat from the coat rack and tipped it toward her before exiting. Once the inner door closed behind him, Daisy's hand reached for the first dead bolt out of habit, but she caught herself before she could lock it. Letting her hand drop to her side, she stared at the unsecured door, reminding herself that she had made progress, despite what had happened earlier.

Shaking off the residual guilt and shame, she headed back into the kitchen, where Chris was still staring at the stove. Everyone else had left almost an hour ago, and the house seemed oddly quiet without the firemen and deputies stomping around the place.

"Chris? Did you enter a fugue state or something?" She boosted herself onto the counter next to the stove.

Although he turned his head toward her and focused on her face, he ignored her question. "Did anything unusual happen between when I left this morning and the gas leak?"

"Unusual?" She frowned at the cabinets directly across from her, trying to recall. It felt like a week had passed, rather than just hours. "Let's see. You left—and it was more like afternoon than morning—so I finished packing up the dolls. No, wait. Before that, I took a shower, texted my grocery list to Tyler, and *then* I got the dolls ready to be shipped. Oh!" It wasn't really relevant to what Chris had asked, but she'd forgotten in all the hubbub. "I met Bill for the first time—in person, I mean, instead of just over the intercom."

"Bill?" There was an icy edge to his voice.

"Yes. You know, Bill the delivery driver? Beard and belly?"

"Right." For whatever reason, his tone had warmed to its normal temperature. "The dolls are gone, then? You survived. Congratulations."

"Barely," she said in exaggerated relief. "I'm shocked the toothy one didn't chew on me while I was sleeping."

Chris snorted. "Like you ever sleep."

"Hey! I did a pretty good job last night—this morning really."

His smirk turned smug as his eyes narrowed in a way that made her wiggle on the counter. "Yeah, you did. Wonder why that was."

"I'm not sure." Although her cheeks were hot and her stomach was squirmy, she faked nonchalance.

"Whatever the reason, it was nice to sleep so deeply. My dreams were really good, too."

"They were?" He shifted toward her, and her breathing got faster, though not from fear that time. "What were they about?" His next step brought him close enough that her knees almost touched his thighs.

"Um..." Distracted, she stared at the half inch of space that separated them before raising her head to meet his eyes. "Fireman Steve."

With a growl, he lunged forward and yanked her off the counter, turning her laugh into a shriek. He held her steady, but she still wrapped her arms and legs around him, both to keep from falling onto the tile floor and just because she had the right to hold him now.

"I'm kidding," she giggled, hugging him tighter. It was hard to remember how she'd managed to keep her hands off him for eight years. Her willpower was extraordinary, she decided. "Fireman Steve had no role in my dreams, not even a walk-on part."

"He better not have." Although Chris's voice was still growly, she had a feeling the current rasp had more to do with the feel of her in his arms than jealousy. He tucked his face into the crook of her neck and was doing really interesting things with his teeth, things that raised goose bumps from the spot below her ear where he was nibbling, all the way to her ankles. She tilted her head to give him better access.

"Oh!" she breathed when those clever teeth closed on her earlobe. "That's very nice." At any other time, she would've been embarrassed by her inane words, but now she was too preoccupied by how he could reduce her body to helpless shivers with such a simple action.

His chuckle vibrated against her skin, bringing another quiver in her chest. "I aim to please."

"Well, your aim is excellent." She sucked in an audible breath when he bit on the muscle sloping from her neck to her shoulder. "That's a bull's-eye, right there."

With a rumbly laugh, he raised his head from her throat and kissed her square on the mouth. By the time he pulled back a fraction of an inch, she'd forgotten where they were. Her world had narrowed until she was aware only of Chris, the way he was pressed against her, and how his breathing was visibly fast and hard, showing her that he wanted her as much as she wanted him.

Resting his forehead against hers, he said in that wonderful, deep and rough voice, "I have to run out to my truck."

It took a moment for his words to penetrate. When they finally did, she frowned and pulled back her head. "You're leaving?"

He grinned at her. Even in her annoyed state, she was so happy to see the return of his wide smile. "Not to leave. I just need to grab the supplies I bought after I left your house this morning." At her raised eyebrows, he corrected himself. "Fine. Afternoon."

"Supplies?" When the lightbulb flickered on in her brain, she immediately felt foolish. "Oh, *supplies*! Right. I'll just...ah, uncling myself, then."

His laugh regained its gravelly texture. "I like it when you cling." He tightened his arms, as if to demonstrate.

"Me too, but it makes going outside a little tough for you." Although she tried to laugh, one of his hands slid over her butt, turning the sound into more of a hiccup.

His face was in her neck again, and she almost melted, only remembering his necessary errand the second before she forgot everything except his mouth.

Reluctantly, she released him, her legs unhooking from around his waist and her arms dropping from his shoulders. His grip kept her dangling several inches off the floor.

"Chris?"

"Hmm?"

Loving how the sound felt on her neck, she shivered and resisted the urge to reestablish her hold on him. "Supplies, remember?"

For a moment, she thought he would ignore her. Daisy was surprisingly okay with that. Just as she was losing herself in his ministrations, he sighed and gently lowered her until she was standing on the floor. Her legs were as wobbly as they ever got post-panic attack, and she grabbed him to keep her balance.

"Okay?" he asked once she'd steadied.

She smiled up at him. "Perfect."

As he looked at her, his grin turned predatory. He leaned down but then stopped. With a groan, he took several steps back and turned his face to the side. When his gaze met hers again, Daisy could feel the heat of his eyes, even across the space that separated them.

"Be right back." The slam of the inner door came shortly after his words.

Dazed, she stood for a moment, smiling. Then she realized she was wasting precious preparation time. Glancing down at her clothes, she cringed and ran for the stairs. Her usual yoga pants and hoodie did not scream sexy, and she wanted Chris to look at her and not be able to breathe—but in the best, non-life-threatening way, of course.

Skidding around the top of the stairs and dashing into her bedroom, she dug through her dresser drawers.

"Why do I have so many sports bras?" she muttered, slamming one drawer closed and yanking open the next. "Would it be too much to ask to own one thing that's sexy?"

Time was ticking, and Chris would be back knocking on the front door in just seconds, so she gave up on her lingerie treasure hunt. Vowing to do some online shopping as soon as she could, Daisy pulled her hoodie over her head. Her tank top underneath was formfitting, so she was just going to have to be satisfied with that.

When she glanced in the mirror, she bit back a startled shriek. The quick removal of her sweatshirt had charged her hair with enough static to make the strands float around ear level. Her face was red from exertion and nerves, and she pressed her palms to her hot cheeks with a groan as she headed for the bathroom.

A little water and a quick brushing tamed her hair, although there wasn't much she could do about her red cheeks except calm down, which wasn't going to happen anytime soon—not with Chris getting *supplies*. As if the thought had conjured him, she heard his distinctive, aggressive knock. She hurried to the front door, took a second to get herself together, failed at regaining any kind of composure, and pressed the unlock button.

Before she could even take a bracing breath, Chris was inside and had her pressed against the wall in the entry. Her nerves vanished, overtaken by excitement and arousal and sheer happiness as she returned his kiss.

Without letting go of each other, they made their way upstairs, tripping on the steps and bouncing off door-frames as they blindly found their way into her bedroom.

Pulling back to yank his shirt over his head, Chris paused with just his abs revealed as he stared over her shoulder.

"What?" she asked, tugging impatiently at the fabric.

"Your window's open."

She turned to stare at it, unable to believe she'd forgotten. The whole time she'd been frantically searching her underwear selection, there'd been nothing between her and the world except for a flimsy screen. "I know."

His gaze snapped to her. "Did you open them, or did Fire?"

"I did."

He searched her face, and then he smiled. "Good for you."

Although she glowed with pride on the inside, she tried very hard to keep her expression blasé. "Thanks. Now are you going to strip, or what?"

After staring at her for a startled second, he laughed and yanked the shirt over his head. "Happy?"

Her eyes fixed on his chest. In the fading evening light, the shadows and highlights made him look like a piece of artwork. Daisy raised her hand, wanting to touch, but she hesitated before making contact. Losing her nerve, she started to drop her arm to her side, but Chris caught her fingers.

Pressing her palm to his chest, he held it there until she started moving her hand, stroking over the wiry hair and soft skin that covered the muscles beneath. She'd seen him without his shirt before, and she'd wanted to touch so many times. It was hard to believe that she actually had her fingers on Chris now. A laugh escaped as she raised her other hand to join the first.

"What's so funny?" he asked, his smile starting to grow.

"Nothing," she told his belly button as her fingers traced the grooves between his ab muscles. "I'm just glad we're doing this."

Skimming his hands up her arms and over her shoulders to cup both sides of her jaw, he tilted her face toward his. Dropping his head, he brushed his lips over hers, connecting with the slightest of pressure. "Me too." He paused, hovering just over her mouth. "God, you have no idea how glad."

Her fingers dropped low enough to dip into the waistband of his BDUs, and his teasing ended. With the kiss, he took over her mouth. Forgetting about her plan for cautious exploration, Daisy let her hands mindlessly roam over his sides. He walked her backward, his lips never leaving hers, until her legs bumped against the bed.

The need for oxygen forced her to pull away. As she sucked in air, Chris took the opportunity to peel her tank top over her head and toss it aside. Dropping to his knees in front of her, he kissed her heaving stomach, exploring her so thoroughly that Daisy could tell he was as fascinated by her body as she was by his.

"When we were working out in your gym," he breathed, following the line of her lowest ribs with just his fingertips and leaving goose bumps in his wake, "I'd catch myself staring at you all the time. I can't believe I actually get to touch you."

"I know the feeling." Her voice caught on the last word as Chris used his teeth to scrape against her skin. "Especially when you wear those pants that look like they could slip off your hips at any second. It's hard not to stare."

"At least *I* don't wear Spandex," he growled, moving to a new spot to torture her there. "Those new outfits you've gotten since the others started working out with us…" The sound he let out was full of frustration and longing. Although she knew it shouldn't make her happy, she couldn't erase her smug smile. It was just so satisfying to know that she hadn't been the only one wanting what she thought she could never have.

With a final nip that made her gasp in the best way, he stood and circled her waist with his hands. Dipping his head, he kissed her lips as he slid his fingers higher, until they traced the bottom edge of her sports bra. Daisy stood on her tiptoes so she could press her mouth harder against his.

He pulled away as his fingers circled around to her back, still fingering her bra. "What's the trick to this?"

For some reason, that made her snort a laugh.

"No, seriously." Despite his words, he was grinning, too. "Are there hooks? A zipper? A hidden keyhole? A secret password? Because it seems awfully tight just to pull off over your head."

She was almost laughing too hard to be of any help, but she managed to peel off her bra, yanking it over her head and flinging it across the room. "See? It's like magic."

"Yeah." His face was serious, and the heat in his eyes as he stared at her bare breasts sucked all the desire to laugh out of her, leaving only need. "Magic." He covered her with his hands and then his mouth, and her knees went wobbly. Half-sitting and half-falling, she plopped onto the bed, Chris following her down.

As he worked his way up her neck, she stroked his head and down his back, pressing into the muscles running along his spine so she could both feel and hear his groan of pleasure.

"I need to get some pretty bras," she said, her breath catching on the last word as his teeth lightly scored the side of her neck. "I have too many"—she lost track of what she was saying for a moment when he moved to just beneath her ear—"sports bras. They're not very sexy."

"Everything you wear is sexy," he said against her throat. "You could make granny panties hot. Or a flannel, one-piece Union suit. Or those plastic clogs—even the orange ones."

She was laughing again, and he caught the sound with his mouth, turning it into a needy moan. It was different than she'd expected. Even in all her daydreams, she'd never imagined that sex with Chris would be so much fun. When he nipped at her lip, making her gasp, she lost track of her thoughts and just felt.

Taking his time, he explored her body, touching and kissing and telling her why each part was his new favorite. He loved her ears because of the way she'd tuck her hair behind them, and her toes just because they were cute. Her elbows made him a fan when she'd jab him teasingly. He knew she could use them to really hurt him if she tried, but she never did, even when he was at his most annoying. The indentation above her breastbone reminded him of how vulnerable she was, and her biceps of how strong. Chris told her how he loved her knees and her shoulder blades, the back of her neck, and her belly button.

By the time he was finished cataloging her assets, she was panting and sweating and so worked up she was ready to scream. That was when he donned a condom and slid inside her, and she was ready, more than ready.

"God, you feel amazing," he groaned, and then he kissed her fiercely. Locking her fingers in his hair, she pulled his head down, needing him as close as she could get him. Not breaking the contact of their mouths, he started to move, and the wonderful pressure began to build again.

Tangling her legs around him, she tugged at his hair, wanting to make him as frantic as she felt. His breath caught, and he pulled back far enough to study her face. After a few seconds, he bared his teeth in a wild grin and lost control.

His patience from earlier was gone, smashed to bits, but Daisy didn't care—in fact, she reveled in his urgency. She clung to him and lost herself in the heat and pleasure of the motion. It was fast and hard and shoved Daisy over the edge into bliss before she even knew her climax was coming. She clutched at his shoulders as she rode the unexpected wave of ecstasy, aware that she was digging her short nails into his skin again, but unable to let him go. Chris didn't seem to mind her roughness. In fact, he matched it with an intensity of his own, driving into her until he found his own pleasure.

After he disposed of the condom, they lay tangled together, sweaty and breathing harder than after their toughest cross-fit workout, and a breeze from the window swept over them. It would've been too cold if she'd been alone. Since Chris's lax body covered most of her, Daisy felt the air touch only her cheeks and one arm. It was perfect, a sign that she was moving forward—with Chris, with letting go of her fears, with her life. Suddenly filled with such euphoria that she could almost feel her body floating off the bed, she tightened her arms around Chris, her rock.

He stirred in response, pushing himself up so he could look at her face.

"Okay, Dais?" He brushed a damp strand of hair off her cheek, and she remembered him telling her how much he loved that hair and that cheek. She smiled.

"I don't know if I mentioned it tonight." She mirrored his motion on his much-shorter hair. It wasn't long enough to hang in his face, but she brushed it with her fingers anyway. "Since you were talking so much, I couldn't really get a word in edgewise."

With a mock insulted look, he began to tickle her. He seemed to instinctively identify all of her most sensitive spots, and he ruthlessly took advantage of that knowledge. When he'd reduced her to laughing, pleading exhaustion, he finally showed mercy.

"You were saying?"

Wiping the mirth-induced tears from her eyes, she tried to glare at him. It was difficult to do while she was still giving the occasional hiccup of laughter. "What I was *saying*, before that unprovoked attack, was that I love you—as in love-love you."

"You love-love me?" He appeared to be holding back a smirk—not very successfully. "Is the double love different from the single love?"

When she shoved his shoulder, he didn't budge. "I mean that I love you, and not in a just-friends way."

"I know." He rolled off her and stood next to the bed.

She frowned at his smug tone. "That's not the right response."

"Fine. I love you, too, in not a just-friends way. Is that better?" His grin was too contagious, and she fought returning it.

"Not really," she grumbled. "Maybe in about twenty years, when we're an old married couple, and this is old hat, but it's pretty *new* hat right now, so I was hoping for a little more passion—eep!"

He picked her up and swung her off the bed, ending her monologue. "Shower?"

A shower sounded wonderful. Everything with him sounded wonderful. "Okay. Race you."

~~~

"Okay. What is up with you?" Lou demanded.

"Me?" Although she tried, Daisy couldn't stop smiling. "Nothing."

"Uh-huh. Liar. Who else here thinks Daisy's lying?" She raised her hand, and Rory and Ellie joined her.

Laughing, Daisy caved. "Fine. Chris and I are kind of…well, we're dating now."

While Lou whooped with excitement and Ellie called out her congratulations, Rory looked confused.

"I don't get it. Weren't you dating before?" she asked.

"We were just friends," Daisy explained. Lou coughed and raised her hand again. "We were!"

Once the laughter died down, they asked her a million and one questions. When she was blushing hot enough to spontaneously combust, she called a halt to the interrogation.

"Aren't we going to talk about the murder? Isn't that why we're meeting tonight? Please?"

"Fine." Lou conceded, flipping to a blank sheet on the oversized notepad. "Who wants to talk about dead people?"

"First," Ellie said, her expression changing from amusement to concern, "I want to talk about Daisy's gas leak yesterday. What happened?"

Her stomach twisting in remembered fear, she gave the other women a condensed summary of the incident. "Is Ian in a lot of trouble?"

Rory shrugged. "Not as much as after he went into his dad's burning house against orders. He'll have to do some of the nastier tasks around the station for a week or two, and then he'll be off the hook. Chief Early knows he's not going to change."

"I'm sorry," Daisy said for what felt like the hundredth time.

Rory didn't look upset. "Not your fault. Ian's just... how he is." By the sappy look on her face, she liked Ian exactly as he was. "Did the chief determine it was just an accident, then?"

"Probably." To Daisy, it didn't feel like an accident. It was one more way the house was turning from a sanctuary into a trap. "Although the repairman said the damage was strange."

"Strange?" the other women echoed.

"Strange as in deliberate?" Lou asked.

"The repair guy laughed at the idea when Chris suggested it." Although she knew it was ridiculous to think that someone had intentionally sabotaged her stove—had tried to *kill* her—Daisy's stomach was churning.

The other women exchanged uneasy glances. "But did he say it couldn't have been deliberate?" Ellie asked.

Even in her Chris-induced happy daze, the possibility that someone had intentionally caused the gas leak had been poking at the back of her brain. "No. Who would've done that, though? And why?"

"An explosion sounds right up an arsonist's alley," Lou said in a hushed voice, as if she were in danger of being overheard. "And you *were* a witness to a possible dead-body moving."

"But who? And how?" Daisy repeated, unable to wrap her head around the idea that someone hated her enough to try to kill her. "No one ever comes inside. Only my dad, Chris, our workout group, Tyler Coughlin, and that real estate agent." As she listed off the names, Lou wrote them down.

"Real estate agent?" Rory repeated.

Daisy grimaced. "We need to have these meetings more often. The real estate agent was showing the house across the street, and they found blood on the ceiling. Chris wanted to get a warrant to search the place, but the sheriff refused."

"Why?" Lou turned from the notepad. "I would think blood would be suspicious enough to call for a search, especially after what you saw."

"Tyler Coughlin was here?" Rory interrupted.

A little startled by the change in topics, Daisy blinked at her before answering. "Yes. He's my grocery-delivery boy."

Looking grim, Rory stared at the names on the list. "When was he here last?"

The room suddenly felt like all the oxygen had been sucked out of it. Daisy barely found enough air to speak. "Yesterday," she said in a tiny voice. "Right before the gas leak."

"Tyler?" Ellie sounded shocked. "The sheriff's son? But he's a kid!"

"He's sixteen." Lou drew a circle around his name. "Old enough to know how to start a fire. And that would explain why the sheriff would try to cover for him."

"Including the missing arson reports," Rory added.

Swallowing hard, Daisy thought about bashful Tyler, all gangly arms and legs, who pretended he was grown up enough to like coffee. "I don't know. It fits, but... Do you think he murdered Willard Gray, too? I don't think he'd be capable of *killing* someone, do you?"

"If it was him, he tried to blow up your house," Rory said flatly, "with you in it."

Everyone went silent. Daisy tried to wrap her head around the idea that Tyler had tried to kill her. The Tyler she'd seen—the awkward, lonely boy—was a murderer. And Tyler's father...how much had he known?

"The sheriff knew about the arsons," she started carefully. "Do you think he also knew about Willard Gray? Or my gas leak?"

"He couldn't," Ellie said firmly. "There's no way. To cover up something like that, Rob would have to be just as much of a monster as his son."

Rory looked uncertain, but Lou added, "I agree. He seems to really care about people. I don't think he could have known what Tyler was doing—the killing part, at least—and allow it to continue."

"What do we do?" Daisy asked, her heart thumping like she'd just sprinted a mile. She wasn't as sure that the sheriff wasn't complicit in his son's murderous activities, but the other women knew Rob better than she did.

Carefully capping the marker, Lou placed it on the coffee table. "You need to call Chris."

<center>~~~</center>

Chris stared grimly at the notebook with unseeing eyes. "Give me until tomorrow."

The women looked at each other. "He's *killed* people," Daisy said carefully. "If it is Tyler, we need to make sure he's stopped before he hurts someone."

"I know." When Chris turned his head and met her eyes, she almost flinched. Instead of his usual cheery expression, he just looked tired and sad. "Just give me a little time to figure out how to tell Rob, and then we can bring this information to the BCA."

"Don't tell him tonight," Lou warned, her knee jiggling up and down. Since she'd abandoned the notepad, she hadn't been able to sit still. "Rob is a good guy, but this is his *son*. We're pretty sure he's been covering up the arsons. Murder is a whole different thing, and we don't think Rob would defend Tyler for that. If we're wrong, though, he could take Tyler and run."

"I know. I'll tell him first thing tomorrow, and we'll call in the state investigators immediately afterward."

Ellie had been chewing on the side of her thumbnail until she'd grabbed her arm with her opposite hand and pulled both into her lap. "What if it's not him? We don't have any proof."

"At the very least," Chris said, "the case needs to be taken over by someone who'll be objective. If they find that Tyler's innocent, I'll be very happy." He didn't sound like he expected that outcome, though.

"Should we meet here tomorrow at nine, then?" Rory said, and everyone's eyes went to Chris.

"Yes." His cop mask had fallen into place. "I'll plan to talk to him at eight."

"I'll see if Cal's up for a stakeout," Lou offered. "We'll keep an eye on Tyler's house to make sure he doesn't sneak out and commit any felonies tonight."

"If you take from now until midnight, Ian and I'll take the graveyard shift."

Ellie leaned forward. "I'll see if George can do the last four hours with me. If he can't, I'm kind of useless. George doesn't like me to go anywhere alone without asking Rob for a deputy, and telling the sheriff I'm right outside of his house, spying on his son, would be...uh, bad."

Although there were a few chuckles at that, the laughter quickly died. Subdued, the other women left. It was strange, Daisy thought, when normally the group was so loud and boisterous. She looked at Chris, who hadn't moved.

"You okay?" she asked, wanting to hug him. When he was wearing that stoic expression, though, he almost felt like a stranger.

When he looked at her, his cop-mask fell away, revealing the worry beneath. "How am I going to tell Rob his kid's a killer?"

Rushing forward, Daisy wrapped her arms around him, trying to give him that feeling of loving security she always felt when Chris was holding her. "I'm sorry you have to do this."

He hugged her back, a little harder than usual. The items on his duty belt pressed against her belly, a physical reminder of his job, of that huge part of him that would always be a cop. Daisy was aware it would be hard to let him leave for work every day, knowing he could be injured or even killed. She loved Chris, though, and that meant loving the deputy, too.

She tipped her head back so she could meet his gaze. "Can you stay tonight?"

"I'm not going anywhere." His arms tightened around her. "Tyler's targeted you. I don't want you to be alone until they pick him up tomorrow."

"Good," she said, not wanting to let go of him. "I like having you around."

His smile was a ghost of his usual grin. "Love you, Dais."

"I know."

That made him laugh.

Once Rory, Lou, and Ellie had left, Tyler hurried across the street and wiggled under the porch, just like he'd watched his dad do the other night. The cover to the crawl space was in place, but the screws were missing, so Tyler just moved it over and slid into the hole feetfirst.

The crawl space was about four feet high. Crouching, Tyler shuffled forward, shining his flashlight—set to the dimmest setting—on the boards above him, checking for the hatch that would allow him into the house. The stove thing hadn't worked, so he was going to try again. This time, he'd do better. He'd get rid of the threat to his dad.

"You okay?" Daisy's voice made him freeze and flick off his flashlight. Tyler figured he was right beneath her, since her words were only slightly muffled.

"How am I going to tell Rob his kid's a killer?"

Tyler stopped breathing for a second. *They knew!* Chris and Daisy knew, and they were going to tell, and Tyler and his dad would both go to prison. He hesitated as his mind raced. Tyler's plan wouldn't work now that Chris was there. Soundlessly, he retraced his path to the opening under the porch.

As much as he wanted to take care of things himself, Tyler knew he had to tell his dad what he'd heard. His dad would know what to do.

Chapter 21

CHRIS PACED THE KITCHEN AS DAISY UNENTHUSIASTICALLY checked out the options for dinner. Nothing looked appetizing, and she knew they were both too stressed and anxious to eat. Giving up on her search for food, she leaned back against the counter just as Chris's phone rang.

He glanced at the screen, and his face went grim. "Rob," he answered, sounding robotic. It felt like her heart stopped for a second before her heartbeat took off at a gallop.

"Now? Right. Okay." Chris's impassive expression had acquired a few cracks, and he didn't look happy. "I'm already at Daisy's, so just knock when you get here."

Chris's free hand tightened into a fist. When Daisy glanced at his balled fingers, he must have noticed, since he stretched them flat again. Monotone and even, his voice didn't reveal his anger.

"See you." He ended the call and returned his phone to his belt with restrained violence. Once he glanced at her, though, his face softened. "Guess I'll be having that talk with Rob sooner than later."

"What's up?"

He grimaced. "Rob decided I was right about doing a search. He got a warrant for the house across the street this afternoon, but the gas leak put it on the back burner."

She snorted at his unintentional—at least she hoped it was unintentional—pun.

His quick grin didn't clarify whether he'd meant the play on words or not, and he soon sobered. "He's coming over so we can search the house."

"Tonight?" She glanced at the black window. "In the dark?"

"Rob said we'll do the interior tonight and then come back tomorrow to search the yard."

Her stomach was churning as every instinct she had screamed a warning. "Why is he willing to search the house his son lit on fire—and where Tyler might have killed someone?"

"He said we won't be going into the room that burned. Safety reasons." The last two words were heavy with sarcasm. "I can't believe Rob knows how bad Tyler's gotten. Covering up an arson, especially when it's an unoccupied shed, is a much different thing than hiding a murder. Rob lives by a strict moral code. There's no way his conscience would allow him to do that."

She made a noncommittal sound. It seemed that she was the only one who believed the sheriff was capable of covering up his son's murderous tendencies. "Will you talk to the sheriff about Tyler tonight instead of tomorrow morning, then?"

His cheerful expression flattened as he sighed. "I'm going to have to. There's no way I can pretend that nothing's wrong the entire time we're searching."

"Do you think he'll fire you?" Daisy asked, hating that Chris could be punished for doing the right thing.

"Maybe." His tone was even, but Daisy knew how much Chris wanted to stay with the sheriff's department.

"I have no idea how he'll react. He's all about the rules, except when it comes to his son. When I think of everything he's done to cover up Tyler's arsons…"

Daisy's breath caught. "Do you think the sheriff is the one who—"

A heavy knock on the door stopped her words. She turned too fast and almost slipped, but Chris caught her arm, steadying her—physically, at least. "The sheriff's here. How am I supposed to make small talk with him when we've just been accusing his son of murder?"

"I'll go. You can stay here." He gently nudged her toward the stairs as he gave a humorless laugh. "This is going to be fun, processing a crime scene while finding a tactful way to ask my boss if his kid could be a killer. If it's not too late when we finish over there, I'll come back tonight."

"Come back, even if it is too late," she told him, a warm flicker cutting through the chill that lingered in her chest from their previous conversation. "I'll be up."

His smile disappeared almost as quickly as it arrived. His shoulders stiffened, and he headed for the door. Daisy heard the inner door click as it latched behind Chris, and she hurried back up the stairs to her bedroom window, turning off the lamp on her way.

Resting one knee on the window seat, she watched Chris and the sheriff cross the street as they headed toward the empty house. While Chris took a detour to the parked squad, collecting a black case from the cargo area, Coughlin fiddled with the lockbox hanging from the knob on the front door. He must have gotten the code from the owners or the realtor, since he unlocked the door and held it open for Chris.

The two men disappeared into the house, and Daisy sagged into the window seat, knowing it was going to be an endless few hours of staring at the blank outside of the house. The large front window lit, clearly showing the interior of the living room and the two men moving around inside. Room by room, they turned on the lights. When the owners had moved, they'd apparently taken all the blinds with them. The only window that stayed dark was the one that had shown flames the night before.

Once almost the entire house was illuminated, Chris and Rob returned to the living room. It was like watching a muted movie on a very small screen. Not for the first time, Daisy wished for binoculars. She leaned forward until her forehead was pressed against the glass.

Even with the distance, it was easy to tell that the two men had worked together for a long time. They moved around the room in an efficient rhythm, and Daisy hoped that meant the search would be quick, and Chris would be back at her house even before she had a chance to get bored watching them collecting evidence.

There was a thump downstairs. Startled, Daisy jumped from the window seat. She strained to listen, but her heart pounding in her ears drowned out any other sounds. Creeping toward the bedroom door, she flinched as a floorboard creaked under her foot. She paused in the doorway, but she still didn't hear anything.

Daisy started wondering if she was imagining this, like she'd imagined the intruder the other night. This sound had been loud and definitely inside the house, though. Taking a couple of steps out into the hall, she inhaled a deep, steadying breath—and froze.

She smelled smoke.

As her heart began to gallop, she reversed her steps, hurrying back into her bedroom toward the bedside table where her phone was charging. Chris was just across the street. She'd call him, and he'd be inside her house in seconds. Grabbing her cell, she pushed the main button, but nothing happened. Daisy stared at the black screen as she pushed the start button over and over. It was charged and only a few months old—why was her phone dead?

Giving up, she rushed out of her bedroom. There were fire extinguishers. She could use those to put out the fire before it got out of control. As she descended the stairs, the smell of smoke grew stronger.

In the downstairs hall, she flicked the light switch, but nothing happened. Could something electrical have blown, causing the smoke and a loss of power? Strangely enough, the thought was almost reassuring, that there was an explanation. As frightening as an electrical fire might be, unexplained thumps and smoke and power outages were even more terrifying.

As she entered the kitchen, intending to grab a flashlight from the utility drawer, she stopped abruptly. Flames flickered in the entryway, coloring the kitchen red. The smoke was thicker, burning her throat and making her cough. Pressing her sleeve against her mouth and nose, she grabbed the fire extinguisher from under the sink. When she turned around, pulling the pin to unlock the device, a backlit, menacing figure was standing in the kitchen doorway.

With a shriek, she squeezed the lever, dousing the person with foam. He lurched toward her, so she threw the extinguisher at him and ran into the living room. Blinded by the darkness after she'd stared into the fire, she crashed into a chair and tumbled to the ground, landing painfully on her hip and shoulder.

As soon as she hit, she was scrambling to her feet again, running almost before she had her feet untangled from the chair legs. Unable to resist a glance behind her, she saw Tyler moving slowly from the kitchen, pouring something from a rectangular can onto the floor.

It felt like time slowed as he put the container down and pulled out a matchbook. Tyler struck a match, the small flame standing out against the red and orange of the burning kitchen, and looked at her, smiling faintly, as he tossed it to the floor. Fire zipped along the line of accelerant, lighting the fumes in a tiny wall of flame.

"I didn't want to hurt you," he called over the roar of the fire. "But you saw him with King and refused to shut up about it. I had to do it. I had to do what needed to be done."

King? Did he mean Anderson King? She hadn't seen the sheriff with anyone. Her whole body jerked as the realization hit. It hadn't been Deputy Macavoy. The sheriff had been moving Anderson King's body that night.

Slowly, deliberately, Tyler moved closer, leaving a thin trail of gas behind him. Snapping out of her shocked daze, Daisy bolted for the stairs. None of the rooms would be safe downstairs. With their barred windows—or no windows—she couldn't escape even if she'd been able to force herself outside. Briefly, she considered the front door, but terror instantly smashed that idea. Even with her home on fire, the thought of leaving it liquefied her insides with fear.

Sheer instinct drove her toward her bedroom, her

sanctuary, even though she knew it would become her coffin. Her lungs felt tight in the haze of smoke, not allowing her to pull in enough air. After all those miles on the treadmill, all those sessions with Chris, terror and smoke destroyed her fitness, leaving her gasping as she climbed a single flight of steps. At the top of the stairs, she looked over her shoulder to see Tyler, backlit by red and yellow flames, pouring gas in patterns across her hall floor.

"Tyler!" she called, her voice cracking, and he turned to look at her. Heat rushed up the stairs, as hot and dry as if she were baking in an oven. "Tyler, please stop! Why are you doing this?"

"I can't stop!" His voice broke, as well, but Daisy couldn't tell if it was from emotion or the smoke. "I have to take care of this. It's my turn to be a man. Dad protects me, and I protect him. That's what families do!"

The raw emotion in Tyler's voice gave Daisy hope. Maybe she could reason with him, get him to stop burning her house. "Your dad wouldn't want you to hurt me," she said hoarsely. The smoke was thickening, threatening to choke her, and she held off a cough, since she was afraid she wouldn't be able to stop once she'd started. "He wouldn't want you to do this."

"Shut up!" His arms flew wide in a vehement gesture, sloshing gas onto her wall. "You don't know anything. I'm doing this for him! You *saw* him with Anderson King! He didn't want to do it, but he didn't have a choice. King was a blackmailing drug dealer. And what happened to Mr. Gray was his own fault. He'd taken pictures of me at the fires. They would've ruined everything!"

The horror of what she was hearing merged with her hellish surroundings. Despite the fact that she knew Tyler, this *boy*, had stood by while his father killed people, she gave one last attempt at convincing him not to burn her alive. "Please, Tyler. I don't want to die."

"I'm sorry." He stopped playing with the fire and walked to the stairs, his gaze fixed on her face. "You're nice and really hot, and I don't want to hurt you. I have to protect him, though."

"My phone's in my room, and I'm going to use it to call Chris," she bluffed. "He's going to be here in seconds, and he'll be pissed. You should get out while you can."

The sound of his laugh made the back of her neck prickle with aversion. "Good luck with that. Dad killed that phone remotely before he called Chris."

"What?" Confusion made her hesitate. "How could he do that to my phone?"

"It's not your phone." He started climbing the stairs, the flames rolling up the walls next to him. "Dad broke in through the crawl space and switched your phone for a matching one. You can't call for help. You're not getting out of this house...ever."

She reeled back as his words hit her like a physical blow. It was her private nightmare, that she would die alone, still trapped in this house. When Tyler laughed again, Daisy knew it was no use. He was going to burn her house to the ground—with her inside.

Darting into her bedroom, she slammed her door and locked it. Turning, she fought the instinctual urge to hide under the bed or in the closet. It wasn't Tyler who was going to kill her, but what he brought with him. She couldn't hide from fire and smoke. It would find her.

Her frantic glance took in her room, trying to find a way out. Her computer was downstairs in her study, and it was useless for communicating without power to the modem, anyway. Her gaze locked on the window. Even if she couldn't force herself to leave through it, she knew she could open it. If she yelled, surely someone would hear her?

Running to the window, she put her hand on the crank. Before she could turn it, she looked across the street at number 304 and went still. Framed by the picture windows, the sheriff was standing in front of Chris, his face buried in his hands. As she watched, Chris stepped closer, placing a hand on one of Rob's slumped shoulders.

"No!" she yelled, struggling to open the window. "It's a trap!"

Before she could even crack open the window an inch, the sheriff yanked something off his duty belt. In the same motion, he raised it high in the air, and the object extended into a baton. The sheriff swung as Chris stumbled back, his arm rising to deflect the unexpected blow.

Sucking in a breath, Daisy lurched back. Everything felt like it was happening in slow motion. She couldn't take her eyes off the horrifying tableau across the street, but when the sheriff lifted the baton again, something popped in her head, and she was able to move in real time again.

She charged for the door, unlocking and swinging it open, only to come face-to-face with Tyler.

The sheriff's attack on Chris still playing in her mind, Daisy attempted to shove past him, but he dropped the gas can and grabbed her arm. She tried to yank it free, but he held tight.

Daisy didn't hesitate. Lurching toward him, she moved in close. Sent off balance when she quit pulling against him, Tyler stumbled back.

Stepping into him, she drove the heel of her hand upward at his nose, forcing herself to follow through instead of pulling the strike like she had in training. The knowledge that he was trying to kill her helped, and rage added power to the hit. Tyler released a sound that would've made her feel bad if Chris wasn't being beaten at that very moment, and if that punk kid wasn't trying to keep her from him.

Her knee connected with his groin. When he doubled over in pain, she grabbed his hair as she raised her leg again, kneeing him in the face. Using her grip on his hair, she shoved him away from her, and he went down. She didn't wait to see if he got to his feet again, but turned and ran toward the stairs instead.

At the top, she jerked to a stop. Fire was everywhere.

Flames ran across the floor and danced up the walls, making it feel like she was about to descend into hell. Smoke filled the space, rolling in thick clouds at the ceiling. She glanced back at an unmoving Tyler. Even after everything he'd done, she couldn't leave a kid to burn.

Running for the hall closet, she grabbed a couple of blankets and hurried into the bathroom. Daisy turned on the shower and tossed the blankets into the tub before stepping under the spray. The freezing-cold water shocked her lungs, but she forced herself to stay until her clothes and the blankets under her feet were soaked.

She was shaking uncontrollably by the time she grabbed the blankets and ran back to a groaning Tyler. Tossing a soaked blanket over him, she wrapped herself in the other and then grabbed handfuls of his coat under his shoulders. Daisy pulled him across the floor to the top of the stairs.

With a rough jerk, she started pulling him down the burning steps. The first couple were the hardest, until momentum and gravity kicked in, and Tyler started sliding faster and faster. By the time they reached the bottom, Daisy was having to hold him back, fighting to keep his weight from bowling her over. She was desperate to stop and try to catch her breath, but she forced herself to keep moving, reminding herself that there was no catching her breath in a smoke-filled house.

Glancing behind her, she flinched at the flames that had overtaken the hallway.

Chris, she reminded herself. *Help Chris*.

Readjusting her grip on Tyler's coat, she started pulling. His body slid more easily across the wood floor, and she ran backward, the heat of the fire surrounding her. Steam from her clothes and blanket joined the smoke in the air, making it hard to see.

As she turned into the dining room, Tyler's legs bounced off the doorframe. Daisy, her chest heaving as she tried to suck in enough oxygen, felt her arm muscles shake under the strain of his weight.

"Almost there," she told herself, coughing out the last word as the smoke burned her lungs. Just one more room to get through, and they'd be at the front door.

The kitchen was an inferno. Daisy didn't allow herself to pause or even slow. If she did, she'd never go into the kitchen, and then she, Tyler, and Chris would all die. She wasn't about to give Chris up—not for another seventy or eighty years.

Her fingers tightened around Tyler's coat, and she backed into the flames. The heat was incredible, covering her skin and the inside of her lungs in seconds. A piece of flaming debris fell from the ceiling onto Tyler's head, and his hair caught fire.

Grabbing a corner of his blanket, Daisy yanked it over his head, smothering the flames. As soon as it was out, she renewed her grip on his coat and started pulling again. As she slid Tyler past the stove, she thought of the gas lines it contained, how it could easily explode. Moving faster, she pulled Tyler through the entryway until she bumped against the interior door.

Yanking it open, she stepped through and then remembered. The world spun, driving her down to her knees.

Daisy couldn't breathe, much less speak. She fumbled for Tyler, pulling him across the tile until he was closer to her. The outside door loomed above her, appearing as enormous as the entrance to an airplane hangar, rocking from side to side. She fell forward, landing on her hands.

Chris. The thought of his name didn't make it easier to breathe, but it did force her forward. One hand shifted and then a knee. *Chris is in trouble.* Her other hand inched ahead. It helped to focus on crawling, so much that she was startled when her head bumped the exterior door.

Don't think, she ordered her brain as she tilted her head to see the doorknob. *Don't think of anything except Chris.* Bracing her hands on the door, she rose onto her knees and grasped the knob. She tried to turn it, but it slipped in her grip, the sweat that coated her palms greasing the metal. Her fingers tightened, and it finally twisted, unlatching with a sharp click.

She pushed, but nothing happened. It took a moment for her to remember that the door opened inward. When she leaned back, the door came with her, opening until it bumped her knees. Night air rushed through the space she'd created, and she made a helpless sound before she managed to clamp her lips together.

Chris, she reminded herself. *Get to Chris.*

Shuffling back on her knees, she worked open the door until there was nothing between her and the open space. Dizziness hit her again, and her vision started to gray around the edges.

"No!" she said out loud, making herself jump at the volume. No passing out. She was moving too slowly already. How many times had the sheriff hit Chris? She needed to run.

Using the hand still clutching the doorknob and the other braced against the doorframe, she managed to pull herself up until she was standing. Her knees wanted to bend, her body to crouch, as if she were trying to balance on a sloped roof. She had to ignore everything—the breeze, the night sky, the open darkness, and her terror—especially her terror. If she allowed it in, it would take over and make her useless, and then Chris would die.

Chris, she thought, staring at the wood floor of the porch just outside the door. Forcing one foot forward, she crossed the threshold and stepped outside.

Chapter 22

DAISY PROMPTLY THREW UP. THE FORCE OF IT TOOK HER by surprise, and she stumbled forward another step as she vomited, bile burning her nose and throat. Her head buzzed with the violence of it, and she choked and heaved for several precious seconds before turning back toward the door. Leaning down, resisting the urge to run back into the house—the *burning* house—she grabbed Tyler by the coat again and pulled hard. His body lurched forward, pushing her back, and she half ran and half fell down the four porch steps.

At the bottom, she almost stumbled onto the concrete walkway, but she dropped Tyler and caught the railing, afraid that if she went down to her knees again, there would be no way she could get back up. Once she regained her balance, Daisy turned, staring at the ground immediately in front of her feet, and started to run in the general direction of number 304.

The yard was rough and lumpy and tried to catch her toes, tripping her a few times, but she didn't fall. Her breathing was harsh, too fast for the short distance she was traveling. The scrubby brown grass ended, and she stepped off the curb, jolting her whole body when she landed. She watched the asphalt in front of her running feet, and then the tan fender of the squad was in front of her, and she couldn't stop in time.

She bounced off the SUV, stumbling back several

steps before she managed to catch her balance again and plow forward. Skirting the squad, she stepped over the curb onto more grass. The living room window would be right in front of her, she knew. All she had to do was look.

Chris. Repeating his name like a mantra, she forced her gaze from the ground and up at the house in front of her. Although still muted, the scene was much bigger now that she was directly in front of it. To her relief, Chris wasn't dead. He was even on his feet, locked in a battle with the sheriff. As she watched, he landed an uppercut, sending Coughlin's head snapping back with the force of the blow.

The sheriff recovered quickly, though, and hammered at Chris, driving him back toward the far wall. The movement jolted Daisy, and she rushed for the front porch. Her shins hit the first step, sending her sprawling over them. After a stunned moment, she started to crawl.

The front door hadn't been closed completely, and Daisy shoved through the entrance. She'd expected crashes and thuds, or at least some sounds of a fight, but silence greeted her. Furious that she'd let Tyler delay her, frantic about what she was going to find, she tried to lighten her footsteps as she ran left toward the room she'd been watching though the window.

The sheriff had his back toward her as he bent over an unconscious—*please let him just be unconscious*—Chris. Without allowing herself to hesitate, she charged toward Coughlin. In his hunched position, it was easy to reach up and wrap her arms around his neck.

With a roar, he straightened, but she hung on, clasping her hands together and pressing her left forearm against the side of his neck. Although she'd practiced the hold in training, she'd never actually used it until that moment, and she hoped desperately it would work. If her arm wasn't positioned correctly, or if she wasn't applying enough pressure to cut off the flow of blood to his brain, he could shake her off like a fly and then kill her just as easily.

The seconds felt like hours as he grabbed at her encircling arms. Then, just as she worried she'd messed up the hold, he went down hard, taking her with him to the floor. When Chris had taught her the move, he'd told her to help the unconscious person down so they weren't injured, but there was no slowing the sheriff's bulk when he went limp.

His body landed partially on top of hers, driving the air from Daisy's lungs in a pained grunt. She knew she had only a short time before he recovered consciousness, and she fought her way out from under his bulk. Shoving him onto his left side, she managed to wriggle free.

Unsnapping his holster, she slid out his gun. Daisy wasted a precious second debating what to do with the weapon. Except for some practice dry firing and cleaning the pistols Rory had lent her, she hadn't had any experience with firearms. Daisy thought of tucking it in the back of her waistband, but she wasn't sure if her yoga pants would hold the heavy gun.

The sheriff groaned and, in her panic, she slid the weapon across the wood floor away from them both. It skidded to a halt a few feet from Chris's unmoving form. Ripping her gaze away from him, she refocused on the sheriff. If she allowed herself to dwell on Chris's stillness, Daisy knew she'd lose her ability to do anything useful.

With a hard shove, she rolled Coughlin onto his stomach. He was moving his arms slightly, and she knew she had to act fast before he was fully conscious and able to fight her. He kept his handcuff case on the left rear of his duty belt, and Daisy fumbled to remove the cuffs.

Grabbing his left hand by the thumb, she twisted it onto his back and secured the cuff around his wrist. Holding the section between the cuffs in her left fist, she reached for his other hand with her right.

Before she could grab it, he rolled, swinging his left arm and jerking the cuffs out of her hand. The open side of the restraints flew toward her face, the metal forming a dangerous hook, capable of gouging eyes or delicate flesh. Ducking, she brought up her hands to protect herself, falling hard on her shoulder. She tried to roll, but Coughlin had followed her, pinning her back to the floor.

She thrust up her arm, sending a palm-heel strike toward his nose. When he jerked back, avoiding most of the impact, Daisy took advantage of the space he'd created and flipped onto her stomach. In her head, she could hear Chris coaching her. *Keep fighting, Dais. That's the most important thing. Don't give up.*

Pulling her knees up under her, she drove her elbow into the sheriff's ribs, taking a vicious pleasure in his grunt of pain. Without pausing, she swung back her head, feeling her skull connect with something so hard that the impact made her vision blur for a moment. Whatever she'd hit had made him yell and back off. She dragged herself free of his loosened hold and scrambled to her feet.

When she turned, the sheriff was up, as well, his eye
red and already swelling. Chris's voice rang in her head
again. *Don't let up, Daisy. Keep the hits coming.* She
kicked out, not wanting to get close enough to land a
punch. Her front kick drove him back a few steps, and
then she swung her leg in a side kick, hoping to hit that
same place on his thigh where she'd landed the blow
on Ian.

His hand caught her ankle before she connected,
and he jerked her forward. She stumbled, and the sheriff yanked again, knocking her onto her back. The air
rushed out of her lungs when she hit, leaving her gasping. He followed her down, pinning her again, and then
he swung.

His fist hit her face with such force that all her training disappeared. The only thing that remained was the
pain and the bewildering knowledge that someone—*the
sheriff!*—had hit her. She was used to grappling and
punching bags, but none of that had prepared her for the
brain-shattering reality of a true hit.

When her mind cleared and the pain faded enough
for her to have a rational thought, she realized that
Coughlin's hands were around her throat. As she struggled against his hold, she stared at his face, at his normal
impassive expression. The scariest part of everything
was his lack of emotion. If he was about to kill her, he
should at least be raging. There was nothing, though.
His eyes were empty.

"This actually worked out for the best," he said
evenly as his fingers tightened around her throat. "You
had to go next anyway. I hadn't figured out how to
cover up Deputy Jennings's death, but now it can be a

murder-suicide, a tragic possessive-lover kind of thing. It's a shame. He's a good cop. Too bad he's so infatuated with you."

She tried to fight, to shove him back, but his hands held her still. It was so wrong, that people would think Chris had killed her and then killed himself. Her training finally kicked in, and she grabbed his right arm with both hands in the first step toward freeing herself from his hold. The lack of air was already making her limbs clumsy and unwilling to follow her directions, and her fingers couldn't keep their grip.

As her struggles weakened and her vision narrowed, all she could see was the sheriff's emotionless face, and she thought of how unfair it was to be killed right after she'd finally managed to leave her house. To have a *life.* In a final burst of strength, she yanked at his wrists, trying to free her airway from his compressing hands. It was like his arms were made of concrete, though, and her weakening, air-starved muscles were no match for him. Her hands went limp and fell to the floor, and a gray cloud darkened her vision.

A loud boom was quickly followed by two more, and Coughlin's face was covered in a waterfall of blood. She squeezed her eyes closed as it spattered onto her skin, right before his forehead crashed against hers. His hands had fallen away from her neck, and she sucked in air, trapped under his weight.

Then he was gone, pushed to the side, and she opened her eyes to see Chris's face—battered and bloody and grim, but still more beautiful than anything she'd ever seen in her life. Something was running into her eyes, making them sting and water. When she touched the

side of her face with her fingers, though, she winced
and reconsidered any kind of contact.

"Dais." He reached toward her with shaking hands
and then pulled back, as if he was afraid of hurting her.
"God, Daisy. I thought you were dead. I thought I was
too late."

"Hey, Chris." It hurt to talk, but it also hurt to not
move, so she figured she might as well say something.
"You okay?"

"I'm fine." It was an obvious lie. She just had to look
at him to see that, but at least he was conscious and
talking and not dead. "Where are you hurt? Is any of
this your blood?"

She blinked. Her lashes felt gummy, and she didn't
know why. "What?" Raising her head, she looked down
her front. Her hoodie had been light blue, but blood
stained the top half, leaving it wet and sticky against her
skin. If she continued to think about that, she'd throw up
again, so she concentrated on Chris's question, instead.
Everything was aching and sore, but she didn't feel anything that felt critical.

"Keep your head still," he warned, pressing a hand on
her shoulder. "Don't move until Med checks you out."

Lowering her head to the floor, she watched as Chris
yanked out his phone and tapped the screen. As he held
the cell to his ear, he let his other hand brush her cheek
so, so lightly. Although she knew something was off,
that she was *too* calm, Daisy just lay still and enjoyed the
feel of his fingers on her skin as he talked to Dispatch.
She realized how scared she'd been that she'd never get
to experience his touch again.

The ceiling was spatter-painted with chunky red,

and she couldn't keep looking at that. Hoping that Chris was too occupied with the call to notice, Daisy turned her head. Inches away from her face were the sheriff's dead eyes. Caught by his vacant stare, she couldn't look away, couldn't even blink, until hands straightened her face, gently turning her gaze back toward the bloody ceiling.

To her relief, Chris's face blocked her view of the sprays of blood and...other stuff. "You still with me, Dais?"

"Yes." Her voice was flat and as hoarse as a pack-a-day smoker's. "Did you shoot him?"

He nodded. "Three times in the top of the head. It was the only target available to me."

She tried to nod, but his hold prevented it.

His forehead touched hers, and she held back a wince. The throb of pain was muted, though, and she didn't want to lose the contact with Chris.

"I didn't hesitate this time," he said, so quietly she barely heard him. He didn't sound like himself, and she wondered if he was in shock. Daisy was pretty sure she was. It wasn't normal to be that calm. Maybe being terrified for so long had fried all the fear receptors in her brain.

Lifting a hand, she stroked the back of his head, trying not to think of how she was getting blood in his hair. "Thank you."

"That's twice, Dais. Twice in two days that you almost died. Don't do it to me again."

It was a choked hiccup of a sound, but Daisy still couldn't believe he'd actually made her laugh—here, covered in a murderer's blood, lying next to the sheriff who was missing the back of his head. There really was something wrong with her brain. "I'll try."

"You better. I love you too much to lose you."

"I love you, too, Chris." Her hand paused on the back of his head. "Did you see? I left the house."

"I saw. Knew you could do it."

"I threw up on the porch."

He made a sound very similar to her earlier parody of a laugh. "It's okay. I'm proud of you."

"Tyler burned my house. He's on the porch, too."

"What?!"

Before she could explain, the sound of booted footsteps came from the direction of the front door, followed by two voices calling out, "Sheriff's department!"

Chris raised his head, revealing his newly blood-streaked forehead, and Daisy propped herself up on her elbows so she could see. Two deputies charged into the room, guns out. The gory scene brought them up short, and they stared in silence for a frozen second.

"Dad?" A bloody-faced Tyler appeared in the doorway behind them. One of the deputies turned, holstering his gun, and used his body to both stop Tyler from entering and to block the boy's view of the room. "Dad! What's wrong with him? What'd they do to him? Dad!"

As the deputy backed a still-screaming Tyler toward the front door, the other cop finally shifted his shocked gaze from the sheriff's body to Chris. "What the *fuck* happened here, Jennings?"

Chapter 23

I F DAISY HAD KNOWN HOW LONG IT WOULD BE BEFORE she got to go home, she might've reconsidered leaving her house. But then an image of Chris's limp body flashed through her mind, making her shake her head. Even if she'd known she'd never get to return home, nothing could've stopped her from heading to his rescue.

"Daisy?"

"Dad?" She blinked at the bearded face peering around the curtain that made up the wall of her cubicle. "What are you doing here?"

"I heard about what happened on the radio—well, the basics, at least. They didn't mention you, but I called to make sure you were okay. When you didn't answer your cell phone, I tried Jennings. His went to voice mail, too, so I drove to Simpson. The fire chief told me they'd taken you to Connor Springs in the ambulance." He eyed the scrubs a kind nurse had found for her to change into when her gory clothes had been taken away in evidence bags. "He said you were covered in blood."

"Not mine," she explained. "Except for some bruising on my face and…well, pretty much everywhere, I'm okay. The EMTs insisted I come here, though." Under the cover of their professional calm, she'd been able to tell that the amount of gore she'd been wearing had freaked them out. It had taken a while to convince them that they weren't missing a gushing injury.

"How'd…" He rubbed a hand over his mouth and started again. "You're out of the house. Was it the fire?"

"No." After all the horror and shocks of the night, her trek through the burning house and across the street had been pushed to the back of her mind to deal with later. "I saw the sheriff attack Chris. I had to go."

That time, she was pretty sure his face swipe was to wipe away tears. Gabe caught the back of a chair like it was a cane and lowered himself onto it. Propping his elbows just above his knees, he stared at the floor.

"That's…good, Daisy. Really good."

From her spot sitting on the padded table, she reached over and patted his rounded shoulder. "Thanks, Dad."

For a while, they sat in silence. Daisy had to fight back her threatening tears at the sight of her hard-as-nails father crying. Eventually, he gave his face a final, two-handed rub and leaned back in his chair, stretching his work boots out in front of him.

"Where are we going to live?" she asked, wanting to break the silence that had grown awkward.

Cutting off his laugh in the middle, he shook his head. "Don't worry about that right now. We'll stay at the motel if we need to."

"I wonder how Chris is doing." She was tempted to start a search of the hospital to find him.

As if he'd been waiting for an excuse to move, her dad stood abruptly. "Want me to check on him?"

"Sure. That'd be great. Ask"—Gabe was already gone, so she sighed and finished her sentence under her breath—"if I can see him."

And she was left alone again. Although she understood that she was low priority for the medical staff,

Daisy wished someone would let her know she was free to go, so she could track down Chris and see with her own eyes that he really was okay. She wouldn't be able to relax until she felt his arms around her again.

When the curtain moved, she looked up, expecting her dad, but a strange man entered instead. Daisy stiffened, and he apparently saw her unease, judging from the way he lifted his hands, palms out, as if to show he wasn't a threat.

"Daisy Little?" he asked.

As she nodded, she watched him warily. He wasn't a big man, but he exuded authority. His dark hair was tidy and his clothes neat, although fairly casual.

"I'm Paul Strepple." He didn't reach out to shake her hand, and Daisy was grateful for that. Still uncertain of him, she definitely didn't want to touch him yet. "Investigator with the Colorado BCA."

Pulling his ID out of his pocket, he held it out to her. Although she wouldn't know authentic BCA identification from something created by a five-year-old forger, Daisy examined it closely. "Because of the circumstances, we've been charged with investigating."

"Weren't you already?" she asked, remembering Chris telling her about the state's involvement in the Willard Gray case.

"We'd been assisting," he said, returning his ID to his pocket. "We'll be heading up the investigation from this point on."

She nodded, waiting for his questions. It didn't take long. He asked about the usual personal information—full name, date of birth, address—and then he paused, eyeing her closely.

"So, Ms. Little. What happened tonight?"

Her inhale was slightly shaky, and it rasped against her aching throat. She really did not want to relive the evening, but it had to be done. Mentally pulling up her big-girl panties, she told the investigator what had happened, starting from the sheriff's phone call to Chris and ending with the two deputies' entrance.

"Gas leak?" he asked when she'd finished, so she backtracked and explained about her malfunctioning stove and Tyler's quick exit after he'd been alone in her kitchen. "And what did Tyler mean about you seeing his father with King?"

"I'm guessing that the sheriff was the guy I saw hauling the dead body to his SUV," she said.

Strepple's eyes bulged, showing surprise—or any emotion, really—for the first time since his arrival. "You saw Robert Coughlin moving King's body?"

"Yes, but I didn't know it was him." After a moment of consideration, she added, "I didn't know it was definitely a dead body, either. The boot falling out of the tarp made me suspicious, though."

Closing his eyes for a moment, Strepple said with exaggerated calm, "Why don't you go back to the beginning and tell me exactly what you saw."

Daisy did, adding the sheriff's odd behavior toward her. In the middle of her retelling, Gabe stuck his head around the curtain.

"You okay, Daisy?" he asked, eyeing the investigator with suspicion.

"Fine. Thanks, Dad." She smiled at him with an effort, so tired that even lifting the corners of her mouth was a struggle. "Did you find Chris?"

"Sort of. He's getting X-rays, so I found out his

general location, but I haven't seen him myself." After another glance at Strepple, he turned back to Daisy. "I'm going to run to the cafeteria and grab some food. Want anything?"

Too tired to be hungry, she shook her head and gave him a small wave before he disappeared again. With a silent sigh, she picked up her statement where she'd left off.

"So neither the sheriff's department nor the fire department had reports on these arsons?" He seemed more bothered by this than the murder. Apparently, missing paperwork was the ultimate crime.

"That's right." Daisy swallowed back a yawn. "Ian has his own copies of the calls he went on. It's not all of them, but it's a start."

"Thank you. I'll ask him." Since Strepple looked like he was preparing to leave, she assumed the interview was almost over.

"Wait," Daisy said, and he looked over his shoulder at her, an eyebrow raised in inquiry. "Did Tyler burn down Lou's cabin, too, or was that really her stalker?"

"Lou's cabin?" Strepple squeezed his eyes shut as if he was in pain before turning back toward Daisy. "Why don't you start at the beginning with that one, too?"

By the time she'd finished telling the investigator everything she knew about the Coughlins' crimes and possible additional wrongdoing, another forty minutes had passed.

"Thank you, Ms. Little." Strepple moved toward the curtain, looking determined to leave that time. "You've been very helpful."

"Have you talked to Chris yet?"

"Not yet," he told her without pausing. "I'm going to do that now."

"Oh!" Hopping off the padded table, she hurried after him. "Can I go with you? I just want to see him to make sure he's okay, and then he'll be all yours."

Stopping but not turning around, Strepple was quiet for a second. "Fine," he finally sighed. "Two minutes, and then you need to leave."

"Deal." She followed him through a maze of hallways. Her breathing sped up when she left the safety of her enclosed space, so she focused on the back of Strepple's jacket and concentrated on making her inhale exactly the same length as her exhale. It worked well enough to keep her from passing out before they reached a curtained cubicle that matched the one she'd just left. Once Daisy passed through the opening into the exam area, she ducked around the investigator and saw Chris lying on his own padded table, looking weary and cranky and hurt.

"Chris!" Her voice was embarrassingly close to a squeak, but he didn't seem to mind. A grin eased the pain lines on his face, even though his swollen mouth pulled his smile in the wrong directions, and he pushed himself to a seated position and held out his arms toward her.

"Hey, Dais. You doing okay?"

Hurrying into his hug, she pressed her sore face into his shoulder. Under the hospital smell was Chris's usual scent, and she felt herself relaxing against him. "A few bruises, that's all." Pulling away just far enough to meet his eyes, she reached a hand toward his swollen, discolored face. "Ouch."

"I'm fine." He gave her another painful-looking grin. "I'll be ugly for a while, but nothing's seriously damaged."

His tone was a little too light, and she frowned at him suspiciously. "They didn't find anything broken on the X-rays?"

"No." He lifted his hand to run a light finger over her sore cheek, and she caught her breath as she spotted the wicked-looking bruise forming on the back of his forearm. That must've been where the baton hit when he blocked. "Dais." He gently tilted her head so she wasn't able to see his injured arm. "It'll be fine. I'm even getting out of here tonight."

Her laugh was shaky, but she forced it out anyway. "I don't think it's tonight anymore. I'm pretty sure it's tomorrow."

"It is," Strepple said, gaining their attention. "I need to get your statement, Deputy."

"Dad's here," Daisy hurried to tell Chris. "He'll drive us to Simpson once we've been released."

"Okay." He pulled her down for the lightest touch of lips, which still hurt. Daisy didn't care, though. It was worth a little pain to kiss Chris. "See you in a bit."

Reluctantly, she pulled away. It was hard to leave an injured Chris to the mercies of the investigator, but she needed to find her missing father. After all, he was their ride home.

Chapter 24

"SURE YOU'RE READY FOR THIS?" CHRIS'S SMILE WAS teasing. "Lou in her own habitat… It's a little scary."

Daisy laughed and slapped his shoulder. "Lou's awesome, no matter where she is. And I was born ready." At his smirk, she rolled her eyes. "Okay, so maybe I took a detour between birth and a few weeks ago, but I'm definitely ready now."

"Let's do this, then."

Despite her words, it took an effort to open the truck door and an even greater one to climb out of her seat. She focused on the pavement right in front of her feet until her heart settled down a little. With a deep breath, she lifted her chin and took in the front of The Coffee Spot. Although the building wobbled slightly from side to side, Daisy smiled.

"It looks exactly how I pictured it," she said, proud that her voice was calm, although still a little raspy. The doctor had said it would take some time for her trachea to heal. In the meantime, Chris had told her that he thought her husky voice was sexy.

He frowned, eyeing the small structure in front of them. "Kind of a dump?"

"No!" she protested, though she was unable to prevent another laugh from escaping. "It's cute. And cozy. And we should probably go inside before it starts rocking back and forth any more than it already is."

With a concerned look, he took her arm and escorted her to the door. She didn't mind, since the world seemed steadier when he was touching her. Chris pulled open the door, making the sleigh bells hanging on the inside jangle. As soon as Daisy stepped inside, a shriek like a train whistle came from behind the counter.

Lou hurtled across the shop as the few customers ducked out of her way. "Daisy! You're here!"

Daisy barely had time to brace herself before the other woman plowed into her, hugging her tightly. As air was squeezed out of her lungs, Daisy wondered if allowing Lou to use her gym was the best idea. She was already freakishly strong.

"This is so perfect!" Lou released her and grabbed her hand, towing her to the counter. "Sit! What do you want to drink?"

"Um…" She slid onto a stool, trying to ignore the fascinated stares of the other customers. Eyeing the menu hanging on the wall behind Lou, Daisy hesitated. Her heart rate was picking up again, and she rubbed her damp palms over her thighs.

Stepping behind her, Chris wrapped his arms around her upper chest and rested his chin on the top of her head. Instantly, she relaxed.

"Why does it stink in here?" Chris's chin pressed into her head as he spoke. Once he mentioned it, Daisy noticed the stench of body-odor underlying the more pleasant coffee scent filling the shop.

Lou beamed. "Smelly Jim is back! I've been really worried that something had happened to him, but Jim said he's been, in his words, 'lying low' until things settled down here. I tried to give him money, to thank him for pulling me and Callum out of the reservoir, but he wouldn't take it. I finally got him to agree to me buying him anything he wants from here. It seems like such a small thing for saving our lives, but he's happy, so I'll quit bugging him about having a parade in his honor. Sorry, Daisy! I'm talking way too much again, but I'm just excited that Smelly Jim's okay. Drink?"

"Not to be boring, but just a regular coffee, please."

"Good choice," Chris said.

Lou grabbed a cup. "And you could never be boring."

"I wouldn't mind a little boring for a while," Daisy admitted, tracing the edge of the counter with her thumb. "Just going to the grocery store is plenty of excitement for me."

"Even though I must admit that I miss the whiteboard"—Lou handed her the coffee—"I have to agree with you. Summer's coming, and that means more people on the reservoirs, which means more calls for us. Being on the dive team is enough of a wild ride without throwing arsons and murders into the mix."

Taking a sip of her coffee, Daisy just made a word-less sound of agreement.

"And what's your beverage of choice, Deputy Chris?" Leaning over the counter, Lou examined him closely. "Your face of many colors is healing up nicely. The bruises have faded to a kind of sickly yellow." Lou looked back and forth between Chris and Daisy. "You two match. It's cute, in a damaged kind of way."

He snorted a laugh. "Thank you, I think. And I'll have what she's having." His chin dug into her scalp again. She didn't mind the pressure. In fact, it was reas-suring to be surrounded by Chris.

"So…" As she poured Chris's coffee, Lou looked over her shoulder at Daisy, who was equal parts impressed and worried about her careless handling of a hot beverage. "What's the plan, now that you're out and about?"

Her stomach churned at the question, but it wasn't a bad mix of emotions. There was fear, but also excitement and anticipation. "I'm thinking about opening a gym. A real one, not just the one in my house."

Thrusting the cup in Chris's direction, Lou grinned. "That would be awesome! This town desperately needs something like that—as you know from all the people who pile into your training room on a regular basis."

"My dad never let me pay rent, so I have some money saved." Daisy felt Chris release her and shift away so he could drink his coffee, but she'd calmed enough to not need her safety blanket wrapped around her anymore. The conversation was distracting her, too, and talking about her plans out loud was making her even more enthusiastic about the idea. "I thought I could focus on the self-defense aspect—like boxing, MMA, and Krav Maga—but have some other classes, too, for the…well, less violence-inclined."

"Belly, the coroner, used to teach yoga." Ellie slid onto the next stool over, grinning at Daisy's surprised look. "You must not have heard me come in. Lou makes enough noise to drown out the bells on the door." Laughing, she ducked the cardboard cozy that Lou chucked at her head, reaching up to catch it. "Thanks, Lou. Just don't do that with my latte."

Turning to grab a cup off the stack, Lou asked, "What was that about Belly and yoga? Those two don't seem to fit together."

"She used to teach it. When she was in the store the other day, she mentioned it." Turning to Daisy, Ellie said, "I think she misses it. I bet you could recruit her."

"Yoga." After considering the idea for a moment, Daisy nodded. "That'd be good, especially for these muscle-bound guys." She rotated on her stool so she could squeeze Chris's biceps. Grinning, he obediently flexed. "Need to keep them flexible."

For some reason, that sent Lou and Ellie into a giggle-fest. "Flexible is good," Lou said, once she could speak again.

"I'm feeling a little too testosterone-heavy to be a part of this conversation." Chris bent and pressed a kiss to the top of Daisy's head. "I'm going to run a couple of errands." He gave her a questioning look, and she nodded, answering his unspoken question of whether she'd be okay without him for a little while.

The other customers had busied themselves with their phones and conversations, so she was feeling less like a zoo exhibit and more like a normal woman having coffee with her friends.

"See you later." She smiled at him, and his eyes darkened before he kissed her again, this time on the mouth. It was short, but intense, kicking up her heart rate just as she'd gotten it under control.

"I won't be long. Half hour, tops." He continued to hesitate while watching her carefully.

"Sounds good." When he still didn't move, she made shooing motions with her hands. "Now go, so we can discuss you and your buddies."

That must have proven to him that she'd be fine, since he grinned at her and headed for the door. As she turned back toward the other women, she saw Lou was frowning as she watched Chris through the front window.

"How's he been?" Lou asked, her eyes still on Chris as he got into his truck. "He seems...sad."

Before she answered, Daisy took a moment to consider how he really was. "It's going to take a while, I think, before he's back to his usual level of happy. Until the whole mess exploded, he really admired...his boss."

"Will he run in the emergency sheriff election?" Ellie asked, taking a sip of her latte.

Daisy shook her head. "Not unless he changes his mind. Chris likes responding to calls and being in the middle of the action. Turning into a paper pusher would drive him insane. Even having off these last couple of weeks during the state investigation is making him twitchy. He's ready to get back out there."

"Too bad," Lou said, spinning a plastic cup lid on the counter. "He'd have made a good sheriff."

Just the word "sheriff" made her skin clammy, so Daisy turned to Ellie. "How are you doing?" She hadn't gotten a nighttime call from Ellie since before the shooting.

"It seems kind of coldhearted to say." Ellie bent her head over her latte, absently twirling a stir-stick in it.

"Don't worry about offending *us*," Lou told her. "I'm the one who referred to a deceased person as Headless Dead Guy, remember? And Daisy's been dating a cop forever. I'm sure she can handle some plain speaking."

Shooting a wary glance at the other customers, Ellie leaned closer to the two. Lou and Daisy mimicked her until their heads were almost touching. "Ever since the sheriff was killed, and I found out King was dead, I've been so...*relieved*." She leaned back, leaving Daisy and Lou in their craned-forward positions.

"That's it?" Lou said. "That's your confession?"

Looking uncertain, Ellie nodded. "Well, yeah. Two people are dead, and I'm more relaxed than I've been for months. Isn't that a sign I'm a sociopath?"

Since Ellie asked the question so seriously, Daisy tried to turn the amused sound that came out of her mouth into a cough. "No," she answered after clearing her throat. "You are definitely not a sociopath. I'd be relieved if the person who'd *shot* me and tried to kill me was dead."

"Um..." Lou sent her a sideways look. "The person who tried to kill you *is* dead—at least one of them."

Carefully placing her coffee on the counter, Daisy flattened her shaking hands against her thighs, trying to force them to be still. "I'm glad Tyler's going to be okay...physically, at least."

"I guess." The other two looked at Lou, and she grimaced. "I don't wish he were *dead* or anything, but the little brat burned my truck...and my house. Sure, my stalker probably watched him do it and didn't stop him, but Tyler confessed to being the one who lit the match."

"Why'd he go after you? It's a ways out to your place—how'd he even get there?" Daisy asked.

"Apparently," Lou said, still sounding bitter, "he didn't like that I was investigating Willard Gray's murder. He thought he was protecting his dad. And he's known how to drive since he was thirteen. He stole his dad's truck to drive out to my place. That's how he got out to set the wildland fires, too."

"Wow." Daisy shook her head. "I'm not sure why I'm surprised, though. He did burn *and* try to blow up mine. He thought he was helping his dad, but there are still some pretty big chunks missing from the kid's moral framework. Deputy Macavoy's parents filed a missing-person report, and no one is optimistic about finding him alive. They're looking into his mom's disappearance, too."

"Tyler's mom?" Lou asked. "I thought she left them voluntarily."

Pity for the kid rushed through Daisy, almost smothering the anger toward him. "There's no proof she didn't, but Rob walked in on his wife abusing Tyler. After that, no one saw her again. It's enough that the BCA is checking into it."

"How sad," Ellie sighed.

Lou made a sound of agreement. "Who told you that?"

"Strepple," Daisy said. "He called to update me on the investigation."

"Where'd they take Tyler?" Ellie asked.

"A psych facility outside of Denver."

Ellie's eyebrows rose. "Which one?"

"I'm not sure," Daisy answered with an apologetic grimace. "Sorry. Strepple didn't share that. Chris's been trying to protect me from knowing details about the case. It's a good thing I've started leaving the house, or I wouldn't know *anything*."

At that, Lou growled, "Seriously? Why would he think that would help? It makes me nuts to not know stuff."

"Me too. Even my dad is acting all protective, and that's not like him."

"He's still staying with you at Chris's?" At Daisy's nod, Lou scrunched her nose. "Doesn't that get in the way of you and Chris...?" Trailing off, she waved a hand.

"Talking?" Daisy guessed, widening her eyes with mock-innocence.

"No."

"Watching movies?"

"No."

"Cooking brownies together?"

Cocking her head to the side, Lou looked thoughtful. "I guess that could be one euphemism for it."

Ellie wrinkled her nose. "No. No, it can't."

Finally breaking down with a laugh, Daisy admitted, "Yes, when Dad sits on the couch between us, glaring at Chris, it does get in the way of me and Chris"—she imitated Lou's wave—"cooking brownies. Literally in the way. It's just temporary, though. Dad'll be heading out to another job site soon, and he'll find another place in Simpson. Chris's already bugging me to move in with him permanently."

"Are you going to stay?" Lou asked.

"Yes." Living with Chris was pretty much as wonderful as she'd thought it would be.

"Oh!" Ellie slapped her non-latte-holding hand on the counter, startling Daisy. "Speaking of fathers, guess who called me last night?" Positively beaming, she answered her own question before either of the other two could guess. "Dad!"

"Seriously?" Lou demanded, rushing to round the counter. "And you didn't lead with that?" She grabbed Ellie, who lifted her coffee up out of the way just in time, and squeezed her tightly. "That's awesome, El! I'm so happy for you!"

When Lou finally released her and returned to her spot behind the counter, Ellie bounced on her stool a few times, grinning hugely. "I know! I can't believe I forgot to tell you until now. Poor George. I was so wired that I barely slept last night, and I kept poking him to wake him so I'd have someone to talk to about it."

"That's great, Ellie." Reaching over, Daisy grabbed her hand. "You could've called me instead of waking the sleeping beast." She didn't mention that a call would've woken Daisy, too, since she'd been sleeping a lot more soundly recently.

Ellie laughed, a genuinely happy sound. "George was right there, so I just tortured him."

The bells on the door jangled, and all three women turned their heads toward the sound to see Rory entering.

"Rory!" Ellie was the first to greet her. "My dad called last night! He's in Florida for some reason that he didn't explain very well. I mean, Florida? Really?"

A brief, but beautiful, smile flashed across Rory's face. "Good. He's okay, then?"

"Yep. He's even on his meds. We had a conversation that actually made sense."

"I'm glad." Rory took the stool on her right, and Daisy shuffled hers back a foot so she could see everyone without having to turn her head back and forth.

"Not that I'm not wildly excited that you joined us," Lou said to Rory, "but shouldn't you be watching your store? The guns don't sell themselves, you know."

"I was at the store." She frowned, but looked more baffled than angry. "Ian walked in and said that Derek drove by and saw Daisy walking into the coffee shop, so he texted Chief Early, who mentioned it to Soup, who called Ian."

Lou lowered her head to the counter with a thump that made Daisy wince. "This town."

"Ian said," Rory continued without reacting to Lou's comment, "he was going to watch the store so I could come here and have *girl time*." She said the last two words as if they were in a foreign language she didn't know. "Is *girl time* really a thing, or is Ian pretending he knows stuff he doesn't again?"

Lou and Ellie snickered, while Daisy tried to keep a straight face. Rory looked so very bewildered.

"I'm pretty sure it is a thing," Daisy said as seriously as she was able. "Not that I'm an expert, of course, since most of my knowledge of girl time has come from books and movies."

"It is a thing," Ellie confirmed.

Rory nodded. "I have something that I'm pretty sure is girl time appropriate, then."

Three pairs of eyes fastened on her.

"Well, spill it," Lou urged, propping her elbows on the counter and leaning in. "Don't make us drag it out of you. All that training with Deputy Chris has made us a bunch of badasses, so we could force you to talk if we need to."

Rory was actually blushing, which made Daisy even more curious.

"Here." Rory slapped a glossy brochure on the counter. All three reached for it, but Ellie was the quickest and managed to whip it away from the others' grabbing hands.

"What is this?" Ellie looked confused as she flipped it over. "Safe rooms? Is that like a panic room?"

Realization hit Daisy, and she shrieked and grabbed

Rory's arm. The other women looked alarmed. "He actually did it?"

Leaning back warily, Rory said, "By 'it,' do you mean propose? If so, then yes."

It was Lou's turn to scream as she barreled around the counter for the second time. "He proposed?" She lunged to hug Rory, but then paused in midreach. "Wait. Did you say yes?"

Rory didn't look like she wanted to answer, but she finally gave a short nod. With another shriek, Lou dove toward her and hugged her hard, apparently oblivious to Rory's panicked expression and stiff frame.

"Hold on!" Ellie had to almost shout to be heard over Lou's expressions of happiness. "I don't get it. Did Ian propose to you using a safe-room brochure rather than a ring?"

"Yes." Rory's face softened at the thought. "He said he was going to get me a gun, instead, but he figured I had plenty of those."

"Congratulations!" Hopping off her stool, Ellie dove into the hug, turning it into a three-way. As Rory's expression changed from panic to resignation, Daisy grinned at her and wrapped her arms around the cluster of women, joining in the group hug.

Her laugh burbled out of her, sheer happiness making it impossible to hold back. If this was girl time, then girl time was awesome.

Keep reading for a sneak peek at the first book in Katie Ruggle's brand-new Rocky Mountain K9 Unit series

Run to Ground

THE NEW WAITRESS WAS HOT. SQUIRRELLY, BUT HOT.

Theo always got to Coop's early for the K-9 unit's breakfast and informal roll call. Those fifteen minutes before Otto and Hugh showed up usually were, if not exactly peaceful, at least a little break from having to hide the mess he'd become. This morning, though, he was distracted by the way the dark-haired stranger kept trying very hard not to stare at him. He'd caught himself watching her four times now, and he'd only been in the diner for five minutes.

A mug thumped as it hit the table in front of him, and Theo turned his frown toward Megan. They had a morning ritual: He scowled. She delivered his food and coffee with more aggression than politeness. Neither said a word.

This morning, though, as Megan was turning away, Theo was almost tempted to break the silence. He barely caught himself before a question about the new server popped out of his mouth. Stopping the words just in time, he snatched up his coffee and took a drink, burning his tongue in the process. He set down the mug with enough force to make it almost slosh over the rim. *Shit*.

Before Theo could stop himself, his gaze searched out the new waitress again. She was delivering two plates of food to a table across the diner. By the look of concentration on her face and the exaggerated care she was taking, Theo assumed she was new to waiting tables. She was definitely new to Monroe, Colorado. If she'd been around, he would've noticed her. There was no doubt about that.

As she turned away from the table, smiling, their gazes caught for a second before she ducked her head and hurried toward the kitchen. The uniforms at Coop's were designed to be more homespun than sexy, but Theo couldn't look away from the stranger's rear view.

"Who's that?" Otto dropped onto the bench next to him.

Tearing away his gaze, Theo gave his fellow K-9 officer a flat stare. "Move."

"No." Otto stretched out his legs until his lumberjack-sized boots bumped the opposite bench. "I always sit here."

Just for the past two months. Theo didn't want to say that, though. It might've led to talking about what had happened, and he *really* did not want to discuss it. Still, he couldn't let it drop. "I'm not one of your wounded strays."

Otto made a noncommittal sound that heated Theo's simmering anger another few degrees. Before he could rip into Otto, though, Hugh slid into the opposite side of the booth.

"Hey," Hugh greeted both of them with his standard, easy-going grin. "Who's the new waitress?"

"You're not going to squeeze onto this bench, too?" Theo asked with thick sarcasm.

Half-standing, Hugh gave Theo a too-earnest look. "Did you want me to sit with you two? Because I can. It'll be cozy."

Several comebacks hovered on Theo's tongue, but he swallowed all of them. All it would do was convince Hugh to change sides, and they'd be uncomfortable and awkward all through breakfast. Behind Hugh's placid exterior was a mile-high wall of stubbornness.

He stayed silent.

With a slight smirk, Hugh settled back on his side of the table. "Anything fun and exciting happen last night?"

"Eh," Otto said with a lift of one shoulder, "Carson Byers got picked up again."

Hugh frowned. "That's not fun. Or exciting. That's something that happens almost every shift. What was it this time?"

"Trespassing."

"He was drunk and thought the Andersons' house was his again?"

"The Daggs' place, this time."

"Wait. Isn't that on the other side of town?"

"Yep."

"Dumbass."

"Yep."

Only half-listening, Theo let the other men's conversation wash over him. His gaze wandered to find the new server again. She was topping off the coffee mugs of the customers sitting at the counter as she listened to something Megan was telling her.

"I ran into Sherry at the gas station last night."

Otto's too-casual statement jerked Theo's attention back to their conversation.

Rubbing the back of his head, Hugh asked, "How's she doing?"

"Not good. But what do you expect when her dad—"

"Let me out." Theo cut off the rest of Otto's words, glaring at him until the other man slid out of the booth. As Theo stalked away from the table, there was only silence behind him—a heavy, suffocating silence. He didn't have a destination in mind except *away*, but his feet carried him toward the new server as if they had a mind of their own.

The woman watched him, her blue eyes getting wider and wider, until he stopped in front of her. They stared at each other for several moments. She was even prettier and more scared-looking close up. There were dark shadows smudged beneath her eyes, and her face had a drawn, tight look. Her throat moved as she swallowed, and her eyes darted to the side. Theo tensed, his cop instincts urging him to chase her when she ran.

"Theo," Megan barked in her husky voice as she passed, "go sit down. You're being creepy."

He sent her a frowning glance, but most of his attention was still on the new server. "What's your name?"

She swallowed again, and tried to force a smile, but it quickly fell away. "Jules. Um…for Julie."

"Last name?"

"Uh…Jackson." Her gaze jumped toward the door.

"Where are you from?" He couldn't stop asking

questions. It was partly his ingrained cop curiosity, and partly the personal interest he couldn't seem to smother.

"Arkansas."

Theo called bullshit on that. While she'd said her last name too slowly to be believable, this latest answer had come too fast, like he'd asked her a quiz question that she'd studied for. He could see the tension vibrating through her, her body projecting the urge to flee. What was she running from? An abusive husband? The consequences of a crime she'd committed? "What brings you to Colorado?"

"It's...a nice state?" Her eyes squeezed closed for a second, as if she was mentally reprimanding herself for the inane answer.

Every glance at the door, every stifled flinch, every half-assed response of hers just made Theo more suspicious. "You move here by yourself?"

"I...um..." Her hunted gaze fixed on Megan's back, but the other server was occupied with helping a little boy get ketchup out of a recalcitrant bottle and didn't see her new waitress's pleading expression. "I should get back to work."

"Wait." He reached for her arm.

"Theo." Hugh stood right behind him, and Theo felt his jaw tighten as his hand dropped to his side. Why did they feel a need to babysit him like he was an unstable six-year-old? "Food's here."

Theo didn't want to return to the table, didn't want to eat, didn't want to talk about Sherry or anything else. What he did want was to find out more about the new, pretty, squirrelly waitress whose name may or may not—but more likely *not*—be Julie Jackson.

Jules.

He was tempted to send Hugh back to the table without him, but what was the point? All she would do was keep lying...badly. Later, in the squad car, he'd try to run her name, although "Julie Jackson" from Arkansas, without a date of birth or a middle name, would give him enough hits to keep him busy searching for months. They were at the diner every morning. He'd have plenty of opportunity to try to get information from the newcomer. Instead of blowing off Hugh and asking Jules more questions, he gave a short, reluctant nod and returned to the table. He could wait for his answers.

Still, it was hard not looking back.

Chapter 2

One Week Earlier

JULIET YOUNG KNEW THE EXACT MOMENT SHE DECIDED TO commit a felony. It was when Sebastian, her seventeen-year-old, six-foot-two, two-hundred-pound jock of a brother, cried.

"Oh, Sam…"

"J-J-Juju…" His stutter hadn't been this bad since he was thirteen. It killed her that they were talking on the phone and she couldn't hug him—not that he'd probably want to be hugged. "Puh-puh…" His inhale shook with tears. "Please!"

Resting her forehead on her kitchen table, she felt all the despair and hopelessness and frustration that had swamped her after talking with her lawyer consolidate into a hard ball of resolve. She sat up straight. "New plan, Sam-I-Am."

"Wh-wh-wh…" When he couldn't manage the word, he just went quiet, waiting for her to tell him.

Now that she'd decided to do it, to break her life-long law-abiding streak, Jules felt strong again. No wonder people became criminals. "The lawyer said that, with the FBI investigation and without my CPA license, it's unlikely I'll get custody. The money's almost gone, and I'll need a really good, really expensive attorney to even have a chance at winning y'all."

His intake of breath was audible. "I-I-I-I c-c-can't *stand* i-it anym-more, Ju."

"I know. That's why we're going with plan...heck, I don't even know what letter we're on anymore. Probably triple-Y or something."

His laugh was just a short huff of sound, but it still made Jules smile.

"I'm calling the mob."

"Mr. Espina..." Jules's voice cracked on the last syllable. Clearing her throat, she forced her fist to release the crumpled handful of her skirt she'd been unconsciously clutching and tried again. "Mr. Espina, I need your help."

Mateo Espina didn't say a word. In fact, he didn't even twitch a muscle. It was a struggle not to stare at him. He was just so *different* than his brother that it was hard to believe the two were actually related. For over two years, Jules had worked for Luis Espina, and she'd never, ever been this nervous. Luis was a chatterbox who wore a constant, beaming, contagious smile on his round face. His brother, on the other hand, was all hard lines and angles, glaring eyes and stubble. Even the tattoos peeking from his shirt collar and rolled-up cuffs looked angry. Eyeing the man sitting across the table from her, Jules couldn't imagine him smiling. Brooding? Yes. Scowling? Sure. Flashing a cheery grin? No.

Jules realized she'd been staring at him silently for much too long, and she had to hide her cringe. It had been almost impossible to set up this meeting with Mr. Espina, and she was crashing and burning not even five minutes and ten words in. As she opened her mouth to say who knew what, a bored voice interrupted.

"What can I get you?"

Although Mr. Espina ordered a beer from the server, Jules stuck to water. The meeting would be hard enough with all of her wits about her. Besides, the sad fact was that she was broke. Drinks were the last thing on her stuff-I-need-to-buy list. Lawyers were number one. *Good* lawyers. *Miracle-working* lawyers.

"I was hoping," she said, "that you could give me a reference."

There was actually a reaction to that. It wasn't much of one, just the slightest lift of his eyebrow and twitch of a small muscle in his cheek.

"Although I wasn't charged with anything, I lost my CPA license and all my clients when Luis was investigated." The terror and humiliation of being questioned by the FBI flooded through her once again. "I didn't give them any information about Luis's finances, though, even after they'd told me I'd be able to keep my license and my business if I did. My clients' confidentiality is sacred."

Instead of looking pleased or relieved by that, Mr. Espina's entire face drew tight, stiffened into a hard mask. His voice was smooth, deep and as cold as ice. "Are you *threatening* me, Ms. Young?"

Horror flushed through her, turning her blood cold and then hot enough to burn. "No! No, God, no! I'm not an idiot! I mean, it was probably dumb of me to work as Luis's accountant when I knew he wasn't great at...well, coloring inside the lines, but I'm not trying to threaten you!" Saying the words out loud made it sound so, so much worse. "I just wanted…" The sheer futility of what she was attempting flooded her, and she started to stand. "Never mind. I'm sorry to have wasted your time. I'll figure something out."

"Sit." Something about his clipped tone made her obey before she realized what she was doing. "What do you want?"

"A job." Once again, the command in his voice had her answering before she considered whether or not it was wise to be so blunt. "I know Luis would give me a reference and, well, new employer contact information, if he wasn't"—he paused, trying to think of a polite term—"dealing with more serious concerns right now."

Those dark, dark eyes regarded her over his raised beer bottle for a long time. Jules let him stare, determined not to break the silence with more babbling. "You want me to hire you?"

"Oh, not you!" she blurted, and then cringed. "Sorry. That came out wrong. I'd be happy to work with you, of course. It's just…I have expenses, so I need to have more than one client—unless I find a single client with extensive accounting needs. I was thinking I could work for some of the people Luis worked with, since they'd probably not care about the whole FBI thing, as long as I know what I'm doing and can keep my mouth shut."

Mr. Espina didn't hurry to answer her. Instead, he eyed her for another painfully long time before finally speaking. "Anyone specific in mind?"

"The Blanchetts?" she suggested tentatively. Most of Luis's business associates had been names on a computer screen to her. At best, she'd met a few in passing. "Maybe the Jovanovics?"

He choked—actually *choked*—on his beer when she said the second name. Carefully placing the bottle on the table, he sat back and closed his eyes for several seconds.

"So that's a no on the Jovanovics?" Disappointment flooded her. They'd been her best prospect. With their hands in what seemed like every not-quite-legal pie, their empire appeared to be huge. She'd imagined that the Jovanovics needed a good accountant—and a discreet one. As she'd proven in the mess with Luis, Jules was both.

"It's a no. On the Blanchetts, too."

"Oh." Her disappointment was quickly heading toward despair. "Is there anyone you *could* recommend?"

"No."

That single bald word made Jules's eyes burn with threatening tears. She wasn't a crier. Even as a little girl, she'd rarely cried. It was just that Mr. Espina had been her only hope of getting well-paying work, the kind of job she needed to afford the kind of lawyers she needed. Staring at Mr. Espina's expressionless face, she felt the last of her dwindling optimism being sucked out of her, leaving Jules hopeless and plan-less and heartbroken.

She bit the inside of her cheek hard enough to shock herself out of her self-pity. This wasn't the end of her dream. This couldn't be the end. She'd keep fighting for her brothers and her sister until the youngest, Dez, turned eighteen. Even if Jules was broke and lawyerless, she'd still try to get her siblings out of that house.

Jules stood as well as she could with the table in the way, and said, "Okay. Thank you, Mr. Espina."

"Sit."

This time, she managed to resist the compulsion to obey and moved until she was standing next to the table. Digging in her purse, she pulled out a crumpled ten and laid it next to her untouched water. Even though Mr. Espina hadn't been much—or any—help, he had met with her. Also, he hadn't killed her. The least she could do was buy his beer.

"Thank you for your help, but I need to go now." She tried and failed to force a smile. "Job hunting to do." When Mr. Espina didn't return her sad attempt at a smile, she turned to leave.

"Ms. Young." Automatic courtesy made her stop and look over her shoulder at him. "No matter what lawyer you hire, you will never get legal custody of your brothers and sister."

Her entire body jerked as if he'd stabbed her. It wasn't only the shock of knowing that Mr. Espina, a stranger, and a terrifying one at that, was aware of her family situation. Hearing the words out loud, the ones she couldn't bear to consider, even in the wee, sleepless, lonely hours of early, early morning, was more horrible than she'd ever imagined.

"How did you… *What?*" she wheezed, her hand pressed to her chest.

Mr. Espina gestured toward her recently vacated seat, and she managed the few steps back to the table and plopped down on the bench. Her knees had gone wobbly, and she knew she had to sit before she fell.

"As you said, you could've made it worse for my brother. I appreciate that you didn't."

Her stunned brain didn't register the words f

minute. Confused, Jules stared at him. "Then why aren't you helping me?"

"I am helping you." He pulled out his cell phone and tapped at his screen. Even the way he poked at his phone screamed aggression. Jules's cell chirped from her purse. Instead of checking the text, she kept her gaze on Mr. Espina. "Call Dennis Lee. I just sent you his number. He'll get you what you need to take your family…elsewhere."

"Take?" she repeated, knowing that she sounded dazed. The conversation had taken on a surreal cast.

"Ms. Young." His gaze sharpened as he leaned forward slightly. It was the most engagement he'd shown for the entire meeting, and she mimicked his posture before she realized what she was doing. "Your brothers and sister are not in a good place. You need to fix that."

"But…" Her voice lowered until barely any sound escaped. "Kidnapping?"

"Ms. Young, sometimes you have to trust what you feel in your gut to be right, even if others are telling you it's wrong."

The idea was overwhelming, terrifying, and wonderful, all at the same time. For years, through countless frustrating, futile, expensive legal custody battles, Jules had followed the rules. It had gotten her nowhere. Her siblings were still stuck in hell, and Jules was broke and desperate enough to work for criminals. Maybe it was time to change the rules. Maybe, if she started playing dirty, she and her brothers and sister could win for once.

Maybe instead of working for criminals, she should become one.

"Ms. Young." She was jerked out of her thoughts as

Mr. Espina pushed a laptop case across the table toward her. Jules's gaze bounced from the bag to his face and back again as she tried to figure out what he was doing. "In thanks for what you did for Luis. He's a pain in the ass, but he's my brother, and I love him."

Tucking her hands into her lap, Jules stared at the case. The conversation had taken another turn toward the weird and unexpected. Was he really giving her a computer? "But..."

"Consider it a bonus that Luis never got around to giving you." After dropping a few bills on the table, Mr. Espina picked up her crumpled ten and held it out to Jules. With numb fingers, she automatically accepted it. He slid from his seat and moved toward the exit. Jules stared at his back, too bewildered by the entire meeting to call after him. Instead, she watched as he walked out the door.

Refocusing on the laptop bag, she cautiously pulled it to her. It was lighter than she expected, and she lowered it to her lap before tugging open the heavy zipper. It wasn't a computer. Instead, a bulky envelope sat inside the case.

Her teeth closed on the sore spot where she'd bitten the inside of her cheek earlier. She slid a hand into the bag. Her fingers shook, and she almost laughed at how tentatively she reached toward the envelope, as if it might grow teeth and bite her.

Jules unfastened the clasp without taking the envelope out of the bag, feeling safer with the package hidden inside the laptop case. The unsealed flap opened easily, and she tilted the envelope so that she could see inside.

Catching a glimpse of the contents, she restrained a

squeal that would've carried through the bar and down the street. Instead, she made a small sound, part squeak and part sigh, touching the stacks of twenty-dollar bills with a disbelieving brush of her fingers.

Her heart was racing as thoughts ran through her mind, too quickly for her to make sense of any of them. The first thing she was able to grab hold of was the idea that she was staring at a whole lot of money—most likely *dirty* money—in a fairly seedy bar. The reminder jolted her into action. She resealed the clasp and zipped the bag with hands that trembled even more than before. Jules was surprised her entire body wasn't vibrating with nerves.

Gathering the precious bag and her purse, Jules stood and hurried for the door as fast as she could go without looking like she was rushing to leave the bar with a bag full of money. The door appeared to be glowing. Even though she told herself it was the late afternoon sun silhouetting it, her more fanciful self imagined the door as the entrance to a safe zone, a home plate, a magical gate that would keep her—and the money—safe.

She couldn't keep the cash, one part of her brain was telling her. She barely knew Mr. Espina. For goodness' sake, she still called him *Mr. Espina*. Who handed off stacks of cash like that to a near-stranger? Mr. Espina did. That was one more thing she knew about Mr. Espina, then.

A hysterical giggle bubbled into her throat, threatening to escape. She swallowed, holding down the laughter that would only draw curious stares. Jules did not want any stares, curious or otherwise, right now—not when she was toting a laptop bag full of money.

"Miss?" The gravelly voice made her spin around as she clutched the case tighter to herself. A huge man loomed just a few strides away, and he was approaching quickly. *He knows!* She felt her eyes round as she took a backward step closer to the door, but she knew it was no use to run. He was almost on top of her, and running would just confirm that she had something of value on her—something stealable.

She had to tilt her head back to see his face—his angry-looking, stubble-covered face. A knife tattoo followed the side of his neck, the bloody tip ending just under his jaw. The man held out a very familiar crumpled ten-dollar bill. "You dropped this."

It took a moment for the adrenaline to subside enough for her to understand him. She couldn't stop staring at the money in his outstretched hand. "Oh! Thank you!"

She reached out with a shaky hand to accept the bill.

"You really should stop throwing your money around." With a grin that revealed at least three missing teeth, he turned away and left her with her ten dollars—plus the many, many thousands tucked in her laptop bag. Taking a deep, quivering breath, she hurried to the door, determined to get to the dubious safety of her car before she suffered a heart attack.

About the Author

When she's not writing, Katie Ruggle rides horses, shoots guns, and travels to warm places where she can scuba dive. A graduate of the police academy, Katie received her ice-rescue certification and can attest that the reservoirs in the Colorado mountains really are that cold. While she still misses her off-grid, solar- and wind-powered house in the Rocky Mountains, she now lives in Dennison, Minnesota, near her family.